STOLEN BRILLIANCE

A Lady Black Mystery

◆ ◆ ◆

MICHAEL G. COLBURN

I.P. PUBLISHING

I.P. Publishing
152 Deforest Road
Burlington, Vermont 05401

Hardcover ISBN: 979-8-9905420-2-0
Paperback ISBN: 979-8-9905420-1-3
Ebook ISBN: 979-8-9905420-0-6

I.P. Publishing and the colophon are registered
trademarks of IWD Holdings, LLC

Cover design and illustration by Karl Spurzem

In Loving Memory of Lissa C. Bogner (Colburn)

TABLE OF CONTENTS

PART ONE

EDIE BLACK AND BENJI DIAMOND

◆

CHAPTER 1

EDITH

London, 1890

Lady Edith Black instructed her driver to park her carriage by the old communal water pump at Aldgate. *I'm sure I can find my way from there*, she thought, though she had been away from London so long, she wasn't sure. "William, please return in two hours. If I'm not back, please wait."

"You sure you'll be all right alone, ma'am?"

"I survived it once, William. I'm sure I'll survive it today."

Edie glanced down Fenchurch Street deeper into the East London slums. She hesitated, then began walking. She scanned the narrow, winding streets lined with overcrowded tenement buildings, many several stories high with crumbling facades, broken windows, and sagging roofs. Little had changed. Occasionally, she noticed a collapsed roof and wondered if the poor souls there had survived. Piles of rotting garbage lined every street. The sights and smells made her feel sluggish or numb; she wasn't sure which.

She turned down a familiar street. Edie could hear loud voices and cartwheels clattering against the rough cobblestones. Her pace quickened until, turning down the next alley, she stopped abruptly. *Well, I'll be!* she thought. The block was full of cart vendors and peddlers calling out their wares to shoppers visiting from outside the slums. Nostalgia washed over her. She walked toward the alley; she was sure it was the one where the warehouse for the market had stood. It had burned down years ago.

She turned away from the market, walking deeper into the slums where she'd spent her early childhood. People of all ages were gathered in small groups, assembled in doorways, some on stoops or sitting on the ground in alleys. She heard different languages—some she recognized as Italian, French, and German, and others she didn't know. She knew the way home from here. She walked over blocked drains reeking of sewage, mixed with the acrid smell of smoke and coal from factories and workshops. Finally, she arrived at her destination.

Lady Edith Black stood at the foot of the street where she had spent her first ten years. The current residents stared at the sophisticated-looking lady wearing a stylish black jacket, black hat, and diamond hatpin, carrying a walking stick and smiling. She hadn't been here since the day before her tenth birthday, twenty-four years earlier. As vivid memories walked the streets like ghosts, her breath became shallow.

Edie saw her nine-year-old self running down the alley that intersected the street.

She remembered how her torn shirt and stained pants were soaked with sweat from the blistering heat—and how fear clung to her body. Scooting under a discarded dray, she opened a coal chute door and climbed in feet first, bracing her legs against the turned-up sides of the chute to avoid falling into the cellar. Coal dust coated her face, hands, and clothing, but she held her breath and covered her mouth and nose with one hand to avoid choking or sneezing. She didn't know how near her stepfather was or if he was still pursuing her, but she couldn't risk being caught.

She waited for what felt like hours. Her heart gradually slowed, and her breathing became normal. She wondered if her mother was safe. Very slowly, she opened the coal door a few inches and looked around, then a little more. No one was nearby, so she pulled her upper torso out of the chute, then pushed with her feet to clear the door and lay prone under the dray.

On this hot summer day, her stepfather, Cloyd, had been drinking since noon and returned home to get money from her mother, Nell. When Nell refused, he hit her in the stomach. Edie balled her fists and hit Cloyd in the back. He turned and slurred his nasty laugh. He drew his arm back to punch Edie, but, standing up, Nell grabbed his arm from behind. She remembered hearing her mother say, "Run, Edith—*now*! I can handle this." Edie narrowly escaped Cloyd, who had tried to grab her as she ran away.

Now Edie was cautiously on her way home, peeking around corners and hiding behind barrels and carts. She stepped into the open when she saw one of her mother's street friends, an older lady named Beth, walking toward her. Beth put her hands on Edith's shoulders.

"I sent my Abe to borrow a cart from the stable," she said. "She's hurt real bad, Edith; I think some ribs are broken, and her head was bashed hard. Abe and I can pull the cart to the workhouse infirmary."

I never saw Mother again. Beth told me she died on the way to the infirmary. Cloyd was the one who deserved to die! She stopped. *I can't think like that—I can't hate—not now.*

She had to relive this next part: the moment the path of her life changed.

Standing at the alley entrance, she looked at the spot where she had curled up on the ground after Beth told her about her mother. She remembered that her friends had tried to console her about her mother's death. She hadn't seen her stepfather approaching.

He grabbed her around the neck from behind, choking her. She gagged. He picked her up and threw her to the ground. Her friend Rachel jumped on him, but he pushed her back. She fell on top of the other children, tumbling them all over.

"You hid money from me!" he yelled, slurring his words. He pulled the precious coin sock Edie's mother had made for her from his belt and held it in front of her face. "I'm taking it now. Never hide money from me again!" He coughed, and as he cocked his leg to kick her, she drove forward, grabbing his legs with both arms. He stumbled backward, hitting the alley wall. He regained his balance and bent at the waist to catch Edie around the neck again. He dropped the sock. Edie rolled away.

At that moment, a fist slammed into the left side of Cloyd's face; blood gushed from his eyebrow. He coiled back to defend himself, and a second fist slammed the right side of his face.

"Bloody shite!" he yelled, as he covered his damaged eye.

Rachel grabbed the sock and ran to hide. Edie's other friends followed.

Not realizing what had happened, Edie stood up, shaking all over. Tremors racked her body so violently that her bladder released. She pulled a hatpin she had found in the road from her belt and braced herself for the next attack. Her eyes cleared; she was stunned to see that a tall young man had her father up against a wall, holding him by the collar and suspending him off the ground.

"You've beaten her for the last time, old man!" he yelled. "I've seen her bruised face when I encounter her on the streets. If I, or any of my boys—and trust me, they are everywhere—ever see you again in this part of the city, you're a dead man. Do you understand?"

Blood ran from Cloyd's eyes into his mouth, and he began to choke. He managed to nod slightly. The young man punched him again in the stomach, then let him drop to the ground, where he retched.

Edie stared at her stepfather in revulsion. He had taken her mother from her. Her body convulsed from memories of his cruelty and the beatings her mother had endured. A new conviction bubbled up. She felt possessed. She ran at her stepfather with the hatpin positioned to stab him with all her remaining strength. She wanted to kill him. But the young man grabbed her wrist. "I've done enough damage," he said. "You're safe. Keep your innocence."

Edith slumped to her knees. Tears welled in her eyes as she gasped for breath. Her friends came out from hiding and hugged her.

"It'll be all right," Rachel said.

How? Edie could not imagine that anything would be all right.

Rachel handed Edith the sock of coins and turned to the young man. "We've seen you around."

"I'm Benji Diamond. My boys and I run the stall market ten blocks south of Aldgate Pump."

"You've left crates of food here sometimes."

"I do what I can."

"Can you help her?" Rachel said, nodding toward Edith.

Cloyd was bent over, holding his face with one hand and clutching his midsection with the other arm as he walked away. He didn't look back.

"Does she have a mother?" Benji asked.

"Not any longer," Rachel answered.

"Come with me," the young man said to Edith. "Call me Benji." He turned to her friends. "I'll look after her." He took her by the hand and led her down an adjacent street.

"Where are you taking me?" she asked, tugging at her wet pants, wary of trusting this man. She had never known a man she wasn't suspicious of.

"A place you'll be safe."

My dear, dear Benji. He tried to help everyone. I love him so much. Coming out of her trance, she spoke to a mother and two daughters sitting on the nearest stoop, dressed in ragged garments. They were staring at her. "I used to live here, right up there," she pointed. *I should have brought food*, she thought. She took her coin purse from her bag and opened it. She handed the lady three coins, one for each. Suddenly, a small flock of children surrounded her, all talking at once. She couldn't make out their individual words as they clamored around her with their hands out. She laughed and handed out coins until her purse was empty; she held it upside down, open, to show that all the coins were gone.

She took her time walking back to the waiting carriage and the privileged life she now lived. *I wish I could save all of them from this blight.*

CHAPTER 2

CARRIAGE RIDE

"William, I don't want to return directly to the inn. Would you mind touring the city while I do some reading?"

"Of course, Lady Black. I would most enjoy it."

William took her arm as she boarded her carriage and settled into the seat.

Once Benji had taught her to read and write, she had begun writing about her life. His passion was teaching, and many of the gang's boys and the women who ran the stalls had benefited; he rescued and educated them.

She had two of her older notebooks with her in the carriage. It was a day for remembering. She had been back in London six months, leaving Melbourne after learning that the *RMS Quetta* sank off the Queensland coast in treacherous waters near Mount Adolphus with Benji aboard. Benji's name was not among the deceased or the rescued. There were over one hundred and forty souls unaccounted for. She had spent three months visiting every island and mainland facility and cemetery in the region, seeking any information on Benji, dead or alive, with no luck. She was heartsick. She'd finally traveled to London to complete the transaction of selling their farm operations, which Benji had started before sailing home to arrange the deeds and paperwork.

She opened her oldest notebook to when Benji first brought her to the stalls after rescuing her from her stepfather, one of her first memories she captured after she learned to write.

All the people and noise frighten me, she read. She closed her eyes, remembering.

"Don't be afraid, angel," Benji had said. "This is part of my business; the stall ladies are my partners. They'll become your family."

Returning to her notebook, she continued to read. She recalled knowing her life had just changed. How wary and fearful she had been, not trusting what would become of her. She wrote about meeting Maude first, an older stall lady who became like a mother to her. She wrote of the other eighteen ladies she was to live with for more than four years in the warehouse accommodations Benji provided. But mostly, she wrote about the two women who were most instrumental in forming who she was to become, Specs and Britina. Specs's glasses were so thick her eyes looked huge; her hair had streaks of silver mixed with brown, and Edie remembered how long and delicate her fingers were. She never knew her real name. Benji had taught Specs math. She'd later managed the market's finances, calculating a portion for Benji and his boys to pay them for the goods they provided and a portion for each lady who worked there. Edie also wrote about Britina, the beautiful young lady with dark brown eyes and long black hair. Britina was Edie's voice of reason, only three years older than her, with wisdom beyond her years. Edie thought that her knowledge and approach to life probably came from reading the Bible daily.

Lady Black put the notebook down and glanced at the scenery. She hoped Britina would be at the service; they hadn't seen each other in a couple of years.

Returning to her journal, she smiled as she read about her first meal at the warehouse: lamb stew and freshly baked bread prepared by Alice, the cook. She could almost taste it—at the time, it was the most delicious food she had ever eaten. One of the ladies taught her how a "respectable lady" would use her spoon. Another taught her to dunk her bread into the thick broth. She had asked if a respectable lady would dunk her bread, and they had all laughed. "How do I become a respectable lady?" Edie had asked innocently, dipping her bread. They all laughed again. Edie recalled being embarrassed, hanging her head toward her bowl, her face turning crimson. One rough voice said, "You must be born into it." Another sweeter voice said, "You can earn respectability by the good you do for others." It was Britina.

The following day, Lady Black recalled, had been her birthday. She could place herself in the scene as if it were only yesterday.

Maude unbolted the large warehouse doors, letting Benji and eight of his boys into the warehouse with their wagons. "New supplies!" Benji called.

He went to Specs, spoke briefly, looked at the accounting she had done, and took his cut and payment for goods. He gave her an invoice for the day's delivery. Then he sought out Edie.

"Happy Birthday, angel," he said when he saw her.

"How did you know?" She felt warm all over. She formed a cautious smile. "Thank you for bringing me here."

"You're welcome. Maude told me that today was your birthday."

Benji handed her a paper-wrapped package tied with an awkward bow. "This is for you."

Uncertain of what to expect, she unwrapped the gift. It was a beautifully bound book. At first, she was ecstatic, but then she felt ashamed.

"What's the matter, angel?"

"I'm sorry, Benji. I can't read."

"I thought not. It's all right. I'll give you your first lesson tonight after dinner."

Thrilled and more than a little overwhelmed, she hugged her book. Edie was delighted with the prospect of reading, and though she didn't have the words to describe it then, she was filled with gratitude.

Benji read the book's title: "*The Merry Adventures of Robin Hood of Great Renown in Nottinghamshire.*" Then he added, "It's by Howard Pyle. It's a difficult first book to read, but you'll love it—we'll enjoy it together."

◆　◆　◆

Lady Black took a deep breath. She tapped on the roof of her carriage to tell William he could head back to the Riley Inn now. She picked up the second notebook, which skipped over four years to the time when Edie had decided that she had to leave her warehouse family.

"I've decided I will leave the market," Edie told Britina on one of their nightly talks. "I'm so grateful for your friendship, but I can't work here forever." She hugged Britina. Britina hugged back.

"I knew you would have to leave sometime. You have big plans."

"I just don't know what they are yet. Will you stay forever?"

"Nothing is forever, Edie. It's a safe home for now, and we make good money. I aim to serve God. Eventually, God will have other plans for me; until I know them, I'll stay."

"Benji saved me from poverty and educated me; I love him like a brother. I'm afraid to tell him I'm leaving. He's hard to get to know."

"I know some," Britina said. "What do you want to know?"

"Benji has a funny accent."

Britina laughed. "That's what you want to know about?"

"Not just that," Edie said. "Does he have a family?"

"That's a more interesting question." Britina smiled. "He has a Canadian accent. His parents brought him here when he was young, perhaps nine. His father was an accomplished weaver. His mother was a respected teacher before she died."

"Is his father alive?"

"It's a sad story. Russell, his father, injured his arm beyond repair in a weaving machinery accident. Benji left school to care for him. He started a delivery business to earn money. The business grew fast. His father healed in time but had limited use of one arm. He was unemployable. He wanted to open a tailor shop with fabric and a seamstress. A client of Benji's, James Henderson, introduced Benji and his father to a wealthy, sophisticated lady who agreed to finance the shop. Her name is Mrs. Lillian Hill. She lent him the money; Henderson supplied the fabric. The shop opened and was an instant success."

◆ ◆ ◆

Lady Black paused, remembering her feelings when she heard this—*how quickly emotions can change!*

"Benji and his father were arrested," Britina had told her that day. "His father, with a shop full of stolen fabric, was arrested for receiving stolen goods, and Benji for thievery. Eventually, one of Benji's clients named Henderson as the broker. The police had to release Benji for lack of evidence. Henderson had fake receipts for purchasing all the counterfeit goods. Henderson got off. Benji's father was convicted and sentenced to seven years. The police never discovered Mrs. Hill or her gang of lady thieves' involvement in providing the stolen goods."

Lady Black remembered being shocked and angry at this injustice. *But I had more to learn.*

That evening, she told the other ladies she would be leaving.

Lady Black closed her eyes and leaned back against the carriage seat; she could see this next part without reading her entries.

Benji showed up at the market at the usual time on Monday with his crew of boys. When he finished his business with Specs, he sought Edie out.

"What's this I hear of you leaving?" he asked in a firm voice.

"Benji, I can't work at the stall market forever. I need to take steps to improve myself. I don't want to be selfish or unappreciative, but I want to do more with my life."

"What are those steps?" Benji asked.

"I don't know," Edie admitted.

Benji rubbed the back of his neck. He stood and walked a few steps away.

Edie followed with her eyes, wondering what was to happen.

Then he turned and came back.

"What can I do?" Benji said.

"Help me figure out those next steps."

Benji, looking resigned, came back and stood before Edie. "Please pack a bag tonight. I'll be staying in town. I'll pick you up at 7:30 in the morning."

"Where will we be going?" Edie asked.

Benji replied, "The farm. I think you'll like it there. It's where the boys live. Say your goodbyes tonight."

They rode silently; Edie glanced at the countryside she had never seen before.

Edie was curious when Benji pulled the wagon into a shabby farmhouse and barn. She could see three horses grazing in the field; the barn was leaning slightly. She was expecting more from Benji's farm.

"This is the Widow Farnsworth's farm," Benji explained. "She's struggling to hang on. I try to bring her what I can to help when I come by." He climbed down, took a crate from the back of the wagon, walked to the farmhouse door, and knocked. No one answered, so he opened the door, pushed the container inside, and closed it again, returning to the wagon.

"Will she know who it's from?" Edie asked.

"I suspect so; I don't think she gets much help or visitors. I leave a little money in the crates as well."

After a pause, Edie asked, "What happened with the delivery business after you and your father were arrested?"

He looked at her, surprised she knew. "Not now, Edie," he said. "I have work to do when I get to the farm; I need to think about it. We'll talk later."

Benji stopped the wagon and fumbled in the stores until he finally pulled out a book. "I brought you the stories of Auguste Dupin by Edgar Allan Poe. Dupin is a detective."

"Oh, I'm going to like this."

She beamed at him.

She wanted to ask about the work but decided to stay quiet. She was eager to read about this detective person, and she felt warm and comfortable just sitting next to Benji. *How could I leave him? I love him!*

◆ ◆ ◆

"I'll walk from here, William; I won't need the carriage again today. I'll need an early ride to the docks tomorrow. I need to board by 7:00 a.m., and I have three trunks."

"Yes, milady. I'll have them loaded and ready."

Edie walked to the chapel. It was a pleasant, cool, sunny day, and the London air felt fresher than usual. She climbed the steps and entered, wondering what or whom to expect. She was early, but a few people were seated, waiting. Some turned when she entered, but no one she recognized.

"Edie?"

She turned to a figure just entering the chapel.

"Britina." Edie started crying. "I'm so glad you're here." They wrapped each other in a hug that lasted a long while. More people turned to inspect the new arrivals.

The casket was open; they walked to the altar to pay respects. They both smiled, pleased that the undertaker had placed her half-inch thick glasses on her face.

CHAPTER 3

THE FARM

1871

Benji and Edie arrived at the farm in the late afternoon. Edie looked around; it was a far more prosperous operation than the Farnsworth farm. There were two barns and several outbuildings. The farmhouse was old but in excellent repair; an enclosed walkway attached a large bunkhouse to the house. The grounds and fields that Edie could see were tidy. She recognized a field of corn, and another field of tall grass was waving in the distance. A garden near the house held plants and herbs. She could see more rows of green plants on the opposite side of the road. Twelve boys and young men came to greet the wagon. She could see others working in the fields. Benji introduced each by name, and each shook Edie's hand.

"You all have seen Edie at the market. She's come to spend some time with us here at the farm, and for now, she'll stay in the spare bedroom at the farmhouse. I'm sure we can find some tasks for her to do." There were a few chuckles and some nodding heads.

"Mark, will you attend to the horses? And the rest of you can unload the wagon; the kitchen items are apparent, and I've labeled a few crates for the print house; there's feed and fertilizer. The rest can go into storage. I put the personal items several of you requested in the oak trunk.

"Edie, grab your bag, and I'll take you to your room to settle."

Edie's room on the second floor was beyond her expectations, including a four-poster bed with a canopy out of one of her novels! She had a bureau with a gas lamp and a wash basin, a stuffed chair with a side table, and another gas lantern. A woven oval rug was on the wood floor before a small fireplace. A window with white lace curtains looked toward the barns; she could see a small apple orchard.

"Benji, this is wonderful. Will I be staying long?"

"I don't know, angel. We'll talk more, and then you can decide to stay or leave."

He turned to leave. Turning back, he added, "You'll hear the dinner gong at seven. I'll see you in the bunkhouse; the dining area is in the front."

Edie unpacked and put her clothing in a drawer and her accessories on the bureau. She looked at her hatpin and wondered if she needed it any longer. It was her street weapon. She thought of her mother and felt a hollowness in the pit of her stomach.

She placed it on the nightstand by the bed. She sat by the window and read her book for a while. She was distracted by her new surroundings and looked at the barn and fields. *Is this my future?* she thought. It wasn't what she had dreamed, but she had known nothing of this type of place or life before today. She took out her notebook, wrote about the day, and then listed things she wanted to know about. She also wrote, *How can I make my life what I want it to be? Britina said God would provide an answer: is this it?*

The gong was loud; Edie didn't miss it, even though she'd nodded off. She straightened her clothes and washed her face using the basin. She thought, *I need a milk can*, and giggled—they used milk cans for their privies at the warehouse. There needed to be a chamber pot somewhere. She glanced up and down the hall; there was a door open, and inside was a wooden chair with an oval cutout that contained a chamber pot—clean with a bit of water inside. There was also a stand with a water basin for hand washing. *How modern!* she thought. She used the facility. *Even better than a milk can!*

Walking to the bunkhouse, she thought of her friends at the market. They had been her family for a long time. She longed for their company. She missed Benji too, but she would see him soon. She wiped a tear away and walked in. Like the market women, everyone talked simultaneously, and she instantly felt more at home. Someone yelled, "Welcome, Edie." One of the boys handed her a mug of beer. She hesitated. "I've never had a beer."

Benji stepped up behind her; he had streaks of black on his hands and ink on his overalls. "Have one," he said. "I have to clean up, then I'll join you for dinner." He took a mug of beer with him.

She sat with a couple of the boys she had talked to at the market. Mike handed her a piece of paper and said, "We put a list of things together that you can do tomorrow to help."

"Thank you," she said. "I hope to explore the farm a bit as well."

"You'll have time," Mike said. "Those of us who aren't staying in the city start at 6:00 a.m. with our milkers."

Edie wondered why some of the boys spent the night in London.

Then the food arrived—two boys wearing aprons rolled large wooden tables on wheels from the kitchen. There were baskets of fresh rolls, greens from the garden, sliced tomatoes, and pies with beef, vegetables, and gravy. Everyone served themselves.

Benji joined everyone after most were already seated. He filled his plate, took another mug of beer, and came to sit next to Edie. "We'll take a walk after dinner, all right?"

"Of course. I'm excited to see more of the farm. Will you show me what you do for work?"

"Yes. I'd be glad to. How are you enjoying the book?"

"I love it." She turned toward Benji, her face glowing. "Two women are killed in a room where the door and windows are locked from the inside, and the chimney is too small for passage. No one can have gotten in or out, and yet the women are dead, and witnesses heard other voices coming from the room. Dupin will figure it out, but I can't imagine how. It takes place in Paris; I need to visit Paris someday. I want to see the world. I want to visit Jamaica, where Britina is from. It sounds exotic. By the way, I skipped over some French words because I don't know them."

Benji gave her a half smile. "I'll help with those soon."

She finished her dinner and was anxious to see the farm with Benji. "Can I use the kitchen to wash my hands? Then I'll be ready."

"Take your time," he replied. "I haven't finished my dinner."

The boys broke into groups: one group cleaned up, another went to the sleeping area to play games, and another went outside.

It was a beautiful moonlit night; a slight breeze was sweet with the smell of grass, trees, and dirt. Edie hadn't smelled air so clean before.

Benji walked her toward one of the outbuildings. She looked sideways at him as they walked. She could see he was worried.

Unlocking the padlock, he lit an oil lantern and led the way into his print shop. Edie glanced around in awe: two large presses, one small press, containers of ink and paper, a table with a mechanism with foot pedals of some sort, and stacks of wooden trays filled with metal pieces containing letters in relief and some with symbols and crests. The smell was rich and slightly chemical, new to her but intriguing. Edie walked to the most significant press, touching the large wheel on the side, imagining how all the pieces worked. She felt Benji watching her.

"Who do you do all the printing for?" she asked.

"Mrs. Hill," he said, and waited.

Edie took a step backward; her mouth fell open. She turned and glared at him; her green eyes wide. She snapped, "The criminal?"

"Edie, please take a seat. I'll tell you what happened after my father went to jail."

She did as he suggested, her eyes blazing at him in disbelief. Benji paced back and forth between the presses, not looking at Edie.

"You deserve the truth." He took a deep breath and closed his eyes. "You've become important to me, Edie. I don't want to lose you."

CHAPTER 4

BENJI AND MRS. HILL

Benji took another deep breath and spoke. "It was the street gangs, aided by the police, that ruined my delivery business. I kept at it, but I couldn't make a legitimate business work. Street gangs attacked my boys and me, and packages were destroyed; one boy was beaten up badly and quit. The gangs demolished one cart. They demanded money to leave us alone. One of the bobbies who arrested me offered to help my business in return for a weekly payment to prevent the gangs from interfering. I was cornered. I couldn't get a real job."

Edie lowered her head, understanding his frustration with street gangs and dishonest police. *He must have felt close to hopeless.*

"One evening, I was having a quiet dinner at the Cock & Bull pub, and suddenly Henderson was standing next to my table. I must have looked surprised because he let out a little chuckle. 'Mind if I sit down?' he asked. He signaled the barkeep for a beer, and we talked. He said it was a shame about my father's imprisonment but he wanted me to know that Mrs. Hill had appreciated that my father and I had kept her name confidential. He said Mrs. Hill wanted to talk to me. That worried me because my father and I had never repaid her for the investment in my father's shop. I decided to confront the issue directly with Mrs. Hill. I didn't trust Henderson; I had no reason to doubt Mrs. Hill. I boarded Henderson's carriage when he told me he'd take me to her, and we drove across London into a prosperous neighborhood. We ended up going in through an iron gate to the side door of a mansion—smaller than some, but the property had several outbuildings. It was in the Mayfair district on Park Street, near Hyde Park. We entered through the kitchen door and went upstairs to the sitting room. I gazed at the paintings, the fine woven carpets, and the expensive furniture. Mrs. Hill stood before a small serving table with a silver tea service, looking elegant and composed.

"She instructed me to have a seat and asked Henderson to leave the room, which he did without hesitation. She remained standing. I was even more concerned at that point. She looked at me for a moment, probably recognizing my discomfort. She said that the money she had lost on my father's shop was a business loss: she took the risk and would take the loss.

"I felt a little better for a moment. Then Mrs. Hill said that the money she spends as a favor to someone is different: she expects it to be repaid—and with a premium. I remained silent, not knowing where she was heading. She told me that Judge Singly, who heard my father's case, would dine with her the following evening. She said that she makes an effort to know influential gentlemen. She then explained her plan to me. At some point in the evening, she would claim an old friendship with my father and would ask if the judge could arrange to get his sentence suspended. She assured me it would work but that it would also cost a lot of money, which she would pay. But she expected me to pay it back.

"I would have done almost anything to make that happen. I was also highly anxious. I felt I had to level with her. I told her that I very much wanted my father released. I feared he might die in prison if I couldn't get him out, but I had no means to repay her.

"She smiled and thanked me for being honest. Then she said, 'I invest in people, Benji. I know I can trust you; you've proven that. I intend to provide the means to assure that you will be able to repay me and make a good living.'

"She had two roles she needed me to fill in her organization. First, she could no longer trust outside printers to print documents she often needed; the organization needed its own printer. She understood that I had training in this skill and said she would set up a full printing shop in a barn at a farm she owned outside the city limits."

Edie was stunned—she never expected this. "This is *her* farm?" She put her hand over her chest while she caught her breath.

Benji didn't answer but continued. "I was both intrigued and apprehensive. I said I knew little about her organization and asked her to tell me about it.

"Mrs. Hill seemed to hesitate, then settled in the chair beside me. She told me she was the head of a syndicate of ladies who were highly professional, sophisticated thieves. She arranged jobs for the women. She said that for many, she provided the means for them to come out of poverty and live in comfort. Her ladies were nicknamed the Forty Elephants.

"She told me that for some time, she'd been thinking about a problem in London and the opportunity it might present. She thought the two of us would make a great team. Over the years, the slums and the poverty associated with them had birthed dozens of boy gangs.

"'Most of these boys are crude,' Mrs. Hill said. She got up, turned, and stood in front of me. 'Many are mean and dangerous. They are dangerous to every citizen—and to each other. Besides robbery, extortion, kidnapping, protection rackets, and gambling, some hire out for murder.'

"She wanted me to organize a gang of about twenty of the brightest boys I could find, boys who needed a way out of poverty. I would lead and educate them, and she would arrange lucrative jobs. I would house and feed them here at the farm. I would set the rules and operate similarly to her Forty Elephants.

"Mrs. Hill was animated as she described her plan. 'I am proposing sophisticated crime with a purpose,' she told me. 'Like the women I work with, your boys will mean no one any physical harm.'"

Edie couldn't control her dismay and interrupted Benji. "But you and all these boys are thieves . . . *criminals*." She paused briefly and scowled. "Wait!" she said, quickly standing. "All the goods at the market, are they from your . . . ah . . . activities?"

"The market was my idea, and I put it together, but yes, most of the goods come from our activities or from the Elephants."

"That makes all of us just like your father, unknowingly selling stolen goods." She shook uncontrollably, wanting to scream, but she tried calming herself; her heart was pounding, her teeth clenched. She took a deep breath.

Benji hung his head, ran a hand through his curly brown hair, and finally looked at her. "Edie, I've seen the corruption that threatened honest businesses and the ruination of so many lives from filth and sickness in the slums. We both lost our mothers to poverty. I think of myself as a provider. Through crime—clean, sophisticated crime—I could achieve my dreams of teaching and financial independence and helping people have better lives. Mrs. Hill converted me."

Edie stared at him in astonishment. "You're still . . . still criminals," she stammered.

Benji's voice changed; his words were firm. "And you, all the market ladies, and all the boys here are far better off than if we weren't."

Edie didn't know what she thought about Benji now, and she felt uncertain about herself. She sat down again, pulled her knees up, and wrapped her arms around them. She put her head on her knees, and her long black hair concealed her face and agony.

"What happened to your father?" she asked in a small voice.

"He was released two weeks after I met with Mrs. Hill. He was a broken man, Edie. I had a few weeks with him, but I felt he could only heal and lead a comfortable life in Canada, where we had relatives. I promised to visit as soon as possible, but I knew that wouldn't happen. I put him on a sailing ship for Boston, where his brothers met him and took him to Canada. He died a year later."

Edie's shoulders shook again as she started to sob. She felt sick inside.

Benji went to Edie and put his arms around her in a hug, but she pushed him away hard. Her face was flushed and wet with tears. She stood up quickly, her chin trembling. "Don't touch me!" she said.

CHAPTER 5

MORAL CHOICES

What is it I'm feeling? she asked herself. *I'm hurt, and I'm angry. I trusted Benji, and he's a thief. I trust Benji; he's been kind and caring to me and others, but he's still a criminal.* Back in her room, pacing the floor, her thoughts turned to her future. *I can't just leave. Where would I go? But I can't go back to the market knowing everything has been stolen. I'd be a willing criminal then. Besides, I don't want to be without Benji; he's family, and I love him.*

Edie tossed and turned in bed all night, finally falling asleep just before dawn. When she woke, sunlight was streaming in through her window, illuminating the whole room. Edie got up, put on her robe, and stood by the window looking over the farmyard and the activities underway. Some of her anguish evaporated as she took in the action on the farm. She saw the cows for the first time: several boys were herding eight up the drive from the other side of the road while others were herding a group back in that direction. They brought them into the smaller barn. Edie set aside her concerns. Someone had mentioned milking during dinner. *That barn must be where they do the milking,* she thought. *I'd like to see that.*

Glancing up and down the hall, she went to the commode room and bolted the door behind her. She used the commode; someone had cleaned it and added fresh water to the basin. She washed her face and hands. A tin of tooth powder was on the stand, so Edie took her toothbrush from her knit case and brushed her teeth. She felt a little better.

Returning to her room, she dressed in pants and a light shirt. She had packed a hat, but it wasn't the type the boys were wearing, and it didn't seem appropriate. She would see if she could borrow one. She felt obligated and excited to do her chores, but first, she would go to the milking barn. She picked up her list of duties and put it in her pocket.

"Morning, Edie," one of the boys greeted her when she got to the barn, and another waved. Two boys were seated on three-legged stools, squeezing the cows' teats, sending a stream of milk into a pail on the ground. The other cows were in a walled pen, waiting their turn.

"Mark, do you have a hat I can borrow for my chores?"

"Take mine; it'll fit if you pile all that hair into the hat. I have another."

"Thank you," she said, and did as he suggested.

She had several chores, starting with weeding the kitchen garden. It was wonderful to get her hands into the dirt. It was good clean dirt, not like the filth of the slums. She did a lot of thinking during the hours on her own. She knew later she would take her thoughts to her notebook, but first, she had one last chore: muck out the horse stalls. She finished around five. Returning to the farmhouse, she washed in the commode room, changed into clean clothes, sat in the chair by the window with her notebook, and began writing:

> *Successfully avoided seeing Benji all day—but missed him. Still very angry with him.*
> *Theft is a crime, selling stolen items is a crime, and everyone I know is a criminal. I'm a criminal.*
> *Benji has done and is doing good things for many people; he's a good person, except—*

She stopped and considered what she'd written, then continued.

> *There is so much wrong in London; is poverty a crime? What it does to people is criminal. All the gangs are hurting and killing people,*

*ruining businesses, and harming good people; that's criminal. And the
police helping them for money, are they criminals?
I need a direction and a plan to pursue my dreams of respect, wealth, and
doing good for others, like I promised myself when I said I would be
like Benji. I didn't know.*

She paused and thought again. She wrote.

Can breaking the law ever be the right thing to do?

She recalled the legend of Robin Hood from the first book she'd
read, how he stole from the rich and corrupt and helped the poor. She
remembered how Benji had stopped at the Farnsworth farm and left
a crate of food, supplies, and money.

*Benji is like Robin Hood! He isn't asking for anything in return. Benji's
helping his band of thieves to leave poverty behind, run a farm, and
become educated. It's all he wants.*

Benji's thoughts kept turning back to Edie. She was so upset and
disappointed in him. He'd been afraid she would react that way, but
he'd needed to be honest; she deserved that. *But I care for her more
than I probably should. I don't want to lose her, but she must do what she
feels is right.*

He packaged everything he had printed, wrapped each order in
paper, and tied it with twine. Placing the items in their appropriate
crates, he stacked them so Frank could load the cart in the morning.
He went to the kitchen to clean up. After he was clean he would
approach Edie.

It was early evening when he knocked on her door. "May I come
in?" he asked.

Edie couldn't tell if she wanted to scream no or if she wanted to
put her arms around Benji and accept the hug she'd rejected the night
before. She said nothing.

"Edie, are you there?"

She exhaled and muttered, "I'm here."

I want to see him. "Just a minute." She took her time, preparing herself. She went to the door, opened it, and stood there.

"May I come in and talk with you?"

"I guess. I'm still mad."

"I know."

She backed away from the door, and Benji entered.

"I'm sorry," he said.

"For what, being a thief?" Edie said.

"Well, no—I'm proud of my role in life. I do more good for people than harm to those who hardly recognize their losses. No one gets hurt by our actions, and many benefit. But I am sorry to have distressed you."

Edie walked to her chair and sat down. "Can breaking the law ever be the right thing to do?" she asked.

Benji turned and paced, thinking. "I wouldn't say the right thing. I would say, based on circumstances, it can sometimes be the best option."

Edie looked at him but didn't say anything.

"Edie, have you decided to leave? If you have, I'll drive a cart into the city tomorrow. I don't want you to leave, but I can take you back to the market, and you can decide what to do from there."

She hesitated. "I can't go back there and pretend I don't know they sell stolen goods."

"I'll ask again," Benji said. "What can I do?"

"I need to make decisions and plans. You can give me a job here on the farm, a place to live, and perhaps friendship while I figure out the rest of my life."

Benji was delighted. All was not lost. All was not well either, but this was a good beginning. "Agreed," was all he said. "Will you come to dinner?"

"Yes, now I will."

CHAPTER 6

EDIE AT THE FARM

Edie had taken well to farm life; she loved the challenges, the camaraderie, and the clean open spaces. She was seventeen now, and after
three years of farm labor, she was as strong as many of the boys. The
fall was busy: weaning the new calves, harvesting the hay and corn for
feed and the sweet corn for the table, turning the potato plants with a
single horse plow and harvesting the tubers, picking apples, securing
the cows in their winter barn, and stacking the newly cut wood to
age, moving the older wood so it was ready for the winter. Edie had
orchestrated a project with the help of two of the boys; they built and
established a fully functioning chicken and egg production operation.
She felt proud.

When she ran into Benji on his occasional visits to the farm, her
stomach fluttered. She knew her feelings were more than friendship,
but she didn't know how Benji felt.

In mid-December, Edie approached Benji. "I miss my friends at
the market—I'd like to visit over Christmas for a few days. If that's all
right, I'll surprise them with a few dozen eggs and some fresh chickens
for stew."

"Of course it is," Benji said. "Plan on coming with me in the wagon
next week. I'll pick you back up on the twenty-seventh; how's that?"

Edie's face lit up with joy. It had been a few months since she had
visited the warehouse. "Thank you, Benji." She beamed at him and
looked into his kind eyes. *I do love this man*, she thought.

Benji and Edie each had their responsibilities to take care of at the farm. Days went by when they didn't see each other at all, and he often stayed at the London warehouse, but they had moments when they talked and enjoyed each other's company.

One night just before Christmas, spending time together in the printing barn, she asked him how he had learned to print.

Benji was used to her curiosity.

"It was when my delivery business was doing well," he said. "I was looking for business in a new neighborhood and had the good fortune to stop by a printer's shop. I met Mr. James Lackson, who did print work and sold used books and daily newspapers. He quickly signed me up for delivery service, but I was most interested in his books. It had been a long time since I'd read a good book! I begged him to let me borrow some. Finally, he agreed, probably to keep me from harping at him. He also let me read the newspapers in his shop. We became friendly. Anyway, I was thrilled at having books to read every night.

"One day, he asked me if I'd like to help with the typesetting for an order of printed stationery. I jumped at the chance to learn something new. A few deliveries were late that day, but I started scheduling more time with Mr. Lackson and spent Sundays setting type and working the presses. I had to refuse the formal apprenticeship he offered—by then, I felt that I couldn't spend seven years learning a trade at low pay when my delivery business was going so well."

"Thank you for telling me," Edie said.

Later that evening, Edie reflected on the new piece of Benji's story. She made entries in her notebook about Mr. Lackson and Benji learning to print.

She sat in her chair by the window, thinking. *Benji is accomplished in so many ways. He is kind and caring to others and saves lives, yet he is a criminal. Can it be justified? Where do I fit in? Do I fit in? It's time for me to take a stand, to become independent, perhaps, but what of Benji? Do we have a future together? I need to find out.*

When the day came for Edie's trip into the city, they left early. As they neared the market, Edie asked Benji to stop the wagon. "I have something I want to discuss." Her face was tight, her stomach fluttery. She pulled her hair back and reached one hand around to hold it. She was shaking. *I have to do this just right.*

He pulled the wagon to the side of the street and turned to her, a little concerned. He recognized her anxiety. "What's the matter, Edie?"

"I'm going to say something that you will not agree with. I don't want you to say anything now, but think about it, and we can discuss it when you pick me up." She took a deep breath. "You and your boys steal a lot of what the market sells, yet you charge the ladies for all the stolen items and still take a cut of the profits. Is that fair?"

His jaw dropped. "Everyone does well, Edie. What I charge covers the costs we have, including the rental of the warehouses. Every boy needs to be paid and provided for. And thievery doesn't happen without costs: we pay for information, for conveniences like unlocked doors and contacts on sailing vessels. And a percentage goes to Mrs. Hill."

"Why does Mrs. Hill get paid?" Edie asked.

"Because she financed it; she put up all the money. She owns the warehouse."

"Is Mrs. Hill a good person in the same way that I believe you are?"

"I wouldn't have the market, the boys, or the farm if it weren't for her, but I know she's a little more involved in larger activities than I can imagine. But I don't know her to be a bad person. On the other hand, I wouldn't want to cross her. She would have no mercy."

"Benji, I love you. I always will. I have no right to demand anything from you, but I have decided that I either have to leave the farm or you must include me in the gang activities. I want to know how they work, how you work, and I especially need to see that no one gets hurt except for losing a little money. I must be included. Or take a new direction with my life."

Her voice and face told him that she could not be dissuaded.

She took her basket of eggs, freshly slaughtered chickens, and her travel bag from the back of the wagon.

"I'll walk from here. See you in four days."

Benji hadn't expected Edie's demand. He sat in the wagon and thought about what had just happened. Edie had a strong will and determination. *She means a lot to me. I love her as a brother loves a sister. I fear I could love her as a lover. She's as capable as many of the boys, but it seems wrong to include her.*

He struggled with the thought of Edie in the gang; he could think of little else over the following days. He wondered how the scared but tough little girl he had rescued had turned into the determined, forceful woman who meant so much to him. For the first time in his adult life, he was confused about his future and his feelings.

CHAPTER 7

THE BEST OPTION

Maude let out a yell. "Edie's here!" Maude bounced along the alley toward Edie, arms flapping. Several ladies followed Maude, abandoning their stalls, and they all hugged. Edie laughed. "Can you spare a room for a few nights?"

"Your room is always ready," Maude said.

Alice made dumplings and a delicious stew with Edie's chickens.

After dinner, Edie, Maude, Britina, and Specs settled into their old positions at the table for a game of whist. Edie learned how the market was doing: it was busy leading up to Christmas, but business had been slower. "Not bad," Specs said. "We all made good money, but it's not our best year."

"We don't see Benji as much," Maude said. "You keeping him too busy?"

"Hardly!" Edie said. "He often has a lot of printing projects for Mrs. Hill."

The game stopped abruptly. Maude and Specs looked at each other, and Britina looked at Edie, her eyes wide.

Edie turned to Specs. "You know about Mrs. Hill?" Edie asked.

"We all know, Edie; we just never talk about it," Specs said. "I keep funds from Benji's cut to pay the rent every month, and I know he pays a percentage to her for getting the market started."

"You know all the goods you're selling are stolen."

"Not all of them, Edie," Maude said. "Benji also has some supply sources for legitimate goods, but a lot is stolen."

"Selling stolen goods makes you a criminal. Are you all right with that?"

"If we weren't selling stolen goods, Edie, we would all be sick, hungry, or dead . . . or prostituting ourselves for enough money to survive," Specs said quietly. "Benji and Mrs. Hill have given us a worthy life, an education, a place to live, a livelihood, even medical care at times," she added, pointing to her glasses. "We cannot approve or sanction the activities as morally right, but are they justifiable?"

Edie was quiet. She had asked herself the same question. She turned to Britina, who hadn't said a word, and they looked into each other's eyes. They knew each other more intimately.

Britina held the stare and said, "The Bible says that theft is a sin. From John 10:10, 'The thief comes only to steal, kill, and destroy. I have come that they may have life and have it to the full.' I believe thieving is wrong, but in this case, the acts it empowers are righteous. Benji brings us life and the means to fulfill it."

"Will you tell me about Mrs. Hill's operation, please?"

Specs spoke, "It's called the Forty Elephants."

Edie nodded, and Specs continued.

"Mrs. Hill maintains the persona of a socialite. She entertains the city's elite, sits on some business boards, and is known for making substantial investments in legitimate businesses and organizations. But her primary business is shoplifting from the high-end stores where her women, wearing garments with hidden pockets and spaces to stash goods, lift items and leave. None of the authorities know of Mrs. Hill's involvement. She arranges the targets and the sale of the stolen goods, and she takes care of her women."

Edie spent the next three days enjoying time with her old friends while anxiously wondering what Benji would say about her ultimatum. With the input of her friends, her anger and worry over his criminal activities lessened. She was anxious to be a part of the operation and relieved that she didn't have to leave Benji, the boys, and these ladies—if only Benji agreed.

Benji returned on the evening of the twenty-seventh. He tied the horses to a post and sought Edie in the warehouse. The women knew about the conflict between Benji and Edie, and they sat quietly and watched as Benji approached Edie and handed her a bag. He looked red in the face; he didn't look Edie in the eyes.

"I'm not happy about this, but put these clothes on."

Edie took the bag to the privy stall she had shared with Britina and changed into black pants, a black shirt, and a flat black cap with a rim. She was uneasy; she had forced her position but, in doing so, disappointed Benji. *At this point, I have no option*, she thought.

When she came out of the privy, Benji was standing outside. "Tuck all your hair up into the hat," he said, handing her a pair of black gloves. "You're working with the boys and me tonight. I told them your demand, and I took a vote on including you . . . I voted no." He turned and headed back outside.

He wants to protect me. He knows I'm capable—I'll just have to show him. The boys support me.

Edie said goodbye to all her friends. Britina was last. They hugged each other tightly, Britina nestling her face into Edie's shoulder. "Be very careful," she whispered.

"I will, my good friend. I love you," Edie replied.

Edie climbed to the buckboard seat beside Benji, placing her bag in the wagon bed. She glanced up at his face. He still didn't look at her. *Stubborn.* She gripped the side rail. *What will this night bring?* she wondered. Her body tingled; she wasn't sure if she was nervous, excited, or both. They met up with two other wagons with four boys in each. Benji led the way. They slowly drove twisty lanes and alleys toward the Docklands. They hid the wagon and Benji's buckboard in an alley as close to the quay as possible.

"The docks are so backed up that if sailor merchants don't offload and sell to the likes of us, cargo will rot and be wasted." He pointed to the river and said, "Other ships out there could wait three weeks or more to get a slot to unload their goods; it's a real bottleneck. The sailors want shore leave and money to enjoy themselves— they don't want to wait. We'll take a flatbed raft from the Blackwell docks to two ships we know and offload textiles, furs, bales of tea, hogsheads of tobacco, crates of bouillon and spices. We take just a small portion of each shipment. Are you ready?"

Edie's heart was beating faster than she ever remembered; she knew her eyes were darting in all directions. She was scared but also exhilarated. "Ready," she said.

"We'll have to unload in a hurry when we return to the dock and run crates to the wagon," Will told her. Then he and the other boys went to a dilapidated dock.

The boys pulled a concealed flat raft out from under the unusable dock. It was dark. Edie took one boy's hand and stepped onto the raft. When all were aboard, they pulled out two long poles secured under the dock and started poling into the water. No one spoke. They circled behind two moored vessels and out toward anchored ships. At the first ship, they secured the raft to the ship's lines at water level, and two boys climbed to the deck above. "I'm going!" Edie said.

"No!" Benji said.

She started to climb up. "I have to," she replied.

Edie followed the boys to the ship's cargo hold. Looking at the massive cargo load, Edie whispered, "How do we know which to take?"

"We have help," Mike said. "Any crate, container, or bale with a red X on it is our load."

She found some red X parcels and carried them back to the raft.

Then she returned for more. "Is anyone on board?" she asked Will, who was standing watch.

"Don't know, probably at the saloons."

"And if someone sees me?"

"Yell, dive overboard, and make sure you miss the raft." He grinned.

They each made four trips to the hold, unconfronted, and then they climbed down to the raft.

They quickly poled away to another ship. As they approached, Edie could see five sailors walking around on deck.

"What do we do? We'll be spotted," Edie said.

"Benji will board and deal with the captain," Will replied.

"What do you mean 'deal with the captain'?"

Benji said, "He means to complete my deal with the captain, Edie. We do not harm anyone." He looked at her this time.

They pulled alongside, and Benji climbed a lowered line. He was greeted by the captain. They seemed to know each other. Ten minutes later, sailors lowered six bales of tea to the raft, followed by additional parcels.

Fully loaded, they headed back to the unused dock. "If we're approached, Edie," Will said, "don't yell—just run as fast as you can to the wagon."

She nodded.

After unloading ten to twelve containers to the dock, Edie and one of the boys started transporting them to the wagon. Benji and the other boys continued to unload. On her return, she heard, "Halt, stop there." Edie was scared. She held her breath, her stomach felt sick, and her heart was pounding in her ears. She turned and ran to the wagon as fast as she could and waited. No one else showed up. *Were they all caught?* She carefully peeked around the corner; Benji was shaking hands with the man who had called out to her. Benji handed him an envelope.

The boys were watching for her. Will waved, and then he and Mike carried more cargo toward the wagons. When Will arrived at the wagon, Edie punched him hard in the arm. He giggled. "You giggle like a girl," Edie teased. He giggled more. When they were fully loaded, the two wagons left in different directions.

Edie said, "That was so exciting. Who was that man?" Her words were high-pitched, and she was breathing very quickly.

"He's a customs guard who arranges deals for us with various ships and protects our raft."

"Why are we going in different directions?"

"We don't have protection outside the Docklands. If we're apprehended, we only risk losing part of our night's work. We have our own warehouse where we'll unload, and the boys will sort goods for delivery to various locations later tonight and make deliveries tomorrow morning. It's where we'll stay tonight. We'll make up a bunk for you."

Edie just nodded; she was exhilarated, tingling all over. *Why?* she wondered. She had just committed a crime, yet it was the most exciting thing she had ever done.

Benji was still uncomfortable with Edie participating. It took more convincing from all the boys she had worked with that she could be an asset to their activities.

Then she was part of the team.

Edie was eighteen and wholly converted to her "justified" life of crime.

Two nights later, back at the farm, Edie joined Benji after dinner, accompanying him to the print shop; as they walked, she took his hand. He looked down into her eyes, and he squeezed a little. Benji unlocked the door, lit the lantern, and entered; Edie followed. She placed her hand on his arm and turned him toward her; she rolled on her toes, reached her face up, and kissed him lightly. Benji looked into her eyes longingly. Edie said a simple, "Thank you." Then she added, "Now you have work to do." She smiled. "I'll get the paper supplies."

CHAPTER 8

THE RAID

One early afternoon, Hank—one of the older boys Edie knew from his deliveries to the market—drove into the farm road with one of the three wagons from the London warehouse that had gone to the city earlier that morning. Edie gathered with the others to find out why he was here and alone.

Hank breathed rapidly. "The market!" he managed, gasping for air. He was in a panic.

"Someone get him water," Edie demanded, then turned to Hank. "What happened? Take your time." Her chest tightened, afraid of his answer.

"It . . . it was raided by . . . by the police."

"Get down from the wagon, Hank. Let's go inside," one of the boys said.

Another added, "Someone get him a beer."

When Hank was calmer, beer in hand, he told the group about the events that had occurred earlier that day.

"The market was raided by the police midmorning, at its busiest," he said. "Eight bobbies ran in with their clubs raised over their heads. They destroyed all the stalls."

"Was anyone hurt?" Edie asked, fighting off panic.

"I don't know, really," Hank said. "A few customers and our ladies might have had some direct altercations. The police brought in prisoner wagons and carts after the raid was underway. They loaded merchandise into the carts. The last I saw, all the stall money was being gathered and given to a sergeant."

"Do you know who they arrested?" Edie asked.

Calmer now, Hank said, "I first saw Maude. She confronted one of the constables. 'We're legitimate businesses! What is the meaning of this?' I heard her yell at him. He laughed and cuffed her to a prisoner wagon. I think Benji and Specs were in the warehouse when the commotion started happening at the stalls. I saw Specs run behind the stalls carrying the strongbox of money from the warehouse in her arms. She turned down an alley. I don't know what happened to her. I didn't see Benji after that. Later, I saw Britina run down the same alley, but far behind Specs. There were two bobbies after her."

"Where were you to see all this?" Edie asked.

"I hid when it all started. I climbed a drainpipe to a roof above the stalls and just watched; I couldn't do anything except hide."

"It's all right, Hank. You did the right thing—nothing else you could have done," Edie said. "Did you see who else they arrested?"

"The bobbies took at least a dozen women to a prisoner wagon and six of our boys. The constable in charge sent the customers on their way."

"Not Benji?" Edie asked.

"Like I said, I never saw him again."

"Did the police find the warehouse?"

"I don't know," Hank said. "I couldn't see the entrance in the alley. When everyone had gone, I didn't check. I found one of our wagons still in one piece and took off for the farm. I wasn't followed; I made sure."

"Get some rest, Hank. You did well," Edie said.

Edie's limbs were shaky; she had an intense feeling of unease. She had to do something. These were her friends.

"Mark, please rig up the small carriage. I'm going to town."

"I don't think it's a good idea, Edie."

"I'll be fine, and I'll be careful."

She imagined all sorts of nasty scenarios during her drive to London. *Her friends were going to be prosecuted as criminals!* It took her back to her ethical debates on their work. *What if they went to prison? What would happen to them?*

The market had been operating for years. *Why raid it now?* Edie wondered. Even some of the police and their families shopped there on occasion. *There must be a reason.*

Hours later, arriving in London, dressed in stylish clothes and riding in a lady's carriage, she felt above suspicion. She drove near the market site. The bobbies had destroyed all the stalls and scattered merchandise throughout the alley—the more valuable merchandise they had taken.

She tied the horse to a lamppost and cautiously entered the site. It was heartbreaking to take in. She approached the warehouse and found the door open. She peeked in. She stepped in and saw that everything had been torn down or smashed, the goods gone. Walking around, she looked at each bedroom for signs of life or death. In Britina's space, she saw the corner of her Bible sticking out from under her torn mattress and broken frame; she picked it up and hugged it and again prayed that her friends were safe. *Was it a mistake to have accepted crime as a way of life?*

I must find Benji.

Edie drove her carriage to the lockup. When she arrived, Edie took a few deep breaths to shore up her courage. The police didn't know her and couldn't associate her with any crimes, she hoped. She walked in, head held high, a serious, determined look on her face. A burly, older, uniformed officer stood at the counter.

"What can I do for you, young lady?" he said condescendingly.

"My name is Marie-Nicole, and I teach the Bible for the Catholic Relief Reform School." She hoped this at least sounded real.

"And?" the officer said.

"I believe you have behind bars one of my students, Britina Myers, a promising person."

"And if we do?"

"Will you give her this Bible?"

Edie could tell that she had him then. He wouldn't refuse a Bible for fear of Godly punishment.

"If she's here, I'll give it to her."

"May I leave a note?"

"I'll have to read it first," he said.

"I understand." Edie took a piece of paper and a pencil from the officer, wrote, *Stay strong, make good decisions, and trust your instincts*, and signed it Marie-Nicole. She knew the message would tell Britina who she was. The phrase was one that Britina often used to counsel Edie.

Edie touched the man's hand and said, "Thank you. You're a good man."

She turned and walked to the door, turned back, and asked, "I understand from the nuns that you arrested the man who was the ringleader of this illegal market. Good work."

"We didn't get him, lady, but we will soon."

Edie touched her chest as the tension released. *He remained free. What's going to happen to the others?*

Back at the farm, Edie pulled Mark aside. "Can I talk with you?"

He nodded, and they went to sit in the dining area.

"Mark, I stopped at the lockup. The officer I spoke with confirmed that they don't have Benji, but he implied that a search is on to find him. Does anyone know about the farm location?"

"They could, but we've never been bothered. I don't think any of the boys arrested will reveal the location. I hope not."

"How much trouble are the women and boys in?"

"It depends on the judge. They'll try to use them to find Benji."

"Where would Benji go to stay undercover?"

"I don't know, Edie. He'll avoid contact with you if he thinks it might implicate you in any way. If he's captured, they'll come down hard on him."

"You don't think he'll come back here?"

"I suspect he won't be back here until he feels it's completely safe for all of us."

"I assume you'll suspend raids and other activities."

"We'll just run the farm for now, Edie; it's all we can do safely."

This police raid could ruin Benji. The women and boys in jail, the police after him—he could do something rash. If he avoids the farm to protect the rest of us, there's only one person he'll turn to, Mrs. Hill. She was likely the only one who would know where Benji was, and she'd want to protect him—if for no other reason than wanting to keep her involvement confidential. Edie began forming a plan.

She made her decision. "Mark, will you allow me to take possession of the small wagon and two horses? I'll send word on where to retrieve them."

"Edie, you can do whatever you want. Benji has made that clear."

"I could be gone a while. Will you take care of my things? I'll travel light."

"Of course," Mark said. "Can you tell me where you're going?"

"I hope I'll find Benji. I'll stay in touch by inland mail or messenger. I'll let you know where I end up and how to reach me. If you find him first, I need to know."

Edie traveled again to the West End with just a few belongings, her favorite books tied in her blanket and some of her savings safely hidden in her garments. She dressed in her work clothes. She left her horses and wagon at the Hyde Park stables.

She went to the stately residence of Mrs. Hill in the Mayfair district and presented herself at the front door. She rang the bell and waited. A man in a black suit answered and immediately announced, "You can receive a handout from the cook, Molly, at the back door. Please take yourself there."

She saw no benefit to saying or doing anything except going to the back door. Upon knocking, an older woman with a pleasant, welcoming smile dressed in kitchen garb invited her to sit at the servants' table in the kitchen. She brought Edie fresh bread, a scrap of cold chicken, and a cup of tea. Edie was pleased; she had yet to eat since the prior evening.

Molly sat across from Edie. "And what might your story be, sweetie?" she asked, obviously expecting a tale of hardship that she had heard many times before.

Hardening her voice, Edie said, "My name is Minnie Rose, and I'm here to meet Mrs. Hill and to offer my services."

Molly leaned back with her mouth open in surprise. "Whatever do you mean, young lady?"

"I have talents to offer Mrs. Hill, and I would appreciate it if you would tell her Miss Minnie Rose would like an audience."

Molly was stunned by Edie's grit. She said nothing but headed up the stairs, shaking her head. Edie finished her tea and poured a little more. She had determined that a new name—if only a stage name—was necessary: it would be best not to divulge her association with Benji until she knew more.

Molly returned, saying that Mrs. Hill would see Edie, and ushered her up a staircase and into an elegant sitting room. Edie had pictured Mrs. Hill from Benji's stories but was surprised at how tall and straight she stood. She wore a delicate full-length tiered skirt with gathered material at the back. Her hair was dark and fashioned into a practical bob tied with a ribbon. She was standing in the middle of the room to greet Minnie Rose as the cook presented her. In a calm but rather stern voice, she said, "Young lady, I understand you have something to offer me?"

"I do," Edie replied, looking over her shoulder to wait for Molly to retreat. When she was gone, she said, "I want to join your gang."

Mrs. Hill was startled. "Minnie, I don't know what you think I'm involved with, but you're mistaken."

"Please forgive me, Mrs. Hill, but I know full well what you and your forty ladies do."

"How would you know about my business?"

"I grew up in the slums of London's East End, and the streets know a lot. I ask questions, and I listen."

"You better sit down," Mrs. Hill said. She offered Edie a seat and poured tea from a pot that was now lukewarm. Mrs. Hill stayed standing and fixed her eyes on Edie's face.

"You speak with a more sophisticated voice than I'd expect from the history you claim," she noted.

"A friend taught me to read and write as we worked together, committing a few petty crimes. She was educated before she ended up on the streets when her parents died. My main talent was creating a diversion while she'd steal from our target. The skills I've learned and the language and accent I've perfected can also help your members in their business. I've come to work for you."

"Minnie," Mrs. Hill said, her voice grim, "tell me what you think you know."

CHAPTER 9

THE FORTY ELEPHANTS

Edie faced Mrs. Hill with a steely calm. She had rehearsed this scenario in her mind. Her future depended on displaying steadfast strength and courage.

"You are high-end shoplifters," Edie declared bluntly. "You raid stores for substantial hauls and have never been caught. I've heard that some of your members had been identified but not captured. I heard of Maggie Hughes, who ran out of one store with a tray of thirty-four diamond rings visible, and when approached, she scared off the police detective with a hatpin aimed at his eye. I've carried a hatpin for protection since I was a little girl. Your women are all trained, stylish, and sophisticated. I'm told their clothes are modified to create hidden pockets and spaces. They approach the large stores and upper-class shops around London in small groups. They hide loot in coats, cummerbunds, muffs, skirts, bloomers, and hats. It is rumored their activities net thousands of pounds, and every lady is well compensated."

"I think I need to sit down." Mrs. Hill sighed. She poured herself some tea, put it down, stood back up, went to a sideboard, and poured a brandy.

Edie felt gratified that she had made an impression.

Sitting down, Mrs. Hill said, "Maggie's method is not how we prefer to do business. Maintaining anonymity is all-important, and while most of our women work for us for life, Maggie had to leave.

I'm shocked by your knowledge of us; even the Metropolitan Police cannot deduce our members or my involvement. Their leader attends my dinner parties here without a clue, yet here you are in my sitting room with more knowledge of my operations than the entire legal establishment."

"The illegal establishment knows a lot more," Edie explained.

"I don't know you, and you have private information on my activities; this concerns me."

In a powerful voice, Edie held her gaze and said, "You can trust me."

"My 'gang,' as you put it, has a long history, and we're quite successful, as you know, but we are cautious. We have a stringent set of rules that we enforce, and there are no exceptions. That's why Maggie had to leave."

"I understand," Edie said. She softened her voice. "I have hopes that you'll accept me. I *will* prove my worth."

"I would like you to stay here at my home. I'll have you checked, and I'll consult my partners. Do you have an arrest record?"

"I do not, I'm cautious too," Edie answered.

"You show grit, and I like that. You're attractive and young; you might be useful in diverting guards and clerks while the women work. If you check out, we'll discuss how to proceed."

Edie moved into a spare servant's room off the kitchen until Mrs. Hill was ready to see her again. Mrs. Hill escorted her there personally, telling Molly to take care of her.

"Don't talk to my employees about anything you know about me. I will not tolerate it," Mrs. Hill said sternly.

"I won't."

Edie spent an anxious five days waiting to hear from Mrs. Hill again. She diverted herself by having her meals with Molly, who was always too busy talking to ask probing questions. On her first full day, Edie inspected the property. She visited the barns to see if there was a carriage or a horse she recognized as Benji's. After that, she spent her time taking long walks in Hyde Park.

She became friendly with the stable manager, Willie, at the Hyde Park stables. She carefully observed his care and kindness to his horses and his dog. Her instincts told her she could trust him, and she liked him. Eventually, she asked if he would receive mail and messages for her while she was in the area. He agreed and didn't probe into the reasons why. She wrote a note to Mark and asked Willie to mail it: *Any word? None here.* She told Mark what she was doing with Mrs. Hill and her assumed name and told him to reply to Willie at the Hyde Park stables. She tipped Willie well.

After such a long wait, Edie worried that Mrs. Hill was stalling and that they might have determined she was not who she claimed.

Finally, she received a note inviting her to dine with Mrs. Hill the following day. Edie spent the afternoon considering all the options and how she might respond to them. The next day, she dressed carefully before walking up the stairs to knock on the door to Mrs. Hill's rooms.

"Come in, Minnie," Mrs. Hill said.

A well-dressed lady was already seated in the dining room when Edie entered. "This is Pearl, Minnie. She's been observing you on your walks this past week." Edie panicked—*the stables!* she thought. *A stupid mistake.*

"Hello, Pearl," Edie said. Pearl had short hair, and her pointy face and small mouth reminded Edie of a squirrel. She displayed no humor. She did not seem pleasant at all.

Pearl nodded at Minnie. Mrs. Hill sat down. A soup tureen and a basket of bread were already on the table. A servant entered and ladled soup for each woman and placed a roll on their plates.

I guess I won't dip my bread, Edie thought, still worried about what was to come.

"You like horses, Minnie?" Mrs. Hill said.

"I do," Edie said with all the enthusiasm she could muster. "I've been visiting the stables at the park each day; there are some nice horses, and Willie's good-looking as well."

"You can do better, Minnie, and I don't expect you'll have much time for flirting for quite a while. We found nothing about you that would keep me from giving you a try. Pearl will be your trainer. You'll learn our system and our rules by heart and then have some practice sessions acting out a raid, and finally, you'll observe a few operations without participating. Until you're ready."

She had succeeded! Edie wanted to smile, but she chose a more serious demeanor. She was pleased but nervous that she was entering a higher realm of criminal activity. Most importantly, she knew it would lead her back to Benji one way or another.

After finishing the soup, Mrs. Hill stood and excused herself and left Pearl to take over.

Pearl turned to Minnie, snarling, "You're not allowed one slip, do you understand? You will always do as I say—on the job and off."

Edie held her tongue and said, "Yes, I promise," in her meekest voice.

"We'll start today with a manicure, and we'll get you a new hairstyle and some proper clothing. We'll meet again at eight tomorrow morning and begin your training."

Edie watched the ladies enter the store from separate entrances on her first observation assignment. Each entered and headed in different directions. They casually strolled from aisle to aisle. She saw how swiftly and deftly each woman stored items away in her garments. She had been practicing with the ladies at the mansion, but seeing it in action was impressive. Rings, watches, furs, hats, shoes, cosmetics— they took anything of value. Edie was nervous for the ladies, but she took no risk herself. Her instructions were to leave before the women, get the horse carriage, and drive slowly along the front of the building and down the side street. Each lady would get on at a different spot. It all went smoothly, and they unloaded goods at a small warehouse. It was a sizeable haul.

Edie's first actual theft was at the Liberty Department Store, famous for luxury goods and collections from foreign lands. It displayed a mock-Tudor frontage flying a Union Jack and had multiple floors filled with nooks and crannies full of expensive items.

She was extremely nervous—her stomach was fluttery and her hands sweaty. She didn't want to drop anything. She was thankful the other women encouraged her as their carriage neared the store. Once inside, Edie found that picking up jewelry was easy; she hid away several pieces as she walked past the displays. Fabric was more complex (the store was famous for its Liberty-print fabrics). Edie picked up a folded piece that a clerk had cut off a bolt and placed on the table. As she was about to slip it behind her jacket into her corset, a store clerk said, "I'm sorry." Edie's heart jumped into her mouth, but she maintained a calm bearing. "This piece has been spoken for; may I assist you with another pattern?"

"No, you are kind to offer," was all she could manage. She turned and left the department and the store with just a few pieces of jewelry.

All the women sympathized when Edie described her nervousness; they had all been through it. Through the subsequent few raids, she improved and mastered her techniques. Even the sour Pearl gave her a little praise—Pearl said Edie thought quickly on her feet, adding that it was a good trait to develop.

More stores were employing guards. Mrs. Hill approved Edie's proposal to use her to divert attention. All the women agreed.

She collected a few messages from Mark, but there was no news of Benji or the arrested women and boys. Benji was not at the mansion or in Mrs. Hill's circles. Edie was worried. There was nothing to do except work.

Then, finally, Mark sent word that he had received a message from Benji. Mark asked to meet with Edie at the stables. Her hopes were high, and she tried to keep her emotions in check. When Edie arrived at the stables, Mark had her sit on a bale of hay. Her mood changed. *Is he going to tell me Benji's dead?*

"Edie, Benji asked me to talk to you face-to-face."

Her face tightened; her throat closed. Something terrible was coming.

"Is he all right?"

"Edie, he was devastated by the arrest of the market women and the boys. He went into hiding; I don't know where. He contacted a barrister he knew of through his association with Mrs. Hill. The barrister contacted the head of the London police, and Benji volunteered to turn himself in."

"What!" Edie moaned, a sudden weakness in her limbs. "He can't. Why?" She slid off the hay onto her knees and put her face in her hands. Lifting her head, her chin quaking, she asked, "What can we do?"

"Nothing, Edie; he's exchanging his freedom for the release of all the arrested women and boys."

Edie was crying now, tears streaming down her face. "What will happen, Mark?"

"The barrister is smart, he wasn't going to let Benji's case go to a jury trial, so they settled on a seven-year sentence."

Edie put her face on Mark's shoulder, and he held her until she stopped crying.

Edie wiped her eyes with the back of her hand. "Did he send me a message?"

"Edie," Mark said. "He knows you're with Mrs. Hill. His message was to 'trust your instincts and make good decisions.' I don't know what he was trying to say, but it seemed important to him that I convey that exactly. He also said to tell you he loves you."

Edie almost smiled through her tears. "I know what he meant, Mark. Can you communicate with him again, or can I?"

"No, it's done, Edie. We don't even know where he'll be incarcerated."

"Have they released the ladies and boys?"

"Yes, the judge agreed to the deal on terms of transportation."

"What does that mean?" Edie asked.

"They will be transported to Australia and released to make their way."

Her friends would be impossibly far away. She started crying again. "When?" she managed.

"They're gone, Edie."

She clung to Mark, trying to take it all in. She would dwell on the "I love you."

Edie's rise in the Forty Elephants gang was unprecedented. She was superb at diversion, allowing gang members to increase their haul. And the ladies loved her; she knew where they came from and understood their struggles to become part of the gang. She became a counselor to a few younger women and became a crucial part of Mrs. Hill's social and professional life. Over time they developed trust in each other. She was allowed to stay in Mrs. Hill's residence, and guests were told she was a niece who had come to live. Free from Pearl's oversight and trusted by Mrs. Hill, Edie had increasing autonomy.

She took up a hobby on her occasional days off, taking riding lessons from an instructor engaged through Willie at the stables. The lessons allowed her to keep communicating with the farm, and while she genuinely enjoyed learning to ride, she also knew it could add to her appearance as a lady with social standing.

Mrs. Hill watched as Minnie matured in the organization. Her trust in the young woman grew as Minnie grew in confidence. She recognized Minnie's skill at presenting herself as an upper-class person and appreciated her role as a mentor to the new recruits. As Edie continued to prove her worth as Minnie, Mrs. Hill included her in discussions about the business and financial aspects of the Forty Elephants' operations. Mrs. Hill began to plan for Minnie's future.

Edie buried her heartbreak about Benji in her new responsibilities.

One evening Mrs. Hill summoned Edie to her bedroom office.

"Minnie, I have an assignment. I need you to take several of the women and manage them in the seaside town of Brighton. Brighton is becoming a boomtown for wealthy individuals, and the stores are happy to accommodate them with fine goods. London is getting riskier. I've decided to taper off activity here until it cools down and focus on a clean territory."

Edie was both excited and apprehensive about the move to Brighton. She was confident that her women would do well, but being on her own in a new town was a big responsibility. On the other hand, Edie welcomed the distance from Mrs. Hill and the London operation. She could communicate more frequently with Mark; she would let him know where she was so he could tell Benji once he had contact. And it was a financial opportunity that would increase her wealth.

As Edie set up operations in Brighton, Mrs. Hill continued to handle distribution. She introduced James Henderson into the picture. Edie remembered that he had played a role in Benji's past, and she felt he wasn't trustworthy. To Edie, Henderson seemed too slick. He was to pick up merchandise in an enclosed wagon every two weeks and transport it back to London. Edie knew Mrs. Hill never handled or saw the goods, but she maintained a network of receivers, fences, street market traders, and pawnbrokers. The market raid had taken away one very lucrative outlet, but she had others.

Edie kept an eye on her inventory, documenting every piece before Henderson transported it to London.

After a few months of working with Henderson, Edie began to suspect that he was skimming merchandise before turning it over in London; her documentation and the monies she received didn't match up. She booked a weekend train to London and sent a note to Mrs. Hill that she would be visiting. Mrs. Hill received her as soon as she arrived, and they retired to the sitting room.

Edie didn't wait for formalities. Her voice was a touch challenging. "Mrs. Hill, my receipts are short; I suspect Henderson, but I would like your opinion." She spread out her paperwork on the tea table. She accounted for every item sent to London, the monies she had received, and what she expected to receive.

Mrs. Hill looked amused. "Henderson used to be my top lieutenant. I still rely on him for assistance, and I have a long-range plan shaped around his abilities as an effective con man, planned months ago. He can accomplish things that a woman can't. However, he is greedy and less loyal than I thought he was.

"I suspect Henderson will skim product coming here and monies sent to you. I'll monitor that as well, with your help. I want to see just how much I can't trust him. Don't let on what you suspect; we'll act when appropriate. I'll ensure you and your ladies are made whole on your earnings. Thank you for coming to me."

Brighton was smaller than London, so Edie knew she would need a different approach to her work. She averaged one theft a week, cased each target the day of the strike, and used different women on different days.

She had earned Mrs. Hill's syndicate a lot of money and was an almost-wealthy woman herself. Her financial future looked much better than it had before her time with Mrs. Hill. She started considering how she would like the next few years to evolve. Her feelings for Benji were more than friendship—she needed him. She dreamed that she would eventually leave the syndicate and be with Benji. She frequently recalled the "I love you" in the last message he had sent her.

The months went by, and Edie buried herself in her work. One gray day in early spring, the target was Hannington's on North Street in Brighton. Edie's three best ladies were dressed and ready to shop. They entered a few minutes apart, Edie first. When she'd visited the store earlier, it had been packed with shoppers—the weather was drizzly, and shopping was a good substitute for the beach. She straightened her posture and walked up to the floor guard.

"Please take me to the manager's office," she demanded in her sternest voice.

"What's the problem, ma'am?" the floor guard asked.

"I have a serious complaint; this establishment has improperly treated me, and I want it made right, or my friends and I will never shop here again. Will you take me to your manager or not?"

Ladies Judy, Margaret, and Barbara went to their assigned areas and started covertly filling their storage garments with expensive clothing, shoes, jewelry, cosmetics, and accessories. Women in the finer stores are usually afforded privacy from the staff, so it was easy to stash away a fine collection of goods quickly and undetected. But that day, something was different.

Edie and the guard had just started walking to the manager's office when a shopper yelled, "Thief!" The woman was pointing at Margaret, whom she had spotted stowing a necklace in her dress. A panic broke out throughout the store, with shoppers scurrying toward exits and staff scanning for shoplifters.

The guard grabbed Edie's arm and said, "You're a part of this, aren't you?"

"You're hurting my arm; I know nothing of what's going on; you have no right—"

He didn't buy it. "Come with me until the police arrive," he demanded.

Barbara made it out of an exit quickly. However, Judy and Margaret were grabbed by clerks, and concealed goods were discovered on their bodies, despite their protests. The police held Edie, along with Judy and Margaret. Judy and Margaret stuck to their training and denied knowing Minnie.

Overnight in the local lockup, Edie paced the floor all night. *Being caged is not something I could survive*, she thought. Then her thoughts went to Benji, incarcerated somewhere. Edie hadn't possessed any stolen goods, so she was released the following day.

Margaret and Judy appeared before a judge later that day and were convicted and sentenced to three years of penal labor—they were the Forty Elephants' first convicted thieves.

Edie was heartbroken and ashamed—the women were her responsibility. She was supposed to protect them, and she'd failed. And now her face was familiar as a suspected thief. She didn't want her life with the Elephants anymore. She felt an emptiness. And more than anything, she wanted Benji with her. She hadn't heard from him or Mark in months. She worried she would never see Benji again.

Mrs. Hill sent word to close down the Brighton operation and return to the residence.

Molly greeted Edie coolly when she returned and told her she could move into the old room behind the kitchen until Mrs. Hill sent for her. Days went by, and Mrs. Hill didn't ask to see her. Her meals were brought to her room by Molly, who didn't stay and talk as she used to. Edie wasn't sure how Mrs. Hill felt toward her now. She used her time to read and write in her journals, trying to regain her belief in herself. She started thinking about how to separate herself from the Elephants and Mrs. Hill.

After a week of solitude, Mrs. Hill invited Edie to dine with her that evening.

She arrived in the dining room promptly at 7:00 p.m.

"Drink?" Mrs. Hill offered quietly. Edie couldn't read her mood—she was determined to at least appear calm. She didn't usually accept a drink but thought it best to say yes this time.

"Yes, sherry, please." She fixed a hard stare at Mrs. Hill.

Mrs. Hill gave her a hard stare back and opened the conversation. "Minnie, I'm disappointed that your operation in Brighton was shut down, and we've lost two ladies to jail, though I expected that the time would come when the Forty Elephants must try different tactics. What do you think went wrong?"

"I've been contemplating that over the past few days. There are several possibilities. First, the stores are smaller, so I should have used fewer women. Second, the Elephants were becoming known in London, so it was only a matter of time before the Brighton stores started to watch for them. They've increased guard surveillance, which complicates the typical approaches as well. Lastly, it was pure bad luck having a shopper whistleblowing on Margaret."

Mrs. Hill smiled, "That's good reasoning, Minnie. I've also had setbacks in my career and learned from them. I believe you've learned from this one."

A little relieved, Edie said, "What will happen now?"

"Minnie, you were unlucky at the robbery. As to the future, I have plans. Henderson has skimmed from both of us, but not enough for me to act now. I need him for an operation with some of my partners. I included Henderson because it needs a male lead, but I can't trust him now. I'll let him know that I'm aware of our mistrust at an appropriate time. I want you to become part of the operation, and you and I will monitor all the activities. You'll benefit greatly, providing everything goes as planned. When it comes time to settle, I'll deal with Henderson."

The offer was not what Edie had expected from the meeting. Could this new activity allow her to take more significant steps toward separating herself? "Can you tell me more?" Edie asked.

"I've made plans for a very profitable series of events. My partners and I agreed that I would bring in the talent and finance a portion of the operation. I engaged Henderson, and he brought on a partner of his, Mr. William Walker. Planning and arrangements have been in the works for over a year. I'll keep Henderson in the operation as the frontman because he can pull off the scam. I want to involve you as my direct representative and the person in charge of the money. This twist will be an unpleasant surprise to Henderson, but I suspect he can't refuse. Henderson and Walker will be here for drinks tomorrow to discuss details. I will introduce your role in the plan at that time. You shouldn't comment too much or react to any surprises you may hear. Are you comfortable with that?"

"Yes. The plan sounds intriguing. Thank you for trusting me."

"You haven't given me a reason not to trust you."

Edie smiled at her, hoping she could trust Mrs. Hill too. She drained her sherry.

"Can you tell me what we'll be doing?" Edie asked.

"To start, we'll steal a ship."

CHAPTER 10

MRS. HILL'S PLAN

Henderson and his friend William Walker dressed for a formal dinner, but when they arrived at Mrs. Hill's home, she told them there would be no food. She'd made the excuse that Molly was ill, but the truth was that she couldn't tolerate a pleasant dinner with Henderson. She poured champagne for everyone.

Edie studied the men upon their arrival. There was one striking difference between them. *Faces tell a lot*, Edie thought. Mr. Walker had a turned-down mouth that made him look disagreeable. His eyebrows were bushy and dark. His eyes were dark as well, giving him a sinister look. His speech had an air of sophistication and superiority. He shook Minnie's hand.

On the other hand, Henderson tried to be charming, but she already knew him too well. She appraised him from a new viewpoint on this encounter. He was no longer her superior, and she assessed him as if she were meeting him for the first time. He was tall and powerfully built, his skin bronzed from outdoor exposure—away from London, Edie assumed. His nose was long and hooked, but the two distinguishing characteristics of Mr. Henderson were his deep, penetrating blue eyes and a scar that crossed his right cheek from ear to chin, giving him a buccaneer look. Edie was angry and distrustful after his stealing from her and Mrs. Hill.

♦ ♦ ♦

Mrs. Hill had cautioned Edie to go along with what she said and not act surprised. Edie was curious but didn't let it show. Mrs. Hill addressed the gentlemen: "You've discussed my plan?"

"We have. It's quite interesting and, I must say, ingenious," commented Henderson.

Mrs. Hill smiled. "Thank you, James. As promised, I will fund the operations and expect a return of my capital and fifty percent of the take on trade and the sale of the ship."

"What trade activities have already been arranged?" Henderson asked.

"My bank, Sterling Union International Bank of London, is owned by a group of South African businessmen who are deeply involved in the import and trade of guns. Our ship will provide the opportunity for a very lucrative trade at sea. You should be able to negotiate other transactions for cargo from port to port."

Mrs. Hill was not surprised when Walker objected to fifty-fifty on trade. "You have money at risk, but we have ourselves at risk and must find the other trade opportunities," Walker argued.

"Do you have the money or contacts to pull it off without me?"

"No," Walker answered.

"Then my terms are accepted?"

Walker deferred to Henderson, who nodded.

"And they are fair," Mrs. Hill added.

Henderson shrugged. "We agree, Mrs. Hill. We'll put things in motion in the morning."

"I have a couple of conditions we haven't yet discussed. Minnie is my right-hand lieutenant." Minnie glanced at Henderson to see his reaction to this declaration; he had none. "She will travel with you. She will travel as your wife, James. You will be Mr. and Mrs. Barnett Smith, a wealthy merchant and his elegant spouse. Minnie will be my eyes and ears on the ship and report to me by cable at various ports."

Edie noticed a slight tension in both men and a glance between them. She tensed herself, thinking she'd prefer marriage under different circumstances. Both men nodded but did not comment.

Mrs. Hill added, "During the voyage, Minnie will record all transactions. She will also monitor and control all cash and financial activities, forwarding money to me when appropriate at various ports. Enough cash will remain on board for operations and your personal use, but the majority will be returned here to London. We will split up the shares upon your return."

Walker was visibly upset. He said, "I disagree! You'll have my portion, and I don't know if I'll ever see it."

"Mr. Walker, you will be allocated sufficient money during the trip. Your money is safe with me. Consider me your bank. I'm sure Mr. Henderson will vouch for my integrity and trustworthiness."

Henderson paused briefly, knowing he had no choice but to support Mrs. Hill. "William, your money will be safe. It's risky to keep too much cash on board; if we're ever short of money, I'll contact Mrs. Hill for funds."

Mrs. Hill corrected him. "You'll talk to Minnie, and *she* will contact me."

The financial hierarchy was established.

Henderson nodded but did not make eye contact with Minnie, who was trying not to show her surprise. She was nervous she might be in deeper than she could handle.

Mrs. Hill continued: "I will plant a crew member as Minnie's protector, and only the two will know of this. She will travel with two additional trunks of valuables that are ours alone and shall be stored in a concealed locked chamber, to which Minnie will have the only access. Whatever route you take, you will eventually stop in Melbourne, Australia, where she will depart with our trunks and possessions, leaving you with yours and the ship. After selling the ship, you will wire half the proceeds to me and keep half. Then you'll return to London and claim the balance of your share. Your share will be my collateral that you will execute my directions."

Mrs. Hill did not seek approval or agreement. "I will prepare identifications and marriage documents for you and Minnie as Mr. and Mrs. Smith. It's a marriage on paper only. Do you understand that, Mr. Henderson?"

"Of course," he said, gathering his footing in the conversation. "A young woman traveling without a husband would raise suspicion. And let's use this arrangement: we'll claim that my wife is ill, and her doctor has suggested an extended trip at sea. The illness will be the reason for the ship charter."

"I'm impressed, James. Excellent idea."

Edie was scared. Not of the adventure, not about pretending to be married, but about how she would ever connect with Benji if she left London. *Maybe Mark could coordinate a reunion with Benji in Australia, and I could leave the Elephants and start the new life I've dreamed of. I've never run away from a challenge yet, and I don't want to now.*

The drinks were finished. Mrs. Hill rose and extended a hand to Henderson, a sign that the evening was over.

"Thank you." Henderson stood and bowed slightly. "There's a lot to do. We will take our leave now."

As she ushered the men toward the door, Mrs. Hill said, "I will have Minnie meet you at Sterling Union International Bank of London at 10:00 a.m. next Tuesday. You will meet Mr. Harley Blake, my banker. Minnie will provide the funds to establish the accounts. I have provided a suite of offices on Gracechurch Street in the heart of the financial district, which should be adequate for your cover activities. A proper sign will be hanging over the door this week."

When they had gone, Edie turned to Mrs. Hill—her voice a little shaky, her mouth dry. Edie felt a bit dazed. "May I have a drink and get more details about what is happening?"

"Of course, my dear." Mrs. Hill smiled at Edie's nervousness and poured them each a whiskey.

Mrs. Hill gave Edie a notebook. "Use this code to decipher and write our messages. I have informed my contacts in various ports to expect you to collect messages from me. My contacts are in the back of the notebook.

"I will provide details on the firearms deal when the dates and contacts are settled. I will want you to handle this personally. Other opportunities should arise during the voyage, and the proceeds from the sale of the ship will be a nice frosting on a financial fortune.

"And after the voyage?" Edie asked.

"You've wanted a new life for a long time; I'm suggesting that you take your savings, your share of this venture, and the monies I've invested for you and establish yourself as a wealthy young widow in Australia. It's booming, and you can make a place for yourself in society. You can then set up the Elephants' new operations in Australia. With my help, you can replicate what I have done here and create a financial empire for both of us. Take a chest with valuables; I will store a second chest with your share as monies come in from the voyage. The second chest you are taking will have valuables belonging to me. If things get too risky for me here in London, I will relocate to Melbourne. If you anticipate problems, arrange to store the chests with any of my contacts in your notebook, and advise me. I will direct the investment of my funds at the appropriate time."

Edie was stunned. She sat motionless, not knowing if she should be happy or terrified. On the one hand, her dreams of real wealth were materializing, but a good amount of danger was involved. She was very interested in the prospect of leaving London, experiencing a new country, and establishing a new life—but only if Benji was there too.

As she pushed aside her concerns, Edie began to see that she had been led to this moment. She knew she had to pursue the opportunity, and she'd find a way to reunite with Benji when it was possible.

Mrs. Hill continued. "I have engaged a Captain Wilford Watkins, a master mariner whom a trusted friend recommended. He is to assume command at Cardiff when a ship is acquired, where he will hire the rest of the crew. His presence will be a surprise to Henderson and Walker. He is fully aware of your role and will monitor your safety." Mrs. Hill then gave Edie a small handgun in an ostrich leather case and said, "If the need arises."

After Edie silently stowed the handgun in her bag, Mrs. Hill went on. "A longtime associate, Mr. Mathew Rohwedder, is in Melbourne and will be available to assist you there; he has worked for me for years and is trustworthy; his contact information is in the notebook."

Mrs. Hill rose to end the session but turned and said, "Oh, one more thing, Edie. An old friend of yours will be joining the trip en route."

Edie's breathing stopped; she was shocked. Mrs. Hill had used her real name. She had never revealed her past or her name.

Trying to regain her composure, she asked, "Who is it?"

"Benji Diamond. His printing skills will be useful, and it's time he left London before he dies on the work detail in jail. I've arranged for his release."

Relief and excitement washed over Edie, almost suffocating her. She stood, and her knees buckled. She couldn't speak; she was overcome.

After a pause, she said, "You knew?"

"Of course, Edie. I had to have you checked out fully before trusting you. An alias is often a good idea. And you didn't lie to me. Lying would not be tolerated. You have yet to mention your past in detail, and I chose not to ask about it. Benji vouched for you soon after we first met. I've stayed in touch. Keep Minnie as your name for Henderson, Watkins, and crew, and I'll continue to use it for now."

Edie just nodded, embarrassed. As Mrs. Hill left the room, Edie walked to her bedroom, thinking. *Benji. Thank you, God. Will he be the same? Will he still care for me?* She was shaking all over; her prayer was being answered.

CHAPTER 11

INSPECTION AND PREPARATION

Henderson occupied the offices at Gracechurch Street while he made arrangements. Stationery with a Henderson & Co. Ship Brokers masthead and cards for William Walker, Broker, and William Walker, Purser, were delivered. A package from registered mail included letters of referral and recommendations and a generous letter of credit from Sterling Union International Bank of London, properly executed, signed, and stamped. Harley Blake, at the bank, assured Henderson and Minnie that he would extend any necessary references and assistance if needed as they proceeded with their activities.

Henderson and Walker identified potential ships by scouting the shipyards and owners in Glasgow, Scotland, through maritime periodicals. They wanted to avoid dealings in London or Liverpool, where they might be recognized as imposters. It didn't take a lot of time to find a ship.

After contacting the owners based on an advertisement, Henderson and Walker traveled to Greenock to meet with the owners' representative, David Jones, who had also been the designer of the ship.

Jones met Henderson and Walker and gave the men the history of the *Ferret*. It was owned by a company called the Highland Railway and had been built in 1871 with the intent of running it for the River Clyde ferry service. As the ship's designer, Jones pointed out that he had envisioned the day when people and businesses would no longer need ferryboats. He had innovated the design of the hull to give her excellent seagoing qualities.

Having toured the deck and interior spaces with Jones, Walker asked for some time with his client as they walked the steamer, occasionally pointing at a feature or two as they discussed their next move.

"It's a fine vessel," Henderson said, "and I suspect we can have it fitted up in style. It certainly has sufficient space for our needs and excellent accommodations." They discussed what offer to make with a requirement that the fit-up be completed in six weeks since Mrs. Hill had imposed a critical timeline.

A tentative deal was agreed to, pending review by the Highland Railway's chairman and their solicitors.

Henderson and Walker returned to their hotel in Greenock and sat in the lobby to compare notes on the fit-up. Walker was still dissatisfied with Mrs. Hill's terms, and Henderson felt this attitude could spoil the whole plan.

"This may be the voyage of a lifetime," he said. "We have access to a great deal of money and credit with no cost. We'll make side deals that will be highly profitable and remember that we will sell the ship and keep half the proceeds—that alone would make the trip worthwhile.

"I'll follow your lead," Walker said, "but the young lady is an obstacle to our original plans."

"Yes, she is, but I know her; I've worked with her. She's young and naive, and we'll take care of her."

"She'll have a protector."

"Walker, it won't be a problem, believe me."

Henderson headed for the bar and walked up to five gentlemen playing darts. "Barnett Smith's the name," he said.

"And what's your business, Mr. Smith?" asked one of the men, as he pulled his arm back and studied the target, dart in hand.

"I've leased the steamship *Ferret* and am seeking trade opportunities."

While Henderson was at the bar, Walker went to the hotel desk. He wrote a note and arranged for a messenger to deliver it to Douglas and Company of Union Street, Glasgow, a leading ship chandler.

When Walker joined Henderson, he was introduced to the dart players as the ship's purser. "You can discuss trade deals with him." To demonstrate the wealth of his alias, Henderson made a show of buying a round of drinks for everyone and peeling off notes to pay for them from a large stack.

After planting their story locally, Henderson returned to London to prepare for the voyage.

Walker traveled to Glasgow to meet with Douglas and Company. He took a cab from the train station to the elegant Blythswood Square Hotel, where many wealthy merchants stayed.

"Mr. Walker, it's a pleasure to have you as our guest. Please make yourself comfortable. I'll get your room key and accompany you to your suite."

"Thank you," Walker replied. "I should have a message waiting."

"I'll check," the porter assured him, and left, returning shortly with the key and two messages. The first was from Stanley Potvin, manager for ship stores, stating that he would be honored to meet Mr. Walker at 1:00 p.m. the following day, and the second brought a smile to Walker's lips. It was from Henderson with an extensive list of costly wines that he wanted to order from the ship chandler.

Potvin was a smallish man with round spectacles on a lanyard. He was bald in the center of his head but had bushy facial hair and prominent sideburns. He smiled and seemed genuinely pleased that Mr. Smith and Mr. Walker had chosen Douglas and Company as their supplier. They retired to a private glass room and began discussions. Mr. Potvin explained that to take the ship's supply and stores order, an account would have to be created and Mr. Smith's credit established.

"Of course. I'm more than happy to arrange that," Walker replied.

Walker provided the account information at Sterling Union International Bank of London and a bank reference for Henderson & Co. Walker said Harley Blake was a bank executive and Potvin could contact him. Potvin thanked him and left to present the references to his accounts executive to begin the investigation.

The two men spent several hours reviewing supply lists for the six-month voyage. When Potvin priced the provisions, the total came to nearly £1,500.

"I almost forgot!" Walker exclaimed, as he pulled another paper from his jacket. "These are a list of wines Mr. Smith will require for the voyage."

Potvin looked at the list, then glanced over his glasses at Walker, cleared his throat, and said they would have to source the wines in London since they did not typically provide such high-quality beverages. When priced, the wine came to another five hundred pounds. Terms were agreed to for a ninety-day note on Mr. Smith's account if the references were approved.

Before leaving Glasgow, Walker had identified two merchants interested in a trading agreement. Walker required cash deposits, letters of introduction, and credit to the foreign suppliers they would contact during the sail. He would purchase goods for the merchants and transport the goods back on their return trip in about six months.

The charter was approved, and the parties agreed to terms for the fit-up costs. Henderson did sketches for the required work and sent them to J&G Thomson, the shipbuilders in Glasgow, to enable them to hire the riggers and do the job in their shipyard. J&G Thomson arranged to tow the *Ferret* from Greenock to the shipyard to begin the work.

With the fit-up complete, Robert Wright Carlyon, an acquaintance of Walker who would join them on their journey, was charged with hiring a crew of temporary runners to sail the ship to Cardiff. While Carlyon organized the move of the steamship, Henderson and Walker met with the merchants interested in purchases and transportation of goods. Henderson had added a third merchant. With little effort, they had three deals signed with deposits of £1,200—which they pocketed. They both felt better about their financial prospects beyond their business with Mrs. Hill.

When they arrived in Cardiff, Henderson met up with Minnie, who had reached Cardiff the day before with the luggage and trunks, both hers and Mrs. Hill's. Henderson ordered Walker to supervise the coaling of the ship, something Walker had no experience in. Henderson needed to oversee the hiring of the crew.

Walker approached the coal broker and asked to have him coal the ship.

"How many tons?" the broker asked.

"She's four hundred sixty tons," Walker replied.

"Not the ship." The broker snorted. "How many tons of coal?"

Walker had to admit he didn't know.

The broker did the calculation to the next port, and his men commenced unloading onto the *Ferret*. The unloading lasted long into the morning hours.

Henderson ran into some obstacles of his own. As he and Edie approached the office of the Registrar General of Shipping and Seamen, they were met by a distinguished-looking Black man in a blue captain's coat with bright yellow shoulder epaulets and gold buttons.

"I'm Captain Watkins," the man announced proudly. "I'm here to hire a crew and captain your ship, Mr. Smith."

"Like hell you are!" Henderson growled. "I'll hire my captain and crew. Wherever did you get the idea you would captain my ship?"

"Sir, Mrs. Hill hired me in London," Watkins said calmly. "And good day to you, Mrs. Smith; I hope your journey to Cardiff was comfortable."

The protector, Henderson thought.

Edie bowed her head slightly, signifying that it had been.

Watkins held his ground as Henderson's face turned red.

Edie knew it would surprise everyone that he was already hired. She needed to calm Henderson quickly without making him angrier. Edie drew him aside.

"James, Mrs. Hill personally selected Captain Watkins; he was recommended by one of her partners who is partially funding this venture."

"Why wasn't I consulted?" Henderson demanded. "I want a captain I know and trust."

"Mrs. Hill told me. Perhaps it was my responsibility to tell you. I apologize. I do think it would be best to start the voyage with everyone amicable."

Henderson reluctantly agreed, and he returned to Captain Watkins to shake his hand. "Welcome aboard this venture, Captain. I apologize for my outburst—I was taken by surprise."

The following day, with the coaling complete and the crew aboard, Mr. and Mrs. Smith waited on the dock—both finely attired. Edie felt a sensation of disbelief; inside, she wanted to flee. But she knew if she could act her way through this departure and assume her responsibilities, she would soon see Benji. After boarding, the dockworkers loaded the trunks. Edie supervised their storage in the concealed compartments she had requested in the fit-up.

Henderson formally greeted the captain, introduced himself as Smith to the crew, and gave a brief address in the ship's saloon.

"Captain, seamen: Mrs. Smith and I are pleased to have so many talented and experienced sailors on our voyage. He glanced at each as he addressed them—his gaze lingering on Edie. We'll feed you well, provide improved accommodations, and pay you generously. As we plan on trading along our route, you will have the opportunity to earn a bonus share provided you stay the course and remain employed by the captain and myself at the end of the voyage in six months." He paused and glanced out at the water. He continued. "I expect the best behavior from all of you, the entire journey. As you know, my wife is not well, so please see that she is cared for. Her every request should be attended to."

Edie wondered if Henderson could follow that suggestion. She sat on the bench at Henderson's side as he stood and addressed the crew. She looked at their faces and saw acceptance and respect. She thought Henderson presented himself well with his speech and hoped it was a promising start to their journey. Edie was now eager to be underway and looked forward to being treated as a wealthy lady, albeit a sick one. She wondered what sickness she was supposed to be convalescing from. A case of the vapors would be best—she could claim any symptom that suited her.

Since it was her first trip on the water, it took Edie some practice to stand up and walk in a straight line as the ship set out. The morning departure from Cardiff allowed for an early evening arrival in Milford Haven. If the weather held, the plan was to attend to business there in the morning and be on their way.

The trip had just begun, but Henderson advised the captain that they would spend an extra night in Milford Haven. The Smiths would reside in a hotel.

"Before leaving Glasgow, Captain, I hired a ship's carpenter, Ralph Chance, who resides in Milford Haven. He has sizeable cargo to be loaded and stored in our personal storage area."

Watkins looked surprised by the new plan but just nodded.

The carpenter, Ralph Chance, arrived with three large crates once they had arrived at the dock that evening. He was young and skinny with curly blond hair that hung in ringlets down his back and hands as large as dinner plates. He proved much more robust than he looked, hoisting the crates aboard as if they were empty.

Edie was relieved when Henderson told her she'd have a private room in the hotel—the fit-up of the ship had only provided one bed in the owner's cabin, so she would need to set boundaries with him while they were at sea. As they checked into the hotel, Edie heard a familiar voice. Her heart pounded in her chest. *Benji!* She worked hard to conceal her emotions. Henderson recognized the voice as well and turned to greet Benji. "Aha—my printer has arrived. Welcome, Benji!"

"And the press and supplies are crated and set to sail," Benji said.

Benji greeted Edie more formally, but his eyes told a different story when Edie gazed into them. She was thrilled. She'd finally reconnected with Benji. He had lost weight in jail, but no permanent physical damage showed.

Late that night, Benji came to her room at the inn. She put her arms around him and hugged him tightly. He kissed her tentatively at first, then more passionately. They held each other without saying a word. Eventually, they sat on the bed.

"Edie, I realized in jail that I want to be with you, always," said Benji. "I love you." Before Edie could reply, he said, "We have to conceal that we even know each other from Henderson and the crew," he warned her. "It's crucial that Henderson trust me. As far as he's concerned, I'm here to print documents needed for trade and other activities.

She understood that he was right, but her emotions were boiling over. She wanted to grab Benji and hug him until he couldn't breathe. She wanted to tear his clothes off and ravish him until he begged for mercy. She shook inside, just having these thoughts. But she understood the need to be cautious. She put her hand on his cheek and said, "I love you more than I can express." He kissed the palm of her hand and looked into her eyes.

She craved more intimacy but added, "We'll have time together." Benji squeezed her hand and then left. Edie knew she would lie awake for hours reliving their few minutes together.

When the three of them returned to the ship, Henderson introduced Benji to the captain as an acquaintance of Mr. Smith, whom the Smiths had just invited to accompany them on the voyage and help with their trading activities. The captain expressed no objection.

They set sail on a beautiful November day. Edie strolled the deck, happy that Benji was on board and healthy. The captain knew of her status as representative of Mrs. Hill, as did Benji, Henderson, and Walker. To the rest of the crew, she was Mrs. Smith, an ailing wealthy lady from London.

The first night sailing out of Milford Haven was Edie's first night sharing quarters with Henderson. Edie Black, a.k.a. Minnie Rose, a.k.a. Mrs. Smith, set the ground rules.

"Until I have Mr. Chance create a new sleeping quarter for me, we'll each be confined to half the bed." She rolled up a blanket and placed it under the covers down the center of the mattress like a bundling board. "Do not allow any part of you to cross this blanket."

Henderson sat at his table with a glass of wine; watching her fuss over the bed, he grinned at her. His attitude irritated Edie. "I will not tolerate any contact, James."

"I'm not interested, *Minnie.*" He put heavy emphasis on her name.

They prepared for bed separately; she asked James to go first since she had some paperwork to do for Mrs. Hill. When he left for the privy, she retrieved her hatpin from her luggage and placed it under her pillow.

As the *Ferret* steamed across the English Channel directly toward Brest on the tip of Brittany, the waters were wild and rough. The strong currents and winds slowed progress. The *Ferret,* even with its power and superior bow design, tossed and rocked uncomfortably. Edie spent much of the time in her cabin feeling sick. The coast of Brittany wasn't much better; Edie, feeling slightly better after tea and crumpets brought to her room by the cook's assistant, ventured out to view towering, dangerous-looking cliffs. As they progressed into the Bay of Biscay, heading down the coast of France, the waters became more peaceful. She could see idyllic bays, islands, and small port towns.

She was beginning to enjoy traveling on the water and made it part of her daily ritual to visit Captain Watkins's wheelhouse.

"The Channel and northwestern France can be wild and windswept, but unless there's a storm, the balance of the trip to Lisbon will be very pleasant," the captain promised one morning as they sat together.

Henderson invited Captain Watkins and William Walker to join him and his wife for dinner in their quarters that evening in calmer waters.

The captain showed up at 8:00 p.m. as directed, dressed in his finest, including his dress uniform with gold braid on the sleeves and cap. The dinner was pleasant, with Henderson leading the conversation, first with questions and then with information for the captain.

"Captain, after our port stop in La Rochelle, we'll sail to Lisbon, where we'll take on coal and water; soon after, we'll reach the Strait of Gibraltar. Please take the *Ferret* close to the rock and the town so we can be adequately identified and communicate with the British sentries. I instructed that the ship's owner would receive word that we had safely passed into the Mediterranean."

"Certainly, Mr. Smith," the captain replied.

The cook had prepared a menu on Henderson's orders, including several bottles of costly wine for the evening meal. He did the best he could. *The ship wasn't an ocean liner!* he told himself, but he had to try. He welcomed the job, and Mr. Smith was paying for everything.

The first course was smoked oysters on fresh greens, which would only last for a while in ship storage, followed by squab baked in fennel and white wine, with winter squash and creamed potatoes. Dessert would be a cherry tart from dried sour cherries, served with a sweet winter wine.

The chef shook his head at the wealthy travelers and their indulgences. He helped himself to a portion of everything, including some of the wine intended for the squab, while he prepared fish stew and potatoes for the crew.

Edie appreciated Henderson's impeccable taste in food and wine, even though he was spending Mrs. Hill's money. She would refrain from commenting on the menu in her reports to London.

CHAPTER 12

ABOARD THE *FERRET*

As the voyage went on, Edie continued to visit the captain frequently. Captain Watkins was familiar with the coasts of France, Spain, and Portugal and was pleased when Minnie made her wheelhouse visits to chat about the landscape and its history. She enjoyed seeing the land, the ports, and the cities through the eyes of the well-traveled captain and hearing of his adventures.

The captain claimed that the long stretches of sandy beaches along the Vendées were the most beautiful in the world. As they passed and proceeded toward La Rochelle, he pointed out the tall white limestone cliffs bordering the sea and protecting the deep-water port. "La Rochelle was the largest base for the Knights Templar in the twelfth century, rumored to be the home for more than eighteen ships. Do you know about the Knights Templar, Minnie?"

"I have read of them."

"La Rochelle is now the most important trading port in the West Atlantic."

As they navigated into the port, the sun shone brightly, illuminating the limestone walls. The temperature was warm for November, and there was a slight breeze. Edie was awed by the majestic medieval towers, the ancient ruins, and the modern port facilities in the distance. The captain explained that a chain used to be strung between the towers to close the port at night.

"It's hard for me to imagine things so ancient," Edie said. "It makes me feel insignificant but also honored to be able to see and hear about such antiquities. Thank you, Captain." She touched his arm in appreciation.

When she left the wheelhouse, Edie looked around, hoping for a glimpse of Benji, but most days he was kept busy assisting Henderson.

Henderson and Walker planned a trip ashore in La Rochelle. The stop wasn't on the itinerary, but the two men had personal business. They visited one of the Glasgow merchant's contacts and, using their letter of authorization and credit, bought two dozen bales of beaver furs the French had collected from Canada. Once the furs were purchased, Henderson took the opportunity to stock up on quality cheeses, Madeira wines, and fresh baked goods. Henderson presented invoices to Minnie for payment from Mrs. Hill's funds, including a fake invoice for the furs. Henderson granted the crew shore leave, telling Edie that good morale was important.

"Henderson, tell me about the furs," Edie said, confronting him as they were loaded into the ship's hold.

"Minnie, one of my tasks is to create profitable trades on this voyage," he explained. "This is the first of many. Don't worry—you and Mrs. Hill will get your money back with a profit."

Edie was skeptical but accepted the explanation. "Just provide me with an accounting and receipts," she said, leaving him in the cargo hold with his furs.

Benji and Chance, the carpenter, had built a bunk and small desk and sitting area in her private storage room. Edie was thrilled that she could move out of Henderson's bedroom that evening. The *Ferret* had sailed past the southwest coast of France, Spain, and Portugal toward the port of Lisbon; there they took on the maximum load of coal and replenished their fresh water.

The ship reached the Strait of Gibraltar on the morning of November 11. As Henderson had directed, the captain navigated the steamship close to the rock, clearly showing their registration number and signaling *all's well*. Their message stated that they wished to be reported as having cleared the strait as of that date. They steamed out of sight of Gibraltar's signaling crew and anchored until twilight. The crew was in high spirits, and Captain Watkins, on orders from Henderson, dispensed a double ration of rum to each sailor. They raised their mugs to Mr. and Mrs. Smith and Captain Watkins.

"Men, we have important work to do on this voyage," Henderson told them. "You will all be well rewarded. The mission is confidential. I'll provide some details tonight and more as we proceed. Rest a few hours, and we'll reassemble at 10:00 p.m."

Henderson watched the men leave for their quarters, whispering in small groups about what might transpire. Henderson wondered who he could trust.

Edie, with Benji nearby, watched Henderson. She knew what was underway; it was a critical component of Mrs. Hill's assignment. She also watched the men depart. *Will any of them be a problem?*

Henderson expected that the serious and upright captain would not approve or be pleased with the plan. He would have to be convinced. Robert Wright Carlyon and Ralph Chance, the carpenter, went to work moving materials and supplies from one of the crates in Henderson's storage area to the deck. Henderson, Walker, and the captain had a heated discussion, but ultimately, the captain was powerless to disobey orders.

Edie took Benji to a secluded spot—the only crew member nearby was Robinson, whom Edie had befriended and knew she could trust. Speaking softly to avoid being overheard, she explained that what was about to happen was not a rogue operation by Henderson but was part of Mrs. Hill's plan, and all was well.

The men reassembled at ten.

Edie watched from the saloon windows with Benji at her side. Out of sight of everyone, Benji placed his hand on the middle of Edie's back; she smiled at him and looked back to the action.

"Captain," Henderson said, "please direct the men to commence painting."

Following the captain's orders, the chief officer reluctantly oversaw the duties. Paint, brushes, buckets, and a bosun's chair had been brought from storage.

One seaman was lowered over the side to paint out the *Ferret* name and replace it with *Bantam*. Others painted all the lifeboats white except two, which retained their existing blue. The funnel, the most prominent feature of the ship, was repainted black from its original yellow. Everywhere the name *Ferret* was painted, it was repainted with the new name. Chief Engineer Griffin was ordered to have the official number removed from the hatch and the bell and replaced with the number of the *Bantam*.

Chance, Carlyon, Walker, and a group of seamen went to work on the bridge to dismantle the wheelhouse and chartroom and reassemble them on the aft deck of the ship, changing the ship's appearance further. The chief engineer reconnected the wheel to the rudder assembly.

At 4:15 a.m., the conversion complete, the captain directed the lights extinguished, and the *Ferret*, on its first voyage as the *Bantam*, headed quietly back to the strait. As they sailed, the two remaining blue lifeboats from the *Ferret*, several life belts, a chair, buckets, and multiple small items bearing the insignia of the *Ferret* were lowered overboard as the *Bantam*, hugging the far shore in the dark, sailed back into the Atlantic Ocean undetected. After clearing the Rock of Gibraltar, they slowly sailed under dark skies until the horizon was visible.

Aboard the *Bantam*, the captain set a course for the Cape Verde Islands, as Henderson instructed, off the coast of Mauritania, avoiding the many British ships that made port in the Canary Islands. As the ship steamed down the coast of Africa, a group of nine seamen, distraught over the activities of the past hours, gathered to determine who they could trust and who they couldn't. They were all concerned about their employer, Mr. Smith. The night guard was Robinson. He spotted Benji on a walk around the deck and summoned him.

"Please tell Mrs. Smith that trouble's brewing."

Edie returned a few minutes later with Benji at her side.

"I'm glad you didn't leave your post, and thank you for getting the message to me, Robinson."

"Yes, ma'am. Some crew members are building toward confronting Mr. Smith and Captain Watkins."

"I'll see to it, Robinson. Thank you." She handed him a Brazilian banknote. "You might need this in Port Santos."

"Will we have shore leave?" Robinson asked.

"I don't know, but I'll be going ashore. I'll ask for your assistance for a few hours, and after helping me, you can take a few hours for yourself."

Henderson was having a few glasses of wine in his cabin when Edie interrupted. He was with Walker and Joseph Brown, the second steward who also served as the ship's clerk.

"Excuse me, gentlemen, but I must speak to my husband briefly."

Walker and Brown immediately rose, gave slight bows, and excused themselves.

Henderson acknowledged her presence with a mocking sneer, the corner of his lip curling up. "Just what is so important, Mrs. Smith?" he said.

"Listen, Henderson," Edie said. "I hold you in as much contempt as you do me. I don't care unless it jeopardizes our objectives. The success of this trip is important. You need to show a little more respect for your crew. You have a mutiny brewing. You need to bring everyone together, explain, and get support behind you."

"They just need to follow orders."

"And you need to heed my words for once, or you could find yourself drawn and quartered by the crew—or me," Edie snarled. "We will not succeed if you tell the crew to follow orders and keep them in the dark."

Henderson was not pleased to take orders from Minnie. Despite the directions given by Mrs. Hill, he felt he was in control. He would have to deal with her later. He left the cabin, slamming the door. "Dratted woman," he said to himself.

Ten minutes later, Henderson had the entire crew mustered in the saloon. He was seated at the head of the table, upon which were two casks of rum and two pistols. Henderson stood, put one foot on the chair he had been sitting in, and beckoned Captain Watkins and Walker to join him at the head of the table. Then he began a very forceful and emotional speech.

"Gentlemen, my true name is James Stewart Henderson, and I will use my name from now on except during certain business transactions, when I will introduce myself as Smith. I could not share this with you until I was safely at locations unknown to port authorities. I am a political refugee from the United States, where I, as a British national, volunteered and served as a cavalry colonel in the United States Civil War. I am hunted by those who wish me dead, and I have a price on my head. After my injury, which resulted in this scar on my face, I left the fighting but traded guns for the British. I became very wealthy. I own this ship, and it was important to make it appear that the ship foundered and that we all perished so those plotting my death will be thrown off the scent."

Standing against the exterior wall next to Benji, Edie stared at him; except for not owning the ship, she had no idea if the story was true.

Henderson picked up the two revolvers and held them in the air.

Several of the men shuffled their feet, alarmed and cautious. Another cleared his throat to speak but didn't. Those in the back stepped toward the exit.

"We're sailing on a highly sensitive secret mission for the British government, which will be revealed in time. Anyone not wishing to support me and keep these secrets can step forward, and I will be glad to put a bullet through their skull."

There were no takers. The men looked at each other, deciding if they should put their plans into action.

"Any of you who pledge to be true and faithful to me and my mission can pass these jugs around and take a drink to seal your pledge. At the end of our mission, we will sell the ship; upon doing so, I will pledge a bonus to double your pay." After a pause, two seamen stepped forward and passed the jugs after taking a swig. Within minutes, the entire crew had pledged loyalty.

Henderson turned to Minnie. "Satisfied?" he whispered.

"Quite a performance," she whispered as she turned and left. Then Henderson handed a jug to Benji, who took a sip.

The following day, Henderson, Chance, Brown, Walker, and Benji gathered at the work area adjacent to the private storage areas and the owner's cabin. They removed one of the storage crates that Chance had brought on board at Milford Haven, and Chance pried open one long side. The men removed a printing press and its legs and assembled it. Benji directed the placement to ensure it was stable and level. They then unpacked trays of lead type and quantities of different styles and sizes of paper and inks. Most impressive was the collection of revenue stamps from various nations to signify the authenticity of documents.

Henderson clapped Benji on the back. "Very well done, Benji! Start with printing the ship's papers and a manifest for the *Bantam*, and we'll need new identification for each person on board. Walker will provide names. We'll need them in a few days."

Watkins again mustered the men to the saloon that night, and Henderson provided another jug of rum.

"The authorities will check our manifest when we dock in Santo Antão," he told them. You'll be listed under new names to avoid anyone tracking us from the paperwork produced at Cardiff." Walker handed out slips of paper, assigning a new name to each person.

"Use this name on ship and shore. If questioned on this leg of our voyage, say that we just sailed from Cape Town and are sailing to Marseilles and then back to England, port of Liverpool. Our young printer will have new identification documents for each of you and a new ship's manifest for your assignment on the *Bantam*. Sign the manifest in your new name."

William Walker took a new name as well—William Wallace. Edie became Mrs. Minnie Henderson, and Benji chose the name Russell Weaver. Henderson was the only person on the ship using a real name, though "Mr. Smith" survived on the ship's manifest.

◆ ◆ ◆

Minnie spent time in the wheelhouse with Captain Watkins as they approached Santo Antão, which was in the Cape Verde Islands off Africa. "It is a pleasant group of islands and one of the first to abolish the slave trade, so I'm safe here," he said, chuckling.

They docked at Port Mindelo and anchored for several days after clearing customs. Walker, since he was serving as the purser, went into the village to buy pigs, poultry, fruit, and vegetables. He ordered coaling. The ship took on freshwater storage, and he paid for all goods and services with ninety-day notes from Sterling Union International Bank of London, producing papers of bank guarantees in the name of Smith. Henderson meanwhile spent his time negotiating a deal for the furs. He expected it to be lucrative because local industry manufactured beaver hats for export to England. Henderson received £400; he requested a receipt for £300 and received it without question. He was paid in cash. He presented Walker with £50 and pocketed £50 back on board. He gave Minnie £300 and a receipt.

Edie had yet to learn of the value of furs, but the transaction seemed undervalued. She didn't argue but would convey the details to Mrs. Hill for her opinion.

When all was ready, they sailed for Port Santos in Brazil, arriving on December 26. The port authorities at Port Santos scrutinized the *Bantam*'s papers more closely than had those in Mindelo. Captain Watkins stood by and waited nervously, but after some delay and discussion, the customs authority found the papers to be in order; Benji had done a masterful job.

Edie knew Brazil was a hotbed of crime and thievery, but she had a mission here for Mrs. Hill, one critical to the voyage's success. She asked her most trusted shipmates, Benji and Robinson, to escort her. Henderson, knowing her task, had no objection. Walking on solid ground felt good, but her body still thought it was at sea. The weather was quite pleasant, and she enjoyed seeing a new city. Benji, for his part, was less lighthearted. He was there to protect Edie and was constantly alert for unexpected trouble. He was glad to have Robinson's help.

She first sought out Mrs. Hill's Sterling Union International Bank contact. The bank had branches all over the British Empire and South America. Instructions were waiting for her that had been entrusted to the bank. She deposited funds from the fur pelts to Mrs. Hill's account. She then visited the local telegraph office. Following instructions she had received before leaving London, Edie sent a coded message to a contact in Cape Town and a second coded message back to London reporting that she had sent it. She gave an accounting of the fur receipts and expenses. She appreciated how detailed her instructions from Mrs. Hill had been. The big test lay ahead.

The trip thus far had been relatively smooth, despite nervous sailors and Henderson's arrogance and pigheaded ways. Edie expected more disruptions ahead, but she felt confident in her ability to work with Henderson if she had the protection of Benji and the support of Robinson—and the captain. She was unsure how this next step might play out here on shore.

Edie had filled Henderson in on Mrs. Hill's instructions for this port stop. He disembarked later in the morning and exchanged a sizeable sum of British pounds for Brazilian banknotes with funds provided by Edie.

Now as Smith, Henderson contacted local shipping agents, presented his credentials and financial references, and began negotiations. Smith claimed the ship left Cape Town in ballast and was seeking a shipment for delivery during their return to England. He succeeded in receiving a large consignment shipment of coffee beans: 3,992 bags to be received in Marseilles, France.

Meanwhile, Edie, with Benji and Robinson, made a trade of her own. She went to an address Mrs. Hill had received from Harley Blake. Edie continued to feel anxious, not knowing what to expect. She knew this was a significant part of Mrs. Hill's plans for the voyage.

They entered a vast warehouse full of crates of varying sizes stacked in long rows, many containers high. Two large and thuggish-looking

Brazilians closed in to block the path of the visitors; they crossed their arms and stood erect. Edie thought they looked like trouble, but she stepped toward them, taking the lead.

"António Velez is expecting me," Edie announced in an authoritative voice.

They said nothing. Edie suspected they didn't speak English, but they certainly understood the name.

One guard held a hand up toward Edie's face to indicate she should stay where she was.

Benji stepped forward to her side.

"Wait," the guard said, in heavily accented English. He turned and left, leaving the other thug to guard them.

In perfect English, she heard a yell. "Are you afraid of heights, Mrs. Smith?"

She looked up to where the voice had come from. At the back of the tall warehouse was a steel box with a man at an open door. He looked the size of a pigeon on a rooftop. He pointed to a ladder along the wall that scaled about three floor heights connected to a railed walkway at an angle to the box.

"I am not," she yelled back.

"Can you climb a ladder?" was the reply.

"Of course!"

"I am Velez. Join me. Just you."

"I need this man!" she called. "He controls the money." She put her hand on Benji's arm. "And my brother," she put a hand on Robinson's arm, "is very well behaved."

Velez hesitated, laughed, then yelled, "Very well. I never win an argument with a beautiful woman."

Edie smiled to herself. She knew the type.

The three ascended the ladder to the walkway. In truth, Edie couldn't remember ever being this high up. She knew it would make her dizzy and her stomach queasy if she looked down, so she didn't. They proceeded up the walkway from the ladder to the metal box, where António Velez greeted them with a smile as big as Edie had ever seen. One gold tooth glimmered.

"It's a pleasure to meet you, Mrs. Smith." He bowed and kissed her hand. He just nodded at Benji and Robinson.

Once in the box, she could see that the walls had slots that provided a clear vision of the entire warehouse floor. There were wider spaces she assumed were like arrow loops in a castle, providing space for rifle barrels. It was a metal castle in the sky. Velez couldn't escape from here if attacked, or at least it didn't appear so, but he could deal with whoever entered the warehouse. Two dozen rifles were leaning against one wall near his desk. She saw boxes of ammunition stacked against the opposite wall.

"Not many are invited to my little fortress," Velez said.

"Why am I so privileged?" she asked.

"You're a friend of Harley Blake, are you not?"

"I've met him on several occasions, but he is a friend of my partner, Mrs. Lillian Hill, and she has sent me."

"To help our cause."

"To complete a transaction."

"A beautiful lady, but all business."

Edie smiled. "I only have a little time."

"Perhaps you will visit again with more time."

"Perhaps. Shall we proceed?" She produced an inventory of the freight she intended to purchase.

Velez took the list. "You should understand that this is a risky mission. There is a war being fought on the other side of the continent. There are Chilean warships prowling around this coast. The current War of the Pacific, as it is referred to, is a war of resources, but also of independence. Peru has powerful support in England, but Chile is winning. The Chilean Navy successfully blocks Peruvian ports, preventing supplies from reaching troops. Now supplies are taken by foot and horses through the jungles of Brazil, a long and dangerous journey. If the Chileans catch you, you will be murdered." He paused to study her.

Edie felt she needed to act calm and in control, but she hadn't known about the danger Velez spoke of. She did know that Chile and

Peru were far away on the other side of the continent. *Why are they a danger here?*

"Mr. Velez, we are aware of the dangers. We would not be here if we felt concerned about dealing with the risks." Inwardly, she was terrified. She hadn't known this gun deal would occur in hostile waters. "Please continue, Mr. Velez," she said calmly. She glanced at Benji and Robinson; their faces reflected her calm, although she expected they weren't.

"Very well! On behalf of British supporters, an African banking associate of Mr. Blake arranged this sale. The *Bantam* is to take delivery, following darkness, from several of my freight pole boats in the harbor, sixty crates of British Snider-Enfield .577 breech-loading rifles with steel barrels, plus many crates of ammunition and one crate of a disassembled Gatling gun. It's a big load."

Edie had read of Gatling guns; they could fire two hundred rounds of bullets in a minute from multiple barrels. She paid a deposit in British pounds and assured Mr. Velez that the balance would be available on board in Brazilian notes after a successful—and undetected—delivery.

Velez assured her, "There will be no slipups. My men are armed, and I will have many men around the port observing. I have asked the customs inspectors to avoid the area and to take an extended dinner at my expense."

"Mr. Velez, you must keep the delivery silent and fast, and all will go as planned," Edie said.

"You are helping good people, my beautiful friend."

"And you are doing well yourself, I presume," Edie said, smiling.

Velez nodded.

"After the *Bantam* successfully transfers the weapons to representatives of the Peruvian Navy, the rifles, ammunition, and Gatling gun will be transported through jungle footpaths in Brazil to Peruvian troops in northern Bolivia. It is an important cause. Do you have any preserved food you can sell? The troops are starving."

"I do not," Edie replied, "but I'll send a couple of cases of wine."

"Also appreciated," Velez laughed. "They can forget their hunger. Be cautious of the contacts you make. First, ensure you are dealing with Peruvians; second, know they are desperate. Protect your ship, men, and cargo."

"Thank you. We will heed your advice."

Edie turned to leave, and Velez said, "One more thing, beautiful lady. My friend Harley Blake and your friend Mrs. Hill made arrangements with me to give you an important package to be delivered to a colleague in Cape Town by your Captain Watkins. Did Mrs. Hill provide you with an address?"

"She did, but she didn't tell me when I would receive the package," Edie said.

Velez reached under his desk and slid out a small wooden box with a sliding top, tied with rope and sealed with sealing wax. A pool of wax in the center of the top was stamped with a crest. "It's confidential and very urgent."

"We'll keep this to ourselves, and it will be promptly delivered when we reach Cape Town."

"Thank you. I hope we meet again."

Relieved that this part of the transaction was over, Edie felt shaky. Descending the ladder was much more challenging than the climb; she looked down and was overcome with the thought of flying off into the air. She stopped twice to close her eyes and regain her composure.

Reaching the floor, she glanced up. Velez was standing at the railing, and she knew he was smiling. He waved. She didn't.

Leaving the warehouse, Edie handed Robinson more Brazilian notes. "Robinson, enjoy yourself for a few hours in Port Santos. Use cash to buy canned meats, whatever you can carry, and bring them back to the ship."

Robinson nodded and took off at a jog.

Benji put his arm around Edie's shoulders, and she immediately felt better. They walked slowly back, enjoying the time together. They said little.

The coffee was successfully loaded, and the following evening five cargo rafts poled up to the ship's starboard side. Henderson, Walker,

Benji, and Robinson (who now, at Edie's insistence, was reassigned as permanent assistant to Mrs. Henderson) unloaded the crates with help from Velez's men. They dispersed the cargo to every available storage area on the ship. Not all the containers could be concealed. Edie delivered the remaining payment in Brazilian notes that Henderson had exchanged—which Velez's man counted with excruciating slowness—and the transaction was complete. The transfer and payment were completed in the darkness of a cloudy night without a word spoken, unobserved by the dock and customs personnel—who apparently were busy dining and drinking as Velez had planned. The captain and several of the crew were on shore leave. Edie hoped no Chilean spies were observing the exchange.

The *Bantam* sailed from Santos and set a course for Cape Town instead of Marseilles.

Edie, Benji, and Robinson kept watch as the *Bantam* sailed away from Brazil, mindful of Velez's warning. They spotted a schooner. Robinson identified a British flag with a telescope, and the ship ignored them. Edie just wanted this sale over and done with. She was angry with Mrs. Hill for not advising her of the risks associated with the gun trade.

After about three-quarters of a day of steaming toward Africa, Benji spotted several smaller ships angling toward them. There was no telling if they were friendly, but they were moving quickly.

Knowing they would not outrun the vessels, Edie told Captain Watkins to cut their speed and hold steady. She ordered Robinson to take several crewmen he trusted, open a crate of rifles, load them, and pocket additional rounds.

As the engines were cut, Henderson came out of his cabin, a napkin tucked into his collar and wine stains on his lips. "What are you doing, Watkins?" Edie heard him shout. She walked over to the wheelhouse. "Henderson, we're either about to be murdered or make a trade. We should try to do the latter." The approaching ships did not look friendly: open top, powered by an inboard steam engine, they each had a deck with bench seats on three sides. They were built for speed, not comfort. There was a large, mounted gun on the bow of each ship, and eight gun-bearing men crewed each boat, all looking quite rough in ill-fitting and shabby military garb. Edie counted six boats in total. Robinson and his men stood guard on the deck of the *Bantam* with rifles at their sides; they were so overpowered by the boat guns that the rifles would be useless if these visitors decided to attack.

Edie asked Brown to check the fighters' flags and uniforms and verify that they spoke Peruvian Spanish; Brown had sailed South American routes. Leaning toward Edie's ear, Brown said, "Language checks out, and the flag is Peruvian, Mrs. Henderson." She was satisfied that the boats and men were of Peruvian origin.

As the lead boat pulled alongside the *Bantam*, Brown lowered a rope ladder into the center of the war boat, and Henderson descended first, followed by Edie. The apparent leader of the boats communicated in English with Edie, who introduced herself as Mrs. Smith. First, she presented her gift: four cases of canned meat and three cases of wine. "To support the fighters in their cause," she said, then added with sincerity. "I wish we had more." The leader's face and stance softened at the gesture. After some negotiating, Henderson nodded, and the leader went below the ship. Edie returned to the *Bantam*'s deck to arrange to unload fifty-nine crates of rifles and ammunition and one container with the Gatling gun. The leader returned with a chest of gold coins. Crew members brought a small table and two chairs to the deck; Henderson and the leader took opposite seats. Edie returned with two rifles and handed them down to the smaller ship. The two men disassembled the rifles, exchanged some parts, and reassembled the two rifles. The leader loaded shells in each and fired test shots into the sky to check the firing capabilities. The Peruvian leader was satisfied. Returning to the table, Henderson wrote a number on paper. The amount was counted out by the leader and recounted by Henderson. At Edie's orders, crew members began lowering one crate at a time on ropes to the waiting crew members below as each boat pulled alongside for their load. The crews loaded fifty-nine boxes of rifles, plus two rifles from the sixtieth crate, which the men had tested. The rest of the crate was retained on the *Bantam*.

Edie, hoping to escape conflict with Chileans and port authorities, ordered Brown and another seaman to fully uncrate the remaining rifles and ammunition and dump the well-labeled crate material overboard. The British rifles themselves wouldn't indicate any weapons trading. The traded crates were stacked high on the six warships' decks in clear sight. They would have to quickly make land somewhere on the Brazilian coast and unload the cargo for transport by land to Bolivia.

The warships sped off and spread out. Edie breathed a sigh of relief when the rifles and Gatling gun faded into the distance as the warships sped off toward the jungle. She took possession of the gold to lock it away in her storage area. The feeling of relief was short-lived. The warships had disappeared, but Watkins spied a full-rigged sailing vessel coming toward them; he estimated it was a twenty-cannon frigate, nationality unknown.

Edie took back control. "If they are Chilean, we can't fight them. Hide all rifles and ammunition under the mattress in my bedchamber. "She pulled Benji aside and handed him the bags of gold coins. "Hide the gold in the hold; conceal it well. Bring crates of food and wine to my storage area and conceal the wall safe two or three crates deep, whatever you can manage. At four to six knots, they could be upon us in forty minutes. Hurry." She thought of the chests of valuables that belonged to her and Mrs. Hill, but they were concealed in hidden compartments built into the structure of the storage rooms; they were safe.

The *Bantam* showed no hostility when ordered to idle its engines and prepare to be boarded by authorities on the Chilean ship *Rimac*. The Captain of the *Rimac* spoke no English but had an interpreter. Captain Watkins, Henderson, and Edie stood at attention.

Through the interpreter, the captain said, "I am Captain Cordero Plat. We command you to surrender to our control."

He was addressing Captain Watkins, but before he could respond, Edie spoke. "Captain, I am Lady Minnie Smith of London, England, and this is my ship," she said. "My husband and our friend Captain Watkins arranged this pleasure cruise for me because I am dying. We had heard of your conflict with other nations. We have no involvement, and you have many supporters in London. We have food and wine you are welcome to take, we have a cargo of coffee we agreed to deliver, we mean you no harm and ask you to let us continue on."

The captain's face remained stern and unconvinced; he ordered two men to search the ship. Benji and Robinson accompanied them.

Acknowledging Lady Smith as the one in charge, the captain addressed her.

"Have you encountered any Peruvian activity during your travels from Brazil?" he asked, in perfect English.

"We avoided contact, and I am not sure they were Peruvian, but we observed multiple high-speed cargo vessels traveling northwest toward Brazil less than two hours ago." She provided false directions.

The captain softened to Edie; she offered him and the interpreter a glass of wine in the saloon.

"Captain, I am sympathetic to your cause, and if I were going to live long, I might be of service," she said. "But now I can offer cases of food and wine, all the best quality, as a gift to encourage your quick victory. I hope you will accept my offering as support." Edie thought, *He could take it. He doesn't need my offering.*

"Do you have large quantities of money on board?" the captain asked.

"No," Edie answered firmly, holding the captain's eyes. "Our monies are tied up in the coffee cargo we carry."

"Any guns?"

"No," Edie replied. She knew it was over for them if any hidden money or guns were found.

"If my men find you are telling the truth, I accept your kind offer."

Benji and Robinson had successfully given the soldiers a tour, and everyone returned to the deck. They reported not finding weapons or money, only wine, rum, food provisions, and standard supplies.

"Show me," Captain Plat commanded.

Benji suggested they start with the hold; he left with two men and the captain.

"Captain, I have a request," Edie said, and he turned.

"As I have mentioned, I am not well. I must visit my quarters, use my chamber pot, and lie down. Do you mind?"

He directed his reply toward one of his officers. "Go with her, inspect her quarters, then stand guard outside. I will inspect that last."

When Edie was alone in her quarters, the officer standing guard outside the door, she quickly and quietly unstacked several cases of wine in front of her safe, unlocked it, and stuffed all the money and contents into a pillowcase. She left simple personal items. Edie placed the pillowcase under another pillow on her cot. She then slid two fingers down her throat, retched into her chamber pot, and set it next to her bed. She relocked the safe, returned the wine cases, and lay on the cot.

When the knock came, she said, "Enter."

The interpreter said, "The captain is sorry to disturb you in your quarters." He looked at the chamber pot and then away. "But he must inspect the stores you have here."

"I understand," Edie said, and made to get up, feigning dizziness. The captain said in English, "Please stay where you are, Lady Smith. We won't be long. We will take your stores here, wine and food, and leave what you have in the hold." He ordered his men to transport the supplies to their ship. When the captain saw the safe, he spoke harshly, looking Edie in the eyes. "And what have you hidden here? I have been inclined to trust you." She took a notepad from her nightstand, wrote the combination, and handed it to Benji, who went to the safe and unlocked it. Inside were some papers, a few pieces of jewelry, and a little money.

"Nothing valuable, captain," Edie said.

The captain left. The Chileans continued removing crates. Edie lay her head back with relief on the lumpy pillow. She could feel the hard shape of rifles under her mattress.

When the Chilean ship sailed away, Henderson commanded the captain to resume nine knots and to set a course for Cape Town.

At Henderson's orders, Captain Watkins and the crew began changing the ship's look again. The funnel received a red star on two sides, and the bosun chair went over the side. A seaman painted over the *Bantam* name and replaced it with *India*. To further disguise the ship's looks, a tattered yard and a square sail were added to the foremast: it disguised the steam-powered ship as an older version with less power than it possessed.

Benji was busy creating a new manifest and new papers for the *India*, purchasing documents for the coffee from Pinheira & Co. at La Guaira, a small port in Venezuela, and applying the appropriate stamps.

Walker had miscalculated the coal needed for the trip, and it became necessary to burn a small percentage of the lower-quality coffee beans as fuel to keep the steam production adequate to make port. They made an aromatic entry. Henderson felt it necessary to reprimand Walker in front of several crew members. Walker was not amused. The seamen enjoyed the encounter and laughed at the purser's lack of knowledge and experience in fueling a ship.

The *India* arrived in the port of Cape Town on March 2. Henderson, equipped with forged purchase documents for the coffee, went ashore the morning after landing to offer the cargo to the highest bidders among the brokers and traders there. He sold the coffee three days later for the total sum of £13,000. Henderson pocketed £1,000, created a fake bill of sale for £12,000, and turned the proceeds and bill of sale over to Minnie.

Walker doesn't need to know the amount, as he covertly gave Walker a share of £300. Day laborers transferred the cargo, and the transaction was complete. Henderson would now try to secure cargo for transport to Australia and would contact ship brokers to arrange the sale of the ship in Melbourne.

The morning after the coffee transfer, Captain Watkins presented himself to Henderson on deck with his duffle bag packed and tendered his resignation, demanding his wages for his time spent on board.

Henderson was furious. "I can't let you go now—it could jeopardize our entire operation," he declared, his nostrils flaring and his voice seething.

"I am not your slave, Henderson," the captain replied. "It would not benefit me to reveal anything about your voyage or activities, and I have other business here in Cape Town. I've always intended to depart here."

Henderson drew his pistol and pointed it at Watkins. "I'm confining you to quarters, under guard, until we reach our destination. Go there immediately."

The captain dropped his bag, grabbed Henderson's arm, and pointed it into the air, discharging a shot. He pulled his arm down, banging it against the ship's rail. The gun fell into the water.

He pulled out his pistol and held it to Henderson's head. "I want my pay now, thank you very much."

The noise of the shot brought Edie to the deck. "Stop it, you two. You'll draw attention and bring unwanted visitors on board."

Henderson pulled his fist back to strike Watkins.

Edie pulled her hatpin from her belt and stuck it through Henderson's shirt into his side, enough so he would feel it penetrate his skin.

"Henderson, stop it!" She spoke quietly, in a firm, forceful voice. Her teeth were clenched. "We'll end the voyage here, and you will forfeit your share of monies unless you can get yourself together."

"I'll take my money now," the captain said. "I have work to do in Cape Town."

Edie took Henderson to the safe and withdrew the correct amount. "Look, Henderson. You don't need the captain. He is not one of your trusted men, but he will bring you no harm. Appoint one of your own to be captain and leave it alone; I'll handle payment."

Edie returned with the money and handed it to Captain Watkins, along with an extra twenty pounds. He bowed and thanked her.

"You have the box and address I gave you?" she asked.

"Here in my duffle."

"You are expected around three," Edie said. "I wired the contact from Port Santos."

"I'll miss you, Minnie, but I can't say I'll miss anything else about this voyage."

"I understand, and I'll miss you as well, captain. Perhaps we can have dinner, you and I, before we depart," she suggested.

"I would enjoy that. I'll have a message delivered to you as soon as I know where I'm staying."

"Send your message to this person, addressed to me." She handed the captain a calling card from her pocket containing the name and contact details at the bank. "He will keep it until I pick it up. And I look forward to dinner."

Henderson watched this transaction and returned to the deck to watch the former captain disembark and walk off the dock toward the city, holding his head high.

"What was that all about?" he snarled. "This is my command! What are you and Hill and Watkins up to, and what the blazes did you stick into my side?"

"It was just a little prick, Henderson; I could have stuck it clear into your kidney." Edie was feeling assertive. "Nothing involving you, this ship, or even me is happening. I was told in communications with Mrs. Hill that the captain, or former captain, would leave us at Cape Town and that she had agreed to that when she hired him for the voyage."

"He was your protector, wasn't he?"

"Why do you ask? Do you have intentions to harm me? I have several protectors. The one I stuck you with could have killed you if you'd fought me. Just do your job."

Henderson decided he was losing this skirmish.

"I want this voyage over with, and I want my money," Henderson said.

"You could lose everything if you don't control your temper and suspicions. When you sell the ship, you keep half—focus on that."

Henderson turned and left without a word.

Edie was pleased with herself, but it was a show; she feared Henderson could be trouble for her.

"Henderson!" she called after him. "Continue to look for a buyer for the ship with delivery in Melbourne. We'll spend another few days in port—see what you can do." She'd now assumed full command of the actions of the ship.

Edie took two-thirds of the coffee proceeds from the safe and added all the money from the gun sale. It was a large load. Benji was engaged in the print room, so she enlisted the help of Robinson. Robinson went ashore and arranged for a cab to pick them up. They loaded two cases containing the gold and monies and traveled to Mrs. Hill's bankers at Sterling Union International Bank of Africa. In a separate parcel, she brought two disassembled rifles from the purchase in Brazil as a gift to Mrs. Hill's private banker, Silas Browning, to thank him for his involvement in purchasing and selling the rifles to Peruvian representatives.

Upon arriving at the Sterling Union International Bank, Edie was shown into a private room and offered tea. Robinson waited in the lobby. She was left alone until a clerk entered and offered a sealed envelope delivered on a platter. The clerk said, "This came for you a few days ago."

It was from Mrs. Hill. Edie translated the code and read:

Dear Edie (Minnie),

A few changes in plans. I've opened a new account and deposited half of your funds at a bank in Melbourne. I used a new identity for you: Lady Edith Black. You will receive the complete package establishing your unique identity when you get to Melbourne. Our organization is being threatened, I don't know from whom, but I have received threats of exposure. As I learn more, I will communicate with you. In the meantime, it is imperative that the following happen.

Have Benji leave the ship and follow Captain Watkins until he completes his journey back to London. He will be transporting a valuable package. Have Benji protect him and his cargo if necessary. It's best if he is not recognized and Watkins is unaware that he is being observed. Do not involve Henderson or advise him of this action or your new identity. Give Benji sufficient cash for whatever expenses he might encounter and tell him to contact me when he returns to London. Deposit the funds you have for me as planned. I will deposit your share into the chest that you left with me. I will make arrangements for a transfer when you are settled.

Edie, be careful, watch Henderson, and separate from your relationship with him before settling in Melbourne under your new name. I will contact you through the offices of Barrister Carlton Quill at the address in the notebook. Your account in Melbourne is at the English and Scottish Chartered Bank; Johnson Lee is my bank contact. Instruct Henderson to wire half the money from selling the ship to the account number I gave you.

Edie needed to figure out what to make of the change in plans. Her new confidence waned with the prospect of completing the voyage without Benji and losing him again for an extended period. She felt devastated by his departure and nervous about Henderson. She would start carrying the pistol Mrs. Hill gave her and keep her hatpin handy, but it was her heart she was most fearful of being hurt.

Edie met with Mr. Browning and presented the rifles, which thrilled him. He was like a child with new toys.

"Mrs. Hill and Harley Blake have been valuable friends. Give them my sincere thank you."

"I will. I'd like to make a deposit to Mrs. Hill's account, if I may."

"Yes, it has been arranged."

She kept £500 for Benji and £1,000 for any emergency she might encounter.

The banker thanked her for her service, the rifles, and the deposit. "It's a sizeable one," he added.

"Yes, it is. One more thing. A message will arrive for me from Captain Watkins addressed to Mrs. Minnie Henderson. I will come back to pick it up tomorrow."

She and Robinson hurried back to the ship, hoping she could get to Benji before Henderson was back on board. She hoped Henderson was out calling on ship brokers.

Edie returned to the ship and found Benji. Aside from needing to relay Benji's new task, she knew this was probably the last time they would have together for a long while. She took his hand and led him to his private quarters.

She placed her hand on his arm. "I'm so pleased we're together again." She paused, dropping her chin toward her chest. "But you have to leave."

Benji's mouth opened, but no words came out. His dark eyes looked concerned.

"Benji, here is a good deal of money; account for it but use it as necessary. We—Mrs. Hill and I—want you to follow Captain Watkins without being detected until his eventual return to London. Protect him and protect the cargo he'll be transporting. It is crucial to both of us." She leaned in closer, her hand now tightly clenching Benji's arm. She looked into his eyes.

"I don't want to leave you, Edie," said Benji. His voice trembled a little, and he put his hand on hers.

"I don't want you to either, but we don't have a choice. This has to be done."

Benji read the resolve in her voice; he stared into her eyes, saying nothing for a long time.

"Where will I find him?" Benji finally replied, accepting his assignment.

"He will send our banker the address where he is staying tomorrow. I'll pick it up and leave a note for you." She gave him the banker's address. "I know his meeting was later today, so you may be able to pick up his trail before then. Here's the address where he's headed with the package Mrs. Hill arranged."

"What about Henderson?"

"I'll take care of Henderson. You have to pack and leave now before Henderson returns."

"Will you be all right for the rest of the trip?"

"I can deal with Henderson, and I have Robinson—he'll protect me."

Benji gazed at her, feeling a heavy weight on his chest. "Promise me to take care, Edie." He seemed to hesitate. "I care for you."

"I know you do, Benji, and I love you with all my being." She spoke slowly, pausing between each word. "Be careful. In the future, you'll find me under the name of Lady Edith Black, widow and socialite of Melbourne. No one else should know this."

Benji stared at her, then suddenly leaned forward and kissed her firmly. He looked at her, his tanned face starting to color. "I hope I haven't . . . overstepped . . ."

"Don't be silly, Benji. Kiss me again."

Putting his arms around her, he kissed her again, and this time she leaned into the kiss, reaching her arms around his neck and pulling him tighter. She pressed her body tightly against his, lingering over the kiss. She whispered in his ear, "I need you, Benji." She backed toward Benji's bed, sitting, then lying down, pulling Benji on top of her.

"I've always wanted you, Benji," she whispered.

They said little else for the next hour, enjoying the warmth and feel of each other's bodies as they made love, releasing their pent-up desires. When they finally lay exhausted, she said, "We'll have more time together in the future. For now, you should pack and prepare to leave." She said it quietly. Tears ran down her cheeks.

Benji wiped the tears away and kissed her where they had trailed over her cheek. His gaze lingered on her face. "I love you, Edie. I've always loved you, even as a child. Now I love you as a woman."

She tried to say it back, but the sobs broke her speech. She held her hand to his cheek, and tears continued to run down her face. Finally, she said, "I love you too. I'll see you in Melbourne or maybe London."

Benji said, "Following Captain Watkins back to London will mean we may be apart for six or more months. I'll count every hour. I want to spend my life with you, and together we can love, have children, and enjoy life. We'll get away from crime. I'll do my task, find you as quickly as possible, and then we'll—"

Edie put her fingers to his lips.

"I'm sorry you have to leave. Be safe until we can be together," she whispered, kissing him with her hands on his cheeks.

PART TWO

THE DIAMOND HEIST

◆ ◆

CHAPTER 13

JACK CRAMER

Jack Cramer sat on the hard wooden bench in the private railcar owned by the Cape Western Railroad. The car was leased weekly by the British government to transport mail and cargo from Kimberley in the Northern Cape of South Africa to Cape Town. Kimberley was the location of the Kimberley Diamond Mine, rumored to be the largest in the world. Cramer's transport was timed to arrive exactly one hour before the mail ship sailed for England.

He pretended to read a weeks-old copy of the *London Daily Telegraph*, avoiding conversation with the British guards and trying not to think about what would happen if the train fell apart on the trip south. His hands and arms shook. This section of rail was rough, though he knew from experience that the ride would smooth out in another ten miles or so.

How I ever got transformed from an arson investigator in Boston to a railcar bouncing ball in the middle of nowhere, I have no recollection, he thought. He did have a recollection but didn't like to think of it. *Here I am on guard duty. At least it's well-compensated guard duty.*

Two British soldiers with rifles sat on mail sacks with feet firmly planted to keep them upright. Jack hoped the rifles had safeties; he didn't want to get shot accidentally any more than he wanted the train to disintegrate. Jack was American but traveled much of the world on assignments from the Fredrick Taylor syndicate, an insurer under the umbrella of Lloyd's of London. Jack's card read *Insurance Investigator*.

"We usually don't have company," one soldier said to Jack, his voice shaking from the vibrations of the rail. "They call me Woody; come from Sussex initially. Are you American?"

"I am," Jack said. "Boston. Special cargo this trip. Lloyd's wanted an extra guard overseeing its transport and delivery to London."

"Oh," Woody said, looking a little skeptical. Jack assessed his appearance: he was young, very tall, skinny, and had intelligent eyes. A curl of red hair hung down his forehead from under his cap.

"The diamonds?" The second guard frowned at Jack, his face crimson. He was scruffy, with short bristly hairs on his chin. He didn't offer his name, but a patch over his uniform pocket read Sergeant Hall.

"That's right. It's a large shipment, and Lloyd's has had several local robberies in the last few weeks . . . although unrelated to diamonds. Just being cautious."

"We carry diamonds weekly and haven't had any trouble," Hall said.

"Not this many," Jack replied.

"They don't have concerns with us, do they?" Woody said.

The train began to slow, one car after another, as brakemen jumped from car to car to apply the brakes. Jack tumbled off his seat as their car stopped abruptly. He grabbed his shoulder holster to keep it steady, landing on his elbows on mail sacks. His felt fedora fell to the floor and rolled forward. He could feel drag on the train, which meant some of the rear cars had derailed. Now he feared the rest of the cars would tip, but as the train slowed, they remained upright. He looked at the two soldiers—to their credit, they were on their knees with rifles at the ready. They waited.

Jack feared an ambush. It was his job to anticipate bad outcomes. He stood and walked to his hat; picking it up, he combed his blond hair back from his eyes and captured it with the fedora. Twenty minutes went by, and there was a knock on the sliding cargo door.

"Name," Hall called out.

"Hempstead," came the aggravated reply.

"It's the engineer," Woody said, reaching to unlock the door.

Jack grabbed his hand. "Wait!" he said. "Hempstead, are you alone?" He motioned the soldiers to stand guard.

"Aye, we've got a rockslide blocking the rail, and two cars at the rear derailed. We can use all the muscle available to get moving again quickly."

Jack took out his revolver, undid the safety, and unlocked the door. Hempstead looked annoyed with the excess caution when he saw two rifles and one pistol pointing at him. Jack suggested Woody stay with the cargo. "Hall, you come with me."

"Lock the door behind us, and don't open it until we knock," Jack whispered. "We'll use the word *hemlock* to authorize you to unlock the door." It was agreed.

Jack took a minute to walk around the site, looking for anything suspicious. He glanced at the cliffsides to detect any suspicious activity.

Jack and Hall joined the engineer at the front of the train. The train had stopped just fifty feet from the rock pile. A half dozen rail employees were already moving the smaller boulders. It took fifteen minutes to clear most of the rubble, leaving two large boulders that required all the back muscle they could muster. Hall was large and robust; he took the lead. Jack took out his watch, concerned now with the tight schedule in Cape Town. It took another twenty minutes to clear the track. The Royal Mail ships sailed on time, and now time was getting tight. They examined the rail sleepers, fishplates, and fasteners that made up the track. There was some damage to the sleepers, but the train could pass over successfully at a very low speed.

"What about the derailed cars?" Jack asked. "Can we decouple and leave them?"

"Absolutely not," Hempstead said. "Come with me."

The caboose and the cargo car in front of it had jumped the rail but stayed in line and upright.

"This will be easier to fix than the boulders," the engineer said.

Jack had heard of rerailing cars before and thought it would be time-consuming, but it was quick. Hempstead sent men to get the rerailing ramps, and they returned with metal implements. When they were in place, Hempstead instructed everyone to get behind the two cars in teams.

"All it takes now is muscle," Hempstead said. "When you hear me blow the train whistle, you push, and I'll pull with the engine for thirty feet."

Jack found it ingenious: the wheels rolled up a ramped piece of metal that angled them toward the sleeper rail at the top and placed the wheels back on track. He was still concerned about a potential ambush, but something probably would have happened by now if it were a planned attack. He rechecked his watch; they could still make it.

Jack and Hall returned to the car and said "hemlock" before Woody let them in. They were back on their way in less than an hour. However, the engineer took twenty minutes to pass the train over the damaged sleepers. They were going to be late.

Jack felt helpless and frustrated. The engineer had driven the train agonizingly slow for the balance of the trip. They arrived forty-five minutes after the Royal Mail ship had sailed. He would have to make alternate plans for the diamonds. The next ship wouldn't come for a week. Upon arrival, Jack sought out the postmaster, leaving the guards with instructions to stay with the cargo and keep the door locked.

"Where do I find the postmaster?" Jack asked the clerks unloading other mail cars.

"Postmaster Davids. His office is down the street in that building with the flag."

Upon entering, Jack encountered a desk and a uniformed clerk.

"I need to see Postmaster Davids on a matter of urgency." Jack expected the postmaster to be in a private office deeper in the building.

"I'm Postmaster Davids," the gentleman said as he stood. "And who might you be, and what's your urgency?" Davids was a slight man of perhaps fifty, with thinning hair, close-set eyes, and a pointy nose. He had an air of authority.

"I'm Jack Cramer, a representative of Lloyd's of London, and I have valuable cargo that missed the connection with the Royal Mail ship.

I need some help securing a large shipment of diamonds destined for London until the next ship."

"Are they currently in the mail car?"

"They're in a private mail car with two British soldiers."

"How large is the shipment?" Davids asked.

"Twenty-nine Kimberley diamond bags."

Davids's eyes widened, and he puckered his lips.

"That is a large quantity," he said, and paused. "But at least diamonds aren't usually too big—except for that yellow diamond miners found a few years ago, the color of horse piss and worth a fortune! One of the largest fancy diamonds ever found, I understand."

Jack crossed his arms, feeling impatient. "Can you help me secure storage?"

"Come with me," Davids said, standing and striding past Jack, out the door, and into the street. He crossed the road to the post office and called to the clerk, "Jacobs, come with us and bring three men."

Jacobs and three clerks from behind the counter hurried to join the two men as they walked toward the train. Davids marched ahead; the others tried to keep up.

The soldiers had managed to keep themselves locked in. Hempstead was knocking on the door when Jack arrived. Clerks were waiting to unload the car. "We need to be heading back to Kimberley; open up."

"What's the code?" Jack heard one of the soldiers say.

"Code? I don't need any damn code! I'm the engineer. Open this door."

"Jacobs," Davids said, "take your men and carry Mr. Cramer's packages directly to the safe room. We will accompany you."

Jack approached the train door and called, "Hemlock." The door was unlocked. Jack asked the soldiers to bring the twenty-nine sacks of diamonds to the door, where he counted them and checked their seals. The postal workers piled the bags in their arms and headed for the post office, with Jack and Davids following behind.

Jacobs was the head clerk of the registered letter department and had access to a locked storage area where registered mail was sorted and stored. The room contained two patent safes. Jacobs made sure no one was near enough to see the combinations. He unlocked the safes, stored half the diamonds in each, and relocked them.

Then Davids turned to Jack and said, "The diamonds will remain there until next Monday, when they will be placed in shipping bags and restored for loading on the Royal Mail ship the *Pretoria* the next day. You will need to provide Jacobs with details of handling in London."

"I'll continue to travel with the diamonds, Mr. Davids. These diamonds are my responsibility until they are delivered to the Bank of London. I'll handle the delivery." He watched as the men relocked the safe and locked the storage room, and then he thanked Davids and Jacobs for their help. He felt the diamonds were secure. "I'll return next Monday to oversee the packaging."

"No need. No one is allowed in the registered letter room except Jacobs or me. Return Tuesday for transfer to the ship," Davids said.

CHAPTER 14

BENJI AND WATKINS

Edie had told Benji that Captain Watkins's meeting was set for 3:00 p.m. Benji thought he could intercept Watkins at the location of the meeting if he found it quickly. If he missed him, he'd get the address of Watkins's lodgings from Edie's message.

Benji's mind returned to his last few hours with her. He was ready to settle down and begin their new life together. But first he and Edie had to finish their assignments and collect their earnings.

That afternoon, the captain turned onto Loader Street. Benji had staked out a convenient spot on a grass slope down the street to observe the captain's entrance. The captain opened a gate and approached the front door. Benji would wait for him to leave and then follow him. He settled in for what could be a long evening if the captain stayed the night.

Captain Watkins admired the handsome three-story home. It had a wooden fence and a tended yard and was obviously a place of some wealth. He walked up the steps to the veranda, applied the anchor-shaped knocker to the wood-panel door, and was soon greeted by a gentleman in full evening attire, although it was only afternoon.

"Captain Watkins, won't you come in? I am Jacob Robertson; I've been expecting you. Please join me at my desk in the den."

Robertson had short, cropped, curly black hair, and he spoke with a sophisticated African accent.

"Refreshment?" Robertson already had a glass of champagne, and his eyes were bloodshot. The captain took tea. He still needed to figure out what was expected of him other than delivering Minnie's package.

"Do you have a package for me?" Robertson asked.

"I do." The captain dug in his duffel, pulled out the small, wax-sealed box tied in string that Edie had given him, and handed it to Robertson. Robertson inspected it to make sure the seal had not been tampered with, and when he was satisfied, he opened the bottom drawer to the desk, unlocked a metal box with a key, and handed the captain £100. He relocked the box, and locked the drawer.

"If you'll excuse me for a few minutes, Captain, I'll examine the contents of the package in the other room and return promptly."

Robertson sat in a lounge chair in his library and opened the package. There was a note of instructions for him, timetables, a building layout, and contact names with monetary amounts next to them. He had his mission. The box contained gold sovereigns for payments to contacts.

He was gone for about twenty minutes and returned without the package.

"Captain Watkins, my partner in London says you are a man to be trusted. We wish to extend your assignment to include the return to London of a precious package that we'd like you to protect day and night."

"I had intended to stay in Cape Town—retire and settle down for a little pleasure sailing," the captain replied.

"One more trip, Captain, if you will. We'll make it worthwhile. Upon delivery in London, you'll receive £300 plus first-class transportation back to Cape Town. Is that acceptable?"

The captain's expression reflected indifference, though he was mentally calculating what the fee would do for his retirement funds.

"A good sum indeed," the captain agreed. "It must be a precious package."

"It is, to some people," Robertson agreed.

"Then I will protect it to London for £400, and you can count on a safe delivery."

Robertson hesitated, then smiled. "Agreed," he said.

The captain looked at Robertson, trying to determine his trustworthiness. He had learned to read faces well over the years, but he couldn't read Robertson's.

"Should I expect any trouble along the way?" the captain asked.

"Captain, no one will know of your travels or cargo other than me and my partner in London."

"When would I have to leave?" he asked.

"I've booked a room for you at the Brenton House, a prominent inn at the top of Government Avenue. Captain Robert Granger owns it. Captain Granger is a wealthy merchant sailor."

"I know Captain Granger. I've captained for him."

"Ah, that's good. I've arranged private accommodation setting sail on the seventeenth of March, twelve days from now. On the evening of the sixteenth, I'll dine with you and deliver the package into your hands. The package you delivered to me provided the particulars and confirmation that the package would arrive on the sixteenth."

"Mr. Robertson, I want a new pistol for protection, and I'd like to travel under an alias."

"Our thoughts as well, Captain. There will be no record of Captain Watkins sailing back to London. You'll travel as a returning missionary called back by the London Missionary School. I'll provide you with your history of missionary service, a new name from a now-deceased minister, and your story to memorize. You'll have the paperwork and identification to fall back on."

Watkins was comfortable with the cover. "I assume I travel first class?"

Robertson smiled. "Unusual for a missionary, but yes, captain, only the best."

The captain scratched his chin. He wanted this assignment, but he needed to know all the details. "And what do I do when I reach London?"

"A representative of my partner will meet you on the docks in London. Once aboard the ship, dress in accordance with your alias, we'll have clothes delivered, wear a collar. On arrival, switch to your captain's jacket to disembark—it will signal our carriage to collect you. Our representative will take you to a bank. The gentlemen meeting you at the bank will provide your payment."

"Very well," the captain said. "I assume you're covering all my expenses for the stay here in Cape Town. I'm anxious for some real African cooking."

"Enjoy yourself." Robertson smiled and raised his champagne toward the captain.

CHAPTER 15

THE BRENTON HOUSE

After Watkins left the Loader Street house, Benji followed at a distance. The captain still carried his duffel but nothing else. When Watkins arrived at the Brenton House, the manager greeted him as an honored guest and escorted him to the reception desk.

Benji climbed the steps to the porch, picked up a discarded newspaper, and leaned against the railing, pretending to read while observing the front desk through the window. Questions flowed through Benji's thoughts: *What was this whole exercise about? What was the mysterious cargo? Why a personal delivery person? Why Watkins? Was Mrs. Hill involved? Could this be the primary reason for the entire* Ferret *enterprise?* As the Captain signed his guest card, a bellman took the duffle, removed a key from the wall, and led Watkins to the central staircase. Benji noted the location of the key. Once they were out of sight, he entered the lobby and approached the desk. He had never stayed in such a fancy inn, so he was slightly uncomfortable. Benji noted the key location beneath the number 303. He hoped he would have time to explore the room.

"May I help you?" the desk clerk asked.

"Yes," answered Benji. His voice rose unexpectedly; he cleared his throat. "I'd like a piece of hotel stationery to write a thank you to the captain who just checked in. I crewed with him on his recent voyage."

The desk clerk was happy to oblige.

Benji took the stationery to a lobby desk and wrote a note: *Welcome to the Brenton House. We hope your stay is pleasant. The Management.* He folded the paper and returned it to the desk clerk, who inserted it into a hotel envelope and placed it in the cubby below room 303's key hook. "It will be delivered promptly," the clerk assured Benji.

Benji said thank you and tipped the clerk. He turned away, then returned to the clerk, feigning an afterthought: "Can you tell me how long the captain is staying; it might allow me to treat him to dinner."

The clerk looked up from the registry. "I'm not allowed to give out that information, but he's staying a while."

As the clerk glanced back at the registry, he placed a finger on the sheet out of habit. Benji could see the line he had drawn included the balance of the week, but beyond that, he couldn't tell.

Benji left to find accommodations nearby. He wanted to avoid the risk of recognition by not staying at the Brenton, and it was a little rich for him; he wanted to preserve the funds Edie had given him, although they were substantial. Benji walked a few blocks to a pub and restaurant area, found a respectable-looking inn, and booked a room for five days, paying in advance. He inquired about a local message service. Walking to the address, Benji entered the office, wrote a note advising Edie of his actions, and signed it "Love, Benji." He had it delivered to the bank contact that Edie had provided.

When he retired that evening, Benji felt a little adrift—he couldn't be with Edie and had to wait for Watkins to leave, but he didn't know how long that would be. *I wouldn't say I like waiting and idleness,* Benji thought. He thought about his past, his boys, the stall ladies—now free but displaced. His mind came back to Watkins. He had always seemed very proper and kindhearted. *Why does he need protection? The cargo. I have to find out about the valuables.* Benji fell asleep.

Having settled into his room at the Brenton, the captain wrote a message to Minnie. He would ask the concierge to have it delivered to the contact Minnie had provided, requesting she dine with him in three nights at the Brenton. The captain went to bed thinking about his pending encounter with Minnie. He adored her, and though this was a business encounter, not a personal one, he could still dream.

After she received the invitation, Edie prepared a coded message to Mrs. Hill about the upcoming dinner and Captain Watkins's location; in case Mrs. Hill was unaware, she added that Benji was observing the captain. She also noted that she had extended the port time in Cape Town for at least a week and would check for messages at their contact point before departing the city.

Edie also sent a short message to Benji at the pub address he had provided.

Dear Benji,

I miss you. Don't worry about me—I'll be fine. Please be careful and stay safe. The captain's secure delivery of this cargo will guarantee our payoffs from this voyage. I will dine with Captain Watkins at the Brenton House on the evening of the twelfth at 8:00 p.m.

Love, Edie

The night of the dinner, Benji felt it essential to risk being in the lobby for Edie's date with Watkins. He believed the captain to be trustworthy, but there was still a risk of danger. *Was Edie involved in Watkins's mission?* Benji wondered. He decided that he might learn something by observing their dinner unobserved.

Edie arrived, dressed elegantly in a blue dinner dress, her hair in a bun with a blue matching hat, her trusty hatpin securing it at an angle. She was met promptly by Captain Watkins, dressed in his formal captain's uniform with its abundance of gold braid. He escorted her to the elegant dining room. Benji thought that he could observe from the far end of the bar that was adjacent to the dining room. He entered through the separate bar entrance and sat with a clear view of the table, the captain's back toward him. It seemed a cordial dinner—he could see them talking and sharing a few laughs. The captain gave Edie a small box. She opened it and lifted out a brooch. She put her hand on his arm and thanked him.

Benji felt lonelier than he already had.

"Yes, I'm jealous," he muttered.

Edie and the captain dined on oysters, followed by a lobster bisque and an entree of salmon croquettes with a wine reduction and buttered root vegetables. They had a custard for dessert. Benji slowly consumed a bowl of fish chowder, a plate of shepherd's pie, custard for dessert, and several beers to kill time and loneliness.

After dinner, the captain escorted Edie to a cab for her return trip to the ship and paid the fare. Before climbing into the cab, she quickly kissed him on the cheek.

Benji watched the captain head up the stairs to his room. He sulked off to his residence, feeling very alone, and stayed at the bar until midnight.

As Edie exited her carriage at the docks, she looked at the moon and stars. The pleasant night, without Benji, made her lonelier. She'd seen him at the bar and wanted so much to go to him—he looked so unhappy. She would send a message through the banker tomorrow; perhaps they could meet up before the captain and Benji departed.

Walking up the gangplank, she found Henderson waiting for her on the main deck.

"Was Benji with you?" he demanded.

"He was not!" Minnie answered with disdain.

Henderson grabbed her arm, "Where is he?"

"Let go of me, Henderson, or you will pay a dear price!" she said through clenched teeth. She slapped his arm away. Her stare burned into his eyes.

"Where's Benji? Have you been with him?" His face and neck were red. He had been drinking.

"He packed his bag and left after your encounter with the captain this morning. He said he had had enough; he wasn't coming back. I was hoping he might calm down and return. He even left without getting paid—which should please you."

Henderson was livid. "This is some of your doing, Minnie!" he accused.

"Why would I want him gone?" she hissed at him. She took a deep breath and let it out slowly.

"I need documents to sell the ship. I couldn't engage a broker because I needed original purchase and registration documents. I need Benji to create them."

"You'll have to find another printer in Melbourne," Edie said.

Henderson stormed off.

She would miss the opportunity to meet with Benji, but it was best to get the voyage over, sell the ship, and move on. Edie felt in her handbag and touched the handle of her pistol for comfort.

Edie didn't care about Henderson's temper tantrums. She didn't need to have much to do with him. Her private quarters were next to Henderson's, so she would have Chance install a deadbolt immediately, even if she had to wake him.

During the few weeks remaining on the ship with Henderson, she would have to reach a truce of some sort so that the voyage could end amicably for the benefit of everyone.

CHAPTER 16

CAPTAIN GRANGER

If he weren't so concerned for the diamonds, Jack's visit to the Brenton House would be pure joy, surprising an old friend and enjoying stories of his father. One of the great benefits of Jack's early life in Boston was that he got to know many of his father's sailor friends from around the world. His father had been a successful marine merchant who died at sea when one of his ships sank en route to the Orient. At the time, Jack was at Harvard studying maritime law, his father's dream for him, but the family fortune quickly evaporated, and Jack needed a new plan for his life. His father's friends steered him to insurance and Lloyd's, which had a monopoly on marine insurance.

When his father had been alive, one of the many ship captains and owners who would stay with the family when in port was Captain Robert Granger, a wealthy merchant and ship owner based in Cape Town, where he owned a stylish inn. Since Jack had an unexpected few days in Cape Town, he would try to renew an old acquaintance and see if there was room at the Brenton House.

But first, he needed to prepare an update report to Fredrick Taylor at Lloyd's; he borrowed a desk from Postmaster Davids to write the message. He walked to the nearest telegraph office and sent the report to Taylor.

After hailing a carriage, he instructed the driver: "The Brenton House on Government Avenue."

"I know very well where the Brenton House is," the cabbie returned, as he put his horse into a fast trot.

Jack walked into the captain's office unannounced after speaking with the receptionist at the inn. The face that turned up to him was weathered and wrinkled, with a white beard and mustache. But the brown eyes sparkled as Jack remembered. His frown at being interrupted turned into a wide smile when he took in Jack. "Well, I'll be! Little Jackie Cramer, it's been a long time. Come over, sit down."

Jack sat in an armchair facing Captain Granger's wide desk.

"I know it was a long time ago, but I want you to know that I'm sorry about your father," the captain said. "He was one of the dearest men on the sea."

"Thank you, Captain. I miss him. I miss both my parents."

"Oh, sorry, Jack; of course, I felt bad when I heard about your mother. Forgive me."

"Captain, I didn't mean to imply . . . it's the past. Let's discuss other matters. How's trade?"

"I've adjusted; I'm doing all right. The war between the British and the Boers is winding down, but I expect a Boer victory. I'm still determining what that will do with trade between Africa and Britain. Still, I've switched routes for my ships, five of them now: four with stable routes in Australia and the Far East, and one ship running west then north, trading in Brazil, the Caribbean, Bermuda, and occasionally America. It can be difficult for a clipper to sail north in the North Atlantic, but we've developed techniques, and the trip duration is typically half that of sailing back around the Horn. It's very lucrative. Next week's sail will port at Bermuda and load every nook and cranny on the ship with lily bulbs, a precious cargo that generally arrives in London for Easter. This year it will likely be late."

"Complicated!" Jack said.

"Yes, it is. Are you staying here? I want to make sure you have the finest room."

"I've inquired at reception, and they said they would try to find accommodations for me. They were to locate me in the lobby."

The captain stood and took Jack by the elbow, steering him back toward the lobby.

"Give me a minute; then we'll head to the bar."

Jack waited and studied the guests in the lobby: it was a mix of traders, merchants, and the marine elite. He watched the captain as he returned from reception. He was husky, with a slight bend to his back, the result of some ancient injury, Jack suspected. It caused him to look like he was waddling headfirst with his body following at a speed that seemed slightly out of control.

"Suite twelve, third floor," the captain said. "Courtesy of the hotel. I had your bags at reception delivered to the room. Here's your key."

"Thank you, Captain! You don't have to treat; I have Lloyd's paying expenses."

"For a guest as special as you, I can treat. You're the only guest here I used to bounce on my knee."

As they entered the bar, the captain said, "Ah, here's someone I think you'll enjoy meeting." He steered Jack to a table where a man was sitting. "Jack, I have the pleasure of introducing Captain Wilford Watkins, a master mariner who has captained voyages for me and dozens of others. He tells me he's retiring. He sails on my ship, the *Scout*, on the seventeenth as a passenger to London on the northbound clipper I was talking about."

The captain introduced Jack and a brief version of his history with the family, ending with, "I've wiped his nose more than he remembers."

Captain Watkins stood and bowed to the two gentlemen standing at his table. "I would be greatly honored if you would join me."

They drank, dined, and talked long into the evening. Jack loved stories of adventures at sea, and it turned out that Captain Watkins had spent time with his father on several occasions in ports around the globe. For Jack, it was one of the best nights of his life. He happily absorbed the others' remembrances of his father.

Around two in the morning, Captain Granger said, "Gentlemen, I am so pleased the three of us could share this night, but I'm off to bed. I sail for Australia at six."

"Ouch!" Jack said. He was a little drunk, as were the two captains. "Thank you, Captain," he said to Granger. "I appreciate getting a room in your inn. I'll pick up the bar tab."

"Thank you, Jack," Captain Granger said, making his formal goodbyes and asking Jack to be in touch.

Jack promised he would.

Jack and Watkins had one more round to seal their new friendship. Watkins mentioned that he had captained the *India* to Cape Town and then left his command.

"I had planned on retiring here, but my contacts convinced me to take another trip. A lucrative assignment I couldn't refuse. Then I'll return here to a life of sailing the seas alone, enjoying as much of the world as possible." Captain Watkins wondered if one more trip, even one so well paying, would allow him to live his dream.

Watkins and Jack said their goodbyes, and the captain headed back to his room.

A bill needed paying, but Captain Granger had informed the bar manager that it was on him. Jack retired to his suite and fell into bed, lying down fully dressed.

It wasn't until morning that he explored the magnificent suite provided to him and found his belongings safely stored. It was ten o'clock, and Jack thought of Captain Granger on the water; he was glad he was on land. He felt the swaying of waves just standing in his room.

CHAPTER 17

DIAMONDS AND SARDINES

On the morning of the sixteenth, Jack rose early, had a quick breakfast of coffee, sausage, and eggs at the Brenton House, then went to the train station and post office. He had visited twice during the week to comfort his nerves about the safety of the diamonds. Davids assured Jack that the diamonds were in the safes in the post office and that he shouldn't worry so much. Arriving at 6:00 a.m., he headed to the office of Postmaster Davids, but Davids wasn't there. Stepping out to the street, he spied Davids walking down the road from the train station. He called to Jack.

"You had better come with me."

Jack braced himself, anticipating the worst.

Davids was clenching his jaw, his face red. He walked Jack over to the post office and unlocked the door. Walking into the registered letter office, Jack observed letters everywhere and Clerk Jacobs sitting in a straight-backed chair with a hangdog look.

"I told him just to sit there until you arrived," Davids said. "It seems the diamonds are missing, stolen."

Jack's thoughts were wild. "I don't believe it. How can this be? They were locked in the safes."

Davids turned to Jacobs. "Tell him your story, Jacobs. Every detail."

Jacobs started mumbling. His eyes twitched, and his chin quivered like he was freezing to death.

"Pick your head up and talk clearly!" Davids commanded.

Jacobs gave him a woeful look, took a deep breath, and began: "The day before the boat arrives, I always sort and repackage all the registered mail into Royal Mail sacks. Yesterday all the local businesses brought their final mail to the post office."

He slumped further into his chair. "I already had a good deal in storage. When I was done sorting, I had so much registered mail that everything wouldn't fit in the safes, so I hid the diamonds in their Royal Mail sacks under the counter in the safe room."

Now his voice rose to a high pitch. "I've hidden things there before; I was sure they would be safe."

"You felt it more important to lock up the mail than the diamonds?" Jack nearly screamed in Jacob's face.

Davids held his hand up to Jack. "Let him finish."

Jack stepped back.

His voice quivering, sweat running down his face, Jacobs continued. "When I arrived this morning, someone had moved the diamond bags from under the counter to the mail-sorting room in the back. Open bags were everywhere, and the diamonds were removed from the bags; their boxes and wadding were scattered all over the floor."

"Jack, I can add a few details," Davids said. "I searched the sorting room, and the only evidence I found was a stevedore hook and an empty can of sardines. But perhaps more important, I found that the ventilator panel over the door to the registered-mail room was unlocked; the door was still locked. It's always kept locked. I worked late last night and left my office two hours after the post office closed. As is my practice, I crossed the street and checked the front door. I found it unlocked, and it's never been unlocked before. I stepped in; nothing was amiss at the time. I yelled to make sure nobody was still working. I checked the door to the safe room and the sorting room door—all were locked. I didn't think to check the ventilator. I left and locked the front door. When I checked, the thief or thieves must have already been hiding in the building.

"I've sent a messenger to fetch the police to question Jacobs and myself if necessary."

"I didn't do anything!" Jacobs protested.

Jack turned back to Jacobs. "Were you the last to leave the building last night?"

"Yes."

"Did you lock the door?"

"I'm sure I did; I lock up most every night."

So he's stupid or guilty, Jack thought. *I'm sure he knows more than he's saying.*

"Do you or your men regularly eat sardines?"

"Most of us do at lunch."

"Postmaster Davids, I want a guard watching Jacobs until the police arrive."

Jack walked outside to wait for the police; he couldn't believe this was happening. He wanted to do something, but he didn't know what.

The police talked to Jack first. He explained his role, but they didn't seem to care. Jack felt uneasy—they were treating him like he was as much a suspect as Jacobs. They took a statement from Davids and took Jacobs into custody.

Jacobs and Davids had access to the diamonds and a week to put a plan into action, Jack thought. *That many diamonds are very tempting,*

He went immediately to a cable office, wrote a report of the details, and had it wired to Fredrick Taylor, care of Lloyd's. He knew this could be disastrous for Fredrick's syndicate and that it would likely end his relationship with Lloyd's.

CHAPTER 18

DEPARTURE PREPARATIONS

Benji desperately wanted to learn what Captain Watkins was engaged in.

He could make some assumptions. Edie had said that Watkins was to deliver a package to London, and Benji was to follow him and keep him safe. Staying at the Brenton House likely indicated that Watkins was sailing on one of Captain Granger's ships. He decided to approach Captain Granger claiming to be an accomplished seaman and apply to be signed on for the next voyage to London, assuming that Captain Watkins would be on the same ship. Benji would disappear from the crew at the last minute if the captain didn't sign on for the voyage. Benji enlisted the help of a young printer, paying to use his press to modify his sailing papers with his alias, Russell Weaver, and a sailing status as an experienced deck cadet. As a deck cadet, he would have access to the entire ship.

Captain Watkins fell into a routine that Benji soon deciphered. He ate breakfast at the inn and walked briskly to the docks, rain or shine, watching the ships as they came and went. He lunched at restaurants with food from different African countries, often for two or more hours, after which he would return to the Brenton and spend the afternoon in the lobby reading the inn's collection of sailing journals and newspapers from around the world. Benji felt safe leaving his surveillance during the afternoons to attend to other chores. He purchased a new set of sailing clothes to make his appearance suitable when applying for a position on Granger's ships.

He visited the offices of the Granger sailing fleet and requested to speak with Captain Granger. The captain's assistant informed Benji that the captain had sailed on one of his ships to Australia. Benji met with a clerk in charge of hiring and presented the papers he had prepared. He told the clerk he was eager to crew a ship bound for London as soon as possible since his brother was getting married soon. The clerk carefully reviewed Benji's papers and asked him to return the following day.

When Benji appeared the next afternoon, he was handed his papers and told to report to the purser at the sailing ship *Scott*, expected in dock the next day. The purser provided a schedule and assignments. The ship was to sail the North Atlantic route to London on March 17, with one or two trading stops, one in Bermuda. He was third deck cadet. Benji now had to hope that Captain Watkins would be aboard as well.

Benji reported to the purser on March 12 and began work that day. He had to drop his surveillance of Watkins, but he would do some sleuthing to make sure that he was on the right ship to London. He befriended the purser and performed all the duties asked of him with speed and thoroughness.

"You are ultimately responsible to the boatswain, Mr. Philips," the purser told him. "You're at his command whenever work is required on deck." During Benji's duties, Benji sought out a copy of the sailing manifest listing the rooms to be occupied and their guests. Captain Watkins was not on the list, but Benji surmised that Watkins would sail under a different name. He looked for a recognizable alias and didn't find one at first. On a second look, he found a Reverend William Rollins sailing alone in first class. Benji thought a reverend usually wouldn't pay for first class; it could be Watkins. He didn't see any other likely possibilities. He was worried he wouldn't have the means to leave the ship and get back on the captain's trail if he were wrong, but he thought he'd made the right call. The *Scott* was the only Granger ship sailing to London for the next two weeks.

Benji requested the days of the fifteenth and sixteenth off before sailing, saying he needed to put his local affairs in order and say good-bye to friends. He wanted to keep an eye on Watkins.

After the disappearance of the diamonds and the police interviews, Jack returned to his room at the Brenton House to prepare another detailed message to Fredrick Taylor with a request for instructions. Jack received a return cable from Fredrick Taylor. It read: *Attend the inquest of Jacobs. Gather all the information you can, obtain a copy of the police report, then return to London immediately. No delay. Services are needed here.*

Jack inquired into the earliest steamship sailing to London following the inquest and was lucky to book a vacant stateroom. He couldn't afford the weeks the trip could take on a schooner. Jack wired the Riley Inn that he would arrive on the steamship *Adelaide* and requested his regular rooms. He wired Fredrick Taylor with the details of his arrival and said he would report to him immediately. He couldn't help but feel full responsibility for the diamond loss. However, it looked to him like an elaborate plan that reeked of organized crime. Jacobs was likely involved, but he was not the mastermind behind the heist. Jack was convinced that a coordinated effort on multiple levels would have been required to pull off the theft and broker the diamonds, but who was responsible? He suspected it had to be a crime syndicate from London with solid support from local crime bosses in Africa. The theft would be all over the papers before Jack arrived back in London—the public would eat up this type of crime. Jack sent details from the inquest to Fredrick and suggested he post a reward for information leading to the arrest of those responsible and the recovery of the diamonds.

Benji, now with two weeks of neatly trimmed beard growth, a shaved head, and dressier clothes, had been observing his charge from the lobby of the Brenton House. He had booked a room for three nights under the name Russell Weaver.

On the night of the sixteenth, Benji saw a well-dressed, distinguished-looking man carrying a large leather case approach the desk and ask for Captain Watkins.

Benji had just seen the captain the evening before, so he knew he was still in residence. He recognized the visitor as the person who had opened the Loader Street door to greet Captain Watkins. While waiting, the visitor sat on the far side of the lobby from Benji, still within hearing range. Upon his arrival in the lobby, the captain addressed the man as Mr. Robertson. They shook hands and made their way to the dining room. Benji waited a few minutes and approached the dining room host.

"I'm a guest of the inn, but I failed to make a reservation. Can you accommodate me for dinner?"

"Of course we can." The host smiled at Benji.

Benji handed him some coins. "May I have that table beyond those two men?"

"Certainly, sir." The host bowed slightly and led the way to the table. The captain and Mr. Robertson paid no attention.

Benji could see both men's faces, but couldn't hear what they were saying. An occasional word was audible, and their actions were readable.

Mr. Robertson kept the leather case under the table at his feet. After ordering drinks, Mr. Robertson removed a parcel from his jacket pocket. He handed it to the captain, who did not inspect it before he placed it in his jacket pocket. It looked heavy. Benji suspected it was a pistol.

Benji dined lighter than the captain and Robertson, finishing earlier. They weren't in a hurry; he ordered an after-dinner port, then a coffee, lingering while the two men completed their dinner. The conversation seemed cordial and businesslike.

Benji signed his tab and left the restaurant as the gentlemen settled their bill. He noticed Mr. Robertson paid and then carried the case from the restaurant. As the two were saying goodbye at the foot of the stairs, he handed it to Captain Watkins. He waited until the captain had climbed to the first-floor landing before leaving.

The valuable cargo I'm to protect has arrived, Benji thought.

Benji deduced that Robertson was a representative of whomever the principal of this assignment was.

Watkins was the courier, and now he had the package.

Benji had to report to work at 6:00 a.m. the following day. He felt confident he would see Captain Watkins, alias Reverend William Rollins, aboard the *Scott.* They would be on the same ship for weeks; he would find out more during the voyage. Benji wrote a quick report and sealed it in an envelope, asking the manager of the inn to send it to the address Edie had provided in Melbourne. He slept poorly that night. So many things were unknown, and he was taking a journey he didn't want to take.

PART THREE

MELBOURNE, AUSTRALIA

◆ ◆ ◆

CHAPTER 19

THE END OF THE VOYAGE

Edie watched as the port of Cape Town grew smaller, and she wondered what the future had in store for her. The weather was warm, and the breeze created by the ship's movement was gentle on her face. She knew the water would soon get rough as they entered the cape turmoil, typical of the Cape Town waters—but the *India*'s powerful engine could handle it. She feared the threats she might face on this final leg of their journey. She also felt an emptiness, sailing in the opposite direction from Benji. She was staring without seeing, daydreaming.

Enough dreaming! She knew it was more important to deal with the present. As she walked the deck, she considered how she could exert control over Henderson for the balance of the trip.

As was his practice several times a day, Robinson approached her. "Can I do anything for you, Mrs. Henderson?"

"Yes, Robinson, I think you can," she replied. "Call me Minnie; I don't want to be associated with Henderson. Find him and ask him to meet me in his quarters in half an hour. Do you have a gun, Robinson?"

"Yes, I do, Mrs.—I mean, uh, Minnie." He bit his lip to stop his stammering.

Edie smiled. "No need to be nervous, Robinson; I'm just being cautious. Once we're together in his chamber, stand guard outside the door. If I need help, I'll call for you."

Robinson flinched; his mouth opened. He hesitated, then said, "All right." Robinson left, got his gun, then went to find Henderson.

Thirty minutes later, Edie and Henderson sat facing each other across his dinner table. He acknowledged her with a nod. His hair fell into his face, and he brushed his forelock back but didn't look up at her.

"James, we have had and continue to have our differences."

"Oh, so true, Minnie. What's your point?" He pursed his lips and still didn't look directly at her.

"Look at me, Henderson. We have a few short weeks of sailing. I want them to go smoothly and without conflict between us. I have a plan, which I believe you will like."

Now Henderson looked at Edie. "I'm listening."

"You've appointed your man Carlyon captain, right?"

"Carlyon changed his name to Wright. Yes, I have. What of it?"

"You and your partner, Walker, have the most money at stake, other than Mrs. Hill and me."

He tilted his head and raised his eyebrows at Edie. "If we ever see it."

"When you return to England, you'll receive your share from the voyage. You've known Mrs. Hill longer than I have. You know she takes care of her people. And you and Walker will have your half of the ship proceeds after the sale, less what you promised the crew."

"The crew be damned," he said. "Selling the ship without the original construction documents and approvals is impossible. I don't have them, and I don't have Benji here to produce forgeries."

"I understand your predicament, and I have a solution. Here is what I propose. I have Mrs. Hill's contacts in Melbourne; one is someone I believe you know, Mathew Rohwedder."

"I do know him; I recruited him for Mrs. Hill. How did you know about him?" Henderson spoke abruptly, his palms flat on the table as he leaned toward Edie. "And what's your plan?"

"It was noted in my contact notebook. Please calm down. I'm trying to do us both some good. It would help if you quickly rid us of this ship before our charade is discovered—even if it means taking a reduced selling price. Instruct Captain Wright to make an interim stop at Port Louis, Mauritius. You go ashore and arrange a legitimate cargo transport, perhaps sugar for Melbourne. It will serve us well to arrive with a cargo. We'll appear legitimate. From Mauritius, I will communicate with Rohwedder to find the best forger and broker in Melbourne and have them ready for you."

"Go on."

I have kept a good deal of money in my safe; some of it is Mrs. Hill's, some mine, and some is to be sent to Mrs. Hill from Melbourne for the benefit of you and Walker. I have the only access to that safe. Upon our arrival in Melbourne, I want your help to safely remove my trunk of valuables and Mrs. Hill's trunk. I am arranging secure storage for them. I will carry the money from the safe. You work with the forger and broker and sell the ship. Once you accomplish a sale, I will give you and Walker your share of the safe funds instead of sending them to London."

Henderson's face softened, allowing a small smile to cross his lips. "I like that part of your plan." He sat back in the chair.

"But not until our trunks are safely off the *India* and you sell the ship, understood?"

"I may not like you, Minnie, but you have Mrs. Hill supporting you, and I can't get all my money if something happens to you. Therefore, your plan is an acceptable one. I want you to split Mrs. Hill's portion of the money as well, and she can take it from our final settlement. Agreed?"

Edie hesitated, caught between her enemy, whom she despised and didn't trust, and her benefactor, to whom she owed loyalty. She needed a compromise to get through the voyage.

"I'll split half of Mrs. Hill's money with you and Walker and deposit the rest, including my share. I'll send an accounting telling her to deduct your portions from your share of the proceeds she has already received."

"I accept that arrangement. I'll instruct Wright to set a course for the island of Mauritius. You'll be safe for the remainder of the trip. You can call off your guard now."

"Oh, I think he enjoys the duties. Robinson's a good man—I'll keep him as my protector for a while."

During the stop in Mauritius, Edie contacted Rohwedder by cable and put him to work on finding a forger and broker for the ship. She knew she should update Mrs. Hill on the changes to the deal she had agreed upon with Henderson, but she didn't know what to say. The loyalty was still intact, but Edie was living this venture. It was in her hands, and she had to make decisions necessary for its success.

Henderson failed to secure a cargo of sugar. It was the main export of Mauritius, but transport was booked months in advance. The best he could do was a small cargo of livestock, which made the trip more complicated and smellier: chickens in cages and calves in crates. Henderson attempted to put Robinson in charge of the shipment, but Edie made other arrangements. Having failed to acquire any significant consignments, they continued their voyage, stopping briefly at Port of Albany on the south coast of Australia for water and coal. Edie instructed Henderson to pay the vendors in cash. They couldn't afford to risk bogus payments now that they were in Australian waters, where they would end the voyage. They then sailed on toward Melbourne, arriving at Port Phillip. Captain Wright reported to the dock authorities. He produced valid documents for the livestock. The authorities were satisfied and allowed the animals to be unloaded by the livestock broker.

Rohwedder parked his horse and cart at the train station directly across from the dock the following day. He walked to the ship, requested permission to board, and was greeted by Edie and Henderson.

"Did you find me a ship broker?" Henderson asked.

"I did, James, and rumor has it he will bend the rules a little, so he should be perfect for you. I understand you need the original shipyard papers. He has sources."

"Well done!"

"Minnie wanted to make sure I found everything you need to sell this ship—and promised me £200 if you're successful, £100 if you're not."

Henderson glanced at Edie. "Out of your share."

"We split it. Did you expect to get help for nothing?" Edie said with a dismissive tone. She glared at him until he turned away.

Rohwedder smiled at the exchange and handed Henderson a card. "You'll find his office address here. His name is Stanley Lahey. He owns the brokerage—deal only with him. Let's load the trunks, and I'll be off."

"Mathew has arranged safe storage of my trunk and Mrs. Hill's until I call for them," Edie told Henderson. "He can take yours as well if you want."

"And you trust him?" Henderson asked, looking dismissively at Rohwedder.

Rohwedder ignored Henderson. The two men had worked together for a few years in London, and there was no love lost between them.

"Mrs. Hill does—therefore, so do I."

"Oh, very well," Henderson grumbled. "I suppose I can't very well cart it around town."

Edie had Robinson help Rohwedder carry one trunk at a time down the gangplank, across the train tracks, and into the back of the cart. Edie stayed with the cart, covering each trunk with a blanket as they arrived. Henderson watched from the deck.

When Rohwedder and Robinson took his trunk to the gangplank, Henderson grabbed Rohwedder's arm.

Rohwedder looked down at Henderson's grip, then at his face.

With a stern tone, he spoke low and slow. "Remove your hand, or I will remove it for you, permanently."

Henderson let his arm go and said, "Tell me where the trunks are kept."

"James." He smiled at Henderson. "It wouldn't be safe storage if I told everyone where I store things." Rohwedder handed him his card. "If you need access to yours, send me a message." Rohwedder exited down the gangplank.

Minnie gave Rohwedder his cash before he drove off.

◆ ◆ ◆

Henderson got directions to the ship broker's office and presented his card to the office clerk, asking for Mr. Lahey. Lahey greeted him with a handshake and invited him into his office to review the ship's specifications. Lahey's face was round with puffy cheeks, and his hair was slicked back and oily, but his eyes conveyed a sense of competence.

"Let's walk over and have a look," Lahey said.

Boarding the ship, Henderson asked Captain Wright to find Walker to join them.

"I'm afraid the purser has gone ashore—said he needed medicine," Wright replied.

"No one else goes ashore, understood?" Henderson ordered. "And keep the fire stoked. We may move the ship."

"Yes, sir," Wright replied.

Henderson took Lahey on an extended tour of the ship. Chief Engineer Griffin joined them to provide some technical answers.

They returned to the saloon, and Henderson ordered a bottle of wine brought to them from the galley.

"I'm impressed with the vessel," Lahey offered.

"Good," Henderson replied. "I'll sell it to you right now for £10,000, and you know what a bargain that is; you could mark it up considerably." Henderson felt optimistic and smiled at Lahey.

Lahey did not return the smile. "If it had the original construction papers and approval, I could."

Henderson's heart sank a little.

"I'm not buying your ship, Mr. Henderson."

Henderson slumped into his chair.

Lahey let that sink in a minute. "There's a reason you don't have the papers and want to sell the ship so cheaply. I don't care for the details. I have contacts in all walks of life who might be interested. If I sell it for you, I want £3,000 off the top. No contract, no record of my involvement, understood?"

"Agreed," Henderson said. "And place no advertising or sell sheets, verbal only."

"I agree," Lahey said. "I'll need some particulars. I'll get original construction and approval papers forged. I'm surprised you didn't do it yourself. I saw your printing setup—quite impressive."

"My experienced printer finished his tour in Cape Town; I had no one able to prepare them." As Henderson shook Lahey's hand, he cursed Benji and Minnie in his mind.

Walker returned to the ship a little drunk. He sought out Henderson. "We need to talk."

"Yes, we do," Henderson said. "I've good news."

"And I don't," Walker replied.

They went to the saloon, where Walker requested rum. Henderson left, returned with a jug and two glasses, and poured for both.

Henderson didn't wait for Walker's news. "I've arranged for a broker to forge papers and sell the ship at a discount. We should be able to pull that off quickly."

Walker looked at Henderson, his face red and blotchy, his eyes half closed.

"We'll be lucky to see London again," Walker said with a slight slur.

"What the hell are you talking about?" Henderson spat, leaning in close to Walker's face.

"The talk at the pub was about the stolen ship, the *Ferret*. Lloyd's is advertising in papers worldwide, and word is special agents from Lloyd's are investigating ports everywhere to find evidence."

"But the ship sank off Gibraltar; we staged that well."

"That worked for a while. The Lloyd's syndicate covering the ship paid the insurance claims, but when all the notes we issued failed to be paid, they became suspicious."

"Well, you're right, that's not good news, but it's not a disaster. Say nothing to anyone on the ship. Take what you need of your stuff, stores, and money, and find a rooming house not typically used by sailors. I'll get Minnie to pack up all the money in the safe, and the two of us will take rooms at the Collins Hotel. Get me word at the hotel of where you're staying. Do not return to the ship under any circumstances."

Edie was dismayed by Walker's story and agreed that leaving the ship was a good plan. She packed all the money from the safe in a suitcase and her clothing and possessions in a soft pack and prepared to go. Edie was nervous about leaving Robinson but had no choice; she gave him some cash and said to disappear. They had to be clear of the ship if its identity was discovered. They took a cab to the Collins Hotel, booking two rooms.

Fate often plays a role in solving crimes. Constable James Davidson of the Melbourne police, stationed at Queenscliff, where the *India* now lay anchored, had recently returned from visiting relatives in Glasgow, Scotland, where he had read in the Glasgow *Evening Citizen* about the missing ship. Now, back on duty and assigned to the docks, he became curious at how similar the new arrival, the *India*, was to the missing vessel. Observing the ship from shore, he thought it strange that the burner fires were constantly stoked as if ready for a speedy departure.

At the morning briefing the next day, Constable Davidson conveyed his suspicions to his superior, who dismissed them, unimpressed. On duty the following day, Constable Davidson, after again studying the steamship from a distance, decided to take matters into his own hands and walked to the offices of the commissioner of customs and requested a few minutes.

"Commissioner, I've studied this ship in dock, the *India*, and in most details, it matches the missing ship, the *Ferret*. The differences in the two vessels could be easily accomplished to disguise its identity."

"You're fairly confident about this, Constable?"

"I am, sir; I know my ships."

He pulled the *Evening Citizen* article from the pocket of his coat. He showed the commissioner the picture of the *Ferret*. Davidson explained how the modifications could have been made.

The commissioner nodded. "Thank you for coming to me. You have my curiosity aroused. I'll do a little investigating."

"Thank you, sir," Davidson replied, leaving to resume his duties.

The commissioner sent a telegram to the customs department at Williamstown. He received a report that after a thorough search, no vessel of the tonnage given was on the Lloyd's register of ships under the name of *India*. However, the exact tonnage matched the missing *Ferret*.

The commissioner of customs felt he had enough evidence to act. The possibilities energized him. If he could discover the stolen *Ferret*, he'd be in papers worldwide. He'd be famous. He ordered his carriage and driver and traveled to the police headquarters, where he met Chief Chandler in his office.

"Chief, there is enough circumstantial evidence to suspect that we may have the stolen ship *Ferret* in our dock, but we can't obtain any real evidence without seizing the ship and investigating. Will you permit us to do so, and will you provide help?"

Chief Chandler liked to keep his record clean, so he wanted the commissioner to make the call.

"I don't have evidence of criminal activity; therefore, I can't seize the ship. But if you have enough evidence of customs violations and request our assistance, I'll provide the help you request."

"Very well," the commissioner replied. "I'm bringing my men together at 7:00 a.m. We'll consider our options and make our plans. Will you provide us with two of your men, Detective Mackay and Sergeant Daily? I respect the work both men do."

"I'll have the men attend in the morning, and they can advise me of your further needs after the meeting."

The next day, Mackay and Daily arrived a few minutes late and took seats in the commissioner's conference room.

"Gentlemen, most of you are familiar with Detective Mackay and Sergeant Daily from their work on the smuggling case several months ago."

The commissioner detailed the known facts to the team. "We need to prove criminal activity. If we can ascertain that the ship *India* is the stolen ship *Ferret*, we have our case.

"I propose we seize the ship by surprise attack, gather the crew and officers, and conduct a formal investigation. If I'm correct in my assumptions, I expect resistance upon boarding. Once we can inspect the ship and its manifest and logs, we can determine if our suspicions are valid. If they're not, the responsibility lies with me, not with the police."

Mackay spoke up. "Thank you for that, Commissioner. I suggest we use our water police to back up our dock approach. I can arrange for two boat crews of agents to arrive silently at the ship's starboard side and board by hook and cable, while your men approach from the dockside. We'll accompany you with guns drawn."

"Excellent!" the commissioner said. He turned to one of his men. "I want you and one of your men backing us up with rifles as we board."

"Yes, sir," the officer replied.

After dark that evening, the water police approached silently from a nearby dock, poling into place. They climbed aboard and split into two groups to circle the deck with weapons drawn.

Commissioner Clark, Detective Mackay, and Sergeant Daily boarded through the central gangplank—weapons drawn and two riflemen on the dock backing them up.

William Griffin, the chief engineer, walked out of the saloon, followed by Joseph Brown and the chief steward.

"Good evening, gentlemen," Griffin said. "How can we help you?"

Commissioner Clark and Detective Mackay stood with open mouths, dumbfounded. Mackay felt a little embarrassed at the extent of the firepower surrounding the seamen as others joined the initial group and inquired about what was happening. There was no opposition to the visitors' presence.

After Griffin introduced the men and their respective roles, the commissioner asked if he could have two men inspect the ship.

"Of course," Griffin replied. "I will accompany them and answer any questions."

Mackay discovered the vessel's name was filed off the bell, and the registration numbers on the combing of the main hatch had been mutilated and altered. Griffin replied that those actions had been ordered, under penalty of death, by the owner, Smith, and Captain Watkins, who'd left the ship in Cape Town.

Mackay and Sergeant Daily interviewed the seamen, starting with Chief Engineer, Griffin.

They met in the saloon.

Griffin had plenty to say. The officers soon learned that Smith, now using the name Henderson, claimed to be the owner. "He had acquired the ship and had it refitted."

"And where is he now?" Mackay asked.

"We don't know. The trunks belonging to Henderson and his wife were removed the day after we docked. We don't know where they went."

Mackay ordered one of his men to search the local hotels and boarding homes.

"Walker, who also went by Wallace, is not on board," Griffin reported. "Don't know where he went, either."

"What about the captain?" Mackay asked.

"I think Captain Wright is aboard," Brown said, sitting off to the side, waiting his turn. "I saw him an hour ago. I can look."

"Sergeant Daily, please accompany Brown and return promptly." They did not find the captain, but his clothing and belongings were still on board.

The commissioner and Griffin inspected the quarters of Henderson and the adjoining room, which had storage as well as a sleeping section with a bed, a chair, a wash basin, a safe, and a large storage closet that stood open. But the biggest surprise there was an annex space with an elaborate printing setup and a supply of blank legal documents with seals and duty stamps from various dock and port authorities.

"None of us were ever allowed to see this area," Griffin explained.

There were no warrants and no arrests that night. The ship was left in charge of an officer of the police and six water-police constables. Mackay ordered that any attempt to get up steam was prohibited. The watch was to be maintained with a crew change every four hours.

The customs commissioner communicated with the *Ferret* owners in Scotland seeking instructions. Meanwhile, the commissioner and

Detective Mackay continued a series of depositions of the crew and a further investigation of the ship, eliminating any doubt that the ship was indeed the missing vessel. There were many locations where the partially defaced name *Ferret* could still be seen.

Mackay continued questioning Brown the following day and then asked for Captain Wright.

"I'm afraid that the sailing master left with all his belongings in the night," Brown replied.

"What!" Mackay exclaimed. "With six constables and an officer on board?"

"We didn't discover he was missing until just now," Brown replied.

The registration and manifest proved to be forgeries. Mackay arranged for warrants to arrest Robert Wright as shipmaster and captain.

Several crew members told in their depositions of the deceptive entry at Gibraltar, the stolen cargo of coffee, and the various changes made to the ship's appearance.

The crew were released to take minor provisions and move to the Sailor's Home with orders to remain available.

The ship owners had yet to answer the telegram. The customs authorities expected a request to return the ship under its existing crew. A second communication was sent.

Detective Mackay took charge of finding the missing James Henderson, his wife, the purser Walker, and Captain Wright. His constable investigating the hotels learned that Henderson and his wife had taken residences at Collins Hotel on Collins Street. Upon learning this, Mackay put the hotel under constant surveillance. He also learned from railroad guards that the trunks the Hendersons removed were loaded onto a wagon driven away by an unknown person.

The steamship was towed from her anchorage in the bay to the jetty at the government slip, where she remained in the charge of the customs authorities, still under watch until instructions arrived from the ship's owners.

Interestingly, no one mentioned the gun trade that occurred between Brazil and Cape Town during the depositions. It may have been overlooked because most of the crew knew the deal had been made by Mrs. Henderson, and they had no gripes with her.

Later that week, Mackay met with his team. "Gentlemen, something isn't right about this whole *India* affair, but we haven't done our job of digging out the facts. There is little doubt the ship is the *Ferret*, missing from the owners in Scotland. The owners don't seem anxious to communicate with us—we've sent them three messages already. I'll send a more strongly worded one later today. Sergeant Clooney, I want you and three men to inspect the rooms at Collins Hotel occupied by the supposed owner, Henderson or Smith, and his wife. Two rooms, by the way. I have search warrants. Seize anything that might be evidence."

"Should we bring them in for questioning?" Clooney asked.

"We don't have arrest warrants yet. Mrs. Henderson has no testimony incriminating her from the depositions. Henderson is suspect enough, so if he gives you cause, any resistance or confrontation, bring him in."

Sergeant Clooney led the inspection of the rooms at Collins Hotel later that morning. According to the desk clerk, the previous morning, without notice, Henderson had promptly paid his bill, but not Mrs. Henderson's, and left without giving any clue to his destination. Henderson left without detection by the surveillance team; it was later assumed he slipped out a back door. Henderson had not been seen since. The men hadn't yet discovered the trunks the Hendersons had supposedly removed from the ship.

Edie had remained at the hotel. Clooney inspected her room, with Edie following in his wake. "I don't know where Henderson has gone. I suspect away from Melbourne."

"Aren't you married?" Clooney asked.

Edie hesitated. "At the moment," she replied.

Clooney opened the closet door. "What's this?" he asked. He removed a large leather piece of luggage and placed it on the bed. It had the name Henderson embossed on it.

"That's my personal property," Edie said.

Clooney opened the case and stared. He inventoried the valuables he found.

About £8,350 in total.

"That belongs to me and has nothing to do with the ship or Mr. Henderson," she claimed.

Clooney seized the valuables anyway. The hotel manager claimed that no trunks were moved in or removed by either of the guests. Later that day, the manager reported to the police that Mrs. Henderson had hired a carriage and left the hotel; there was no order for the police to restrain or follow her. Edie's destination was unknown. The manager said she did not carry any of the trunks.

A warrant for the arrest of Henderson was issued. Questioning of railroad personnel led to information that after leaving the Collins Hotel, Henderson and another person had traveled up-country by train. A description of Henderson and details of the warrant were telegraphed to all the police stations along the North East Rail Line.

The next day, Detective Mackay received a telegram from Sergeant Purcell of the Seymour police. Purcell had learned that two strangers had arrived by train the previous day.

Mackay saddled a horse and rode for five hours to arrive in Seymour. Mackay entered the hotel, parched and covered with dust. He approached a dining table just as two men were sitting down to drinks. Mackay recognized the man fitting the description of Henderson.

"I am Detective Mackay of the City Police, Melbourne. Mr. James Henderson, I am arresting you for crimes related to the steamship *India*."

"I'm familiar with the ship," the gentleman said. "But my name is George Bolton." He produced identification. "I purchased the ship from a Mr. Henderson in Melbourne; a broker arranged the transaction."

Mackay hesitated, then decided.

"You're under arrest, anyway. If I've made a false arrest, it will be corrected in Melbourne."

Upon searching the man, they found a loaded revolver and £130 in gold coin, which Mackay confiscated. They also found a thick envelope containing currency; the name on the outside of the envelope was M. Rohwedder.

"That's mine," the other gentleman said. "I was about to buy a third ownership in that ship." He showed a bank withdrawal slip from his bank in Melbourne for the amount.

"May I see some identification?" the detective requested.

The gentleman produced a card that read Mathew Rohwedder, gentleman's nurse, Royal Melbourne Hospital, 23 Lygon Street, Carlton. The detective allowed Rohwedder to keep the envelope and cash but took a complete statement from him, requiring a signature, including evidence of him taking possession of the £4,000. Mackay missed the eye contact between Henderson and Rohwedder. Rohwedder was left to return to Melbourne, paying out of Henderson's envelope. Henderson was taken back to Seymour by the night train and placed in the local lockup. He was booked in on charges of forgery.

Rohwedder traveled on the same night train as Henderson and the two police officers, traveling past Seymour to Melbourne.

Constable Brown, walking his rounds, turned down Elizabeth Street. He heard a woman yelling as she ran down the street toward him. A man was stumbling after her, and he was drunk, bouncing off one wall and falling to his knees before continuing his pursuit. Brown ran toward the man until he realized the drunk had a pistol. Brown backed away. He located a rock at the side of the street and waited; the man didn't even seem to notice him. Brown jumped behind him and whacked him on the neck as he ran by. The man fell instantly to the street and dropped the gun.

Mackay took the statement of a Mrs. Honora Ryan, who ran a boarding house on La Trobe Street West. She talked very fast, and her hands and arms emphasized her story. She reported that a "gentlemanly looking man" had approached her that morning and rented a bedroom. That evening, the man returned quite drunk. "I showed him to his room, and upon entering, he grabbed the bed and flipped it over against the wall. He said he would rather sleep on the floor. I asked him to leave, and he drew a bulldog revolver and threatened to shoot me. I ran to the street for help, and he followed me. I ran to Elizabeth Street, and the constable clobbered him."

She simulated the blow with her arm. Mackay chuckled to himself. Mrs. Ryan seemed impressed.

Mackay booked Wright on charges of threatening to shoot Mrs. Ryan. His identity was discovered on a prescription from a chemist with the name Wright on the label. The identification led to additional charges of unlawful and fraudulent alteration of documents that he had made and signed as master of the British ship *India*. His parcel, left at the boarding house, contained identification as Robert Wright Carlyon.

The detectives refocused their search to find and arrest the purser, Walker.

A mistaken identity assisted the police in pursuing Walker, who was escaping disguised as a commercial traveler named George Jackson. Arriving in the town of Wodonga, the police consulted the handbill circulated for the capture of Henderson. He claimed to be a commercial traveler in the employ of Heald and Co., Delft porcelain merchants, London, and had been in their employment for three months. He produced samples of porcelain plates, the same pattern as the one found on the ship. He had no papers to prove the correctness of his statement. He was arrested on suspicion of being Henderson and searched.

Walker's real identity became clear in Melbourne. He too was taken to the city lockup. The three suspects believed to be behind the crimes related to the steamship *Ferret* were now under lock and key and awaiting court action.

No charges were made for the theft and sale of the coffee.

CHAPTER 20

BENJI ABOARD THE *SCOTT*

The seas churned; the *Scott* pitched and rolled. Benji glanced at the bosun, who was yelling directions to several crewmen aft. Some braved the winds and climbed to the upper sails. Benji couldn't hear. The bosun was smiling. He was enjoying this. Benji wasn't. He let go of the guideline he was grasping to stay upright and attempted to walk aft to get directions. The wind increased and seemed to come from all sides. A wave hit the *Scott*—she rolled left, and Benji fell face-first onto the deck before he could regain a hold of a guideline. He lay there embarrassed as the bosun came over.

"Weaver, that was no more than the ocean having a little fun. You must get your sea legs before we experience any real bad weather, or you might end up over the side."

Regaining his feet, staggering to stabilize himself in the rocking, Benji saluted and said, "Sorry, sir. I'll be more careful."

"Forget the salute. Get to the foresail and help the seamen reefing."

His cheek was bleeding from hitting the deck. Benji made his way fore, grabbing every handhold he could. He recalled the warnings the bosun had given them yesterday when they left port. Bosun warned they would encounter rough seas caused by the Indian and Atlantic Oceans meeting east of their location. The oceans didn't like each other, Bosun had said. Benji thought they must hate each other. He lost his balance again and grabbed a line, but he ran into a crewman tending a sail. "Sorry, sir," he said. The seaman frowned and ignored him. Benji pulled himself forward.

They were sailing southeast, which seemed strange since their destination, Saint Helena Island, was twelve hundred nautical miles northwest. He made it to the foresail. He placed himself between two seamen attempting to roll wet blowing sailcloth while they fought the wind; one man tied the roll with halyards. Other sailors were aloft, tending the upper sail squares on the mast.

Benji wished he knew more about how to manage all that cloth. He regretted overstating his knowledge when presenting his papers to acquire the job. *I'll just have to learn*, he thought. *I hope I don't make a grave mistake.*

After his first twelve-hour shift, Benji was exhausted. The salt spray on the sails and halyards made his hands sting like he had stuck them in a beehive, and his cheek burned. His face was coated with a layer of sweat and salt.

The *Scott* continued southeast, and at midafternoon, they encountered slightly calmer waters and more consistent winds. The bosun ordered the tack northwest toward Saint Helena.

Benji wanted to go to bed, but he washed his hands and face and put alcohol on his cheek to stop the bleeding. He needed to complete some tasks for the purser, which he hoped would allow him to determine if Watkins was indeed on board. It would be hell if he *weren't. Swimming back to Cape Town and picking up his trail would be hard.* But Benji was fairly confident that Watkins was traveling as Rollins. The package was time sensitive, and Watkins had no reason to sit around Cape Town.

The *Scott* had only ten first-class cabins, twenty second-class ones, and limited steerage bunks for passengers so the ship could carry more cargo. Benji was surprised to learn that the big cash crop was lily bulbs. The shipment was waiting for them in Bermuda. They had cargo to offload in Brazil before that leg of their voyage. The ship made this cargo run once a year, usually in time for Easter. They wouldn't arrive for the April 17 celebration this year, but the bulbs were still precious.

Benji was relieved when he spotted Captain Watkins at dinner. He was standing in the first-class service kitchen drinking tea he'd grabbed from the sailors' mess. Benji could hear and observe without being seen. There was no mistaking the captain's dark skin and white beard. The men passed platters of roast beef, mashed potatoes, white fish with sauce, and dishes of vegetables.

The first-class passengers ate extended meals together, with conversations continuing over after-dinner drinks and cigars. Ladies, few of whom traveled by schooner any longer, excused themselves to their pursuits. Captain Watkins was telling a fabricated story of his adventures as a reverend returning from abroad. Benji felt there was no reason to delay his visit to Watkins's cabin. He went to the purser's office. It was vacant and the door was open—as he had hoped it would be. Benji picked up a master key to the staterooms. He went directly through the first-class saloon to the captain's cabin and unlocked the door. Closing the door behind him, he locked it from the inside. The stateroom was detailed with rich mahogany and polished brass fittings. There was a coal stove, a richly upholstered couch, and comfortable-looking berths. The walls had gas lanterns. The room was equipped with an en-suite bathroom and basin. A mahogany storage cabinet was built adjacent to the berth. One porthole provided a view of the sea.

Benji found the leather case hidden behind neatly piled clothes and personal items at the back of the cabinet. He carefully removed the case, trying not to disrupt the camouflage so he could replace it without creating suspicion.

The bag was big and heavy. Benji unzipped the case and removed a black cloth and saw six large cloth bags with string pulls. He removed one and opened it. It contained five smaller white bags again with pull strings. He opened one. He was shocked to discover it packed with diamonds. In the six bags, there had to be thousands of diamonds. *Does Edie know what the cargo is?* he wondered. *Is this Mrs. Hill's doing?* He methodically removed one diamond from multiple bags, six in total, and then repackaged the bags. There were so many diamonds that one per bag wouldn't be missed. He would send a diamond to Mrs. Hill and Edie from their first port to prove the cargo was on board and that he had inspected it. Then he replaced the case on the shelf. Looking around to ensure he'd left no evidence of his visit, he unlocked the door, stepped into the passageway, and relocked the door.

"Who goes there?"

Shite! Benji thought.

The purser was halfway down the passageway.

"Sir, checking for rats. Some rooms have shown the presence of vermin. We can't have that in first class."

"Any sign?"

"None here, sir, I'll keep checking."

"Very good, Cadet. Carry on."

He went to the next room, knocked, and announced himself. When there was no reply, he unlocked the door and entered.

The purser continued on his way.

Just a day from Saint Helena, they encountered a squall that required all three cadets on duty at night. The ship was rolling violently as Benji climbed to the main deck; when he opened the hatch, the force of the wind took his breath away. He hung on as the ship tossed and the swells rose to four meters and higher. The night was as black as coal. He pulled himself forward, hanging on to the rail with both hands, searching for a guideline. His body shifted back as the bow rose with a wave and nosed down into the trough. A large wave broke and washed the deck with a flood of water two feet deep. The bosun had set a head-on tack, and sailors were trying to reef in a lot of sail. Benji made it to the mainsail and helped pull the sodden cloth down. He was drenched, and he hung on for his life. The wind changed direction several times, requiring the bosun to assist the helmsman at the wheel to keep the ship headed into the swells.

Benji was scared. Sailors were aloft in the rising winds, struggling with the sails. *How can they hang on and keep their perch on the rope ladders?* Benji wondered. A gust of wind caught him by surprise. He was torn loose from his handhold and landed again on his chest, sliding across the swamped deck toward the rail. A tarp had torn free and was blowing across the deck; it caught Benji, and the wind rolled him and the tarp toward the water. He was wrapped in a canvas cocoon and couldn't breathe. He slid into the opening between stanchions, hitting his back and head hard on the rail. He was in complete darkness, gasping for breath as the tarp clung to his body. He felt a void under him and lost consciousness.

Benji woke in what looked to be a medical ward. He saw eight other men in beds along the same wall as his. His head was bandaged and throbbing, and his chest was wrapped tightly almost to his waist. It hurt even more than his head. He checked with one eye and then the other to see if there were really eight men or if he was seeing double.

"Where am I?" he asked no one in particular. To his left, the man in the bed said, "Military hospital, Jamestown." Then he added, "Name is Ted Compton, Lieutenant Royal Navy."

"I'm Russell Weaver, deck cadet on the *Scott*."

"Yes, I know. Your bosun and purser have been here to check on you; you've been out two days since you arrived. They said some tarp saved your life. Otherwise, you'd have drowned in the drink."

Benji moaned and fell back on his pillow. "Have they sailed?"

"I don't know, but when they came yesterday, they brought a duffle of your belongings. It's under your bed."

"Are you able to reach it for me? I don't think I can."

"Yes, I'm fine—just waiting for discharge and enjoying the rest."

Compton climbed out of bed, squatted down, and pulled Benji's duffle out. "Is this going to be too heavy on your chest?"

"It'll be fine, thank you."

He helped Benji slide up into a half-sitting position.

Compton placed the duffle on Benji's chest and slid back into bed.

Benji grimaced and groaned from the weight on his damaged ribs. He untied his duffel, opened it, found an envelope on top, and read:

Sorry to have to leave you. We delayed a day, but we have to keep to the schedule. Hope you are all right. I've left your pay for two weeks' sail and an amount that the Royal Navy will charge you for transport back to London with Commander Fitzwilliam. Good Luck. Signed, Bosun Philips and Purser Stevens.

He searched his bag; the money Edie had provided was gone. There was no telling when or where it had been stolen. It was a lot of money; he was more disappointed than angry. He was sure one of the cadets had had the task of packing his things. He pulled out his grooming kit, opened it, and found the tin of shaving powder; he stuck his fingers into the powder and found the diamonds safe where he had hidden them.

Benji closed his eyes and tried to get his mind working.

CHAPTER 21

MELBOURNE TRIAL

Henderson, now charged with stealing the steamship *Ferret*, was transported from Seymour to the Melbourne lockup where his mates Walker and Wright were being held.

The story of the ship and crew had become local entertainment since the armed seizure of the *India*. The courthouse was standing room only for the preliminary hearing. Henderson expressed his aggravation about the number of spectators to Judge Williams, but to no avail. After the hearing, he was returned to the lockup in Melbourne.

When the preliminary hearings were complete, the three prisoners were bound over to the criminal court for trial on six counts each.

The prosecution opened the second day of the trial with a complete reading of the charges to the prisoners and the jurors.

The defendants, through their individual barristers, each pleaded not guilty.

A presentation of evidence from the depositions consumed the balance of the day.

Edie thought it best to stay away from the trials, and she hoped her name wouldn't come up. *Time to get on with my life*, she thought. She engaged a barrister named Fink as her representative, who, after the trial was complete, was to claim the funds removed from her at the Collins Hotel. Edie told him she was returning to London and handed him a note: *If successful, please forward the funds to the name and address listed below. I trust you to keep this confidential.*

"Of course, Mrs. Henderson."

Meanwhile, on the third day of the trial, several crewmen testified that it was Captain Watkins who had ordered the lifeboat and other materials tossed into the water near Gibraltar, as well as the ship's remaining lifeboats and the funnel repainted and the name changed to the *Bantam*.

Henderson smiled to himself. *This is going well*, he thought.

The jury deliberated for about an hour and a quarter. Upon returning to the court, the foreman read their decisions:

"On the charge of defrauding the *Ferret*'s owners, Highland Railway Company, the accused are found not guilty. The jury finds the accused guilty of attempting to defraud a purchaser and on the fifth and sixth charges of attempting to deceive the commissioner of customs."

Henderson was stunned. He had believed an acquittal was the only decision the jury could make. He had, however, put contingency plans in place.

His Honor Judge Williams reconvened the court on Saturday morning, first fending off several requests by the barristers to reverse some of the charges. His Honor refused all requests.

"In passing sentence, I do not intend to argue the case further. Since the jury has tried each of you and found each guilty, I must act upon the jury's conviction and pass sentence. As it appears," the judge continued, "that Henderson and Walker were the brains that formed this unlawful purpose and planned steps by which it was carried out, I sentence each of them to seven years of hard labor.

"As to you, Mr. Wright, your case is much different; acting under orders of your fellow prisoners, you were a victim of their actions. You are also much older and would likely suffer greatly with a similar sentence. I sentence you to three-and-a-half years' imprisonment."

Fink rose and was recognized by the judge. He made a motion that the money and valuables taken from Mrs. Henderson at Collins Hotel be restored to her.

His Honor said he was inclined to accept this motion but would wait and rule on it the following week.

The prisoners were removed for transport to the Melbourne Gaol.

CHAPTER 22

THE GAOL

Rohwedder read the accounts of the preliminary investigation and the criminal trial daily in the *Argus* and the *Age* newspapers. Henderson had engaged Rohwedder for an exorbitant fee as insurance when he was apprehended, slipping a written message to a porter on the train after his capture. They didn't like each other, but money talks. As requested, Rohwedder had applied for a medical position at the gaol and presented glowing recommendations from his former employer in Melbourne and several letters of competence and recommendation from prominent London establishments, mostly forged. His résumé earned him the position of chief medical nurse. He worked quickly during the trial to learn who he could and could not trust at the goal. He was prepared in case they weren't acquitted.

A system of bells managed the routine of prisoners; punishment awaited those who disobeyed the bell signals. Those who obeyed were rewarded by being able to work in the yards and stone quarries during the day. The most trusted prisoners moved to third-floor cells. The third floor held large communal cells with up to six prisoners. Henderson, Walker, and Wright were incarcerated on the second floor in three separate cells, sufficiently separated to avoid conversations.

Rohwedder was playing checkers with a warder he had befriended. He let him know he had a friend who had been recently jailed.

"Henderson is a decent person," Rohwedder remarked. "I suspect some of the charges against him were misrepresented."

Ralph remembered reading some of the reports during the trial. "Pretty clever," Ralph commented, "but still illegal."

"True," Rohwedder said. "But I know him, and he's not that clever." Ralph laughed.

Rohwedder felt Ralph was not one to be bribed, but he was a person who would feel obligated to do him favors when needed. And he needed a favor.

Shortly after arriving at the gaol, Henderson learned from Rohwedder which warders could be bribed and which could not. He paid for better food, an extra blanket, and drinking water. He soon had a steady supply, particularly from a warder named Osin. On one visit, after pocketing his fee, Osin said, "You're being moved upstairs next week! That's quick. You must have impressed someone."

"What about Walker and Wright?" Henderson asked.

"No, just you."

"Could five pounds make it happen?"

Osin hesitated. "Let me check." He turned and left. He returned the next day. "Twenty-five pounds will make it happen. Don't ask any questions. Can you produce the cash?"

Henderson feigned concern at the figure. "You know Nurse Rohwedder from the hospital?" Henderson asked.

"I know him, yes. He's well respected."

"If I can talk to him privately, I'll ask him to get the money."

When Rohwedder and Henderson met that afternoon, Henderson explained his escape plan. It began by getting the three men together in a communal cell. Henderson asked for several things to be prepared and for Rohwedder to pay Osin out of the envelope of money Rohwedder held.

The prison yard consisted of a pentagonal tower from which triangular yards radiated, allowing one warder to observe three separate yards of prisoners. The yards were separated by thick brick walls about eight feet high. The outer circumference of this series of triangles was confined by a high iron railing, so a warder walking around had visual access to the prisoners below in each triangle as he passed by. Outside the radiating triangles in the northeastern corner, closest to Russell and Victoria streets, stood a small shed against the prison's outer walls. The shed had locked gate access from all three triangles, allowing one prisoner from any of the triangles to relieve themselves at a time. It was screened with a partition about eight feet high and a lower wooden screen about four feet high to mask the inner space of the latrine. The outer wall surrounding the entire prison was constructed of dense blueish-gray limestone, twenty-two feet tall, with no visible means of climbing to the top.

At the appointed time, the three men worked closely together. A fight, arranged by Walker, broke out between six inmates in the triangle most distant from theirs, distracting the two guards on duty in the tower and attracting the attention of the warders on rounds.

Henderson, Walker, and Wright dropped their tools and ran to the nearest brick wall. Henderson, the tallest, jumped and grabbed the top of the wall, pulled himself up, and lay on his belly, extending his arms to assist Wright and Wallace. The three ran the length of the brick wall and jumped over the iron rail into the open space between the inner and outer brick walls. They ran the thirty yards to the back wall of the latrine. Hearts pounding and sweating profusely, they disrobed to civilian clothes under their work uniforms, and each unrolled the blankets they had wrapped around their bodies. They tied the ends of each blanket with laces acquired from Rohwedder to form a rope. Working quickly, Wright climbed up the latrine wall and stood on the top of the privacy screen, stooping with his hands against the outer stone wall.

Wallace climbed up his back, stood on his shoulders, and assumed a similar position. Holding one end of the rope, Henderson climbed up the two men, reached the top of the wall, and pulled himself up. Sitting with the rope hanging down the inner wall, he pulled up Walker, then dropped the rope end back to Wright.

"Hurry up, Wright."

Wright was struggling.

"I'm trying, James," he said, his voice choking with the effort. "Please don't leave me."

Henderson repositioned himself with two legs hanging over the wall toward Wright; he started to pull the blanket rope hand over hand. When Wright was about eighteen feet off the ground, the rope split at one of the seams, and Wright fell backward, crashing against the privacy screen. His face filled with fear and anguish. They had to abandon him. With no time to spare, Henderson and Walker jumped to the ground outside the prison, landing in a flower garden facing Victoria Street. Wallace screamed as his left ankle cracked on landing, and he fell to the ground. "Damn," Henderson exclaimed. Henderson could see a bone sticking out of Walker's ankle. He knelt and examined it. Walker had passed out. "Sorry, Walker," Henderson said. "I have to leave you." He turned and ran to the street. Looking left and right, he saw the expected carriage, and Rohwedder came quickly.

Henderson jumped in. "It's only me. Wright and Walker didn't make it—let's get out of here."

Rohwedder turned the horses away from the gaol and toward the piers. Upon arriving, he pulled his carriage up in front of an alehouse called the Last Storm. Rohwedder gave Henderson a satchel of clothes and other goods, including a book for reading and £900 remaining from the original envelope. He handed Henderson an old newspaper article from the *London Times*. The headline read "Daring Diamond Robbery Nets Fortune, Lloyd's on the Hook."

"Know anything about it?" Rohwedder asked.

"No," Henderson answered, curious about the question.

"It took place in Cape Town when you were there."

He paused, reflecting on the activities of Minnie, Watkins, and Benji those last few days in Cape Town. "I suspect I know who's involved," he replied. "Find Minnie and make her talk. I'll go after Mrs. Hill. Did you pay yourself?"

"I took my fee from the remaining funds; I left a receipt for the fee and expenses," he informed Henderson. "Olaf is the proprietor of the alehouse. He's a trusted friend. Go directly up the stairs to the first bedroom on the left; the key is inside. Olaf will bring you food and ale. Do not leave the room tonight—they'll search for you everywhere. You sail on the steamship freighter *Ram's Head* in the morning. It's faster and safer transport than a passenger ship. There is a port stop in Cape Verde, perhaps others, and then you sail directly to the London Docks. Wear a disguise tomorrow. You'll find materials in the bag. Board the ship at 6:00 a.m. at Dock 12. Your new identification as Alexander Bolton is in the bag. You're an actor. I thought you could handle that. Stay in touch."

"I will," Henderson answered. "Please undertake a search to find Mrs. Henderson, possibly using the name Minnie Rose. She has money that belongs to me from the voyage, and now we have an additional fortune to find. We're partners on this, and I'll compensate you if we can find those diamonds." Henderson took another fifty pounds from his envelope and handed it to Rohwedder. "In case you need to buy information."

Rohwedder looked at it; he leaned forward, hands on his knees. "I helped get you out. I'm providing the information on the robbery, and I have three trunks—I want a share of the diamonds."

"Find Minnie and follow her until we're back in touch. She was involved with this diamond heist. I know it! She trusts you. Find out all you can. While you're at it, take possession of the trunks. We'll split that up, except mine."

Rohwedder's nose wrinkled, and his chin jutted out as he tried to hide his skepticism. "How will I reach you?"

"I have contacts who will arrange accommodations outside London. Not ones I'm happy with, but it'll be safe for now. I know your address; I'll send a message once I arrive."

Henderson paused. "Give me a couple of sheets of paper." Rohwedder retrieved a notebook from the carriage floor. Henderson wrote a name and an address and a full page of details on it. "Send this message to this address, to Cap Alf."

"Wery well. I'll send it and search for Minnie." He looked at the note. He knew the name. It was a notorious one.

"I've worked with Cap Alf and the Vipers on and off for several years. I can count on them for a price. I wasn't always content just to do Mrs. Hill's errands."

The next morning, Henderson sailed for London as Alexander Bolton.

The newspapers ate up the news of Henderson's escape and the failed attempt of his partners in crime. He had only been in gaol for four weeks. The public had escalated Henderson to the status of a master criminal and was enjoying every newspaper report, accurate or not. After sitting on it a few days, Rohwedder sent the wire Henderson had requested. He hadn't seen Minnie since the trial began. He was surprised she'd never returned. Rohwedder was aware of the judge's award of £180 to her, the amount she had on her person at the hotel. The court records showed the £180 had been distributed to Barrister Fink. He realized Henderson didn't know about the judge's order on the funds seized at Collins Hotel. He pondered ways to ensure his place in the diamond venture. The trunks were safe, as he had stored them himself.

Minnie had promised to contact him when it was time to recover the trunks. He had yet to hear from her and had no idea where she was. Mrs. Hill had been generous with him over the years; he trusted her and Minnie more than he did Henderson. Working for multiple people with conflicting interests was a dangerous game. Still, the diamonds would be the haul of a lifetime; he wouldn't have to work for anyone again if he could get a share. But knowing Henderson, that seemed unlikely. It was even more unlikely now that Henderson was aligned with one of the most notorious gangs in England, the Velvet Vipers. Thinking it over, he felt that if he could get critical information to assist Henderson, he might bargain for a guarantee in some fashion. Either way, he had to find Minnie. If she was involved, he might have a better chance at a diamond share if he cooperated with her. As collateral, he thought he would follow Henderson's advice and take possession of one of the trunks—Henderson's.

♦ ♦ ♦

Rohwedder needed to find out where Minnie's lawyer had forwarded the monies. Fink had an assistant whom Rohwedder had briefly encountered months earlier. The assistant liked to gamble and usually lost. Rohwedder assumed he was in debt and looking at little chance of getting out. He waited until the barrister was in court and entered the offices.

"Arch, remember me?"

Arch looked surprised and a little scared.

"No worries, Arch. I want to give you back some of the money you lost to me," he said as he slapped a quid on the desk. "It's yours." Arch took it.

"Want another like it?"

"What do you need?"

"I need to know where Mrs. Henderson is. Your boss represented her at the *Ferret* trial."

"We don't know where she is, and that would be a lot to ask if we did."

"I'll settle for an address where Fink sent the funds—and Arch, I mean her no harm. We've worked together, and she trusts me. I need to get information to her that she needs."

Arch looked a little more comfortable. "Ten pounds, and I'll pull the file."

"Do it!" Rohwedder said.

Fink had sent the money to the interest of Lady Edith Black c/o Barrister Quill of Melbourne.

Rohwedder gave Arch ten pounds, thanked him, and turned to leave.

He paused and turned back. "And Arch, never draw to an inside straight—you'll lose."

Arch's eyes narrowed; his lips quivered as he mumbled.

Rohwedder assumed he had a new alias for Mrs. Henderson. He made plans to visit Quill's office.

He made an appointment for an official interview, saying he needed to retain counsel. He received an appointment with solicitor Dutch Hamill two days later.

"How can I help you?" Hamill asked.

"I need you to locate a business associate I've lost touch with. I have vital information for her."

"What's the name?" Hamill asked.

"Lady Edith Black," Rohwedder replied. "It's an urgent matter. She knows me."

"I'm afraid I can't help you. She's a client, so we can't represent you in this matter. Her contact information is confidential."

"I assure you; she would want to know how to reach me and would want the information I have."

"You can give the information to me, and I can try to get it to her."

"I can't do that. Will you tell Lady Black it's urgent to contact me immediately? Here's my contact information." He handed Hamill a card.

"I can try, but it will take a while, as she is out of the country."

The news wasn't what Rohwedder had hoped to hear, but perhaps she would get in touch. Meanwhile, the information would be valuable to Henderson, so there was still a chance he could capitalize on that. He assumed Minnie was on her way back to England.

He would send a message to Henderson's contact, Cap Alf. He would introduce himself as a partner of Henderson and provide him with the new alias of Mrs. Henderson and the information that she was probably traveling to London. Henderson might not like that he contacted Cap Alf directly, but Rohwedder didn't care.

CHAPTER 23

BERMUDA

The Royal Mail ship docked at the Royal Navy dockyards on Ireland Island, at the west end of Bermuda. The trip had been fast, and Benji hoped the *Scott* would still be at Hamilton Wharves across the Great Bay in Kingston Harbor. Still, when he arrived, he was disheartened to find it was not among the forty ships in the harbor. Stepping onto the dock, he walked along Front Street, seeking out the Port Authority office. There was a chance the *Scott* had yet to arrive.

Benji climbed the steps and entered the double doors to a large room bustling with sailors. Making his way to the desk, he spied a bald, red-faced attendant with a flattened nose, obviously annoyed with any disruptions. "What do you need?" he barked.

"I would like to speak with the harbormaster," Benji replied.

"*Everyone* here wants to speak to the harbormaster, young man. For you, it's not going to happen today."

Benji knew he had an obstacle to overcome, and it stood before him.

"I understand. You probably know more about what's happening in the port than anyone; can I ask you a question?"

The attendant softened a little.

"I just need to know if the clipper *Scott* has arrived and sailed."

The attendant nodded. "I can answer that. It arrived, sailed, and arrived again. It's in dry dock for repairs—storm damage."

Benji's heart raced. He was about to ask directions when the attendant added, "A couple of the crew are over in the far corner." He pointed and went on, "Trying to find new crew members."

He recognized the purser and Bosun Philips with several other sailors. As he approached, Philips exclaimed, "Heavens above, it's Weaver! I never expected to lay eyes on you again. How's the head?"

"Never better—it works now." He couldn't just ask about Watkins or his missing money; it would appear too strange. He inquired about the storm and the ship.

"We were lucky! A rogue wave that big could sink a ship. They can happen anywhere, but it's only the second I've seen," the purser said.

"The wave looked like a mountain with snow on top," the bosun said. "It was a hearty storm with thirty-foot swells, and I'd decided to ride the wind and hope it would carry us to the edge of the storm and out. The rogue caught us from the aft and snapped the mizzenmast, tore the spanker clear off, but drove the ship forward without adding more damage."

"She had to be fifty feet high. If we were sailing into the waves, we'd have sunk." The purser shook his head at the memory.

Benji asked the purser, "What of the cargo and passengers?"

"We had to transfer the crates of lily bulbs to another ship. They wouldn't have lasted; the rest sit in the hold, some water damage but a salvageable cargo. Some passengers have sailed with other ships; some are in the Hamilton Hotel on Church Street. A dozen crewmen resigned to take positions on ships sailing sooner, including the other two deck mates."

Benji guessed that one deck mate left much richer, so there was little chance of finding his money.

"What of Reverend Rollins? I had lent him one of my favorite books. Is he at the hotel?"

The purser and bosun looked at each other.

The purser turned to Benji. "When we limped back into the harbor, I went stateroom to stateroom to check the health of each passenger and inquire as to their desire to wait out the repairs in a hotel room or to have alternate transportation arranged where possible. I started with the first class. When I came to Reverend Rollins's cabin, I knocked. There was no answer. I knocked a second time, and with no answer, I used my master key and let myself in. The room was a mess, with bedding and clothing scattered around. The mattress was leaning against the couch. A pillow on the floor had feathers falling out, and when I turned it over I saw it was stained with blood. The room was empty of all the reverend's possessions except the clothing on the floor. I don't know what to think. It came to me that I hadn't seen the reverend since we originally sailed from Bermuda before the storm. We were only out a day."

Benji's heart was pounding in his chest. He couldn't speak right away.

The purser continued: "We turned the evidence over to the harbor police; they talked to the passengers and the crew and sent everyone on their way. They may want to talk to you."

Finding his voice, he said, "I'll check with them."

"Will you be sailing with us, Cadet? It'll be about another two weeks, perhaps three."

"Thank you for the offer, sir. If I can find faster transportation, I must get to London earlier. I'll let you know."

Benji was stunned; he didn't know what to do. *Is the captain dead? Who could have done that? Where are the diamonds? Mrs. Hill will be devastated and blame me. How will this affect Edie?* He knew one thing: he wasn't going to the police.

He needed money. All he had were the remains of the two weeks' wages and the six diamonds. He needed to get word to Edie. He needed to figure out whether to contact Mrs. Hill.

He made his way to a public house near the dock. He booked and paid for a room with meals for the night.

He approached the publican. "Sir, I have a valuable stone that I inherited. I need cash to book a passage back to London. Are you interested?" Benji glanced around to see if others were listening.

"I don't crimp, young man."

"It's clean, honest."

The publican studied Benji. He rubbed his bald head, then wiped his hand on his apron, apparently coming to a decision. "At your dinner tonight at seven I'll arrange for a person to join you who may help."

"Thank you, sir." He took his key and carried his bag to his room on the second floor.

Benji arrived promptly at seven. The publican directed Benji to a dark corner booth. His hands were sweaty. He tried to look calm as he glanced around the pub. Soon after he sat, a tough-looking man wearing an old sailor's hat approached and sat down across from him.

"What can I do for you?" the man said.

His voice was husky, a blend of English and island accents.

"I have a diamond that belonged to my mother. I want a good price for it."

"I don't give good prices for stolen merchandise."

"I didn't steal it," Benji answered, looking the man in the eye. "I need the money to sail to London."

"Let's see it."

Benji shifted in his seat, realizing he was in a vulnerable situation. He was alone, no one knew him, and he didn't know who this man was. He was thinking he might have made a mistake.

"I don't have it with me."

"Of course you do! Take it out. I'll step over to the bar, and you have it in hand when I come back."

Benji put it on the table. The man returned with a beer. He held the diamond up to the light and squinted at it.

"One pound."

"Give it back; it's worth far more than that. I'll take it somewhere else."

"Two diamonds are worth more than one. Got another?"

They settled on six pounds for two diamonds, far below value. But Benji relaxed when the man left.

He wrote a detailed report to Edie, enclosed his third diamond, and sent it to Lady Edith Black, c/o Barrister Quill's office, Melbourne.

Benji decided to inform Mrs. Hill directly of events when he returned to London.

He could pay for passage now but would try to secure a short assignment if he could find a ship with a quick departure date. Benji went from one shipping office to the next, thinking this might be faster than seeking work through the harbormaster. After a dozen visits, he secured a deckhand position on the steamer *Acadia* of the Cunard Line, heading to London the next day. The purser provided a meal and a bunk for the night.

They would make good time to London running two steam engines and aided by the ship's sleek modern design. He planned to head directly to the farm for news. Then, he would visit Mrs. Hill to update her on the captain and the missing diamonds. It would be a challenging conversation, but he had to do it.

CHAPTER 24

ARRIVALS AND DEPARTURES

Although she had plenty of money in the bank account Mrs. Hill had established under the Lady Edith Black name, she took up residence in a modest hotel near city center Melbourne when the trial started. She purchased appropriate clothing and began her new life. Edie walked to Dutch Hamill's office to check on messages every day.

Every day Edie didn't receive word from Benji, she became more concerned. *Why wouldn't he communicate? He had several ports on his voyage.* Edie prayed nothing was wrong with him. Mrs. Hill sent messages more frequently; Mrs. Hill was becoming irritated that she had yet to hear of Benji, the *Scott*, Captain Watkins, and the cargo. Edie felt like she needed to be doing something more useful than sitting in Melbourne.

A new message arrived from Mrs. Hill:

A source of mine advised that the Scott *was delayed. After leaving Bermuda, it encountered a storm and was hit with a rogue wave; I was told it was forty feet high. The ship limped back to Bermuda for repairs to sails and masts. As I write it's still there. My contact in Bermuda says Benji, traveling as Russell Weaver, was not aboard. He said the police got a report from the ship's captain that a passenger was missing with presumed foul play since there was blood and a sign of a struggle. It was Reverend Rollins (Watkins). He had no further details. I am very concerned about Benji and deeply worried that we have no word on the diamonds. I hope one doesn't involve the other, but I fear it does. The* Scott's *arrival in London is at least five weeks out.*

Diamonds? Until now, it was cargo, Edie thought. She was worried. She hoped that Watkins was safe, but Benji and the cargo of diamonds were both missing—and Mrs. Hill seemed to suspect him. This scared her. She knew Benji would not betray her or Mrs. Hill. She had to find him before Mrs. Hill did if he was alive. Just the thought caused her to stop breathing; she forced herself to slow her heart and breathe normally. *I have to play my role until I can do something; I must keep from obsessing and thinking the worst.* Edie tried to control her thoughts.

She checked the date on the message and then said, "Dutch, my new life will be here in Melbourne, but I'm not quite ready. I will require one additional trip. Can you assist me in arranging the fastest available transport back to London?"

"A fortuitous request, Lady Black."

"Dutch, you know you are to call me Edie."

Dutch smiled. "Edie, we have a client, the Aberdeen Line. They've built the first of what they hope to be a fleet of passenger ships of the highest quality. They completed their initial cruise to Melbourne and are now seeking passengers for a return trip to London. The fare is more than reasonable, the service and personnel are exceptional, and it will be fast. You'll be among the first to experience this mode of travel."

"While I'm gone, will you forward all messages received to Mr. Harley Blake at Sterling Union International Bank in London, to my attention?"

"I certainly will."

"Please wax seal all messages."

Jack watched from the main deck as the *SS Adelaide* maneuvered into its docking location; Jack admired the recently christened Royal Albert Dock in the Docklands at the east end of London. He marveled at how the city had modernized and cleaned up since he'd first visited. It didn't smell as bad as it had a few years ago. *Less waste and horse dung in the streets and fewer bodies in the Thames.* Jack had studied the development of the Royal Albert Dock since its inception. The dock was one and three-quarters of a mile long, which he thought was appropriate for the most significant capital of the largest and most powerful empire the world had ever known. The dock served the largest ships and was built principally for trade. Jack spotted hogsheads of tobacco, pine boards, and ship masts from America, along with live cattle, meat, wine, fruit, and vegetables from Spain and Italy, textiles from India, fur pelts from Canada, tea from China, wool from Australia, goods from around the world for the insatiable appetites of the prosperous and privileged. His father, a lifetime marine merchant, would have loved this port had he lived to sail here. The port had opened just a few years earlier; its modern electric lights cast a welcoming glow on the deck as the *SS Adelaide* docked. It was the only electrically illuminated dock Jack knew of. Edison himself had supervised the installation. Once again, he wished he was improving the world as an engineer instead of following unsavory people around the globe.

Jack watched as the crew tied the lines tight so that passengers could have a comfortable disembarkation.

Walking down the gangway, Jack identified his trunk on the dock just in time to spot an urchin trying to open it unobserved. *Ah yes! London has a seedy and impoverished side as well.* Racing down the gangway, he caught the young boy by the back of his tunic, keeping a solid grip as the child tried to squirm away.

"Let go!" the urchin yelped.

"The trunk is mine!" Jack barked. "You can't open it."

"I was moving it to the cabs for you," the urchin managed. "Hoping for a tip."

"Is that right? I don't believe you, but I'll give you a farthing to drag it to that growler carriage on the other side of the landing."

"Two farthings," the urchin demanded sulkily.

"You're in no position to bargain." Jack snorted. "Haul the trunk, or I'll turn you in."

The urchin glared at him briefly, then nodded and started pulling the trunk toward the cab. Jack could have easily done it himself, but perhaps this would help a starving family—or, more likely, a budding criminal. Jack gave the boy a half-penny when the trunk reached its destination, and the urchin flashed a semitoothless smile.

"Tour of the city?" the urchin asked.

Jack was impressed with his spunk.

"No, thank you," Jack replied. "I know London. But tell me your name. I may have errands for you over the next few weeks."

"Name's Trunk," the urchin chortled, "because it's me specialty. I can get into any trunk and quickly."

Not quickly enough, Jack thought. "How do I find you?"

"I'm usually around these here docks. Ask any docker. They'll find me."

"I'll do that. We could do some business."

The urchin took off running, clutching his earnings.

When the cab driver loaded the trunk onto the carriage's roof, Jack asked him to transport him to Mrs. Riley's boarding inn and provided the address. Climbing aboard, he sat back to enjoy the ride as the cab entered the winding streets toward the Royal Market in Central London. He loved traveling through London, with its crowded, carriage-filled streets, bustling taverns, and hawkers yelling at the top of their lungs.

Upon Benji's arrival, Mrs. Riley welcomed him with a warming smile. "Welcome back, Jack."

He liked Mrs. Riley. She was a short, rotund woman with a shock of gray hair, and she always welcomed him as if this were his home. She reminded him of his late mother in some ways, although with a different shape and accent.

"Thank you, Mrs. R. I brought you a gift." He pulled out a decorative wool scarf, which he had carried with him from Boston to Cape Town and back to London, and handed it to her. "It was my mother's and seemed just right for you. The embroidery shows ducks on the Boston Common Pond, and it'll warm you this winter."

"You're a darling boy, Jack." Mrs. Riley beamed. "It's beautiful, thank you."

A boy! he thought to himself. *Boyhood is long gone.*

"You're too late for dinner, but I'll assemble a plate for you. I'll also have Johnny take your trunk to your room. It's not something I do for everyone, you know. Have a seat, and I'll pull you a beer."

"Thank you, Mrs. Riley. You're very kind, as always."

"Will you be staying long this time?"

"I'm not sure. I'll go to Lloyd's in the morning and find out. I was in Cape Town for a couple of weeks. With the complications we encountered, I expect I'll be here for an extended period."

"Good!" she said, and went to fetch Johnny.

"Jack!" Johnny exploded into the room. "Too tired or weak to bring your case up?"

"Getting old, Johnny," Jack said. "I'm not a strong young buck like you. Besides, your prices are so high, I think the extra service is warranted."

"You've gotten to the privileged stage of your career, I see."

He laughed. "I'm getting there!"

Johnny was in his early thirties, very muscular, and with a mop of untidy red hair. At six foot three, he towered over Jack's five foot eleven. He laughed again, sounding more like a girl despite his manly appearance. "All of forty, is it?"

"I'll have you know it's only thirty-eight." Jack snorted. "Although I'm aging fast."

The only son of Mrs. Riley, Johnny made his career as overseer of the inn, caring for the guests and the building. He was the family member designated to keep an eye on and care for his aging mother. He had three married sisters and was the youngest of the lot. Johnny's sister Jenny and her family lived nearby, and she often helped with the cooking, buying supplies, and bookkeeping (although Mrs. Riley double-checked every entry). Jenny was there to help whenever Johnny asked.

Johnny had helped Jack on his last case, where a dock warehouse had to be observed over the course of several nights to catch a gang of thieves skimming goods from dock storage and fencing them to local receivers. It had been a quick and successful case; Jack was paid well and provided Johnny a fair share for his services.

◆ ◆ ◆

The *Aberdeen* left port a week after Edie met with Dutch; she had to plan her packing quickly. Once on board as Lady Black, she was treated as a dignitary and was given a tour around the ship by Captain Dern. In the elaborate dining room for first-class passengers, the captain pointed out that the ship was the first equipped to carry frozen food, so the meal choices were varied for all tastes.

"We're about comfort, courtesy, and safety," the captain said. "Not in that order. Oh, and we're about speed as well."

"Tell me about our port stops, Captain, and when you expect to arrive in London, please," Edie said.

"Lady Black, we first sail to the port of Colombo in Ceylon, where we'll take on additional provisions, including their most wonderful tea and cinnamon, for transport to London. You'll enjoy sampling these on the voyage. A shore visit there would please you. Then we have the privilege of traveling in the marvelous Suez Canal, an engineering feat of magnificent magnitude."

Edie was beginning to understand that the captain was prone to using superlatives.

"We then arrive at Port Said in Egypt at the northern tip of the canal. I recommend staying on board there, as it is a city of vice and sin and very dangerous for a respectable lady."

"Thank you, Captain." Edie enjoyed his choice of words.

"Our final port is the beautiful island of Malta in the Mediterranean. Have you ever visited the Mediterranean, Lady Black?"

"Once, Captain, briefly. I'll enjoy seeing it again." She smiled.

"We do all this and deliver you to London in about five weeks. A lot different from the clippers and far more comfortable." He hesitated, then asked, "Would you give me the honor of dining at the captain's table this evening?"

"I would be delighted." She curtseyed, and the captain bowed.

Edie enjoyed her status on board. She walked the ship's upper deck, awed by how travel had progressed. Edie was pleased to learn that the British post office kept a lad on board who would take messages from passengers and send them from any port where they docked. She would receive messages if she arranged for the lad to expect one from parties who knew the itinerary. She would write messages that evening to send from Colombo.

Her fascination with the ship and the activities aboard helped Edie keep her worries and concerns suppressed.

The dining on the *Aberdeen* was elegant, with a wide selection of choices, fine crystal and china, and an excellent variety of cocktails and wines. Edie relished the lifestyle and felt proud that her efforts to appear a sophisticated and wealthy woman had succeeded, and the evenings provided a selection of entertainments with organized table games for the women. The men would retire to their smoking room for drinks, stories, and perhaps a little gambling. There was a concert in the grand saloon every third night. Still, the performances became repetitive since the orchestra and singers were the same. The captain said he would have greater diversity once the cruises were fully implemented into the line's offerings. The lectures had more variety. The talks covered topics from stories of travel, geography, and the British empire to current updates on conflicts in Africa and other locations. Edie enjoyed listening to a young electrical engineer, James Trackson, who was returning from installing the first telephone exchange in Australia. It was a private installation in Melbourne with a hundred lines built for its owners, W. H. Masters, and T. T. Draper. It had been operating for less than a year and had twenty-three subscribers. Edie was particularly interested in one of the scheduled talks, "The State of Crime in the British Empire Today." The speaker was Captain Raymond McElroy of the Metropolitan Police of London.

In the port of Colombo, Edie provided messages to the post office lad and tipped him not to read them, which he assured her he would never do.

A message was sent to Mrs. Hill advising her of the following two ports of call and approximate arrival dates. She asked if she had received any updated information on the *Scott* and Benji.

At Port Said, the lad returned with a message from Harley Blake. The message read:

Mrs. Hill's whereabouts are unknown. The butler says she is traveling and will return later this month. I suspect she will be in touch at some point. I will try to find out more. Let me know how I can assist. I have booked my suite at the Connaught for you if that is suitable. Please direct all future correspondence and information for Mrs. Hill to my address.

Edie felt more removed than ever. She had to keep acting her part on the ship, but inside, she was torn to pieces by doubt and dread. She had to locate Benji, find out about the cargo, and then find Mrs. Hill.

The lecture on crime was given between Port Said and Malta. Captain McElroy spoke about the status of gang action in London and warned visitors to take precautions. He told of the causes of crime in London, primarily the excessive poverty. In addition, conflict between immigrant cultures in the slums led to violence. Edie could relate to everything he said, reflecting on her childhood and Benji's stories; she pushed the thoughts out of her head. She lived a different life now. McElroy then turned to organized crime, major thefts, and syndicates of criminals that spanned the entire empire and conducted elaborate schemes. He gave two examples. One was what he called the Royal Mail diamond theft in Cape Town, a heist of immense proportion with no immediate suspects. The second covered the theft of a steamship by fraud and deception. At the reception following the talk, Edie introduced herself as Lady Edith Black and asked Captain McElroy if he would like to share her dining table the following evening.

He was delighted.

Dining with Captain McElroy was very cordial. Edie enjoyed his company, and it seemed the feeling was mutual. He told some hilarious stories of mishaps and mistakes during police actions. He was very self-effacing, which Edie found endearing.

"What about these syndicates of crime?" Edie asked. "Are you ever able to identify them and arrest the criminals?"

"It's difficult and time-consuming. You won't believe this, but many include prominent socialites and businesspeople. They control criminal activities in India, Africa, New Zealand, Australia, and unknown parts. They generally leave Canada alone, but I wouldn't be surprised if they had affiliate gangs in New York and Boston. The syndicates in Great Britain are mostly untouchable because they orchestrate and finance the crimes. Still, we can't prove it, and we can't often catch them in their activities."

"Fascinating!" Edie said, and she meant it. *I hadn't thought of myself as a part of a major crime syndicate, but it seems I am*, she thought. *The diamond theft happened when we were in Cape Town. Could Mrs. Hill have pulled that off? She mentioned diamonds in her last message.*

When Edie discovered Captain McElroy had been widowed two years earlier, she commiserated by telling her fabricated tale of her beloved laird in Scotland. She enjoyed the role-playing, but it felt empty when she thought about Benji.

When McElroy asked her reason for visiting Australia, Edie replied that she was contemplating relocating to Melbourne and starting a new life.

"Intriguing," McElroy said. "I, too, am considering moving to Melbourne . . . a little more than considering. I was there to be interviewed for the chief inspector position at the Metropolitan Police in Melbourne—it's opening up next year. I have a daughter living there and a beautiful two-year-old granddaughter."

"This could be the beginning of a long friendship," Edie replied.

After dinner, Edie decided not to attend the evening's concert, claiming the desire for an early bedtime, so McElroy walked Edie to her stateroom. They agreed to dine again during the cruise and make plans to meet in London. Edie had no doubt the captain envisioned a budding romance, which would have been fine if she weren't in love with Benji and if she and McElroy weren't in diametrically different lines of work.

They docked in Malta and remained in port for a couple of extra days while the ship adjusted its engines. Edie was anxious to get to London and couldn't sit still—she paced the upper deck for days as they steamed onward. When the *Aberdeen* finally arrived at the London docks, she said goodbye to her new friend Captain McElroy. Captain Dern took her arm and escorted her off the ship, and a crew member assisted with her trunks.

Edie was surprised to find Harley Blake waiting for her. He assisted Lady Black into a carriage and loaded her trunks onto the roof rack. "Stay low, I've pulled the shade." He banged his cane on the carriage roof, telling his driver to proceed. Edie looked at him with concern.

"Just a precaution, Edie."

"What's going on, Harley?"

"A lot, Edie. Hill's mansion is under surveillance by the Velvet Vipers, so she went into hiding. I'm not sure where, and I'm not sure about the Vipers' motivation, but don't go near the property."

Edie nodded.

"Lloyd's has an investigator, an American, looking into the diamond theft. I assume Mrs. Hill informed you about the diamonds."

"She never told me they were diamonds until her last correspondence; she called it valuable cargo. I sent Benji to follow the cargo and Captain Watkins at her request, and now both are missing."

"Or missing with the diamonds," Blake said.

"Neither one would do that to Mrs. Hill . . . or me!"

Blake looked at Edie, shaking his head. "Perhaps not, but it's a big temptation."

"I'm concerned about Benji."

"Be concerned about the diamonds—without them, all investments in the Lloyd's syndicate are lost. Benji is my suspect."

Edie paused, realizing her wealth and relationships with Benji and Mrs. Hill were all at risk. She saw no point in arguing, and she needed Blake.

"Who's the investigator, and where is he staying?"

"Why?"

"I'm not sure, but if somebody is looking for the diamonds and Benji is a suspect, I want to follow the investigation. He could keep me informed."

"You could become a suspect if you reveal your involvement."

"I won't do that. Harley, if I can't find Benji, perhaps he can. Benji went quiet on me and on Mrs. Hill. He may know more about the diamonds that could help us all find them. If we find the diamonds, our investments are safe, right? If we can help him, we help ourselves."

"Perhaps," Blake replied. "If we find Benji, we may find the diamonds. I agree. The investigator is Jack Cramer; he's staying at Mrs. Riley's boarding house."

"I know the establishment. I met Mrs. Riley a few times at the stall market."

"Give me a few days before you contact Cramer. I think he's being followed. I'll check it out further."

"Who's after Mrs. Hill and why?" Edie asked. "If it was Henderson, I could understand, but he's locked up."

"Not anymore. He escaped." Blake said. "There's a manhunt for him in Australia and London, but nothing has turned up yet. He could be working with the Vipers, and that'd explain why the mansion is under surveillance." He handed Edie two newspapers, one on the diamond theft and a second on Henderson's escape from jail.

Just about the same time I left on the Aberdeen. He didn't waste any time.

"Damn," Edie uttered. "That complicates things. Harley, Mrs. Hill trusts you, and so do I. Did Mrs. Hill arrange the diamond theft?"

"I'm pretty sure she didn't; she has much at stake," Harley said. "She said she was contracted to protect and transport the *cargo*."

Edie decided she'd do some investigating on her own to give Harley time to determine if Jack Cramer was being followed. She'd wait until she knew more before contacting him. She allowed Harley to accompany her into the Connaught and check her in. Harley, addressing the manager by name, said, "Lady Black's privacy is of the utmost importance. Please have the staff avoid conversations with anyone asking about the lady and keep her name secret."

"Mr. Blake, you are one of our most valued customers. We will have all the discretion in the world."

Once moved into her suite, Edie begged forgiveness but said she was exhausted and needed to retire. Harley wished her a good sleep, adding that he was going to Liverpool on business and would be gone for a few days.

She waited long enough for Harley to clear the lobby, then went to the manager's office.

"Can you arrange for me to rent a single horse carriage for my use during the next few days? I would like to have it available by 7:00 a.m."

"Do you require a driver?" the manager asked.

"No, I can drive myself, thank you."

"The carriage will be waiting for you in the morning. See Charles, the morning bellman; he will assist you."

In the morning, she dressed casually and had breakfast in her suite. She dropped the pistol Mrs. Hill had given her into the pocket of her riding skirt, which she felt was appropriate for a carriage ride in the country. She locked the door on her way out and went to find Charles.

"Good morning, madam," Charles said with a pleasant smile. He led her to the hotel's stables. "I'm sure you will be pleased with Dormouse. Don't let the name fool you—she's a spirited but well-behaved beauty, and I picked the best small carriage available."

"Thank you, Charles. She's beautiful. I'll be back in a few days; I have friends to visit in the country." She handed him a fourpenny bit.

Charles assisted Edie onto the driver's bench and watched as she drove off.

Edie was panicky; she needed to visit the farm to find Benji or find out if anyone knew where he was. *He couldn't have taken the diamonds and abandoned me or Mrs. Hill.*

As Edie rounded the first corner, a young man wearing a newsboy cap stepped up to Charles. A few words were exchanged, and then Charles backed up and held his hand up to the young man, who spoke again, then turned and left.

As she drove through the gate of the farm that she remembered so fondly, two young men she didn't know approached her, recruits perhaps.

"I'm Edie Black," she said. "An old friend of Benji's."

"You're Edie!" one of the boys exclaimed, breaking into a big grin. "Let me help you down. I'll take care of the horse. You're a legend around here."

Edie blushed. "Her name is Dormouse—she's a wonderful little horse."

She looked around fondly, recalling the joy she had felt living a life farming the land with the companionship of all the boys and men and Benji.

"Is Benji around?"

"Afraid not. Brian's over there." He pointed toward the potato garden. "He's one of the older guys you'll remember."

"Thanks," she said, somewhat sarcastically. She thought she was still young, and Brian wasn't much older.

Edie approached the field and walked between a row of plants to where Brian was squatting down, his back toward her.

"Brian," she said.

He stood and turned. "Oh my," he said, putting his arms around Edie and surprising them both by hugging her. She hugged him back.

"Sorry," he said. "It's just so good to see you."

"No need to be sorry. Can we talk?"

They made their way to the kitchen and heated water for tea.

"Benji was here for a couple of days last week, but he was so distraught—he'd had no news of you and had been unable to communicate when he was in hospital in Saint Helena."

"This is new information to me, Brian; please tell me everything. Where is he now?"

"He was planning on visiting Mrs. Hill, telling his story, and asking how to help. We convinced him that some boys should check out the mansion before he went there."

"Is he with her now?"

"No, we found that the mansion was under surveillance day and night, and not the police but a dangerous gang, very dangerous—the Velvet Vipers. We don't know why. We heard some rumors that Mrs. Hill was away, presumably avoiding the surveillance. Benji set out to find her. He was going to get some supplies, spend the night with Specs, and set up surveillance the next day."

"Specs wasn't caught and sent to Australia?"

"No, she escaped. But she's been hiding since the stall raid."

Edie felt a little relief that there was some explanation for why Benji hadn't been in contact. But with all the strange things that had happened, she hoped it was the real reason.

The mention of Specs gave Edie an idea. Could Benji still be at the old warehouse, or was that too dangerous? The next day, she prepared for a trip back to London and loaded her carriage with gifts from the boys. Edie wasn't sure what she would do with fruit, smoked meats, and fresh vegetables, but they wouldn't let her leave without their tokens and hugs. She drove her carriage into London's East End. After tying Dormouse to a post, she slipped into a hidden boarded-up doorway and surveilled the alley for any activity. She thought about her earlier life in the slums and at the market—she'd wanted to become a lady of importance and wealth, of respectability. She spotted a couple of rats slinking along as it got darker, and soon after, she was pleased to see a tricolored cat in quiet pursuit.

She decided to head back to the carriage, eat an apple, and wait to see if anyone showed up. As she approached, she saw her carriage door standing open and a cloaked figure rummaging in the food crates.

"Hey," Edie said softly.

The woman jumped and turned toward Edie. There was no denying who it was; her glasses were as thick as the bottom of a pint glass.

"Specs, it's me, Edie."

Specs stared.

"I don't believe it. You're all grown up," She dropped the produce back in the carriage. "What are you doing here?"

"Looking for you and Benji."

"We better get off the street," Specs said. "Bring the carriage."

They walked up to the old door, which was more boarded up than when Edie had last seen it. Specs took a flat metal rod she had concealed along the edge of the door, inserted it between two overlapping boards, and lifted it upward. Edie heard a latch let go, and the door swung forward a few inches. Specs looked around again, then grabbed the edge of the door with both hands and pulled it open.

"Go ahead, Edie."

Edie led Dormouse into the dimly lit interior. Dormouse hesitated a little at the door, but the warehouse was huge, with ample room for horses, and with a little encouragement she walked in.

Specs followed. She grabbed a bar inside the door and leaned back as the door swung shut and the latch clicked into place. She leaned the metal bar against the inside frame.

"Made that latch myself," she said proudly. "We're safe here, Edie. I'm the only one left."

The insides of the warehouse were torn apart; they'd never been repaired after the raid. But Specs had made a comfortable corner with a cot, table, stand, commode, and several oil and candle lamps lined up. The storage areas were destroyed, but the old stove stood against the front wall. Even some of the center table was still intact. Specs had a barrel for heat and used the stove occasionally.

As Edie looked around, Specs said, "It's comfortable and safe, but it's lonely. I can usually find enough food one way or another. Sorry about the carriage."

"Let's put together a meal," Edie said, "and you can fill me in on what happened to everyone."

They ate cold smoked beef, sliced apples, and greens; Specs told of the raid and how the women had scattered. "Several were locked up, but it was Benji the police wanted. I ran behind the building with the cashbox. There was a ladder leaning against a first-story roof. I climbed it, pulled the ladder up, and hid overnight in a loft."

"Smart!" Edie said.

"Lucky is more like it," Specs said. "Britina ran by, but the police followed her, and they took her away."

"What of Benji?" Edie finally asked. "I know the history, but have you seen him lately?"

"Yes, I have. He was here a few nights ago. It was good to see him.

He gave me some money. I didn't want to take it; he didn't have much, but he insisted."

"What did he say?"

"He wanted to find Mrs. Hill, but she never comes here. He didn't know if you were in Melbourne or had returned to London. He asked me to keep an eye out for you. I sure didn't expect to see you—but here you are!"

"Do you know where he is now?"

"No."

"Did he leave a way for me to reach him?"

"When he can, he'll check with Brian at the farm."

"If you see him again, tell him not to contact Mrs. Hill or Harley Blake, her banker. Just leave word with Brian about where and when we can meet."

"It may be too late—he went to try and find Mrs. Hill."

Edie was disappointed to be so close to finding Benji, but it seemed there was still no way to reach him. She had to warn him that Harley Blake and Mrs. Hill suspected him of taking the diamonds from Watkins.

Edie felt she should avoid travel in the late evening; it would be safer to go in daylight. She would head back to the Connaught in the morning to set up a meeting with Jack Cramer.

PART FOUR

THE INVESTIGATION

◆ ◆ ◆ ◆

CHAPTER 25

JACK CRAMER IN LONDON

Jack slept fitfully on his first night back in London. It had been his responsibility to protect the diamonds, and he had failed. He dreaded facing Fredrick Taylor, who was a powerful man. Lloyd's was a marketplace and overseer of groups of investors that formed syndicates to provide insurance under the Lloyd's umbrella. And Fredrick Taylor was the president of the largest syndicate sanctioned by Lloyd's.

Jack wasn't hungry but forced a light breakfast—coffee and a roll. He found that the walk to the Royal Exchange improved his mental state. He recalled how much he enjoyed walking the streets of London, especially the bustling area near the business center of the city. He glanced at the Old Lady of Threadneedle, better known as the Bank of England. Then at the stock exchange, which had been operating in the area for many years.

As he entered Lloyd's subscription room, people were scrambling everywhere. Some were waving papers and shouting, some were in private conversations or negotiations. He breathed deeply. He loved taking in the energy at Lloyd's. He spotted Herbert Archer, Fredrick's head broker and second in command, exchanging documents with a sea captain, who was likely covering his next voyage with loss insurance. Fredrick Taylor had created the largest syndicate at Lloyd's by recruiting wealthy primary investors, some representing unknown quantities of silent investors. Fredrick's syndicate wrote the most insurance of any syndicate and took the most significant risks. Of course, his premiums were calculated to cover those risks. Jack waved to Herbert, who quickly concluded his business and approached.

"Jack!" Herbert exclaimed. "You're here. I'm so pleased. Let's go to a private room where we can talk."

"Is Fredrick joining us?" Jack asked.

"No," Herbert replied. "He's indisposed now. I'll explain."

Herbert led him into a nondescript room with a desk and two guest chairs, a sideboard for tea, water, or drinks, and a secretary's desk for notetaking and paperwork. There were no windows. They sat in the two guest chairs provided at the desk.

"Jack, the news you sent us from Cape Town on the diamond theft was about all Fredrick could handle. We've been plagued with losses this past year, and that heist could be the killing blow. It made Fredrick physically ill."

Herbert looked scared. Jack leaned forward and spoke calmly and quietly, focused on his face.

"Herbert, I feel terrible about the theft, but there had to be some masterminds behind it to pull off something so substantial and complicated. I intend to find out who those people are. I'm sorry about Fredrick, but surely your reserves will cover the loss. When can I see him?"

Herbert leaned away from Jack and averted his gaze. He seemed almost guilty or defensive—not at all like his usual self. Jack leaned forward.

"Herbert, you're acting strange; tell me what's wrong."

Herbert hesitated, then spoke very quietly. "Fredrick has been at a friend's summer home for a few weeks. He doesn't come to the office. He's under a doctor's care. He's been waiting for your arrival to call an investor meeting."

Strange behavior, Jack thought.

"Fredrick has asked that you make yourself available to attend."

"Of course."

"I'll let you know when I receive confirmation from key investors regarding their availability." Herbert paused. "Jack . . . some blame you."

Jack was startled. It was one thing for him to hold himself to blame, but he didn't commit the crime. It was a shock that the syndicate investors blamed him for the theft.

Jack decided to change the direction of the conversation.

"Herbert, I want to meet with your actuary."

"I'm acting actuary until we hire another—if we do," Herbert mumbled.

"I'm your investigator, Herbert. I need details. How bad is this loss?"

Herbert sighed and looked away again as he spoke. "In the past year, we seem to have become a target of criminal activity aimed at our larger coverages. We've had a series of losses and little success tracing responsibility or recovering any lost property. Some have been more serious than others. Recently, many of our losses have been centered in Cape Town, which is experiencing a boom in diamond and gold mining and, therefore, is a prime target for theft. It's why we sent you there to protect the diamond shipment. But that's not all. We paid claims on a ship considered destroyed at sea a few months back—it was a major loss for the company. It's now suspected the ship didn't sink but was stolen. Fredrick feels that our losses are probably orchestrated by organized crime, financing and controlling these activities out of London. I believe information must leak out of Lloyd's for some of these crimes to occur. The criminals know about the major policies we write. They have to have a source, or sources, of information inside these halls."

"What about the police? What are they saying?" Jack asked.

"The London police have no jurisdiction in Cape Town or other territories where our major losses have occurred, and the Cape Town police are almost worthless to us. Those who are trustworthy hate the English. We can't count on any assistance there. The ship's theft originated in Glasgow; the vessel was called the *Ferret*, then the *India*, and it's now in custody in Melbourne, Australia."

Jack became animated. "*India*! After the diamond theft, I saw that ship in port in Cape Town; I was trying to book my trip back. There may be a connection. Were the thieves caught?"

"They were caught, convicted, and jailed. One's dead, one's still in the Melbourne Gaol, and the ringleader, James Henderson, escaped. It's suspected he'll make his way back to London; the police have a search operation going."

Jack put his hand to his chin. "Can you get me the transcript of the trial?"

"We have it; no one's read it."

"I will," Jack said. "If the ship has been recovered, can you reclaim the payment for the loss?"

"Perhaps someday. The Australian government impounded it to protect against other claims against the thieves. The owner doesn't want it back. It'll end up in court, I suspect."

"I'd like to examine all the losses this past year, and I would still like to confer with Fredrick."

Herbert nodded. "Fredrick will contact you shortly, I'm sure. He said to make the insurance vault available to you as needed."

"I'll also need complete access to your employee records," Jack added.

"Employee records are a little tricky. Lloyd's protects employee privacy."

"I'll start with just a list of your investors," Jack said. "Can you do that?"

Herbert avoided the question.

"Jack, one thing you won't find in the financial ledgers is the diamond loss. We're delaying entering the details until we see what you can uncover. The underwriting files are there, but we haven't yet registered the loss or paid the claim."

"Why not?"

"It's what Fredrick requested. Lloyd's conducts periodic inspections of each syndicate to ensure adequate financial strength, and we want answers before we enter the particulars. It would be best if you acted fast. The loss exceeds our reserve; Lloyd's will revoke our syndicate license immediately if they know."

"I see," Jack said. "And the investors would lose their investments."

"Yes," Herbert said, now looking Jack in the eye.

"One other thing: Fredrick ordered a revolver for you. I contacted Johnny to pick it up. He'll give it to you tonight. Fredrick expects you may need it."

"Am I in danger from the investors?"

"Perhaps, but more likely from whoever orchestrated these crimes."

Jack laughed. "My fee just went up."

"Take it up with Fredrick," Herbert said, unsure whether Jack was kidding.

"I need that list and contact information on all your investors," Jack added with authority.

"I'll get on it right away, Jack. Remember, there's sensitivity to sharing it."

"It may lead us to the parties that have targeted you. I want to read the report on the other losses—can you get that and the transcript to me?"

"I'll put it all together, but you should read them here. Files shouldn't leave the offices."

"You've just told me information is leaking from Lloyd's; I'm uncomfortable working out of here. I'll make the inn my headquarters, as I have in the past."

Herbert looked defeated. His chin drooped, and his eyes narrowed. He was obviously stressed.

"I'll assemble the paperwork and send it by private messenger when complete. "Now I have to get back to work."

"Herbert, I need to review everything before the investor meeting."

Herbert stood, walked for the door, stopped, and turned. "Do you think the registered-letter clerk is involved in the theft?"

Apparently he has read some of the report, Jack thought.

Jack shook his head. "He's involved because of his actions, but is he part of the theft? I doubt it, although he could have been paid to be stupid. The police released the clerk and only charged him with negligence. He will lose his job, but I doubt he'll face charges."

◆ ◆ ◆

At dinner that evening, Jack and Johnny ate together. Mrs. Riley and Johnny's sister Jenny were serving. Jack enjoyed the fried cod, chips, and fresh baked beans, washed down with a couple of beers, just right for a welcome back to London. However, he felt less than welcome worrying about the upcoming investor meeting. Johnny talked a little about items that would normally have interested him, but Jack wasn't absorbing much.

"Johnny, are you willing to help on this case?" Jack asked.

"Ready as a pig in fresh mud," Johnny replied. "Just waiting for you to ask."

"Do you still have the room we used for the other cases?"

"I do. It's a supply closet now. It just needs to be cleaned and tidied up. I can get on it after dinner."

"Great, and did you get a package for me from Lloyd's?"

"The gun?" Johnny said, a little too loudly.

"Quiet, please! We don't want to scare your mother or alert the other guests."

"Sorry. It's in your bureau drawer."

Jack spent the evening reading his notes and the Cape Town police transcript for the interviews and investigation of the diamond robbery he had acquired before leaving Cape Town. He made notes of items of interest in a case notebook. He reminded himself that something would reveal itself at some point. *Identify what isn't known, study the facts, look for motive, and ask good questions.*

Jack had breakfast while Johnny worked the shift. Sitting at his table, he decided there was one very minor drawback to a family inn: leftover beans were served the next day as part of breakfast.

Mrs. Riley brought Jack a coffee refill. "Do you want more beans?" she asked. "We cooked too many."

"I couldn't," Jack said.

"More eggs?"

"I could." Jack smiled.

Mrs. Riley's eyes widened. "Oh, I almost forgot, there's an envelope for you. It was hand delivered this morning by a private delivery boy. It's here somewhere."

Rummaging in the shelves behind the reception desk, she handed it to him. It was an expensive envelope; inside was a handwritten message scented with lavender. He read the first couple of lines as Mrs. Riley approached with a new dish of eggs, then finished reading the letter after she left.

Mr. Cramer,

I am Lady Edith Black of Melbourne, Australia. I learned your name from Harley Blake—my banker and investment counselor.

I have knowledge that will assist you in your work for Lloyd's. I can help you, but I need your help in return. If you are willing to meet, please reply to the offices of Mr. Harley Blake at the Sterling Union International Bank of London. Mark the correspondence for my eyes only and seal the envelope. If you agree, I will send you instructions as to where and when a meeting would be convenient. Please keep this communication confidential.

Jack wrote a reply accepting the proposed meeting and placed it in an envelope. He returned to reception. He took three wax beads from a jar on Mrs. Riley's desk. Placing them in a spoon he lit a candle, and then dripped a small amount of wax over the envelope flap.

Two days had passed since Jack had met with Herbert. A large package arrived at the inn for Jack while he was out at the *London Times* reading rooms, gathering more background on the thefts connected to Lloyd's. The message on the envelope read, *Confidential and Important—Deliver to Jack Cramer at once.* Mrs. Riley decided to take it to his suite of rooms while he was out.

She made her way to the second floor, gripping the railing and the package. Her mind wandered. She climbed the stairs slowly; her knees complained without cease, shooting pain with every step. Usually,

Johnny would be doing this delivery, but he had stepped out to run other errands for Jack. The boys were teaming up again to investigate some goings on at Lloyd's. She was pleased they were working together; she knew it made Johnny happy—he needed more friends.

Lloyd's had been good to Mrs. Riley and her small inn, located blocks from the Royal Market in Central London, where the Lloyd's exchange stood. They kept her rooms full when out-of-towners visited, as they frequently did. Jack Cramer was her favorite visitor. She liked Americans. They were not as demanding as other guests, but she also liked Jack because of his pleasant demeanor. And he brought her gifts. *He isn't a bad looker either.* She chuckled to herself. In her youth, she'd favored tall blond men. Her husband had been tall with red hair, which she didn't like much. Jack's hair was a brownish blond. He would have made her a fine beau in her day. She giggled to herself again. Upon reaching the second-floor landing, still vertical, she felt a sense of accomplishment. She stood and caught her breath. She hadn't done that in a while! Making her way to the suite of rooms assigned to Jack when he was in town, she pulled a set of keys from her apron and unlocked the door. Her attacker came at her so fast she didn't see the quick arc of movement that slashed her throat. There was no sound other than the gurgle of blood that was suddenly choking her, and she barely felt the perpetrator grab the package she carried as he pulled her into the room and shut the door.

Sergeant Lindy knocked and let himself into Detective Wells's office at the Metropolitan Police headquarters. Detective Wells looked up from his desk. He looked slightly irritated at the interruption.

"The chief just received this from the Royal Navy police commander in Bermuda." He placed a crumpled-up newspaper clipping on Wells's desk. Wells flattened the newspaper, and a diamond fell to his desk. The newspaper heading read, "Daring Diamond Robbery Nets Fortune." It was a Bermudan paper with byline credit to the *Cape Town Guardian*.

Lindy handed a note from the Bermudan commander addressed to the London chief of police. "It says that one of their regular informers brought him the diamond. He purchased it from a young sailor seeking money to return to London. The informer demanded reimbursement of twenty pounds for the diamond plus mail charges. The chief refunded him and charged your account."

"Of course he did," Wells said.

"The chief said you should deal with it. The informer also enclosed a description of the sailor with decent detail. Their follow-up found that the sailor had arrived on the Royal Mail ship from Saint Helena Island, where he was hospitalized after injuries in a storm while sailing on the clipper *Scott* from Cape Town. The name was Russell Weaver."

"Good report, Sergeant. But next time, wait to be invited in; I may have guests."

"Yes, sir. Sorry."

After a pause with no comment from Wells, Lindy continued. "I checked with the dock master. Russell arrived here in London aboard the steamship *Acadia*. Arrived a week ago, no word of his whereabouts."

"Lindy, please get an artist to turn this description into a likeness. Let's get some press coverage."

"Yes, sir," Sergeant Lindy said.

Jack was in the reading rooms at the *London Times* devouring accounts of the theft of the *Ferret* and other robberies Lloyd's had experienced in Africa and elsewhere to see if there were connections. A messenger arrived with a note from Johnny that Mrs. Riley had been attacked. Jack's heart sank; he felt weak all over. He just knew it had to do with his being at the inn. Jack left immediately and took a cab to the hospital to check her condition. He hoped he wasn't the cause of the attack. He found Johnny and Jenny on the ward; they greeted him warmly. "We saw her briefly but were asked to return tomorrow," Jenny said.

"How is she?" Jack asked.

"She's holding her own, but the doctor's concerned with her heart," Johnny said. "Her breathing seems stable, and the slice to her throat didn't penetrate deeply. The rest was superficial, but she's not allowed to talk yet."

"When you're ready, I'll return to the inn with you." They walked to the exit.

"I cleaned up the blood in your room the best I could," Jenny said. "You can change rooms if you want. We have a couple of vacancies."

"I'll be fine, Jenny. Don't worry."

Johnny was lost in his thoughts as they walked back to the inn together. Jack asked if the case room was ready for them. Johnny replied that he had cleaned out the storage room they had used previously—cleared the cobwebs, swept the wooden floor, and stripped the walls of shelves and everything else that had hung there.

Back at the inn, Johnny brought in two unused bar tables and two wooden dining chairs from the dining area.

"The dining room never fills up anyway," he told Jack.

Jack had a parcel full of supplies. Following Jack's instructions, Johnny unrolled two four-foot spools of old parchment wallpaper and nailed the corners, design side to the wall. He put a collection of fountain pens with red and black ink, various pencils on each table, scissors, and more small nails.

"We'll each enter what we know or think as we progress," Jack said. "It's important to enter what we don't know, as well. If we're together, we'll talk it through; if not, it's a way of communicating. Eventually, the parchment will reveal answers. Shall we start with the *Ferret*?"

Johnny stepped to the first strip of paper, drew a red circle, and wrote *Ferret* inside—he knew Jack's techniques from the last case.

Jenny stepped into the room, surprising both men. "There's a gentleman to see you, Jack—a Mr. Herbert Archer."

"Thank you, Jenny," Jack said. "Please tell him we'll be right there."

Johnny locked the room as they headed for the reception area. He handed Jack a second key.

CHAPTER 26

HENDERSON ARRIVES

Cap Alf, the London faction leader of the Velvet Vipers gang, read the note sent on behalf of Henderson. Then he leaned on the table and reread it. His first instinct was to disregard anything that came from Henderson. They had done business over the years, and Henderson had done his part, but Alf didn't trust him. He knew of Henderson's association with Mrs. Hill. He assumed this *Ferret* gig was her doing, and now Henderson was a fugitive. And then there was this second note from some associate of Henderson. He was a little uncomfortable with the arrangement, but he couldn't do anything until Henderson arrived. This was a big opportunity, and if Henderson had an inside track, he'd take the risk.

His chief lieutenants were watching the docks for Henderson's arrival; he should have been there two weeks ago but hadn't shown. As Henderson had suggested, they had put a twenty-four-hour observation on the mansion of Mrs. Hill, and they were watching for anyone who might be Minnie Rose or Benji Diamond from descriptions Henderson had sent. They had an encampment in Hyde Park, near Mrs. Hill's mansion.

"The park guards we bribed to work around us are cooperating, but we can't stay there much longer," Cap Alf said.

He was sitting at a tavern table with Cap Irv and Cap Lee.

"What other actions should we take until Henderson shows?" Cap Irv asked.

"You have someone watching the Lloyd's investigator, Cramer?"

"Yes, not much happening there either."

"Cap Lee, what about the safe house?"

"We secured the property Henderson suggested and paid the farmer to take a holiday. He didn't object."

"Good, I'm going to the docks. I want to be there when Henderson arrives. It's got to be soon."

Henderson found traveling excruciatingly slow—he needed to have his feet on the ground pursuing the stolen diamonds. The ship's engines constantly needed repair, causing port delays. They were over two weeks off schedule.

When it finally arrived in the port of London, they were delayed receiving a berth. Henderson had waited long enough. He paid one of the crew to row him to shore. He was surprised to be met on the dock by Cap Alf.

"Get in the carriage before someone sees you," Alf said. "There are posters all over London with your face on them."

He handed Henderson a copy of the *London Times* with the head-line "*Ferret* Thief Escapes: London Police on Alert"—accompanied by a drawing of Henderson. Henderson pulled himself into the carriage and Alf got in next to him. Out of the shadows, a young gang member with the same cap as Alf mounted the buggy seat, slapped the reins, and sped out of the dock area. A horse was tied to the rear of the carriage.

"We've got over twenty miles to go," said Cap Alf. "There's some food, water, and whiskey there; help yourself. I'll talk, you listen. The diamonds are a big haul. I don't know your involvement, and it doesn't matter. If you think you can get these diamonds, we'll help—but we want half. And you cover expenses, even if we don't get the diamonds."

Henderson waited to see if he had more to say. When he didn't speak for a while, Henderson said, "I know who's involved, and I was there when it all happened. If you follow my lead, I'll agree to half of the take, but I can only pay half the expenses."

Cap Alf held his hand out, and Henderson shook it. "No one cheats a Viper, you know."

"I know," Henderson said. His odds of acquiring the diamonds had just gotten much better with the power of the Velvet Vipers behind him.

"We've had the Hill mansion staked out since I got your first message," said Alf. "She's not there, just the servants. There's no sign of a Benji Diamond, but I have Vipers looking for him. We're also following an investigator for Lloyd's, Jack Cramer. Lloyd's sent him a parcel of papers about all their losses and a list of syndicate investors."

"Interesting!" Henderson said.

"We went to Cramer's room to intercept the package, but our guy got there a little early and was surprised by the landlady. Afraid we hurt her."

Henderson fixed his gaze on Alf. "Did you kill her?"

"No, and we didn't blind her either—just a quick slit of the throat with our razor cap to keep her quiet."

Henderson winced.

"We're very proficient with razors. She'll live, at least from the throat wound."

Cap Alf reached into a basket on the floor of the carriage, pulled out an envelope, and handed it to Henderson. "Hope you don't mind the blood stains. You can read it while I drive; we can talk later. One final thing. I got a wire from Mathew Rohwedder; he said he was your partner in Australia, working on the diamond case."

Henderson was furious but kept it inside. This was pressure from Rohwedder.

"He does jobs for me. He's not a partner."

"Good," Alf said. "We don't need too many partners. But he did a good job of investigating—your Minnie Rose is now going by the name of Lady Edith or Edie Black."

When the message from Benji arrived, Harley Blake closed the door to his office. He lit the small oil burner under his teakettle and waited for it to steam. Dutch Hamill had forwarded the message for Lady Black from Benji Diamond, sent from Bermuda. Blake held the seal over the steam until it softened, then carefully removed the seal. He removed a diamond from the envelope and placed it on his desk. Then he read the letter, which was signed *Love, Benji.*

He has the diamonds, and he's coming to get his lover and partner, Blake thought. *I'll be ready.* Harley had no intent to share this information with anyone. He placed the diamond back in the envelope, resealed the letter, put it in the center drawer of his desk, and locked it.

Jack and Johnny met Herbert in the reception room of the inn. They took seats in the bar, and Jenny offered tea, which they all declined.

"Jack, I should have delivered those papers myself; many were originals and can't be duplicated. I have a few papers from my desk and Fredrick's that might be useful." He handed over a much smaller envelope than the original. "Here is a duplicate list of investors. I'm sickened that the list is in the hands of criminals. Fredrick will be furious, as will the investors. Just added kindling to the fire you're about to step into. The investor meeting has been arranged for after business hours tomorrow evening, 7:00 p.m. Fredrick will meet you at 5:30 outside the trading rooms on the south side of the building. He will brief you. About a dozen investors will attend, but several represent many additional silent partners."

"Will I need my gun?" Jack smiled.

"Hardly, but a suit of armor might be good," Herbert countered.

Jack and Johnny returned to the case room to review the paperwork and update the case notes. Jack was concerned about the investor meeting and wondered who needed the stolen notes—and why. He wrote this question on one wallpaper scroll. He then sat quietly, watching as Johnny added case notes Jack had culled from newspaper accounts of the robberies and the article on Henderson.

CHAPTER 27

THE INVESTOR MEETING

Jack arrived outside the trading rooms early. He was waiting at the south entrance at 5:15 when a carriage with blinds drawn pulled up at the curb. Fredrick opened the carriage door and leaned out. He looked both ways and summoned Jack with a hand motion. "Please get in."

Jack went to the street side of the carriage and opened the door; he stepped in, sat, and offered Fredrick his hand.

Fredrick's handshake was weak, and he gave Jack an even weaker smile. "I'm pleased you're early," Fredrick offered.

"Fredrick, you look awful!"

"Nice to see you too," Fredrick replied. "We'll go where we can talk."

He looked ashen and drawn; his eyes were heavy, his face drooped, and he had little of the spark that Jack had always admired. He was once a tall, husky man but appeared to have shrunk since they last met. "I could use a drink before the meeting, Jack. How about you?"

"I'll join you," Jack said, not having much choice. "Perhaps you can give me some insight into the investors attending tonight's meeting and what I can expect."

Fredrick's driver pulled up to a nearby pub, apparently knowing exactly where to go. The men exited the carriage and stepped into a darkened interior smelling of stale beer, gin, and urine. Fredrick led the way to a booth in the back. The bartender apparently knew Fredrick well and brought a whiskey over to him. Jack ordered a beer.

"I need it," Fredrick said to nobody. "Jack, I'm pulling you into the lion's den. The investors are angry, and I don't blame them. Some blame you—it's unfair but still a concern. Just tell your story as written in your report and answer any questions. The level heads will prevail."

"I may have some questions for them," Jack said.

"This meeting wouldn't be the time for asking questions."

"Fredrick, do your investors know about your coverages before they're issued?"

"We usually meet twice a month, most months, to review the pending larger coverages. Smaller policies are written daily, but anything exceeding £1,500 goes to an underwriting committee of several investors for voting approval."

"Tell me about the investors who'll be there. Who are they?"

"Some of the more important are Craig Williams, a wealthy property owner and merchant, sometimes volatile. He's the current chair. The chair rotates annually. Mrs. Lillian Hill is a prominent, wealthy, and sophisticated socialite—she'll charm you. She's the third largest individual investor, but I think some funds come from her silent partners. Rankin Hoskins is an investor who also represents a sizeable group of anonymous investors whom he manages money for. He's a nervous sort, always worried. I suspect he's under some pressure from his group. Harley Blake, a wealthy banker, will attend; he's very connected. He's invested substantial money and represents the interests of some of his clients, who remain anonymous. There will be a few more who you'll meet there, but the names I just gave you and myself represent most of the ownership."

"Thanks, Fredrick."

Fredrick waved his hand in the air to order another whiskey.

Jack realized that Lady Black had already introduced the name of one of the investors, Harley Blake, in her note. Still, he would only mention her name in the meeting if Blake brought it up. And he suspected Blake wouldn't.

"Jack, I have one additional piece of information for you and only you."

"What is it?" Jack asked.

"I received this yesterday."

Fredrick reached into his jacket pocket and withdrew a note card. His hands were shaking. He handed it to Jack. The message was formed with dark, thick ink-block letters on rough pulp stock. It read:

MR. TAYLOR

YOUR LIFE IS IN DANGER, AND WE KNOW WHERE YOUR CHILDREN
    HAVE BEEN TAKEN. ABANDON ANY INVESTIGATION AND TAKE
    YOUR LOSSES

GET RID OF THE INVESTIGATOR

IF YOU GET TOO CLOSE TO OUR OPERATION HARM WILL COME TO
    YOU, THE INVESTIGATOR, AND YOUR CHILDREN

WE ARE VERY SERIOUS AND WON'T WAIT LONG

DON'T INVOLVE THE POLICE, OR WE WON'T WAIT AT ALL

THE MAGPIES

"Who are the Magpies?" Jack asked.

"I don't know. I suspect it's not a real name. Or possibly it's one of the newer gangs."

"Are your children staying with you?"

"They're with my wife . . . she's left me."

"Fredrick, I'm sorry, but if they are serious, and there is no reason not to assume so, you need to protect your children, immediately. Do you know someplace they can go and be taken care of? Your wife too."

"I've arranged with a friend to move them tonight. He has a walled mansion with a guardhouse. They will be safe there. I'm telling no one who it is. We should get to the meeting."

"May I keep the card, or are you turning it over to the police?"

"The police would be too risky. You keep it."

♦ ♦ ♦

Fredrick and Jack entered the building from a rear alley door, avoiding public streets. "Every investor has a key," Fredrick said, locking the door behind them. They descended a dusty set of stairs that seemed little used. Fredrick led them to a nondescript door and entered.

The investors were milling around with tea or water, talking in small groups. Jack counted fifteen, including Herbert. One gentleman approached Fredrick and Jack. He was of medium height and seemed in good physical shape, with short gray hair and a clean-shaven, stern face. He held his hand out to Fredrick.

"Welcome, Fredrick."

"Thank you, Craig; this is Jack Cramer, our investigator."

"I presumed," Craig Williams said, as he turned and shook Jack's hand. He didn't smile or exude any warmth at all.

"Shall we get started?" Williams said to the group.

Williams sat at the head of a mahogany meeting table that could seat twenty. He banged a gavel on a wooden block and called the meeting to order.

"We will dispense with the reading of the last meeting's notes. Please welcome Jack Cramer. As you all know, he has investigated crimes for us over the past few years. I wish we were meeting under better circumstances, Mr. Cramer. Someone stole the Kimberley diamonds on your watch, and we need a report."

"I take this loss very seriously and will give you a full accounting," Jack said, "but please understand that possession and protection of the diamonds belonged to the postal service at the time of the robbery."

Williams responded, "I think most of us feel you were responsible until the diamonds were safely onboard the Royal Mail ship and arrived back here in London, Mr. Cramer. Just start at the beginning and give us all the details."

Jack did as he suggested, providing every detail he could think of. The investors remained silent.

"Mr. Cramer, you say you sent a report on the sixteenth of March." Williams turned to Fredrick. "Fredrick, you didn't inform us until April."

Fredrick replied, "We needed to investigate, and I waited for the police transcript."

"It would have been prudent to bring it to our attention immediately," Williams said, his upper lip curling in disdain.

"The postal service was a poor choice," Rankin Hoskins said. "A bank might have been better, and if I had been you, I would have slept with those diamonds and not in a fancy inn."

"The Royal Mail and the African postal system work together. I believed it was better not to move the diamonds too far away and risk involving persons unaware of their existence," Jack countered.

"Mr. Cramer," Hoskins continued, "are you bonded and insured?" Jack hesitated. His forehead tightened, and he stared into Hoskins's eyes.

"I am not personally responsible for your loss, Mr. Hoskins, and I resent the implication."

"Resent all you like! A court may decide how responsible you are," Hoskins said angrily.

Harley Blake spoke up. "Let's keep this civil, Rankin."

"I have a couple of questions for the investors, if I may?" Jack said, ignoring Fredrick's warning. He didn't look at Fredrick.

"Proceed," the chairman commanded.

"Are you aware of any connections between your loss payees for your major recent losses, particularly the Cape Town losses?"

"None," Herbert Archer replied.

"I'm curious about the stolen ship, the *Ferret*. For what purpose would someone steal a ship? I saw the ship *India*, now known to actually be the *Ferret*, in port at Cape Town at the same time as the robbery of the diamonds was taking place." Jack glanced at each investor.

"What's that got to do with the diamonds?" Mrs. Hill asked.

"Perhaps nothing," Jack replied. "But it is curious that another of your large losses was present for your largest loss. My experience suggests there may be a connection."

Mrs. Hill raised her voice. "I think that is senseless! We need you to focus on the diamonds. The ship has been located, and the thieves have been arrested and convicted. There was no evidence of diamonds on the ship."

Jack thought, *She's not charming me.*

"Perhaps they were better at hiding them than Mr. Cramer," Hoskins spat.

Mrs. Hill continued, "Mr. Chairman, may I redirect the board to the crisis, please?"

"Proceed," Williams said.

Mrs. Hill turned to Fredrick: "What is our financial status and our reserve balance?"

"This is the part I dread. You are all loyal investors and friends. You have done well over the years, but we do have a crisis. We cannot avoid paying the claim of £100,000 much longer. When we make that payment, our reserves will be negative by about £45,000. And you all know we can't just make that whole—we need sufficient reserves to cover any potential losses on other active policies, or we forfeit our right to be a Lloyd's insurer. The ship payment has been made, and when the diamond claim is paid, we'll need £180,000 to reach our minimum reserve limit."

There was a groan around the table.

"How can we be that far in the hole?" an investor asked. "It's policy always to maintain the reserve. It's a Lloyd's requirement."

"The reserve fluctuates," Herbert answered, "and some money is in investments, which haven't done well. Losses have exceeded our wildest expectations and calculations. It's all added up to where we are today."

"Not the best answer, Mr. Archer, but thank you for trying," Williams said. "Why did our actuary quit, and why weren't we informed immediately? Fredrick, you've been less than forthcoming. We deserve to know why he quit!"

Fredrick spoke softly and looked down at the table as he spoke. "We argued about the deficit. He wanted me to approach Lloyd's about the issue. I asked him to quit."

"I see," Williams said. He looked around the table. "All the investors are fiscally responsible for the losses and keeping the reserves whole." He turned back to Fredrick, "Fredrick, I think you have not been diligent about keeping the board apprised of details. As chair, I believe that is a mismanagement of your duties."

Fredrick started to respond, but Blake stepped in.

"Let's stop pointing fingers and finding fault; it won't fix the problem. First, we fix the financial problem; then, we can deal with how we manage going forward. Until now, we've all made substantial profits under Fredrick's leadership. Plenty more will be made, provided we remedy the situation quickly. There will be an audit of all accounts at the end of the quarter—in about seven weeks."

"If my money can be secured, I can bring in £25,000," Mrs. Hill offered, perhaps hoping to start a round of contributions.

"My investors already want out," Hoskins said. "I've stalled them, but certainly they're not in for *more*, and nor am I."

"Rankin," Mrs. Hill said, turning her gaze toward the man. "You do realize that if we don't recover the diamonds or replenish the reserves, your investment and the investments of your silent partners will have no value at all."

He said nothing, looking down at the table.

No one else spoke up.

"What about you, Fredrick?" Williams asked. "You formed this syndicate and profited greatly; how much can you offer?"

Fredrick looked defeated. Not like the person Jack knew.

"My dear friends and investors," he began. "This may be the end of the line for me and the syndicate. My life is a mess. My wife left me several months ago with the children and a lot of money. I apologize for bringing up my personal issues at a business meeting. Still, you need to know that I have no money to invest. Thank you, Lillian, for your support, but—"

Blake interrupted. "I'll provide the syndicate with the money needed. Every investor must sign a personal guarantee that I'll be repaid with interest in less than a year. Those of you with silent investors must take responsibility for their investments. This loan will keep the syndicate profitably operating and save your investments. It will also allow time for the investigation to hopefully recover some of the loss. We'll rely on Jack Cramer for that. My bank has the money but will not take on a risk of this size—I need everyone on the line with demand notes."

There was surprise among the investors; Jack wasn't sure whether they were relieved or afraid.

"I'll put my £25,000 in for an equivalent amount of ownership as collateral," Mrs. Hill replied, "and avoid assignment."

"Lillian, your holdings are far greater than that. That's fine for the £25,000, but you'll need to put in your full share or assign the balance of your ownership as security."

"I prefer not to do that, Harley. Let me see if I can gather funds for a larger investment."

"I'll work it out with you," Harley said. She nodded.

"Lloyd's can't know about this," Herbert said. "Invested monies cannot be encumbered in any way. The funds can't come from debt."

"These will be private transactions," Blake said. "My bank board will be upset, but I'll manage that. However, they *will* need to have the demand notes. I'll manage the internal politics. Documenting it in the syndicate files is unnecessary since these will be personal loans. As syndicate members, you're already responsible for the deficit funds. The syndicate records will show additional investments from each of you."

Seeing no other way out, everyone agreed; Mrs. Hill said she would discuss her additional investment that evening if Blake were available.

Harley deferred, suggesting a breakfast meeting the next day.

"I'll prepare the paperwork and gather the money," Harley said.

The meeting was adjourned.

Seeing Fredrick shuffle off, Jack felt sincerely concerned for him; his life was crushing him. Blake approached Jack.

"I'd like to speak with you in private. A quick pub dinner, perhaps?"

"My pleasure," Jack replied.

Jack made his excuses to Herbert and asked him to proffer his good wishes to Fredrick and to let him know that Jack was on the case until there was a resolution.

Jack and Blake left and found a pleasant pub to continue discussions. Jack thought Blake was an engaging person, entertaining and intelligent. He hoped it was mutual.

After some beer and food, Blake turned serious. "Jack, I appreciate you not mentioning Lady Black at the board meeting. I know she's mentioned my name to you. She is one of my blind investors in the syndicate and a friend. I know Mrs. Hill also has money from Lady Black invested, but she doesn't want Mrs. Hill to know she has invested with me. I spoke confidently, but it will take a herculean effort to pull that much money together in seven weeks. I'm not sure I can do it. I bought you some time. Things will get a lot simpler if you recover the diamonds before the audit. Since I'm going out on a limb here, I'll ask you to inform me about your activities and discoveries. I'll help you in any way I can."

"I'd normally only report to Fredrick, but I'm not sure that's going to be possible," Jack said. "Fredrick doesn't seem accessible or stable at the moment."

"The investors employ you, not Fredrick, so reporting to a lead investor is appropriate. I'm also afraid that Fredrick will receive a vote of no confidence at our next investor meeting, so there will likely be a new head."

Jack felt terrible for Fredrick, but he needed a powerful supporter on the board.

"I'll stay in touch and share what I find, Mr. Blake."

"Call me Harley. And one more thing, Jack. A person close to Lady Black, one Benji Diamond, has instrumental information about the location of the diamonds. Finding him should be a priority. It's best not to mention to Lady Black that I've told you this. She's too close to him."

CHAPTER 28

JACK AND EDIE

Jack and Johnny spent the next day working in the case room. Jack had a dozen notes related to the investor meeting and the investors. On the wallpaper chart, he drew a nasty face in the circle for Hoskins. Next to the circle about the *Ferret*, they drew a circle for the Kimberley diamond heist; Jack drew a dotted line between the two. He drew a circle to one side, wrote *Lady Edith Black*, and connected it with Harley Blake's circle as an investor. He drew an additional circle in red and entered *Benji Diamond*.

He drew a rectangle to the side, entered *Lloyd's audit seven weeks*, and added the approximate date.

"That's our ultimate deadline, Johnny, and sooner would be much better."

"Fredrick deserves his own circle, as does Archer. There's more to learn from both. The circumstances with the actuary are suspicious."

Johnny added *Actuary* as a dotted line connected to the two circles.

"I still think the *Ferret* theft is a key to discovering more about the diamond theft," Jack said. He noted this on the scroll with the *Ferret*. "I saw it sitting there as the *India*." He added *Benji Diamond on board?* "It's just a hunch, but it won't go away."

They listed a dozen facts gathered from the few papers from Lloyd's and the newspaper archives they were both researching. Johnny drew a circle to the side, wrote *James Henderson: thief, Ferret ringleader?*

and connected it with a line to the *Ferret*. He took a newspaper likeness of Henderson he'd acquired at the reading rooms and nailed it to the wall beside the notes.

Again, Jenny interrupted them. "A private delivery boy in the reception says he won't give me the message—he has to hand it to you."

The three went to reception. The boy was young but wore a white shirt, bow tie, and black shorts. *Quality firm*, Jack thought.

"I was instructed to wait for a reply," the boy said very formally, standing erect and looking past Jack at the food being served to guests in the dining area. Jack took the envelope. He now recognized Lady Black's signature scent of lavender.

"Will you sit down and have a bite to eat?" Jack asked, recognizing the boy's hunger.

"I couldn't, sir."

"Of course you can. It's going to take me some time to construct a reply. Jenny," he called, "please bring the young man a plate of stew and coffee."

"Where will you be delivering the reply?" Jack asked.

"I'm not allowed to say, sir."

Jenny placed a bowl before the boy, smiled at him, and poured the coffee.

"Thank you, ma'am," the boy said. "Thank you, sir." He started to scoop up the stew hungrily.

Jack opened the envelope and read.

Dear Mr. Cramer,

    I would enjoy your company tomorrow evening. I will have a hansom cab pick you up at 8:00 p.m. at the inn if you are available. Please advise the delivery lad of your availability. And please dress for dinner.

    Lady Edith Black

Jack welcomed the opportunity; he felt he was getting into the teeth of the case, somehow. He wrote his acceptance on the back of the message and placed it in the envelope.

"Do you know the lady who sent the note?"

"I am not allowed to say, sir," the boy replied again.

Jenny came over with more coffee for Jack and the boy, saying, "Don't pick on the boy, Jack! You know they have strict rules."

"I understand," Jack said to both of them. He handed the envelope back to the messenger with a nice tip. Jack wondered about Lady Black and the upcoming meeting. *She thinks she can help with the diamond heist, and she's a silent investor with two major syndicate investors. She says she needs my help. Why? All very mysterious, all unknowns.* He would add the questions to the wall scrolls.

"Johnny, I'm going to the docks to find a young man named Trunk to do some research for us. Want to come?"

"I'd better help Jenny for a few hours and visit Mum. I've been neglecting my duties lately."

"Give your mother my best."

Jack made his way to the docks to find Trunk. After wandering for half an hour, he finally found him eating a sausage and, true to his name, sitting on a trunk.

"What have you got there, Trunk?"

"Call it *bag o' mystery*." Trunk said.

"Not the sausage, the trunk!" Jack said, laughing.

"Oh, it's empty. I checked. I don't know who it belongs to, but it's been abandoned. Maybe someone got to it afore me."

Jack rolled his eyes.

"Can you find out if any gang called the Magpies is operating in London?"

"Don't know of them, but I have sources. Cost you thruppence."

"Highway robbery," Jack smiled.

"A boy has to eat," Trunk said, pointing the half-eaten sausage at Jack. "Want a bite?"

"No, thanks. I like to know what I'm eating. And keep your ears and eyes open for any information you can provide me on James Henderson or a Benji Diamond."

"All right, but it'll cost you."

"Of course it will, but I want everything you can find. I want to locate both of them."

Trunk left to begin his investigation. Jack decided to visit Herbert at Lloyd's. He found him on the trading floor and took him aside.

"Herbert, do you know anything about a gang called the Magpies?"

"Never heard the name, Jack, and I've heard of most of the gangs."

"What about a Benji Diamond?"

Herbert put his hand to his chin and nodded, thinking. "Yes, that goes back a long way. Benji was an industrious young man who started a delivery service; we used him to deliver policies and pick up items occasionally. I haven't seen him in years. I recall hearing something about some illegal activity, delivering stolen goods. His father, Russell, a weaver, went to jail for selling stolen fabric. Don't know what happened to Benji."

"Thanks, Herbert. Very useful."

"Sorry about the nastiness at the meeting."

"No problem, Herbert, not your fault. I hope Fredrick is all right."

"I do as well," Herbert answered.

Later, Jack and Johnny had a bowl of curry stew and bread for dinner at the inn, and each pulled a beer to retire to the case room.

Jack studied the paper that Johnny had nailed to the wall. He wrote a note about the threat from the Magpies and connected it to Fredrick's circle. Next to Benji's circle, they added the delivery service notes, and *Father went to jail—Russell Diamond, formerly a weaver.* Jack added the questions regarding Lady Black.

The next evening, Jack dressed in his best suit and cravat. It was also his only suit and cravat. *She told me to dress for dinner, and when you're dining with a mysterious lady, you need to look your best,* Jack thought. A hansom cab arrived at the inn a little before eight. Jack stared out the cab window at the streetscape as they passed, lost in thought. Something would be revealed tonight, and he was anxious to find out what it would be. The cab drove to Covent Garden and onto Maiden Lane, stopping near the door to Rules Restaurant. When Jack presented himself at the reception stand, the maître d' said, "Welcome, Mr. Cramer. Lady Black is expecting you at her table. I will take you there."

Jack recognized the woman he presumed to be Lady Black before they reached the table, and studied her as they approached. She was very elegant, dressed in a simple black dress without the frill of proper London evening wear. Her only adornment was a gold and diamond pin in her hat. Her ink-black hair hung to her shoulders and curled under—not a typical London style of the day, but very attractive. Her face was regal and playful at the same time.

Lady Black had selected a secluded table where she could see the front door through a pair of potted plants. Jack took in his surroundings as he walked. Every inch of every wall at Rules was covered with paintings, medals, hunting gear, antlers, stuffed pheasants.

When the maître d' delivered him to the table, Jack gazed at the woman, bowed slightly, and said, "Good evening, Lady Black."

"Good evening, Mr. Cramer. I trust you like champagne—I've ordered for us both."

He eased himself into the chair the maître d' held for him. "The maître d' made it sound like this was your regular table."

"It is," she replied, brushing a stray hair from her face. "I'm friends with the owner, but my earlier visits were due to invitations by my former employer, Mrs. Hill."

Jack was surprised but said, "I met her at an investor meeting. She's very forceful." Jack hadn't liked her much.

"She can be. I'm surprised she was at the Lloyd's meeting. She's no longer at her residence, and no one knows where she's staying—no one I know. I'm trying to locate her."

Jack changed the subject. "London isn't your home any longer?"

"Too soon in the evening to provide so many details, Mr. Cramer." She gave him a long look, the hint of a smile lifting the corners of her mouth. "Cramer—that's Irish, isn't it?"

"Probably, but I'm American."

"Harley has told me." Lady Black's eyes widened slightly. "May I call you Jack?"

"Of course, and how may I address you?"

"Lady Black will do just fine." She smiled broadly for the first time but with a twinkle in her eyes. She hesitated. "After a dinner together, you might be allowed to call me Edie."

A waiter appeared, poured champagne for Jack, and then placed the bottle back in the wine cooler wrapped in a towel. Jack noticed a second bottle on ice in a cooler by the wall.

Lady Black addressed the waiter, "We'll have a dozen oysters in a little while, but we need some time first. Then we'll have the stuffed pheasant and potatoes. Thank you, Randall. Give us half an hour before the oysters, please."

"Of course," the waiter replied.

"I hope you don't mind that I ordered for you. I know the menu well. Much of Rules menu is game from their hunting estate in the High Pennines."

"I don't mind at all. Your selections sound delicious." He gazed at her for a moment.

"How is Mrs. Riley? I heard of her injuries?" she asked.

"She's doing all right. The wound will heal, but her heart is irregular, and the doctor's concerned. I'm concerned with why it happened at all."

"I have my suspicions, and it *is* concerning."

Randall came and refilled their champagne glasses. More people arrived to be seated; Lady Black studied the new arrivals each time someone entered the dining room and listened as the maître d' spoke each name.

"Lady Black, you *are* involved with some of Lloyd's problems on some level, I assume," Jack prodded. "You said you have information for me."

"I have knowledge, Jack, and I *will* inform you in detail, but I need assurances."

Jack cocked his head. "Lady Black, I also need assurances. The injury to Mrs. Riley was for the purpose of stealing an envelope containing information on the theft of the steamship *Ferret* and the diamond heist in Africa that have been all over the papers. Were you involved?"

Lady Black's face and shoulders tightened; she lost her look of playfulness, and she took a deep breath. "I was not involved with the attack on Mrs. Riley," she answered with an edge to her voice.

"Then you had nothing at all to do with her attack."

"Oh, I suspect I had a lot to do with it, indirectly, but I did not cause it to happen. I've been told members of the Velvet Vipers may be to blame, but they would be working for someone else seeking the information. I'm also told they desperately want to locate me. I'd prefer not to be killed or kidnapped if I can help it."

Randall appeared just as the words *killed or kidnapped* were spoken. His face dropped its usual indifference, and he shuddered slightly. He poured champagne, opened the second bottle, and left without a word.

"I think we've upset the dear man, Jack," she smiled. "I'm sure the attack on Mrs. Riley was at least in part an attempt to find out if the package they stole contained any information on my whereabouts or the location of the diamonds. Certain parties believe I know where the diamonds are."

"Then you have involvement in the diamond heist."

Randall returned, a little ashen faced. "The oysters are ready, Lady B—Black. Would you like them now?"

"Five minutes, please, Randall."

He turned quickly and left without further comment.

"You know of James Henderson?" Lady Black asked.

"I do," Jack replied.

"James Henderson thinks I'm involved in the theft of the diamonds. As you know, he's escaped jail in Australia and is now in London, seeking me. I keep checking the door, fearing he will show up. He probably hired the Velvet Vipers to steal that package."

"What do you know of the diamond theft?"

"I know *when* the diamonds left Cape Town and in whose possession. Do you recall that I told you that I need your help in return for my assistance."

"First, tell me how you have this information."

"Jack, I was deeply connected with persons involved in the crimes that led to the Lloyd's syndicate's losses."

"Well! That gives you some credibility, I suppose," he remarked.

The oysters arrived, and more champagne was poured. Jack slid a fresh Scottish oyster into his mouth, chewed, and swallowed. Lady Black took the second and did the same.

As she was swallowing, Jack asked, "Did you steal the diamonds?"

She almost choked. "I did not!" she said. "But, as I said, I was associated with involved individuals. I need your help to find them."

He took a sip of champagne and waited for her to continue.

"Jack, I turned to you because you're in a position to resolve this crime. Our interests are linked, and we can help each other. What I tell you about myself is only known to a few others. I'm taking a chance by confiding in you, and I hope my trust is warranted. I need you to put me in touch with Mrs. Hill, and I need you to find a man by the name of Benji, Benjamin Diamond. He's the only one with any clue about what happened to the diamonds."

Jack didn't indicate that he recognized the name.

"Is he the thief?" Jack asked.

"No, he's not. I should start at the beginning. If I give you the information you need to get to the bottom of the diamond affair, will you agree to help me and not disclose your knowledge of my involvement in this matter, or that of Benji Diamond?"

"It seems like it's part of my investigation, so if you're telling the truth that you're not involved in the diamond theft, then yes."

She cleared her throat and raised one eyebrow slightly. "I *am* involved with the *Ferret* theft." She looked at Jack, uncertain of how he would react.

Jack sat back in his chair, breaking eye contact with Lady Black. He felt conflicted. He decided he needed to know everything this lady could tell him about the case. After hesitating, he said, "I guess it's best if you start at the beginning."

Edie told Jack about being involved in the *Ferret* theft as the representative of Mrs. Hill.

"Did she have a purpose for the ship? Could it be to facilitate the diamond robbery?"

"I believe someone else arranged the diamond theft, but I could be wrong. Before we left, the stated purpose was to conduct lucrative trade deals, including a sizeable transfer of guns to Peruvian soldiers. There was no mention of a major robbery."

Randall had showed up with dinner in time to hear the words *major robbery*—he was having a tough night. She asked him to let them dine and talk until she signaled. He gladly left.

The stuffed pheasant was delicious, and Jack commented on how wonderfully flavorful and tender it was. He hoped to slow the conversation down and listen.

"Lady Black," Jack asked, "will you tell me again about the events in Cape Town? And please elaborate. You've been very frank with me, and I'm fully on board to assist you in return for your help."

Lady Black, now more relaxed than during the first telling, continued. "In Cape Town, Captain Watkins left the ship, as was intended by Mrs. Hill. Henderson was furious. They fought. Watkins had to keep an appointment set up by someone who hired Mrs. Hill—or perhaps set up by Mrs. Hill herself; I don't know which. I confirmed the meeting at Mrs. Hill's orders. I had a coded message to send by wire from Brazil, no name but to an address in Cape Town."

"You have the address?" Jack asked.

"Yes, I'll give it to you. Watkins had no diamonds when he left the *India*. Again, on Mrs. Hill's orders, I sent Benji to follow him back to London incognito. Benji knows who Watkins met with at that address and who delivered the diamonds to Watkins before he sailed. Neither Benji nor Watkins knew what the cargo was before they sailed, nor did I."

Lady Black signaled Randall, and he approached the table. She smiled at him. Randall poured the last of the champagne, and they ordered orange custard, cookies, and coffee for dessert.

"Jack, we have yet to discuss a vital piece of information."

"I'm listening," he said calmly, sipping his coffee.

"The stolen diamonds have disappeared. Watkins disappeared from the *Scott* sometime between Cape Town and its second docking in Bermuda for repairs. That's where the diamond trail goes cold. As I mentioned, Benji has yet to contact Mrs. Hill or myself. He wasn't on the *Scott* when it docked in Bermuda. There were signs of a struggle in Watkins's cabin, and all his possessions were missing."

Jack thought for a minute. "That's a major complication. Watkins and Benji seem the likeliest suspects to have possession of the diamonds, and they could be working together."

"I understand how it could seem so, but I know Benji well, and he is not involved. The captain was a loyal, trustworthy supporter of Mrs. Hill. He doesn't have the attributes of a criminal."

"Most criminals don't," Jack countered. "Yourself included."

Her face hardened and then relaxed. "I guess I deserve that."

The crowd was thinning, but some guests were still finishing up their meals. "How did you meet Benji?" Jack finally asked.

"He rescued me from the South London slums and an abusive stepfather when I was ten."

Jack didn't know what to say. He hadn't suspected that the elegant lady before him had been born in the slums. He sat there for a minute without saying anything, his coffee cup halfway to his mouth.

"Not what you expected?" Lady Black asked with a smile.

"Not quite," Jack said. "Will you tell me about it?"

Edie summarized her early life, and Jack listened with a keen interest. He was won over by this attractive, articulate, and accomplished woman.

"You can call me Edie now," she said, smiling.

"How will we stay in touch?"

"Tonight, I'm at the Connaught. I'll move elsewhere in the morning. Correspond with me through Harley's office, but seal all notes. I'll come to you when I'm needed."

"I'll accompany you to your hotel and take the cab to Riley's. Thank you for your honesty—and the great meal." Jack felt genuinely grateful to have met the lady.

At that late hour, the only cab waiting at the front of Rules was a growler. The doorman hailed the large four-wheeled vehicle across the road from the entrance. The four-horse carriage pulled up and stopped slightly past the restaurant door. Jack tipped the doorman, took Lady Black's arm, and led her to the carriage. As he opened the door and guided her up the step into the compartment, he noticed the shades were drawn on the carriage door. He saw too late that the carriage compartment wasn't empty. A hand grabbed the front of his shirt and pulled him in. He felt a searing blow to the back of his head and fell to the floor of the cab—on top of the prone body of Lady Black. The driver slapped the reins, and the horses took off at full speed.

A tall man in a top hat stood under the gas lamp and watched the unconscious body of Jack Cramer being pushed from the speeding carriage into the road. He had followed Jack since his arrival in London and now knew where Lady Black was and where she was headed.

Sergeant Lindy knocked, then waited to be invited into Detective Wells's office.

"Enter," Wells called.

Lindy held two drawings in his hands. "The artist drew this likeness from the informer's description and took a stab at creating a second likeness of the face without the full beard. No way of knowing how accurate it is, but here they are."

"It's something," Wells said. He scribbled a few lines of text and handed it to Lindy. "Get this to our contacts at the papers to see if we can make tomorrow's editions. Offer a ten-pound reward for information leading to the capture of Russell Weaver, suspect in the Cape Town diamond theft. Post the likeness around the city as well."

"Yes, sir." Lindy left.

The hunt for Henderson and Weaver soon became the talk of London. Reported sightings and stories, fabricated or not, became headline news. Whenever a significant crime lacked a suspect, the newspapers blamed one or both fugitives. Both men commanded a sizeable reward for information leading to their arrest.

CHAPTER 29

DETECTIVE WELLS

Jack regained consciousness with a pounding pain in the back of his head; every heartbeat felt like an explosion in his skull. As his senses cleared, he realized he was in his bed at the inn, and when he reached up to touch his head, he discovered that it was bandaged. His right arm had a wrap on it as well.

"You're awake, I see," a male voice exclaimed. "Your head took a double beating, one from your abductors and one from hitting the ground when you were thrown out of the moving carriage."

"Who are you?" Jack asked, his voice raspy.

"I'm Dr. Bosch, Mrs. Riley's doctor."

The doctor gave Jack a mug of water and held his head up for him to drink.

"Johnny is downstairs entertaining a detective from the Metropolitan Police, who's waiting to see you. Drink this water to help clear your thinking and throat."

"How is Mrs. Riley?" Jack asked, grimacing a little with the effort.

"She'll be released soon . . ." The doctor scratched his chin. "Even if I don't want to release her. Speculation has it that a gang called the Velvet Vipers attacked her. I don't know what they would want from *her*."

"They were after a package intended for me," Jack said, rubbing his head. "I'll need to find out who hired them."

Dr. Bosch shook his head. "I'd advise not taking that on yourself. Perhaps your detective friend downstairs can help."

"Perhaps. I'm seeing double in my right eye."

"That's normal," the doctor said and continued his report on Mrs. Riley. "The worst part of this encounter for Mrs. Riley is her heart," the doctor said. "The beat just takes off running periodically, uncontrollably, then slows. Probably started when she was attacked. As for you, I'd advise a week of bed rest. A concussion can have long-lasting side effects if you're too active too soon."

Jack just looked at him and said nothing.

The doctor excused himself and called through the open door to tell Johnny that Jack was awake. Moments later, Johnny appeared, followed immediately by the detective. "This is Detective Wells," Johnny announced.

"I'll be back later," Johnny informed everyone, glad to shake the inquisitive companionship of the police officer.

"Bit of a nasty set of bruises you got," Detective Wells exclaimed. "Not very hospitable of our city."

"No, it isn't," Jack replied.

"Are you American?"

Jack nodded. "Yes. I do regular work for Lloyd's syndicates"—he groaned, clutching his head—"so I visit quite frequently."

"I see. The doorman at Rules said you entered the carriage after an attractive lady. Did she do this to you?"

Jack shook his head and decided that was a mistake; every slight movement caused stabs of pain. "No, she was hit first and was lying on the floor. I remember falling on her before I blacked out."

"The maître d' and the doorman say they don't know who she is, that you two just dined together, and neither had seen either of you before. What was her name?"

The question sent up a warning that he should be very cautious. Lady Black needed to remain as invisible as possible. What little he had learned told him she wouldn't be friends with the police. Her network of support and veil of secrecy included doormen and maître d's.

"Sergeant, I would rather be discrete."

"It's detective, and I know of no crime I can charge you or her with, so I can't make you tell me. But she may be in danger. We can't help without cooperation."

"Perhaps an angry husband if we've been discovered," Jack said.

"Perhaps." Detective Wells sounded skeptical. "Did you see anyone in the cab before you were knocked out?"

"It was dark. I saw a dark shadow just before I was pulled in and struck, but I didn't recognize who hit me. I remember the curtains were closed."

"Where were you headed?" asked the detective.

"Browns," Jack said, quickly coming up with the name of a different hotel to steer the detective away from Lady Black's lodgings.

"Fancy," the detective offered. "Under your name?"

"No," Jack replied.

"Want to tell me under what name you were registered?"

"No. I'm sorry, Detective. I think I'm going to be ill. Can we end this now?"

Wells scowled; his eyes narrowed. He was clearly annoyed with Jack. His voice turned a little more formal.

"Let me show you a wanted poster we're hanging around the city. It's for a suspect in the Cape Town diamond robbery, which I believe you're investigating. May I?"

Jack was interested now. "Yes." Jack looked at the drawings and read the name Russell Weaver. "Can you give me any more information, Detective?"

The detective scratched behind his ear and looked back at Jack. "I don't want you to get sick. Why don't you come to my office when you're up and about, and perhaps we can exchange some details?"

"I'll be glad to do that," Jack said.

"I won't pressure you on your lady friend. I have no authority over matters of the heart or bed. If you find your lady friend is in more trouble than an angry husband with a streak of violence, contact me." He handed Jack a card with his name and badge number written on it.

"I'll do that, Detective. Could you hand me one of those basins?" Jack pointed.

"There's only one," Wells replied, realizing it was time to leave. He handed the basin to Jack and made a quick exit. Jack watched the detective go, and moments later, Johnny reappeared to ask if he was all right.

"I'm fine, Johnny. I just wasn't prepared with answers for the detective. Is your mother's heart still a problem?"

"Yes," Johnny replied. "And she's had these heart things before, dozens of times. Mum always snaps back. I suspect she'll be all right when her neck heals. She'll have to stay in bed after she gets home. That won't be easy!"

Jack eased himself into a more upright position.

"Johnny, I learned some details about Benji, his father, and the *Ferret* theft, plus information on the diamond robbery that could be useful. Will you hand me that notebook and I'll write them down? I'd like you to transfer them to the case-room notes. I also discovered that the stolen diamonds went missing from the thief's courier, along with the courier."

Johnny handed the notebook to Jack. "That's big!" he said. "The parties that arranged the theft must be steaming."

Johnny read the notes. "I'll enter them," he said.

"Finding Benji is essential. He disappeared off the *Scott* as well. However, Edie—Lady Black—has been in touch with two parties that talked to Benji in London. Whatever you can find out about his past may give clues as to where he is now. I don't want to go to the police for information yet. I'll feel better tomorrow. I'll visit the docks and see if Trunk has found out anything."

Benji was thankful for the warning his boys had provided him about the Hill mansion. He'd been observing the observers for several nights. Benji promised the stable manager a few shillings daily to be discreet and provide water and some food. He recognized the Velvet Vipers gang from his London stall days. They were a nasty group of men known for sewing razor blades into the rims of their caps so that they always had a weapon handy. When they wanted, they could slash the eyeballs of any victim in seconds. *Why were they staking out Mrs. Hill's residence? Are they looking for me and Edie? Or Mrs. Hill?*

Something different was happening as Benji watched from his roughly constructed platform perch in a tall English oak tree on the park's border. Two wagons had pulled into the encampment, and the Vipers were tearing down camp, loading the wagons, and getting onboard; they were abandoning the surveillance. Why? Something else was up.

He wanted to find Mrs. Hill and convince her he was not responsible for the disappearance of the diamonds. Perhaps his detailed report had reached Edie from Australia and she had conveyed it to Mrs. Hill; perhaps not.

Benji climbed down from his observation deck and cautiously approached the cart path around the park. He stopped short. Nailed to a tree next to the path was a wanted poster with his likeness on it. *Wanted: Russell Weaver, suspect in the Cape Town diamond theft.*

Great, Benji thought. *The police suspecting me won't help convince anyone. How did this happen? It had to be the pawn broker in Bermuda—or maybe some scheme by whoever really has the diamonds.* He ripped the poster off the tree and pocketed it. He ran to the stable, quickly saddled one of the rental horses, and left on horseback, just as the second wagon was leaving the encampment. He would follow at a distance. They could lead to Mrs. Hill, Henderson, and perhaps Edie, but he was sure the diamonds were on everyone's mind. It occurred to him that Mrs. Hill and Edie could be working together to recover the cargo.

CHAPTER 30

JOHNNY

Johnny often began his day with a visit to his mother, and today, he was relieved to find her awake and smiling to see him.

She sat up in bed. "My heart's beating like a steam engine," she said. "It's not going to stop yet. How is it back at the inn?"

Johnny wasn't surprised at her recovery speed, nor was he surprised that she was pretending she hadn't heard the doctor telling her she needed a couple more weeks of rest. Johnny assured her that everything was under control at the inn so she shouldn't worry.

"If I didn't have something to worry about, I probably *would* die," she managed, her voice a little hoarse and her hand reaching to touch the bandage on her throat. Johnny gave her a drink of water and said he would visit again the next day.

"Can you bring ale tomorrow? I understand it's good for the throat!"

Johnny smiled at her and left. The doctor said she needed a few more days under observation. She'd threatened several times to leave without permission.

"I'll release her tomorrow if she comes back weekly for a while for me to check on the heart," the doctor advised Johnny.

"I'll make that happen," Johnny promised, doubting he could.

At the Weaver's Guild, Johnny had found the location of Benji Diamond's father's former shop. It was now a smoke shop with tobacco, cigars, pipes, and accessories. The proprietor had heard of Benji and his father but didn't know much else. He said several other businesses had used Benji's delivery services. He suggested that Johnny go door-to-door. Johnny found several people who remembered Benji Diamond, but no one knew what had happened to him after his arrest; he'd just disappeared. On the second day of knocking on doors, Johnny got lucky: he stepped into a bookshop, stationery, and printing establishment operated by a young man named Sam, who had apprenticed with the owner, James Lackson. Sam knew of Benji because Mr. Lackson spoke often of him, usually in unfavorable comparisons, such as, "Benji learned that in two days! What's taking you so long?" The young man spoke good-naturedly, and Johnny learned that Mr. Lackson would return around four to check on Sam, as he did daily, and that he should return then.

"Thank you, Sam. I'll be back."

While he was waiting to meet Lackson at four, Johnny stopped by the offices of the *London Times*. He knew Robbie Dickens, one of the writers for the *Times*. He arranged for guests of the newspaper to stay at the inn from time to time, and he had dinner there occasionally.

"Johnny!" Dickens exclaimed. "It's good to see you. I was sorry to hear about your mother. How is she doing?"

"I think she'll be fine, Robbie. I'll tell her you asked."

"What brings you here? Got a hot one for me?"

"Not yet," Johnny said. "I need your help. I have to research a group of people and may need some help, but I have to keep all the names confidential."

"I understand, Johnny. I'll make sure anything you request is kept private. Celia Ling can assist you. She's very discreet. If you need me, just come and get me."

Celia brought Johnny all the references he requested. He searched papers starting three years back, primarily looking at headlines. Johnny would have to go deeper into the archives to research Benji and his father. He didn't find anything useful and left when it was time to return to the printer's shop. Celia said she would continue to search.

Mr. Lackson was waiting for him. His hands were crippled with arthritis, and he was permanently bent at the waist, so it was hard for him to look up into Johnny's face. Johnny sat down to make talking easier for Lackson.

"You've seen Benji since the arrest?" Johnny asked.

"Many times, but not for a while," the old man replied. "He used to stop in, always with a gift of fresh fruit or vegetables, occasionally a pastry or loaf of bread in the winter. Benji said he was running a series of market carts across town near the East End. Such a nice lad. He seemed very happy. He usually had a request for me when he came by. He continued advancing his printing skills and said he had his own press, which I took some pride in. He hoped to take it up as a career when he was ready."

"What type of requests do you remember?" Johnny asked.

Mr. Lackson closed his eyes to think. He brought one hand to his chin. He sat like that for a while; Johnny feared he might have nodded off. "I recall once he was trying to do official papers—identification papers and the like. Benji wanted to know about paper stock and where to buy such stock. He wanted to know how to acquire seals for documents. He was a good boy. I don't believe the charges that were made against his father."

"Do you remember what the charges were?" Johnny asked.

"Yes," Lackson said. "Receiving stolen goods. He was convicted. I believe Benji was charged with fencing, but he was delivering for customers. He was acquitted."

Johnny thanked the man and told him his apprentice was very professional. Behind Lackson, Johnny saw Sam smile. He told Lackson that his mother ran a good-sized boarding inn and restaurant, and he'd bring some printing work by. Mr. Lackson looked pleased.

Johnny walked back toward the inn, contemplating what he'd learned. He remembered the stall market; his mother had taken him there years ago so he could carry her purchases back to the inn. It was a lively place. The exchange with Lackson had been interesting; learning that Benji was an accomplished printer might be valuable. Looking up briefly, he noticed a new wanted poster nailed to a telegraph pole.

He took it down, folded it, and put it in his pocket to nail to the case room wall at the inn.

Johnny woke Jack up. Jenny said he'd been sleeping most of the day and was dizzy when he came down for lunch.

"Not recovering quite as quickly as you hoped, I presume," Johnny said.

"I'm fine. Just letting my mind work on the facts of the case," he said, smiling weakly. "No, I'm lying . . . I blacked out once when I tried to walk a little. I didn't make it to the docks."

"I'll go in the morning. I have some interesting information if you're up to the case room."

"More than ready, Johnny. It's a bit boring, this recovery business."

"Probably better than the alternative," Johnny said.

Jack sat in a chair while Johnny filled in notes about his visits.

"I think the information on Benji's skills as a printer is important," Johnny said. "The press from Australia emphasized the elaborate printing setup aboard the *Ferret*."

Jack agreed.

"I have one more thing to add," Johnny said.

He took the poster from his pocket, unfolded it, and carefully nailed it to the wall near the notes they had made on Benji a couple of days ago. "What do you see, Jack?"

"Wells showed me that poster, but I couldn't focus on it then."

Johnny took a red pen and circled the name on the parchment of Benji's father, Russell Diamond, then circled his profession of weaver. Turning to the poster, he circled the name of the wanted man, Russell Weaver. "This is our Benji," Johnny said.

"Terrific work, Johnny! We need to track Weaver back to his arrival. We'll give Detective Wells some time with the Weaver search, then pay him a visit. We have to find Benji before the police do."

"Fine, but you still have to take it easy for a few days."

"I know, but someone is holding Lady Black captive, presumably Henderson, and we need a lead to find her. I'll retire early."

The next day, Jack began with chicken broth for breakfast. He decided against any coffee; he was still nauseous and dizzy occasionally, mostly when he moved around.

Johnny went to the docks to find Trunk, and after twenty minutes of walking around his usual stomp, he asked a docker if he had seen the boy.

"Said he had some investigating to do for a client, acting all important. Hasn't been around for a couple of days."

"Does he disappear often?" Johnny asked.

"Hardly ever. His customers usually come here to see him."

Johnny asked the docker to tell Trunk that Jack Cramer was looking for him.

Taking a cab, Jack spent several hours at the reading rooms of the *London Daily News*. He noted names from the reports on Mrs. Hill's social gatherings. It wasn't a surprise that Harley Blake and Fredrick were often in attendance. Some of the other names could be silent investors.

Jack returned to the inn late. He was exhausted, dizzy, and still seeing double. It was Friday, and the inn was full. Johnny was still out. Jenny had left Jack a note that Mrs. Riley had returned from the hospital. It appeared that she had gone to sleep. There was a note from Johnny: *I'll be late, but don't go to bed. Mum's doctor sent a bottle of elixir for you. It's behind the bar—said it would make you feel better.*

He went behind the bar, found the elixir, took a shot glass, and downed a dose. It tasted awful. *It needs a chaser,* he decided. He took a pint glass, pulled himself a beer to wash down the medicinal taste, and carried it into the kitchen. He intended to raid the pantry for food but found Jenny fast asleep on a straight-backed wooden chair, her head hanging back and her mouth wide open, snoring. *Catching flies,* he thought, an expression his mother had used. He tried to wake her gently, but she didn't respond. He tried again, and she jumped from the chair, knocked it over, and started bustling around aimlessly, uttering something unintelligible.

"Jenny," Jack said, "are you all right?"

"Oh, Jack," Jenny's mind cleared with a start. "What are you doing here?"

He didn't know how to answer. "I'm staying here, I hope."

"Oh, that's right, I forgot." She was bleary-eyed, not fully aware.

Jack picked up the chair. "Sit down, Jenny. I'll make tea."

Jack put a kettle on the hot burner of the wood range. It was soon boiling, and he made a pot of tea from the bin on the shelf. He let it steep and waited. Jack poured Jenny a cup—a little weak, but the second would be more robust.

"Jenny, tell me what's wrong."

"Oh, Jack, nothing's wrong. Mum's home. Could be stronger—she wants to help, but she's mostly just bossing me around. She keeps ringing her bell for me to come. We've been busy. Johnny's gone all day and half the night investigating, which I know he loves. I've always wanted to run the inn, but I'm exhausted with the guests, putting on three meals a day, and my kids, not to mention my husband and Mum. I was going home, but I must have fallen asleep. I'm here twelve hours or more a day. Linus will be mad—it's so late."

Jack felt a rush of adrenaline from the medicine; it felt good. He took a sip of beer. His vision cleared.

"Jenny, tell you what. The weekend is upon us. I'm not going anywhere until Monday. I've got case-room work to do with Johnny. We can run the inn, cook the meals, and take care of guests until Monday. You go enjoy your family and get some rest."

Jenny hesitated, giving Jack a quizzical look. "You sure?"

"Yes, I am. I've always wanted to run an inn."

Jenny stood again and hugged Jack. "You are the best guest, Jack."

He laughed. "Go home."

After Jenny left, Jack realized he was starving and raided the icebox. *I like that medicine!* He found some kippers, put them into a pan, cracked three eggs out of the basket, and found the leftover beans in the icebox. He started a proper English breakfast.

Johnny walked in and said, "Add some more eggs. I'm starving."

Jack did, and they sat at the kitchen table to eat. Johnny had his beer in one hand and a newspaper rolled up in his armpit. As Jack ate,

Johnny unrolled the paper, held it in two hands, and put it in front of Jack's eyes. "My contact at the *Times* wasn't in today, but Celia, his assistant, told me he would be back tomorrow and it would be a big news day. This is tomorrow's front page. She gave me a proof copy."

The front-page headline in the Saturday *London Times* read, "Hill Mansion Raided, Police Suspect Home Was Forty Elephants Headquarters." Underneath was a subheading: "Lillian Hill missing, reward offered." Below the article were updates on the lack of progress in the search for James Henderson and Russell Weaver.

"The public will have a field day with this," Jack said.

"I waited for the copy since you mentioned she was an investor in Fredrick's syndicate. What do we do?"

"I don't know," Jack said, and proceeded to tell him about finding Jenny and his promise to take care of the inn.

"I guess we could wait and see if anything new comes of the police investigation," Johnny said. "We can bring the case room current in the downtime."

"Let's get some sleep. We have breakfast duty starting at 6:00 a.m."

"I'll check on Mum. See you in the early morning."

Jack finished his kippers and eggs and went to bed.

He couldn't sleep; he suspected the medicine was keeping him awake. He went to the case room and stared at the notes. *I have to find Lady Black*, he thought. *There isn't a person on this wall she isn't directly or indirectly connected with. Where are the other connections?* He stared for a minute or two. *Everyone is connected to Mrs. Hill. It looks like she's involved in all the action. What caused the police to raid the mansion? How did she manage to disappear before the raid?* He stood up and wrote these questions on a new strip of wallpaper that Johnny had nailed to the wall.

Breakfast was late; they both overslept. They made apologies to the waiting guests and took orders as new guests entered the dining room. One patron complained that a Yankee couldn't be depended on for proper service.

They got through the weekend, with Johnny taking the lead and Jack taking his elixir. They talked a little about the case, but mostly they enjoyed running the inn. Jack thought that a little distance might make connections clearer when they got back to the case room. They felt mentally restored by Monday morning, and Jenny returned—smiling and rested.

"Thank goodness it's Monday and I can get back to work—my family is driving me nutty!" She gave Jack and Johnny each a peck on the cheek.

Johnny headed back to the reading rooms to quiz Robbie on what he knew about the Hill raid that wasn't in the papers. Robbie's response was a surprise: "I'd say that was another botched job by the police, but I won't print that. The Forty Elephants have been impossible to identify for years, and they robbed at will. No one knew who the leader was. Mrs. Hill was part of the social elite in the West End. No one ever suspected her. My contact at the Metropolitan said they received an anonymous note detailing Mrs. Hill's role as the gang's leader."

"Someone informed on her?" Johnny asked. "That's important to know. Any idea who?"

"My contact says that the note appeared on the chief's desk; no one saw it delivered. The police did find stolen goods in the house, but not much. They found a small bundle in a closet with a note addressed to James Henderson. It said, 'Take the bundle to the warehouse.' There was a street name. The package was old, but they found the warehouse in another part of town. A search of the warehouse found goods identified as coming from recent robberies. The gang's been around a long time, and I suspect it won't go away, but I also bet Mrs. Hill won't show up again. The mansion is locked and guarded and will remain in police hands until a court decides what to do with it."

The question becomes, who ratted on her and why, Johnny thought.

CHAPTER 31

CAPTIVE

Edie woke to total darkness, unsure how much time had passed. She was prone—her head throbbed, and her body ached. She reached up and encountered a solid surface above her face. It felt like wood. Her heart raced, and she panicked. *Am I in a coffin?* She reached behind her head and touched another solid surface about six inches back. She wiggled to the right and then back to the left. The width was enough for an additional body; it was too big to be a coffin. She breathed deeply and blew out slowly, trying to calm her heart and thoughts. She was imprisoned in a box, and what was that horrible smell? She slid down until her feet struck a surface. She tried a kick to see if the end would move, but it was solid. She fought off panic with a few more deep breaths, then, wondering if the air supply would run out, she panicked again.

"Let me out of here!" she screamed. There was no response. She felt sure she wasn't meant to die in the cramped space, and she clung to that thought as she continued to breathe deeply. Someone would be along, someone who wanted something from her. The box was big enough to allow her to roll over, but she lay back to conserve her energy and air until her jailer arrived.

She must have slept or passed out again, but she suddenly woke with a start. Had she heard noises? She listened. There was movement outside her crate.

"Let me out of here!" she screamed, near panic.

There were a few whacks of something on the outside of the crate, then a snort. And several more snorts from other areas around the box.

"What the devil?" she said out loud.

"It's pigs," a male voice answered.

"Who are you?" she shouted.

There was no answer. "Please. I need air."

"You can breathe, but let me help." He popped a cork out of her box's roof, allowing a tiny streak of light to enter. "Put your mouth below the hole, and I'll give you some water."

"Why not just let me out? Why am I here? Please, please let me out."

"I have orders not to let you out, and you know why you're here."

"I certainly do not!" Water began to stream through the hole; she quickly opened her mouth and took what she could hold. "I need to pee," she said.

"Go ahead," the voice said.

CHAPTER 32

JACK VISITS WELLS

Jack presented Detective Wells's badge number at the desk of the Metropolitan Police Department in Whitehall. He was asked to wait on a bench with a lady of the night and a street bum who smelled of horse manure, vomit, and urine.

Five throat-gagging minutes later, Detective Wells appeared. "Hello, Jack. How's the head?"

"The injury's doing fine; I don't know how well the rest is working. I'm sorry I was a little abrupt the other day—I was a bit confused."

"I didn't notice," the detective remarked, with a hint of sarcasm. His eyebrows arched, and he smiled at Jack. "What can I do for you?"

"I'm casting about for details on the case I'm currently working on for Lloyd's."

"Come to my desk. We'll see what we can do."

The detective's desk was covered with piles of papers, not just case files and notes but also newspapers, as well as inkwells, a small wooden stand of pipes, and an ashtray that, for some reason, was clean. The rest of the office was orderly and neat. The chair Jack sat on was padded and comfortable, which Jack thought was strange in a detective's office. The walls had several woven hangings that brightened the stark room.

Wells caught Jack looking. "My mother died a year ago, and I couldn't bear to get rid of her things. My wife didn't want them at the house, so I decorated my office."

"I'm sorry about your mother, but her artwork makes your office pleasant looking," Jack said.

"Thank you. I'd offer you coffee but would advise against it—and the tea is nearly as bad."

Jack laughed and said, "No, thank you."

"Have you found your mistress?" He sat across from Jack.

"No, and you know she's not my mistress. She's a critical part of my case, and I don't doubt she's in danger. I need to find her—*and* find her safe. I'll provide details of my investigation if I feel they're important to you, but I can't reveal her identity. The crimes we're investigating are not London-based, so unless I find out any more local details, I don't think I have anything useful for you. As it is, I have little information that would help me find her either. Can I ask a question that might provide clues that I can follow up on?"

"You can ask." Wells looked a little annoyed; his forehead wrinkled. "Jack, the information you have may be more valuable to me than you comprehend. Or perhaps not, but I'm not willing for this to be a one-way exchange."

Jack nodded. "I won't hold back information that I feel is important to your cases if I'm not violating a client's confidence." Jack went on to his question. "On the night of her abduction, my companion mentioned a name from her past here in London, from her childhood, I believe. Benji Diamond. He had a delivery business a few years back, and his father was a weaver."

Wells leaned back in his desk chair. He seemed to relax. "That brings me back a little! I walked a route that included his father's shop." He recounted the story Jack already knew. "I liked them both; I don't think they knew they were doing anything illegal."

"You raided the Hill mansion and warehouse the other night. Do you think the stolen goods Benji and his father were charged with possessing could have come from the Forty Elephants gang?"

"Interesting question. We arrested James Henderson, who claimed to buy on the underground market and had proof. Benji testified that he picked up deliveries from Henderson at a small warehouse several times a week. Because of the raid, the warehouse is now tied to Mrs. Hill, as is Henderson. This discovery casts some doubt on Henderson's testimony, but those cases are ancient."

"You have a manhunt ongoing to find Henderson. As you know, he was convicted of the *Ferret* theft, one of the cases I'm investigating for Lloyd's. I'll provide you details on anything I learn about Henderson." Jack paused. "Any leads on him yet?"

"Nothing. As you mentioned, we're currently conducting a countrywide search for him. We've sent wanted posters to other stations, but we have no leads."

Jack looked disappointed.

"I understand," he said. "I know this is asking something out of the ordinary, but I believe you received a note informing on Mrs. Hill's suspected involvement. Is there any chance I can see the note?"

"I can't do that, Jack. It's evidence, and if Mrs. Hill is found, there will be a trial."

"Can you tell me if the note was in fancy handwriting and smelled of lavender?"

Wells grinned. "Your lady friend?"

"Could be."

"If the note *was* from her, she may be a person of interest here in London."

"I realize that," Jack said. "But first, I must find her. Let me know if it appears to be from her."

"Give me a few minutes." Detective Wells left the office, returning twenty minutes later. "No luck, Jack. There was no lavender smell, and the note was carefully written in block letters on a rough paperboard. No reference to the source."

"Thanks, you've been helpful. I'll stay in touch."

"Good! I'll do the same, Jack." His words to Jack sounded like a warning.

♦ ♦ ♦

Later that evening, Johnny and Jack met again for dinner and then retired to the case room. Jack felt much better but took a shot of the elixir anyway. He added Detective Wells to the circles and wrote *a note to the police on Mrs. Hill in block letters on a rough paperboard.*

"Didn't Mr. Taylor say his threat came on a card with block letters?" Johnny asked.

"He did. I have it here." He nailed it to the wall next to the wallpaper. "I suspect we're dealing with the same individual or gang. We need to find Trunk to see if he discovered anything on the Magpies."

Jack drew a circle from Benji's space on the case map and added *accused of handling stolen goods.* In a connected circle, he wrote, *Suspected source of stolen goods — Lillian Hill — Forty Elephants? — James Henderson involved?* He added *a wide manhunt for Henderson.*

Jack filled in more details about the crackdown on the stall market and the arrests that Lady Black had told him about. They both had a list of names from the social page articles on parties at the Hill Mansion; they compared lists and nailed the list of attendees to the wall with the wanted posters and the list of investors. Jack was pleased that Rankin was never included.

"Bankers, politicians, business leaders, the chief of the Metropolitan Police—all the cream of the crop," Johnny said.

"What's unknown, Johnny, is who would benefit from informing on her."

Looking at the *Ferret* notes, Jack said, "Ultimately, the steamship thieves were caught largely because the notes they had issued for the *Ferret* lease and fit-up were dishonored. The Sterling Union International Bank dishonored them; that's Harley's bank. Before the bad notes surfaced, the *Ferret* was presumed sunk and the crew dead." He drew a line to Blake. "I owe Blake another visit."

Jack was concerned about the welfare of Trunk. Johnny had been unable to make contact twice. Jack decided to head to the docks to check on the boy and see if he had any information before he approached Blake.

◆ ◆ ◆

Trunk had been busy on his own mission. When Jack had first visited with his request, Trunk contemplated the best approach. The Magpie question was an easy one to answer. Trunk was sure they didn't exist, at least in his realm. But he would do a little investigation on them to earn his fee. Trunk's more significant concern was that Jack had mentioned Benji Diamond. Benji was an old friend of Trunk's—as old as a friend can be when you're thirteen. During the stall years, Trunk took many of his acquisitions to the ladies at the stalls, who would sell them, keep a percentage, and pay Trunk. He missed the convenient outlet that Benji had created. Trunk hadn't seen Benji in more than two years, but he had to try to find him to see if he was all right and warn him that Lloyd's investigators were looking for him.

Trunk spent a couple of days quizzing his contacts without any new information. He was unsure how to proceed, so he decided to visit the site of the cart stalls to see if anyone in the nearby neighborhood knew of Benji's whereabouts.

He climbed a drain spout and found a roof position where he could observe the warehouse alley without being noticed. It was early dusk when he saw a lone figure, a woman, bent over a parcel that looked like a cloth-wrapped bundle, hurriedly walking close to the warehouse wall. She placed the bundle on the ground and took a long bar from the edge of the door, inserted it between some boards, and gave it a two-handed jerk upward. The door opened and the woman turned, bending to pick up the parcel, and Trunk could see her face.

It's Specs!

He hurried to the downspout and slid to the ground, losing his balance and landing on his backside. He got up and ran around the corner toward the door. Seeing someone running in her direction, Specs hurried to enter the space and lock the door.

"Specs!" Trunk yelled. "It's me—Trunk."

She hesitated and stared through the crack in the door, ready to pull it shut.

Trunk? The little boy who would bring pilfered goods for sale. She squinted, trying to focus, frown lines forming on her forehead.

"Specs, please. I need to talk to you."

She opened the door wider, allowing Trunk to run in.

"I try not to make too much noise," Specs said. "Don't want anyone to know I'm living here."

"Sorry. I needed to get your attention."

"I remember you, a cagey young lad."

"I do my best." Trunk smiled.

Specs relaxed and smiled back.

"I need your help," Trunk said. "Benji's my friend, and I need to speak to him."

Specs made tea on the wood stove, and they sat down at the remaining section of the center table. Trunk told her that investigators from Lloyd's had questioned him about Benji.

"That doesn't necessarily mean he's in trouble," Specs said.

"I need to let him know." Trunk looked concerned. "I need to help him."

Specs thought a moment, let out a long sigh, and decided to tell him what she knew, hoping that was what Benji would want.

"Benji was here. He left to track down Mrs. Lillian Hill, who financed the stall market."

"I know Mrs. Hill," Trunk said. "I've done work for her."

Specs's eyes opened wide, and she sat up straighter. "I'm surprised."

"I work for a lot of people," Trunk said proudly, lifting his head higher. "This is helpful information, thank you. I'll visit again soon. Please tell Benji I'm looking for him if he returns."

Trunk walked toward the nearest trolley stop and boarded the car toward the West End. Reluctantly, he paid his fare like all the other passengers. He knew where Mrs. Hill's mansion was; he'd been there. He wanted to observe the estate before approaching. He got off at the Hyde Park trolley stop, entered the park, and walked the footpath. The stands of trees shielded him from the street where the mansion stood.

He stopped short, stooped, and hid behind a bench. The woods were full of Velvet Vipers. *I don't mess with Vipers*, he said to himself. They had an encampment set up, and it looked like they'd been there awhile. It looked like they were staking out the mansion. He avoided the woods and entered the Hyde Park stables. "Willie," he called. No answer. He called a little louder. Willie came in from outside with his English setter bouncing in before him. "Keep it down!"

"Willie! It's me—Trunk."

"I see that, Trunk. I just don't want any unnecessary attention drawn to the stable. The area's crawling with Vipers. They've been here over a week. They scare me. They're looking for Mrs. Hill."

"They scare me too. Have you seen Benji Diamond?"

"Friend or foe?"

"Good friend, honest."

"Benji's up a tree."

"You mean trapped?"

"No, he's up a tree watching the Vipers. He's also looking for Mrs. Hill. Popular lady! It's a large English oak about five hundred yards down the tree line. He has a platform and can keep an eye on the Vipers and the mansion. I send him water and some food when it's safe."

Trunk waited until it was pitch dark and carefully started toward Benji's tree.

"Stop!" someone yelled. Two Vipers had spotted him.

He took off running; he was fast, but the two Vipers in pursuit were catching up. He saw Benji's platform ahead of him; he wanted to avoid leading them to Benji. He stopped quickly, turned, and ran right at the Vipers. Startled, one skid to a halt and fell into the grass. Trunk bumped the second as he ran past, but the Viper grabbed Trunk's shirt. Trunk adeptly wiggled out of the shirt, avoiding the grasp, and continued to run. He ran back in the direction of the stable, angling into the park away from the woods, but it had taken too long: the Viper was right on his heels. He grabbed Trunk's shoulders from behind. Trunk fell, bounced up, and turned to face the Viper. He grabbed both of the pursuer's hands so he couldn't go for his cap and slash him. The Viper was much stronger. He pulled a hand free.

Willie's dog hit the Viper in the side, snarling, holding his shirt in his teeth. The Viper yelled; he seemed terrified of the dog. He pulled his ripped shirt free and backed away. "Down, dog. Down!" he shouted, his voice wavering. The setter advanced slowly, growling. Carefully watching the dog, he told Trunk, "You better disappear. No one spies on the Vipers; I'll be back with friends looking for you."

Willie must have signaled the dog, Trunk thought, shivering with relief. The setter backed off the Viper and sat down next to Trunk.

Jack found Trunk at the docks. He wasn't as visible as usual, but a few coins to a docker helped him ascertain his location. He had set up camp in an unused warehouse.

"Jack, my friend, you took a while to find me."

"Why are you hiding?"

"I like living."

"What's up, Trunk? Tell me."

"How much money did you bring?"

"For God's sake, Trunk. Is money all you think about? I'll try to help you."

"I've got valuable information. There's no gang called the Magpies. Someone made it up."

"Not extremely helpful," Jack commented.

"I was concerned with your interest in Benji Diamond; he's a friend and a longtime client. I decided to find Benji to see if he needed help."

"And you found him?" Jack asked.

"Of course," Trunk answered.

Jack shook his head in wonder at the young man's talents.

"Can you take me to him?"

"Sorry, Jack, too late."

Jack was filled with dread.

"You don't mean . . ."

"No, no. He was healthy when I saw him ride off on a horse, chasing the Velvet Viper gang," Trunk said. "Nasty bunch of men, them. I can't help him, but you probably can."

"You better start at the beginning," Jack said.

Trunk told Jack the steps he had taken to find Benji and about the chase. "Which is why I'm in hiding," he added.

Jack was thinking Lloyd's should hire Trunk to do investigations.

"I didn't dare get too close. The Vipers know who I am. I did what Benji did—I found a tree where I could hide way up in the limbs and keep an eye on the Vipers and Benji. He didn't come down that night to get food and water from Willie, so I stayed put. I stayed there all the next day. The Vipers were everywhere, but they seemed to be breaking up their camp. They had tents and everything. By the time it was dark, two wagons had arrived. When all the Vipers and all their stuff were loaded onto the carriages, they took off. I figured this was my chance to get to Benji. I climbed down and headed to the stables. Before I got there, I saw Benji mounted, galloping in the direction the Vipers took. I lost him, so I came back here and set up camp in this warehouse. I have a few friendly dockers screening my visitors in case the Vipers are after me."

"Trunk, this *is* valuable information. Do you know where they're headed?"

"Nope, sorry."

Jack was disappointed that Benji's whereabouts were unknown, but Trunk had given him critical information, so he paid him well. Feeling a little tired, still healing, he took a cab to the offices of the Sterling Union International Bank of London. Entering through the main door, he glanced around at the marble interior with its white stone pillars. The teller cages were made of polished walnut wood with black iron customer gates. The tellers were smartly dressed in white shirts, black bow ties, and black pants. They were all very proper and somber.

Jack walked to the desk next to the teller windows and presented his card. "Would you inquire whether Mr. Blake could see me?"

"Do you have an appointment?"

"No. Harley said to come by when I could. Please check now." It took effort to be friendly, and Jack didn't have it in him.

The attendant's face took on a look of someone eating a lemon, but he rose and headed up a flight of stairs.

A few minutes later, back in Harley's plush office, Jack and Harley sat in leather chairs before a fireplace. Harley's desk was on the opposite side of the office. *Mahogany*, Jack thought. It was highly polished and very neat. There was a wall of bookcases behind the desk. A set of double glass doors with lace curtains was beyond the fireplace, and Jack could see a balcony overlooking the city.

"Drink, Jack?" There was a small, tidy bar next to the fireplace.

He would usually pass, but he hadn't brought his elixir, and a drink sounded good. Besides, they were supposed to be cooperating to solve the Lloyd's problem. "I'll join you," Jack said.

"Have you had any success, Jack? I haven't heard from you since your assault."

"We've gathered a lot of facts, Harley, but I need a breakthrough. Benji was located, but he's now in parts unknown again. He's seeking Mrs. Hill by following the Velvet Vipers gang, who are also after Hill."

"That's not encouraging. What of Edie—Lady Black? Any leads?"

"I'm sure Henderson has her. We need to find her, but I don't have any information to guide me. I've established an information exchange with Detective Wells of the Metropolitan, and they're actively seeking Henderson, with all the police stations in the country alerted. I hope something comes of that."

"That's good," Harley said.

"How's it going with raising the money?" Jack asked.

"Not well. The Hill bust was a setback. I was planning on her assistance, and now the revelation that she's a suspected criminal increases the risk for the bank, and we won't be able to get her guarantee on the new money. I have Herbert working on an angle that might help. I'll get it done, just not sure how yet."

"Harley, can you help me understand something?"

"I'll try, Jack."

"The files on the *Ferret* theft report show that Henderson opened an account for Henderson and Company, Ship Brokers, at this bank."

"That's true, Jack." Harley took a sip of his whiskey. Jack did the same, looking into Harley's eyes.

"An account was also opened for Barnett Smith. That's an alias of Henderson's. How could someone open an account under an alias?"

Harley hesitated just a little. "I didn't know it was an alias then, Jack. I was presented with signed paperwork and deposit money."

"Was it a lot of money?" Jack asked carefully, studying Harley's face.

Harley looked calm and answered quickly. "Both accounts had substantial amounts."

"Where did the money come from, Harley?"

"They were transferred from accounts in the name of Minnie Rose."

Jack let that go for the moment. "Harley, Henderson and his partner Walker issued many credit letters on this bank to lease the ship and remodel and supply it at various ports throughout their voyage, all dishonored by the bank. Aren't you obligated to pay notes once accounts have secured them?"

"I think I'd better go get the paperwork so I can give you an accurate answer." He drained his whiskey, rose, and left the room.

Harley returned twenty minutes later, laid a folder on the table next to their chairs, went to the bar, and poured himself another whiskey. He turned to Jack and held up the bottle. Jack shook his head no—he'd barely touched his first glass. Harley sat down.

Jack took a sip and looked at Harley—questioning, waiting.

"Typically, what you say is true, the bank honors letters of credit. But in this case, the accounts were closed and the funds transferred out, legitimately, before any notes were known or presented. The bank knew nothing of the notes. They were all forged."

"Who closed the accounts, and where did the money go?" Now Harley looked nervous for the first time—his left eye twitched and his lips were tight. He opened the folder and reviewed the papers. He rubbed the back of his neck and looked at the floor.

"Jack, I didn't handle or know about that transaction."

He handed the folder to Jack.

It contained a power of attorney from James Henderson to Minnie Rose, a second from Minnie Rose to Mrs. Lillian Hill, and further paperwork for slips transferring the funds to the accounts of Mrs. Lillian Hill and Lady Edith Black at a bank in Melbourne, Australia.

CHAPTER 33

THE CASE ROOM

Jack was shocked by what he'd discovered in the meeting with Harley Blake. It was his understanding that banks guaranteed letters of credit at the time of issue, but if the notes based on the letter of credit were done after accounts were closed without any registered use of the credit letter, the bank might be liable. He would have to check. The bigger surprise was that the money was transferred to Mrs. Hill and Lady Black in Melbourne. He noted all of this on the wallpaper scrolls, but he needed to figure out what to make of it.

Jack and Johnny discussed their progress, or lack of it, as they added notes to the case-room map. The information from Trunk was compelling. Jack added a circle for the Velvet Vipers. "Trunk is afraid of them, but I promised him a big payday if he could find out where they're currently holed up."

"Why were they there to begin with?" Johnny asked.

"I assume they're after the diamonds, and they must think Mrs. Hill is the key to finding them. More importantly, they wouldn't know that connection without Henderson. If we find the Vipers, we find Henderson, Lady Black, and perhaps Benji. We might even find Mrs. Hill."

"And we might get killed in the process," Johnny said. "They scare me too."

"We must be careful, but this could be our breakthrough lead. So far, we have a lot of information, but only a little we can take action on. Solutions happen this way in cases. You gather a lot of apparently unimportant and sometimes unrelated information. Eventually, a detail reveals itself that leads to a solution."

"You always say that, but can you make it go faster?" Johnny said.

"Let's finish the notes and then decide what to do," Jack said. "Is there a Minnie Rose on your list of party attendees at the Hill mansion?"

Johnny checked his notes. "Yes! Almost all of them last year, and they stop in October. She's mentioned as a niece of Mrs. Hill."

Jack drew a circle for Minnie Rose and one for the Sterling Union International Bank accounts for Henderson and Smith with the details he'd obtained from Harley Blake. He drew a dotted line from Minnie Rose to Lady Black with a question mark. He added, "Blake is having problems raising funds for the syndicate without Mrs. Hill's money."

"I hadn't thought about that," Johnny said. "What happens if he can't?"

"I assume Lloyd's dissolves the syndicate, and all the investors, Fredrick included, lose their entire investments. Fredrick would certainly go broke. He might not survive it. We'd better find out where he is and visit him soon. In the meantime, I'll return to Detective Wells tomorrow and casually quiz him on the Vipers and find out if he has any new leads."

Looking over all the notes, Johnny said, "If we could tie the two block letter notes—the threat to Mr. Taylor and the information given to the Metropolitan on Mrs. Hill that caused the raid and her unveiling—we'd have something valuable."

"I'll try to bargain a little more with Detective Wells. I need to get a look at that note. Maybe there's something I can trade."

Jack figured Wells already knew, but he opened his conversation with Detective Wells the next day by telling him that the Velvet Vipers had been staking out the Hill mansion for days before the night of the raid. He didn't mention Benji or Trunk.

"We had a couple of bobbies watching from a distance," Wells said, "Except for trespass, the Vipers committed no crime, but we try to keep an eye on them."

"Do you know where they're headquartered?"

"They change locations frequently. They have one property in the East End, but it's been weeks since they've been there, so they're likely set up elsewhere now. If you find out . . ."

"I'll be sure to let you know."

"Jack, they're dangerous. You saw what happened to Mrs. Riley. And they do far worse. She was lucky. It would be best to involve us and not take them on yourself—for any reason."

"They may have custody of my lady friend, and Henderson may be involved."

"Do you think Henderson and the Vipers are working together?"

"I do, but I don't have any evidence."

"I have no leads on Henderson's whereabouts yet."

"Detective Wells, you've said that you wish something would break. I will share valuable information to help your efforts, but I need your support in return."

"I can't promise anything, Jack."

"If my information leads to the discovery of an individual you're seeking, I would like you to inform me immediately. I don't want this information to get out. We keep it between your team and us. And Detective, I need to be there if you go after him. It's important."

"Are you talking about Henderson?"

"No. And one last request. I need a look at the note card you received. It might be important to us both."

Without committing, Wells said, "What is it, Jack."

"The Russell Weaver you're seeking is Benji Diamond, and he didn't steal the diamonds in South Africa." Jack thought that he might have stolen them after that, but he wouldn't mention that. "He is following the Vipers to find Hill."

Wells showed Jack the note card about Mrs. Hill. It looked very similar to the Magpie note to Fredrick, but it provided no obvious clues.

"I appreciate the information on Benji Diamond." Wells escorted Jack to the entrance.

Jack and Johnny met in the case room and updated the map. Jack sat in his chair and stared at the data they had entered. He tried to push his concerns for Lady Black, whom he now called Edie, out of his mind. She had been missing many days now, and he was concerned that she might not be alive. He felt desperate to find a way to locate her. The Vipers seemed like the only lead. His thoughts wandered. *Mrs. Hill is hiding, Benji is chasing the Velvet Vipers, and Fredrick is hiding. The clock is ticking on the syndicate's survival, and here we sit. What am I missing? All lines directly or indirectly run back to Mrs. Hill. Why would anyone involved expose her unless it was the Vipers, and for what purpose?*

I can't think of a motive for anyone involved to implicate Mrs. Hill.

CHAPTER 34

LADY BLACK AND HENDERSON

Fear raced through Edie's body, as it did whenever she woke and remembered where she was. Once again, her breathing became rapid, and she was terrified that she was running out of air. She felt like she had been captive for many days now. She remembered sleeping and waking in the cramped space many times, but she'd lost count of how many. Her body felt numb, except for her legs, which were cramping. She flexed her muscles one at a time; she had to keep her strength. She had to think.

The hinged lid of the box had been opened at least once daily. A man in a cap, not always the same one, would provide her with a plate of food and a goatskin of water—never saying a word. She had a bedpan to use, but it was emptied when she was asleep. *How do they know when I'm sleeping?* she wondered. Using a bedpan lying down wasn't easy, but she managed. At least there was plenty of air. She lay there regulating her breathing and assessing her situation again.

Footsteps approached.

"Good morning, Minnie. Or should I address you as Lady Black now? Perhaps we know each other well enough for me to call you Edie. I trust you find your accommodations to your liking."

She immediately recognized the voice. "Henderson, *you bastard*, let me out of here, *now!*"

"How unladylike . . . more like Minnie than a lady."

"Henderson, *now*." Her body was tense, and heat raced through her.

"I have to settle in now and take care of my friends who have taken care of you. They'll be heading out to find your friends Hill and Diamond. Any guidance on their locations? It could save your life." Edie didn't answer. "The less you cooperate, the harder it will be for you." Edie gritted her teeth.

"I'll return, and when I do, I want answers. I want to know how to find Mrs. Hill. I want to know where Benji Diamond is. And most of all, I want to know about the diamonds. I want the money you took from the ship. And while you're at it, you can tell me how to find my trunk from the ship in Melbourne."

Over his shoulder, he offered a parting line: "If you don't cooperate, I would enjoy killing you."

It seemed like hours before Henderson returned. Edie planned on trying to bluff as best she could, but she didn't hold very many cards in her hand. Henderson opened the box lid, sat in a chair, and aimed a gun at Edie's head.

"Ready to talk, Lady Black?" He spoke the name in a mocking tone.

"If I tell you everything I know, will you let me go?"

"Of course," Henderson said.

I believe that! Edie thought cynically.

"Think about what happens if you don't give me all the details. I want those diamonds, and I know you know where they are. I watched you and Watkins in Cape Town, and I know you sent Benji off on a mission. You're in it together with Hill, I know it! I pieced it all together."

Edie's mind was racing. She was near panic, even as her body was shutting down from lack of movement. *I'm never going to convince him.* She had to buy time.

In a raspy voice, she said, "The money from the hotel was confiscated by the police and distributed to creditors at the court's order after your sentencing."

"That's not what I heard. The judge favored restoring the funds to you."

"He changed his mind when creditors filed claims to be paid for fraudulent notes." Edie's voice was shaking, but she continued.

"Rohwedder has the trunks safely stored," Edie said. "I told him to release yours when you requested."

"He's stopped responding to my correspondence. I think he may have absconded with the trunks."

She decided to try something. "He sent me a new contact address. It's with my luggage."

"And where is your luggage?"

"At the Connaught."

"What room?"

"Suite 212."

"I'll prepare a note for you to sign requesting release of your luggage to my partners."

Perhaps they'll get caught and arrested, Edie thought. But Henderson didn't leave yet.

"Tell me about Benji," he demanded.

"I don't know where Benji is. I tried to find him. We lost touch after he left the ship."

"You, Benji, and Watkins planned this diamond heist with Mrs. Hill, didn't you?"

"You give me too much credit," Edie said.

"What has the Cramer fellow discovered?"

"I don't know, Henderson. I only met him once, and your friends interrupted that."

"The diamonds?" Henderson repeated gruffly.

She continued to stall. "Mrs. Hill has the diamonds." She knew this wasn't true, but perhaps it would delay Henderson. "You have to take that up with her."

"And where is she?" he demanded, his voice seething.

"I don't know that either," Edie said, as calmly as she could. "She has your money and my money from the *Ferret* voyage. You've known her longer. Does she have hideaway houses?"

Henderson was quiet. He closed and locked the box lid and left.

As she lay there, Edie thought about what would come next. The schedule was predictable. Every day, she was fed by one of Henderson's goons, and then she slept. She was beginning to suspect that she was being fed a sedative in her food. The feeling of it starting to work was distinctive. At some point, her captors would return, open the lid, take the plate, exchange bedpans, and then lock her back up. She started planning.

After what felt like a few hours, Henderson came back. "I have your dinner, and I have a plan. You gave me an idea. If you're telling the truth, we need to find Mrs. Hill. She cares for you. You'll be my bait. You're going to help me find her."

"How will you do that?" she asked, stalling, as she stretched and flexed her muscles.

"I'm going to make you visible to her as our captive. I know all her properties. We'll visit, threaten to kill you if she doesn't cooperate. We'll have you both—and perhaps your lover Benji."

As his cronies had done, he unlocked the lid and lifted it, pointing a gun at Edie. That was a new touch. With his hand on her chest, he held her down; he put the gun into its holster. Edie cringed at the feeling of his flesh on her body.

He handed her a note. "Sign this." He took his gun out and held it to her temple, allowing her to sit up to sign the release. She placed it on the floor to her left, pulling her head away from the gun. "Don't be stupid," Henderson said. She signed the paper and returned it to Henderson. He again held her down and reached for the plate of food, placing it on her stomach. He tossed in a goatskin, closed the lid, and locked it.

As on other nights, the metal plate contained a quartered raw potato and cold pork. Edie couldn't tell whether the sedative was in the potato or the pork; she would eat neither. *Is the water safe?* she wondered. She hid the food under her torso, placed the plate on her stomach, and waited. Although she was parched, she avoided the water.

Henderson had the remaining Vipers split up—one to scout Hill properties with a list Henderson drew up, the remaining two to the Connaught to get Edie's luggage.

As the Vipers had done on previous nights, Henderson gave the sedatives enough time to work; he had upped the dose. He returned to the pigsty, opened the lid to the box, bent over, and reached for the plate.

Edie opened her eyes, reached up, grabbed his collar at his throat, and pulled him down with all her strength. He was much stronger, but he was caught off guard. His feet slipped on the damp hay and pig dung. His head fell toward Edie, and his belly came to rest on the edge of the box. With her left hand, Edie swung the metal plate with everything she had, catching Henderson with the edge of the plate and slicing a wide gash in his forehead. He jerked backward, grabbed his forehead, regained his footing, and stood as the blood gushed and ran into his eyes, blinding him.

Edie sprang to her knees; momentarily, her legs failed her. *I'll die if I fail!* Adrenalin rushed through her body. She balled her fists and swung a hard left and then a hard right into Henderson's groin. He screamed, grabbed his crotch, and bent over the box again. Edie stood in the box and kneed Henderson as hard as she could in the throat; he fell backward. She jumped from the box, but her legs crumpled, and she collapsed on the dung-covered floor. She rose to one knee, regaining her balance, then ran for the open side of the pigsty and into the muddy pen. A dozen pigs were lying down or walking around. She saw a stone water trough in the middle and at the far corner a gate. She ran for the gate, swung it open, and proceeded down a damp grassy slope toward a river she could see in the near distance. She looked over her shoulder; Henderson was standing in the pen, wiping blood from his eyes, looking for her. He spotted her and started in pursuit.

Edie saw a dock and a small wooden punt tied to one of its pilings. She couldn't hear footsteps behind her yet, but she pushed harder. Reaching the dock, she untied the punt and jumped in, pushing off against the piling.

Henderson had spied Edie running toward the river. He ran for the gate, still half blind with the blood running into his eyes; he failed to see the five-hundred-pound sow step in front of him. She took him down at both knees: he did a half flip, landing on his back in the mud and dung.

Henderson was angry and more than a little uncomfortable, covered with mud, dung, and blood. He slowly and painfully stood up. *How could I have let this happen? I should've shot her. I should've had more Vipers stay with me.* He was too late to chase after her; he needed a different plan. The old sow waddled back in front of him, probably expecting to be fed. Henderson kicked her in the belly, turned, and walked away.

The punt reached the current in the center of the river. The rushing water directed the bow downriver, propelling the punt forward. Edie found she was without a paddle or pole; she tried leaning over the bow and paddling with her hands, which did a little good but not much. She needed to get some distance in case there was another boat Henderson could use.

Edie was still in her dinner clothes from the night at Rules, although barefoot and without hosiery. She shed her dress and, wearing just her chemise, lowered herself into the water. It was invigorating. She kicked while hanging onto the stern of the punt until she had no strength left. Then she pulled herself back into the boat and collapsed to the floor. She held the sides of the punt with both hands and looked around. It was still twilight, and she looked upriver. She didn't see any boat in pursuit. She looked at the shore—it was lined with bushes and trees. She was making good speed. She expected it would be hard to follow her on foot. Her body tingled from the cold water; her circulation was being restored. She was exhausted, her limbs cramping from exertion after days of inactivity; she lay on her back on the bottom of the boat between the seats and let the current carry her. Luckily it was a warm evening. She saw the moon in the twilit sky, which turned darker as the sun fully set. Edie slept and then awoke to a night sky filled with stars; the shore was pitch dark all around her. She was moved by a sense of freedom and thought, *How beautiful.* She felt for the first time the enormity and mystery of the heavens. Then she realized she wasn't moving.

As the river turned east, a sandbar had formed near the eastern shore. The punt's bow was lodged on the outer edge of the sandbar, and a fallen tree trunk extended past the sand, its tip in the moving water.

Henderson knew she was headed downstream; he could be waiting anywhere. She stepped onto the sandbar; it was solid. She pushed the punt from the bow back into the water, intending to climb in when it could float with the current again. But it sprang backward. She slipped and fell into the water face-first, and the punt kept moving. She rose and stood in the shallow water. Stepping forward and reaching toward the punt, she hit a drop-off in the river bottom and was completely submerged. She couldn't swim but made it back to shallower water and stood. She watched as the punt caught the current, passed the fallen tree, and picked up speed. As the punt continued its journey toward the Thames, she remembered her dress was still in the boat.

CHAPTER 35

THE HILL MANSION

Johnny joined Jack at a table in the back of the dining room. Jenny saw them sitting together and pulled two beers and delivered them.

Jack smiled. "Thanks, Jenny. You're one step ahead of us."

"Always!" she replied, batting her eyelashes, then walked away.

Johnny turned to Jack and asked, "Where have you been all day?"

"I couldn't sleep again last night. I went to the case room and stared at the notes for hours until I fell asleep in my chair. I left early—went to Hyde Park and walked the rim path. I stopped at the stables and talked to Willie, got his take on the Vipers and Benji. On the night they all departed, he heard two Vipers talking near his stables. They said Cap Alf had instructed them to meet at the farm and split up from there. Two wagons and several mounted Vipers left, heading north. I checked out Benji's tree in the woods. The platform was still there. Then I walked around the mansion fence and said hello to the guard; there seemed to be only one. The gate was padlocked behind him, and there's a second padlocked gate on the park side. There are several buildings on the property."

"I sense trouble," Johnny said. "What are we doing?"

"Officially, breaking and entering," Jack replied.

"Oh dear," Johnny moaned. "The Hill mansion?"

"Yes. Everything seems to revolve around Mrs. Hill, and yet someone exposed her. We're looking for clues as to motive, her whereabouts, and any connection to the diamond heist. I'm sure there are clues the police haven't discovered somewhere in the Hill mansion, and we'll find them. Do you have black pants and a jacket?"

"Yes," Johnny said, rather meekly.

"Why don't you change into them and get your gun. I'll change and meet you."

Both men got dressed in black and then met in the case room. "I went shopping," Jack said. He unpacked two black hoods and gave one to Johnny. He unloaded two lanterns, two claw hammers, a coil of heavy rope, a set of wire cutters, and his pistol.

Since it wouldn't get dark until about nine, Jack and Johnny waited until eight-thirty and took a cab to the Primrose Hill and Regent's Park area. They walked casually along the footpaths to the residential streets of posh homes and gardens, eventually strolling past the gated entrance to the home of Mrs. Lillian Hill. Jack's jacket concealed the rope that was wrapped around his body from chest to waist, which was a little uncomfortable but manageable.

Walking down Park Street, opposite the mansion's gate, they nodded to the hired guard sitting in a chair in front of the gate to the property. He was smoking a pipe and relaxing at his duties. There didn't appear to be any dogs on the grounds, which had been a concern of Johnny's. They crossed the street and continued walking down Avenue Road. They entered Hyde Park, where they circled back on a footpath until they had a view of the rear of the Hill property. It lay about one hundred yards from the park. It was fully dark now. Jack left first; Johnny followed, keeping an eye out for pedestrians. Jack stepped off the footpath behind the Hill mansion and down a small embankment leading to a stand of sycamore and plane trees lining the boundary of Avenue Road and the park. They climbed up a steep embankment to face the black iron fence surrounding the Hill property. Jack uncoiled the rope under his jacket, tied a loop on one end, and quickly tossed it over the top of a picket. He pulled the loop tight. Next, Jack slung the strap of the canvas bag that held their supplies over a shoulder and pulled himself up the fence using the picket crossbars for toeholds. He jumped from the top to the grass inside the fence.

"Johnny," he whispered through the iron pickets, "when you get to the top, remove the loop and toss it down to me."

Johnny sighed, clearly uncomfortable.

Once Johnny was in, Jack curled the rope and put it in the bag. They stayed low and quietly walked to the back of one of the outbuildings.

"I'm curious about this carriage house," Jack whispered to Johnny. "It has doors on both ends and a path out the back gate leading to Avenue Road and the park. We'll start here."

The barn wasn't secured in any way, so they slowly slid one side of the barn doors open just wide enough to wedge in sideways. They closed the door, and Johnny lit his lantern, keeping the flame low. The barn had space for three carriages; two were missing. There was also an attached stable and tack room, which showed signs of recent use but was currently empty.

The remaining carriage faced the carriage house's front door, and the two missing carriages would have had direct access to the rear doors.

The tack room and stables were one step up. Jack began by examining the wooden floor of the tack room, then the stables themselves. The carriage room had a dirt floor. There was a corridor between the stables and the back doors of the carriage room. It had tack, keys, and lanterns hanging on the wall and a door at the back. The grain bin looked oversized to Jack, so he looked closer. It had two sections: one nearly full of oats, the other empty and very clean. Examining the divider, he recognized it was sectional and installed in grooves so that you could remove the boards to make one bin. Leaning in, balancing on the rim with his waist, he fiddled with the floor panels; they were loose. There was a gap at the front where he inserted his fingers and pulled up. The panel lifted on concealed hinges, and he leaned it against the back of the grain box. He shone his lantern over the opening below the hinged panel, revealing a ladder.

Jack walked over to where Johnny was examining the tack room. "I've found something."

They returned to the grain bin. Casting his light around, Jack spotted two paraffin lamps and lighting sticks hanging on the wall. They looked at each other.

"Must be an escape route," Johnny said.

Jack grunted. "Highly likely, and a way people can come and go undetected, provided it leads to the mansion."

"After you," Johnny said.

They left one lantern burning very low and hung it on a wall hook over the bin in case they needed light for their return. Extinguishing the second lantern, they climbed the ladder, and Johnny lit the paraffin lamps with a spark stick. The tunnel was quite broad, with wooden beams and wood-paneled walls. The floor was packed earth.

"Quite elaborate!" Jack exclaimed.

The tunnel didn't take them directly to the mansion but to a size-able room, perhaps sixty or eighty feet from the carriage house, with a desk, a vent, and a shaft, presumably for fresh air. There were several chests, each open and empty. The floor also had indent marks where other chests or trunks had been placed. Behind the desk were shelves, presumably for books or recordkeeping, now empty. A gas lantern hung on the wall by the desk. Johnny took it down and lit it with a fire stick. They extinguished the paraffin lamps. A metal ladder was secured to the wall. Jack estimated it was at least two floors tall.

"Johnny, check the walls for hiding spaces. I'll check the desk."

The drawers were empty, so he removed them and found in the base beneath the drawers a small notebook, several crumpled invoices, two banknotes, and one gold coin of foreign origin. He put everything in his pocket except the notebook, which he opened and studied. It had pages listing one-word descriptions and currency amounts with dates and two sets of initials next to each. He pocketed it to review later.

They stared at the ladder. At the top was a double door flush with the top of the ladder.

"We should go one at a time," said Jack. "There's no space for standing up there." He very cautiously climbed the rungs.

Reaching the top, he studied the door. There was a square recess in the seam where the two doors met. Inside the cavity was a verti-cal metal rod. There were no door handles. He pushed the rod up, down, left, and nothing happened. But when he pushed it right, the rod movement activated a mechanism that pulled both doors back a couple of inches, then sideways into the walls that housed them. *Ingenious,* Jack thought. The opening revealed a landing about four feet deep with a solid painted wall at the back of the flooring and open space to the left and right. *This has to be a false wall,* he deduced. *Likely the entire rear of the building is fake.* The wall in front of him had no visible means of moving, no door handle or hinges. It was about five feet wide. He signaled Johnny to come up. Reluctantly, Johnny did.

The two men stood in front of the blank wall. "It doesn't seem to have an opening," Jack said.

"The space to the left and right is all full of boxes, obviously not found by the police. It must not have been important enough to evacuate when the trunks and treasures were removed below. There has to be more."

"I hope it's not booby-trapped," Johnny said.

"The space serves no other purpose," Jack said. "It must open somehow." Pushing didn't budge the wall on either side. He felt around the perimeter for a latch or release mechanism. But there was nothing and no gap of any kind.

"Let's think this through, Johnny. If it's an escape route, the opening probably wants to come toward us and close easily. If that's a treasure room down below, they would want to deceive anybody looking for a hidden door on the other side of this wall. It's the only painted surface here. Why?"

Jack went to the wall again, tracing his fingers from the painted center to the floor, then along the floor toward the ladder. He grasped the board on the edge of the landing and pulled. It moved about two inches. There was a pull ring in the gap between where two boards abutted the wall. Jack pulled the ring; the bolts on both sides of the wall could be heard moving, and the wall pivoted open. It was hinged in the middle, top, and bottom and provided an opening on each side. They looked at each other. "Clever!" Johnny said. "You first," he added, looking toward the opening. "In case it is booby-trapped."

Jack walked ahead and into the back of a dressing-room closet.

There was a mirror on the wall to the left of the door, and shelves ran down the back wall about ten feet, filled with hatboxes and shoes. Hanging rods ran down the middle, filled with hanging clothes and bags. Both sides of the revolving wall were identical; a touch and slight push swung the large door closed in either direction. Johnny pushed it closed with two fingers. The bolts reengaged. The vertical seams were identical to the remainder of the wall, giving no hint of a door.

"Hope we can find the inside release," Jack said. "The trick will be to find the pull ring on the closet side, but we know it exists."

Johnny shivered.

They stepped out through the hanging array of ladies' clothing and into a beautifully decorated bedroom with a small couch, two wing chairs, a serving table, a desk, and a large canopy bed with a lace tester. Several oil paintings hung on the walls. The wall with the closet was hung with decorative lace and tapestries. The closet behind the wall ran the entire length of the room; it would be hard for anyone to detect that a false wall existed.

Jack assumed the mechanism for the door would want to be in a straight line from the center of the door to facilitate the pulling of the wire to release the bolts. The door was spring-operated to open when the bolts were released. The center led to the seating area, and they found the access board beneath the serving table in front of the couch. Jack reached below the serving table and fiddled with a couple of boards until one long board slid back two inches, with the rear end sliding into the wall behind the couch, revealing the pull ring under the serving table. He pulled and heard the hidden door open. He slid the board back into place.

"Johnny, Mrs. Hill may not have been here when the raid occurred, but we don't know that for sure, and whoever was here at the time had to leave in a hurry. We're likely to find something somewhere in the house. I expect they cleared out all the goods in the treasure room below before the bust. I'll inspect this room. Will you check other rooms to see if there is something we should look at, like an office or safe? Keep the light low, and don't get lost."

Johnny nodded in reply, relit one of the paraffin lamps, and left the bedroom.

Jack checked pockets and handbags in the closet but found nothing. Removing paintings, he looked at the back of the canvases and inspected the wall for a safe. He again removed desk drawers one by one and had some luck with the center drawer. Attached to the bottom of the drawer was another small booklet with a series of letters and numbers in blocks of four, with words next to them. He put it in his pocket.

Johnny entered a library. It had three walls of books to the ceiling, with a sliding library ladder. Bookshelves along the back wall framed a double window looking out over the rear of the property. There was a leather couch and chair, and wall-mounted gas lights extended into the room.

There was a dictionary stand, but it contained a sketchbook instead of a dictionary. Johnny saw beautifully drawn pencil sketches of buildings, landscapes, and farm animals.

Where do I begin? he thought.

He looked to see if a safe could be concealed behind the cases or the books and did a quick walk along the three walls. He felt the tops of book pages to see if any of the books were fake and might be hiding places. The floor-level books revealed nothing.

He climbed the ladder. Nothing. He climbed down the ladder, slid it five feet along the bookcase, and climbed again.

Something caught his attention. He glanced out the windows and saw movement: several figures were preparing to climb the fence behind the carriage barn. He couldn't tell if they were police, but the police probably wouldn't be climbing the fence.

"Damnation!"

He climbed down quickly and headed for the door. On a whim, he grabbed the sketchbook, balancing the heavy book in his free hand. He ran down the hallway back toward the bedroom. He tripped, the lantern smashed, and the paraffin oil spilled. It ignited. He dropped the book and pulled a wall hanging off the wall, tossing it over the flame, extinguishing the fire. The flame had singed the book, but just a little. He started to run again, then realized the wall hanging had concealed a safe. The door of the safe was not fully closed; it was mostly empty except for one crumpled piece of paper. He grabbed it, picked up the book, and ran to Jack in the dark.

"There are men in the garden," he said aloud. "We've got to hide or get out of here."

"We left the grain bin open and our lanterns on the floor," Jack said.

"They may not be coming to the carriage house," Johnny said.

"We can't chance it. Let's go."

They stepped back into the secret passage room, swinging the wall door shut. They started down the ladder; a slight touch of the concealed doors closed them. They grabbed the wall lantern they had left burning over the desk and ran full speed down the passageway toward the stable. Reaching the area before the new visitors arrived, they climbed up the ladder, closed the trapdoor in the grain bin, lowered the lid, removed the hanging lantern, and sought hiding places in the stables. Jack figured that whoever the men were, they were there for a reason and not to get hay for the horses. They put the lanterns aside and quickly rearranged hay bales into a fort, with their bodies in the middle, covered on all sides. Jack had his pistol if it came to that. Johnny had forgotten to get his when he changed. "They might not even enter the carriage house," Johnny said again, his voice shrill. But they did.

Crouching down and hidden by the hay bales, they couldn't see the new visitors but could hear them. From the footsteps, Jack calculated five individuals. They listened.

"Henderson said there were two trunks of valuables that Hill kept for him and his Lady Black friend. They're hidden in pits under the floorboards of stalls six and nine."

"Are they numbered?" a man asked.

"Yes, Cap Alf. They have plaques with numbers."

God, what stall are we in? Jack wondered.

But no one came into their stall. They could hear rustlings, the rattle of wooden planks, and more whispering.

"Got one," someone said.

"Got the other one," Jack and Johnny heard.

"Let's look!" the man they were calling Cap Alf said. Jack and Johnny could hear the men examining the contents of the trunks.

"Cash and gold!" Alf said. "This will more than cover Henderson's debt to us. Lock them up, and let's get out of here. Just in case, check for loose boards in the other stalls."

Jack and Johnny tensed. Jack held his gun at the ready. Someone entered their stall but didn't touch the hay bales; he just checked the floorboards in the center and left.

"It was worth a try," Alf said. "Two of you at a time, take the crates to the wagons, one trunk to each wagon, and cover them with hay. Depart at two-minute intervals. I'll follow in my carriage in two more minutes. Take the same route back into the park and out to the ring road, but stay a distance away from each other in case of any trouble. We must take these back to the farm now. If you're detected by the guard or anyone else, make a run for it, but don't lead anyone to the farm. The key to the gate is on the wall there; leave it open."

"I need more hay," one of the Vipers said, entering Jack and Johnny's stall. He grabbed two bales, exposing Jack and Johnny sitting there, mouths open, eyes wide, and gun pointing. The Viper turned and headed for the exit with the bales in his arms, never looking, never seeing them.

Four had left. *Could Cap Alf be here alone?* Jack wondered. Very slowly, he stood up and, in a breathless moment, stepped out of the stall and pointed his gun at the man's head. Alf turned, surprised, and stared at Jack.

"Jack Cramer and Johnny Riley, how convenient."

"Put your hands up. Johnny, get the rope. We'll tie him up. If he moves, I'll put a bullet between his eyes."

Johnny turned and hesitated. "Ja—Jack," he managed to stammer, "new plan."

"Cramer, I'd drop the gun if I were you," Cap Alf said.

Two Vipers had stepped in from the corridor and had rifles pointed at Jack and Johnny.

"I always travel with bodyguards, Cramer. You should try it."

Alf took a rifle from one of the men. "Tie their hands behind them and tie their feet, then tie each standing against a stable post."

Alf found a coil of thin wire and wire cutters in the tack room; he cut two strips and handed them to one of the Vipers. "Secure this tight around their necks and around the post. If they move too much, they'll slit their throats."

Cap Alf leaned into Jack's face. "I won't kill you now; I'll leave it to Henderson. He has your lady friend. We want the diamonds. If you want to save her, you should help us find them. We know Benji Diamond has them. Do you want to tell us how to find him?"

Jack felt beads of sweat forming on his lips and forehead. His voice trembled. "We don't know."

"How about Mrs. Hill?" Cap Alf asked.

"Not her either."

"Not much of an investigator, Cramer."

"Guess not," Jack replied, trying to calm himself.

"Cap Sam, go to the East End warehouse. Get a couple of other men and a body box."

Johnny shuddered when he heard the words *body box*.

Cap Alf continued, "Bring our hearse wagon. That way, we can safely transport these two fine investigators through the streets of London to the farm."

Cap Sam took off, jogging down the corridor to the door.

Alf turned his attention back to Jack again as he leaned into his face. Looking into his eyes, Jack felt the evil that lived there.

"Let's go," Cap Alf said to the other Viper.

Once they left, the stables were pitch dark. "You all right, Johnny?" Jack asked.

"Just scared. How do we get out of this mess? We'll kill ourselves trying to get untied."

"Stay calm. We'll find a way. They want us alive to help find the diamonds. We must wait for them to return for us and look for an opportunity."

"I don't know, Jack."

They were quiet for a while; the sound of the mice, or worse, rats, increased as time passed. Dread replaced fear. Johnny had a sour taste in his mouth and was having difficulty breathing.

"Johnny, did you hear that?"

"What?"

"There it is again."

Jack could hear movement outside the building, then the door opening. Jack saw the movement of a light coming toward them. *Could the Viper be back?*

A stranger entered the stable from the aisle; he carried a lantern. He assessed the situation. "Don't move or talk until I get those wires undone." He went behind Jack, carefully untwisted the wire, and removed it from his throat, then did the same for Johnny.

"Thank you," Johnny said. The man untied Johnny first. Jack seemed in better shape to wait. When he finished, he took the rope that tied Johnny and said, "You untie Jack, I'll be back. I can make my way without the lantern." Johnny untied Jack.

"Who was that?" Johnny asked.

"I can guess," Jack said.

The man returned, pushing a Viper with hands tied behind him. "I clobbered him when he ran out alone. I pulled him around the side of the building and waited."

"Face down, Sam," the man said. Sam dropped to the floor.

He held out his hand to Jack. "I'm Benji Diamond." He reached to shake Johnny's hand as well.

"How did you know we were here?" Johnny asked.

"I didn't know you were here at first. I've been following the Vipers for several days, hoping they would lead me to Edie Black and Mrs. Hill."

"Trunk told me you were watching the mansion," Jack said.

"That boy has a bright future ahead of him," Benji said, smiling, "or a long sentence. I borrowed a horse from the stable when they broke camp and followed one group of them when they split up. I followed the wrong group—that's why I'm here."

"Meantime, they're looking for you. They think *you* have the diamonds."

"When you're being tracked, the best place to hide is tracking the trackers," Benji said, once again smiling. "I don't have the diamonds, never have. I was disappointed that I wasn't led to their current hideout. I heard them say it was a farm. I might find Edie and Mrs. Hill there."

"Edie, yes, but not Hill," Jack said.

"I think I heard Cap Alf saying Henderson was there. Is that correct?"

"That's what he said. How did you hear?" Jack asked.

"I followed the gang and waited until they were all in here. I climbed the fence, leaving my horse tied. I lay on the ground by the carriage doors back there. There was enough of a gap, so when I looked, I could see what they were doing but not hear what they said. When I placed an ear up to the gap, I could hear but not see. I did a little of both."

Jack nodded in appreciation. "We're truly thankful that you were here to help us."

"That just happened. But I could use some help. Shall we work together to find Edie, Henderson, and Hill?"

"I think we should," Johnny said, relieved to have another party for protection.

"I do as well," Jack said. "Johnny, is there a way we can house Benji at the inn without anyone knowing . . . and hide a hostage for a little while?"

"I'll have to involve Jenny, but she'll keep it quiet. There are rooms in the attic that used to be for live-in help. We could make them useable. There's a back staircase."

"How many rooms?" Jack asked.

"Five."

"Perfect," Jack said. "The Vipers may come looking for us and possibly Sam here. I suggest we go undercover. We can move the case room to the attic, and perhaps Jenny can quietly sneak us food, or we can raid the kitchen at night. It won't be long—things are moving quickly now."

They gagged Sam and blindfolded him.

"Benji, can your horse pull this carriage? It's rigged for two horses."

"We can make it work. Poor mare—she's worked hard. She'll need a reward."

"Can be arranged," Johnny said.

Benji left to retrieve his horse. Jack and Johnny escorted Cap Sam down to the carriage and had him lie face down in the footwell of the passenger compartment. They waited for Benji.

"Drat!" Johnny said. "I left some things I found in the house behind in the rush, there in the treasure room."

He took a lantern, returned to the grain bin, opened the trap door, and climbed down the ladder. He found the sketchbook in the treasure room on the floor, slightly damaged. Johnny had placed the crumpled paper from the safe inside the book like a bookmark. He rejoined Jack and Cap Sam just as Benji walked his horse back to the carriage house.

CHAPTER 36

VERN AND RACHEL

After losing the punt, Edie had no choice but to venture inland. The riverside growth contained vines and thornbushes, nearly impossible to walk through in her bare feet. She forced her way through the dense bushes and trees lining the river. It was tough going—her bare feet stepping on broken branches and her bare arms hacking a path through the thorny undergrowth. The only light came from the moon and stars. She reached a clearing that appeared to be fallow farmland. She trudged forward through the hard soil toward a small knoll at the end of the overgrown furrows. She could see a light in the distance and headed toward it, praying she wouldn't regret it.

Edie pressed her back against the rough boards on the side of the farmhouse. Only one window had light showing. She carefully leaned forward and turned her head to peer into the space. She saw a short lady with her back to the window, bent over and elderly. The lady removed two dinner plates from the table, so at least one other person was in the house. It seemed late for dinner. Edie pulled her head back and waited. Her bare feet hurt, and she knew they were bleeding. Her thighs itched more than hurt. She peeked around the side of the window again, and this time, she made eye contact with the woman. Startled, the woman dropped one of the dishes. It bounced on the wooden floor. A young lady, probably in her late teens, much taller than the older woman, with shaggy blond hair, raced into the kitchen. Knowing she'd been discovered, Edie walked past the window around the corner of the house, up two steps, and knocked on the door. The older woman had also made her way to the door and opened it wide. She looked up at Edie's face.

"Who have we here?" she asked.

Edie hesitated. *Who am I at the moment?* She decided. "I'm Edie Black."

"Well, Edie Black! What in hell are you doing at my door, in the middle of nowhere, mostly naked and barefoot, peeking in my window?"

The younger lady stood behind the elder one—Edie assumed they were mother and daughter. She was dressed in barn clothes and boots and had grabbed a broom to clean the floor or to use as a weapon.

"I escaped captivity upriver and got away in a punt, which I lost on the river after striking the sandbar. I need help."

The pair stared at the stranger, standing at their door in her underwear. The older woman raised her eyebrows, thought for a second, and said, "It's as likely a story as any other, and you certainly aren't hiding any weapon. Wait there a minute." She backed away, grabbed rags from a box next to the stove, and spread them on the floor before Edie.

"Your feet are bleeding. Step on these and come in," she said. "My name's Vern, and this is my granddaughter, Rachel." Rachel nodded shyly, then returned to staring at Edie but didn't put the broom down.

Vern put another cloth on the floor and walked Edie to a wooden chair. She ladled a pan of water out of a barrel next to the stove and added hot water from a kettle. She dropped a clean cloth into the water and set it at Edie's feet.

"You capable of cleaning yourself?" Vern asked.

"Yes," Edie said.

"You don't look like you're in any shape to harm us, but if you're playing tricks on us, know that we have a gun and know how to use it. We don't get company here. We're not trusting of strangers."

"I'm sorry for imposing. I had no choice. I must return to London, away from the men holding me prisoner. I need clothing, sleep, food, and a ride to the nearest town. I can pay. I don't have money on me, that's obvious, but I do in London."

"I don't want any of your money. God must have sent you our way. I trust you'll not take advantage. Are you a God-fearing woman?"

"No," Edie answered. "I'm a people-fearing person. I find it more practical. But I do need your help."

Vern stared at her, narrowing her eyes and studying Edie's face; she set her mouth and nodded.

Vern said, "You're too big to fit any of our clothes. I'll fetch some of my late husband's garments to cover you up."

The late husband explains the untended fields I walked through to get here, Edie thought.

The water was clean, so Edie took the cloth and washed her face and hands. She put her hands in the water, ran wet fingers through her hair, and washed her hips and legs. Finally, she put her feet in the basin. Streaks of red ran into the water as dirt fell from her feet. She had a few deep cuts that would need bandaging.

Vern returned with a set of folded clothing and sat it on a chair by the table. Rachel spread sawdust on the liquid spilled on the floor, swept it up, opened the stove door, and dumped the mixture onto the coals.

Vern had also brought a box of torn cloth, and she knelt before Edie. "Rachel, bring me one of Gramp's beers from the shed and the tin of boar fat."

Rachel had yet to say a word. She left and returned in a few minutes. Vern pried off the cap of the warm beer. Edie could smell the yeast—she was hoping for a sip, but instead, Vern lifted one of Edie's feet and carefully poured beer into each of the deeper, bleeding cuts. She then smeared foul-smelling boar fat on each cut with her fingers.

"You can start telling me your story while I finish this, then you can get dressed, and I'll get you some food." She wrapped Edie's foot in the cloth strips and sealed the edge of the bandage with a little more grease, then tied a clean strip around her ankle and wrapped her foot to secure the dressing.

"You haven't started talking yet," Vern said. "Give me your other foot."

Edie began. "I don't know how to start, but I've been captive, sealed in a box in a pigsty for I don't know how long. I was kidnapped in

London by criminals hired by someone I once knew, and I was brought to the pig farm upriver."

"Farmer Gray couldn't have done this. You could have squashed him with one hand, and he's no criminal."

"I didn't see the farmer. The kidnapping was set up by a man I had dealings with for a few years. He tried to force me to help him."

"Help him what?" Vern asked.

"Find people I know. He wants to hurt them."

"Did he take your clothes?" Vern asked.

"No, I took off my dress to get in the water and kick the punt—I didn't have a paddle or pole, and I was afraid he was pursuing me. The dress was still in the punt when it floated away."

Vern walked to the chair with the clothing. Even though the weather was warm, she handed Edie an oversized flannel shirt. "This is big enough for a nightgown. Put it on. It'll come to your knees. My Clyde was a big, handsome man. Then give me your chemise. Rachel will wash it."

"Grandma?" Rachel managed. It was her first word since Edie's arrival.

Vern continued to focus on Edie. "I believe you're sincere, and you are safe with us. I have some venison stew left from our dinner. I'll stoke the fire and heat it. It's cooked in beer—do you mind?"

"Not at all," Edie said. "Can you spare one to drink?"

"My Clyde would be proud to have you enjoy it. We have many bottles. Rachel can fetch another from the shed. Rachel and I don't like it much, except for cooking and wounds. There's no farmhand here anymore, so you can use his bunk room behind the kitchen stove. Tomorrow you can try on the rest of the clothes, although there isn't much else to choose from. We'll have breakfast in the morning and discuss what we'll do with you."

Edie nodded. She ate a small bowl of stew and some excellent bread Vern had baked, washing it down with the beer. She could barely muster a thank you as the exhaustion of her frantic journey settled on her.

At first, Edie slept fitfully, worried about Henderson showing up at the door. She didn't know how far she had come down the river. Still, she was so exhausted that, nestled in the comfortable bed, she finally fell into a deep sleep. In the morning, the chair by the door held her clean, dry, folded underwear and the remaining clothes Vern had gathered the night before. There was a fresh basin of wash water and a glass of water to drink. She washed up and put on her chemise, rebuttoned the flannel shirt she had worn to bed, and slipped on a pair of work overalls that were two times bigger than she was. Thankfully, they had shoulder straps to keep them up. Vern had thought to include a smaller belt, probably Vern's, that Edie strapped around her waist and pulled tight. She rolled the pant legs up. The wool socks were huge, but they fit over the bandages; she rolled the tops over. Vern had provided a large pair of boots—too big, but they would do. Edie couldn't imagine how she looked. She opened her bedroom door and stepped into the kitchen.

"Good morning, your ladyship!"

Edie's heart leaped into her throat; Henderson's voice nearly caused her to faint. In the middle of the kitchen floor, Vern was bound to a chair and gagged, her head listing to one side. *Unconscious or dead?* Edie thought, horrified. Henderson was covered with mud and muck, his hair greasy and flattened to his head with dried blood. His eyes were red and droopy; he hadn't had a comfortable night.

"You should have kept going," Henderson said. "I spent the night searching for you. I found the boat tangled in some trees downriver. I worked my way back here, property by property; there aren't many. You looked so peaceful sleeping. I thought I'd wait for your grand entrance, and you look spectacular, I might add."

"Is she dead?" Edie asked. *I wonder where Rachel is.*

"Out cold, I think," Henderson answered. "I try not to kill too many people, but, in your case, I could make an exception. Except you're my only connection to my missing money and the diamonds."

Henderson shoved Edie into another chair with one hand, holding the pistol at her face with the other. He wrapped a rope around her upper body, still holding the gun at her head, then moved behind the chair to tie her hands.

"Don't move, or I'll use it!" he said. He set the gun on the floor and tied her tightly.

Stalling for time, she said, "Henderson, that's too tight. I'll die from lack of circulation."

He loosened the ropes a bit.

Where the hell is Rachel? Edie wondered.

Vern stirred. Henderson moved to her and lifted the butt of the pistol, poised to conk her on the head.

"Don't hurt her further," Edie said. "I'll tell you as much as I know."

Henderson smiled and lowered his pistol. He looked Edie in the eyes. "I'm waiting."

"I trust you got my luggage and the address of Rohwedder."

"You're stalling. I want to know about the diamonds."

"You must believe me—I don't know."

"I'm a hunted man. I can't show myself in Australia or London. I don't mind adding your death to my crimes. If you want to live, I want the diamonds. I saw you orchestrate the transport with Watkins and Benji. I followed you to your cozy dinner with the captain. I saw Benji sitting at the bar. You were all in it from the beginning."

Edie was about to answer as best she could when a shovel slammed into the side of Henderson's head.

Edie hadn't seen Rachel enter the kitchen from the open door behind Henderson. *He isn't having a comfortable week at all!* she thought.

"Oh, Rachel! I'm so glad to see you! I thought we were all done for."

"He showed up an hour ago," Rachel said. Gram was awake—she hasn't slept well since Gramp died. I was asleep in my room and heard the commotion. I thought it was you at first, then I heard Gram's voice raised and angry."

"I'm surprised I didn't hear anything," Edie said.

"You were out cold, snoring loudly, when I brought the clothes in. I knew I couldn't win a fight with him and couldn't get to your room undetected, so I went to the barn and hitched up my horse Sally to our buckboard in case we needed an escape. I got this shovel as a weapon. I hid and watched, waiting for the right moment. I was afraid for Gram, but I saw her move a few times through the knothole in the wall over there. Oh, and I set his horse free with a little switch to the flank."

Edie was impressed.

"Rachel, please untie me, and let's tie him securely. I have a plan."

CHAPTER 37

CAP SAM

"Where's the farm where Lady Black is being held?" Jack asked Cap Sam for the tenth time.

Cap Sam remained silent.

"Tell us, Sam, and we'll assure your safety."

Nothing.

Johnny placed a plate of food and water on the table before Sam but didn't untie him. "If you ever want to eat again, I suggest you talk to us."

Cap Sam relented a little. "She's as good as dead. She's not cooperating."

"Where *is* the farm?" Jack asked, leaning into Cap Sam's face.

"I don't know where the farm is. I rode in the wagon. I don't know the towns."

They had questioned him for over two hours. He was finally speaking. They decided to explore their options. Jack and Benji went down the hall to the new case room, and Johnny kept guard while Cap Sam was allowed to eat.

"Do you think he's lying?" Jack asked Benji.

"I don't know. I'm beginning to think it's hopeless. If I had the diamonds, I'd trade them for Edie."

"I know you would," Jack said. "Let's review what we know and figure out how to find her. We can't hole up here long; I'm afraid the Vipers will suspect we're here and come calling. We can't babysit our boy Sam much longer. If we don't get some information, we have to move on."

"We can't let him go. He'll lead the Vipers right back to us!"

"Or he could lead *us* to the farm," Jack said.

"Perhaps," Benji said, "but if they get Sam back, they might not take him to the farm; they might just kill him."

Jack changed the subject.

"Did Mrs. Hill arrange the diamond robbery?" he asked.

"I suspect she did, but I'm not sure," Benji replied, shaking his head. "I assume she's involved in the theft, but I knew nothing of a robbery at the time, and to my knowledge, neither did Edie."

Jack remembered the notebooks he'd found. He went to the table where he'd emptied his pockets and picked up the notebooks. One was full of dates and financial amounts. It was like a deposit book; each entry had two sets of initials. Most of them were HF and FT. He suspected FT was Fredrick Taylor. The names weren't of people, but they could be places or properties.

Johnny had tied Sam to the chair again, and he came to join them.

"Johnny, do you remember any name on the investor list with the initials HF?"

Johnny shrugged. "I can't remember any, Jack."

"How about you, Benji? Do you recall any HF?"

"No," Benji replied.

They reviewed the list of Mrs. Hill's function attendees from the scrolls on the wall.

"No luck there," Johnny said.

Picking up the other notebook, Jack leafed through it. It appeared to be a codebook to disguise communications. He showed it to Benji and asked if he knew anything about it.

"Edie and Mrs. Hill only communicated in code. Looking at these blocks of numbers and letters, I assume it's a guide to the code they used. We'd need time to study and break it, and a sample message would be useful." Benji shook his head. "I don't see the connection, just looking at it."

"Do you think Fredrick Taylor knew of Mrs. Hill's illegal activities?" Johnny asked.

"I would think he had to know," Jack said.

Johnny picked up the crumpled paper he had removed from the safe. "This seems to be a bill of sale for a property with a title passing from Henry Fitzgerald to Mrs. Lillian Hill."

"That's our HF!" Jack said. "What's the address?"

"It's not the farm, unfortunately," Johnny said. "It's a London address," he read the address.

"That's the address of my stall warehouse!" Benji said.

Benji looked at the evidence table, picked up the sketchbook, and began to look through it. "This is interesting," he said. "Here is a sketch of my farm. I consider it mine, but Mrs. Hill owns it. There are initials at the bottom in pencil: LH and HB."

"Lillian Hill and Harley Blake?" Jack guessed.

Benji flipped through additional pages. "Here's the warehouse, initialed HF and LH."

"This must be a pictorial record documenting Mrs. Hill's property investments," Johnny said. "Perhaps the farm where Henderson has Edie held is in here."

Jack took the book and looked through the sketches. "There are several farms, a couple of mansions, and some commercial buildings," he said. "Several have FT initials. If that's indeed Fredrick Taylor, he may not be as broke as he professed."

"I have an idea," Johnny said, taking the book and heading to the prison room.

"Sam, you don't know the farm's location, but you were there, right?"

"That's right."

"Would you recognize it if you saw it?"

"I would," Sam said.

"Do you want to get out of here?"

"Yes," Sam said.

"I'm going to show you sketches of several farms. I want you to point out which one you were at with Henderson and Lady Black. We know some of these farms, so we'll know if you lie."

Sam looked surprised. His muscles stiffened.

Jack started with Benji's farm. Sam shook his head no. *A good start*, Jack thought. He showed Sam three more sketches; there were a couple left. "That's it," Sam said.

"You're sure?" Jack said.

"Yes," he said, slightly animated. "It shows those damn smelly pigs."

"What direction did you travel?"

"North then west."

"We'll be back for you."

"You said I could go."

"I said I would get you out of here, and I will."

The initials on the sketch were LH and HF. It was noticeable that FT had been erased and replaced by HF.

The three men gathered in the case room.

"I'm going to suggest we split up to cover more ground," said Jack. "With Sam's identification of the farm, we have a hot lead on Henderson and Edie. We have to pursue that quickly. We need to identify where the farm is, but we have a direction, and it's a pig farm. We also have to find a diamond thief and the diamonds if possible. Let's look at the evidence quickly before heading out. We suspect Mrs. Hill arranged the diamond theft, but we need proof. She's in hiding, probably at one of these properties." He put his hand on the sketchbook. "We know she doesn't have the diamonds. We also know Fredrick and his syndicate are in trouble with Lloyd's, and he's also in hiding. I'll find out where today because he also knows the address of the pig farm."

"How are you going to do that?" Benji asked.

"I'm going to threaten Herbert Archer."

"We know," Jack continued, "that Harley Blake has promised to bail out the syndicate but is having trouble assembling enough money without Mrs. Hill."

"And we know someone ratted on Mrs. Hill, taking her out of the funding picture and shutting down her illegal gang," Johnny added. "Who would benefit from that?"

"Right," Jack said. "Why would anyone here"—he pointed at the scrolls—"have the motive to do that? If we knew that, I think many things would become clearer."

"Fredrick was close to Hill. Perhaps he can provide a clue to a motive and her whereabouts," Johnny said.

"I hope," Jack said.

"I'd still like to know more about the note cards," Johnny said. "I think there's a clue there. Someone is threatening Fredrick to keep us from searching for the diamonds. The reveal about Mrs. Hill's illegal activities probably came from the same party. The motive may have been to get her locked away to protect whoever stole the diamonds the second time."

He paused, then said, "I'll turn our friend Sam in for assault and alleged kidnapping. It may not hold, but we're done with him. Then I'll go to Archer and meet you back here."

"You might want to do that without mentioning where we are," Johnny said.

"And without mentioning me," Benji said.

Jack scratched his cheek while thinking. He had to protect Benji and all of them; breaking into the property was a criminal offense. "I'll figure out an approach," Jack said.

"What do you want me to do?" Johnny asked.

"See if you can find deeds for Lillian Hill, Henry Fitzgerald, or Fredrick Taylor at the National Registry. If so, try to find an address for a pig farm."

"On my way."

"If you get something, come back here as quickly as possible," Jack said.

Benji said, "I'd like to try a different approach."

Jack and Johnny looked at him.

"I'm going to enlist the help of my best informer."

"Trunk?" Jack and Johnny said together.

Jack borrowed the inn's carriage and had Cap Sam lie face down in the footwell with his hands tied behind his back. He covered him with a blanket. He pulled up to the police headquarters in Whitehall, tied the horse to a hitching rail at the front of the station, and helped Cap Sam out of the carriage and to his feet.

"You said you were letting me go!" Cap Sam said as he realized where he was.

"I said I was getting you out of there, and I did."

He marched him into the station and up to the constable on duty. He tossed the cap with the razor blades onto the counter. The constable just looked at Jack. He'd seen him here before.

"I'm pressing charges for assault, tying me up, threatening my life, participation in the kidnapping of a friend of mine, bonking me on the head, and dumping me out of a speeding carriage."

"I didn't do all that," Cap Sam said. "That was Cap Alf."

"I suggest you shut up, Sam, for your own good."

The constable just shook his head in disbelief. "I'll put him in a holding cell. You take it up with Detective Wells," he said to Jack.

Jack sat down with Detective Wells. He needed the detective's help.

"Jack, I'd love to have some Vipers behind bars, but do you have any evidence?"

"Nothing I can share, but I know the Vipers kidnapped my lady friend and gave me a concussion at the direction of Henderson. He has her captive at some pig farm I think I can find. Can you hold him to give me some time?"

"Are they after you?"

"Yes, they had us, but Johnny and I escaped, taking Sam with us."

"I don't want to know any more until you have firm evidence. I can hold him up to seventy-two hours—I can bend the law a bit."

"If you have to let him go, I'd suggest following him; he may lead you to at least one of your fugitives."

"Perhaps," Wells said.

"Thanks," Jack said. "Have you discovered any additional information on Mrs. Hill's location?"

"I don't have any more on Hill. We have an active arrest warrant, and the plainclothes officers are working on it."

"I have a request that could provide valuable information for both of us."

"And it is?" Wells asked.

"If you could see fit to join me on a trip to a local printer, Mr. James Lackson, around four this afternoon, and are willing to bring the note you received alerting you to Mrs. Lillian Hill's involvement in the Forty Elephants, we may be able to narrow down where the note came from—which could be useful to us both. It's just a hunch."

Wells frowned. "It is highly unusual to remove evidence."

"It'll be in your hands and safe. It may provide valuable information."

"Very well. You've been cooperative. I give in, I'll be there. I've known that gentleman for a long time. It'll be good to see him."

"Thank you. I'll see you there."

Jack left and headed to the trading rooms at Lloyd's.

Upon entering, Jack got the same thrill that he always did entering the beehive of activity: the sounds, the noise, the smell. He looked around the floor for Herbert but didn't see him.

He found him in the quieter office space dedicated to Fredrick's syndicate, working on a thick pile of papers.

Herbert sensed his presence and looked up. "Jack! You've been a missing element of late," Herbert said.

"I have. I've been following up on some of your losses and some of your investors."

"We could use some good news."

"I don't have much of that, Herbert. I may make it worse for you."

"You can try," Herbert said. "But time is running out, and we don't yet have the money that Blake promised, partially due to the bust of Mrs. Hill—which I have a hard time believing is legitimate."

"Finding her could be very helpful. Any clue as to her whereabouts?"

"None, Jack. What of your investigation? Can you bring me up to date?"

"The investigation is ongoing. I have to be honest with you, Herbert. Many criminal thefts associated with your policies were abetted by information leaks from inside these halls, and you're not above suspicion."

Herbert looked shocked; he jerked his head up and stared at Jack. "Suspicion of what?"

"Someone here at Lloyd's is leaking information on insurance policies and details of coverages, allowing robberies to be committed. Any individual providing information would be an accessory to the crimes."

"Why would I do that? Any of the investors could do that!"

"True, but to what purpose?"

"I don't know, Jack. You're the investigator," he said indignantly.

"Did you inform the police about Mrs. Hill?"

"What?" Herbert nearly screamed. "No, I didn't! You're grasping at straws!" Herbert's voice was shaking.

"Perhaps I am, Herbert."

Jack smiled to himself. It was the reaction he'd been looking for. He continued, "I'm also working with the Metropolitan. There are multiple crimes associated with losses from your syndicate. I don't believe you have any illegal involvement, but I must rule that out."

"How?" Herbert asked nervously. "I provided you with the list of investors, *and*, by the way, did so without Fredrick knowing!"

"I assumed that," Jack said. "But doing so took my attention off you and onto the other investors."

"I've done nothing wrong. What can I do to convince you?"

"Tell me about Henry Fitzgerald. Is he a real investor or a front-man for Mrs. Hill?"

Herbert shook his head. "Mr. Fitzgerald is a real investor. Not in the syndicate. He invests in property with Mrs. Hill. She also invests in real estate with Harley Blake, and they all have their agreements."

Jack took a deep breath. "That's good to know, thank you." He paused. The next part was critical. "Herbert, I have a critical request. I need you to give me the location where I can find Fredrick. I don't want him to know, and I want it now."

Herbert suddenly looked horrified. "Surely you don't suspect Fredrick of criminal activity."

"I have evidence I need him to review and verify, and only he can do it," Jack replied. "There are details that only he possesses, and he seems reluctant to give me the contact I need with him. I need to know how to find him, Herbert."

Herbert studied Jack's face, chewing on his lips. Jack noticed his hands were shaking. Seeming to come to a decision, Herbert said, "Wait here." Herbert went into Fredrick's office and returned a few minutes later with an address written on card stock. It was similar to Jack's card from the Magpies, but it had a black border around the perimeter. He wasn't expecting that, but he would discover more during his visit with Lackson.

Benji picked up his carriage. He paid the groom to change the tack to a single-horse harness. He hooked up his borrowed horse and headed for the port. Trunk found Benji before Benji saw him, and he beckoned Benji into the warehouse where he lived.

Trunk got right to the point. "Benji, my friend. Here for some information or got a job for me? My business is slow."

"Trunk, I'm working with Jack Cramer and Johnny Riley on their investigation."

"You going legit?" Trunk smiled.

Looking at Trunk and smiling back, Benji answered, "I like to think that I'm right on the edge of legit. I've got some questions."

"It'll cost you."

"Only for answers," Benji said.

Trunk's grin grew wider, exposing his missing teeth. He nodded.

"I'm trying to locate a Lady Black, also known as Edie—tall, dark-haired, beautiful."

"I can't help you get a woman, Benji," Trunk teased. "I have my principles."

"She's a close friend, and she's in trouble."

"I don't recognize the name."

"How about James Henderson."

"I know a little about him. Escaped from jail in Australia, right?"

"That's right."

"This Henderson," Trunk continued. "I think I seen him get picked up a while back. I think by a Velvet Viper in a carriage: Cap

Alf, one of the leaders, plus one of his boys as a driver. Took off like lightning."

"Do you know where they went?" Benji asked.

"No, but I can find out."

"How much?" Benji asked, thinking it best to set the price ahead of time.

Trunk raised his eyebrows in thought. "They're a dangerous bunch. It'll cost you six shillings for me and six for my source."

"Can you get the information today?"

"I'll have to pay upfront."

Benji dug in his purse and pulled out twelve shillings. "Don't let me down. I'll be back in a few hours. We're also looking for a pig farm, a temporary location for the Vipers, where they may have my lady friend captive. It may be the same place Henderson was taken to."

Jack and Wells met at Lackson's print shop a few minutes before four. Sam was working intently; he smiled and nodded but didn't pause in his work.

"Several large orders to get out," he spoke over the sound of the press.

Mr. Lackson arrived a few minutes later, walking slowly with a cane. "Detective Wells, how nice to see you. It's been too long."

"It has James, it has. I miss our chess games when I was on the beat."

"Me too," Lackson said. "Perhaps a game again soon."

"I promise to try," Wells said.

Jack introduced himself and mentioned Johnny's visit.

"I remember," Lackson said. "He brought us some printing work since we met. Nice to meet you as well. What can I do for you?"

Jack pulled the card with Fredrick's address from his pocket and asked the detective to show the other card to Lackson. Jack kept the note threatening Fredrick hidden; he hadn't shared that with Wells.

"Can you identify this stock? We think it looks to be the same on each card."

Lackson handled both pieces of card stock, holding each close to his face and examining both sides.

"Not an expensive stock but of a nice weight. It's quite common, and several mills produce it. It's made from rough pulp, so it's less expensive and more absorbent than finer stationery or cards. The buff color makes it less formal than white or cream, so it was probably intended for commercial trade or notes other than formal correspondence. The black ink on both is a standard color choice; the block lettering on this one is uncommon. Usually, a script is used. It might be to disguise the handwriting. Steel points are used instead of quills on both. And one other feature of this card," he said, holding up Jack's card with the address. "This black border around the perimeter indicates that the card was intended to be a communication from someone who was in mourning or to be delivered to someone bereaved."

As they left the print shop, Detective Wells said, "I'm not sure what we accomplished."

"I'm not sure either," Jack commented. "I was hoping for more."

Jack thanked Detective Wells and headed back to the case room.

What had he learned? He didn't know. The block letters used on the Magpie card, which Jack had kept hidden, matched the letters on the note exposing Hill. Jack decided to focus on getting to Fredrick and learning the location of the pig farm.

Benji returned to the port two hours later and again found Trunk. "Any luck, Trunk?"

"All talent, Benji, but luck is good to have," Trunk said. "One problem. I had to pay my source twelve shillings. We're risking our lives. Discussing the Vipers is dangerous. It gets expensive."

"Right," Benji said. "Tell me what you've got first."

"When he picked up Henderson, Cap Alf picked up two more of his men who followed the carriage on horseback out of town. My trustworthy source says they went to a pig farm past the town of Tilehurst, outside Reading. The farmer's name was Gray, but the Vipers encouraged him to take a holiday and maybe paid him. He didn't refuse."

Benji was sure that the farm where Henderson was taken by Alf and his Viper pals was the same place where Edie was being held captive. He paid Trunk fifteen shillings for his trouble. Benji was anxious to get on the road to Tilehurst before anything happened to Edie, but he couldn't leave without letting Jack and Johnny know what he'd learned.

"Can you get me something to write on and a pencil?" he asked Trunk, who'd turned to leave. "I want to hire you to deliver a message to Jack Cramer at the Riley Inn."

"Give me ten minutes," Trunk said.

True to his word, he returned with a note card and a pencil. Benji didn't ask where they came from. He wrote down all the details and told them he was on his way to the farm. If they could follow, he might need the help. He folded the note and gave it to Trunk.

"It's vital, Trunk. Please deliver it at once."

"I'm on my way. No charge."

Trunk was feeling rich.

Benji patted his horse and boarded his carriage. He wished he had a gun, but he couldn't wait any longer. Benji had to try and save Edie now that he knew where she was. There was no time to spare.

CHAPTER 38

ON THE MOVE

Rachel was furious that this dirty, bloody man had hurt her Gram, perhaps beyond healing. Rachel heaved his body over onto his stomach on the floor. She took the ropes that had secured Edie and tied Henderson's hands behind him. Rachel forced his legs to bend at the knees and bound his feet together. He was still out but moaned as she tightened the ropes. Edie untied Vern, who was also moaning, which assured them she was alive. Rachel took the rope that had been wrapped around her Gram and ran it through the ropes at Henderson's wrists, looping it down through the center of the bindings at his feet. She pulled the rope tight, bringing Henderson's arms and legs closer and bending his torso backward into a *C*-shape. She secured the connecting rope. "That's how we tie hogs," she said.

"Rachel, we need to get your grandmother to a doctor. Do you know one nearby?"

"Doctor Wright in Tilehurst. He delivered me and attended to my mother when she died in childbirth. I'll get the buckboard."

They laid Vern in the back of the buckboard on a horse blanket and covered her with another, putting a bedroll under her head. Edie took water and bandages in the back to attend to her while Rachel drove.

Rachel drove to the outskirts of Tilehurst where the doctor had his practice. Edie helped Dr. Wright and his wife bring Vern into the surgery, while Rachel tied Sally to a fence rail. Once the doctor had done a quick examination, he told them that Vern had a concussion and needed her wounds tended to. Dr. Wright suggested that Vern recuperate for a few days at his home with him and his wife, and Rachel was welcome to stay with her. Edie felt desperate to escape to Benji's farm and safety.

Outside the surgery, Edie spoke with Rachel. She asked to borrow the horse and buggy for a few days. Edie wrote out contact information for Harley Blake at Sterling Union International Bank, explaining he was her banker and a friend. She gave Rachel a note requesting that Harley pay an amount far more valuable than the horse and buggy were worth. Edie assured her it wouldn't be necessary to collect: the horse and buggy would be returned in a week. Rachel hesitantly agreed. "I can't sell Sally," Rachel said. "Not for any price! Please bring him back."

"Sally's a him?" Edie asked.

"Not my doing," Rachel said. "Just please bring him back."

"I will," Edie said. "One more thing . . ."

Sergeant Lindy handed a telegram to Detective Wells. It read: *Fugitive from justice James Henderson is hog-tied in the kitchen of a farmhouse outside the town of Tilehurst, currently knocked out. Please hurry.* Directions to the farm were provided. It was signed Rachel Daffern.

"Constable, see what you can find out about this property and this Daffern name. In the meantime, we have to get it checked out. Reading is the closest station. Wire this information to the chief there and ask him to take custody of Henderson immediately, on my authorization. And let him know we'll arrive on the next train to verify his identity and question him before bringing him here. I'll book the train. You'll come with me. Have the Black Maria sent to the York lockup for transporting him after questioning."

The next train was scheduled for the following morning. Wells went to the train station and purchased two tickets. He spent the next hour and a half putting pertinent paperwork together, including the wanted poster drawing and the file on Mrs. Hill. He wondered who this Rachel Daffern was: maybe the mysterious lady that Henderson supposedly held captive. He thought of sending a note to Jack, but there would be time enough after he confirmed the captive was Henderson.

CHAPTER 39

BACK TO THE FARM

Edie felt that the best and safest action would be to head to Benji's farm. She hoped the police got Henderson before he escaped. She didn't know who the capped men were. They might still be around. She worried they might pursue her or free Henderson. She was frightened and sore from the box and her escape and longed for the comfort of the farm and the camaraderie of the men and boys there. It was also her strongest geographical tie to Benji; he would eventually go there, she knew it.

She couldn't think straight. Everything that had happened was swirling around in her head. She needed help. Edie was dressed like a shrunken farmer. She had no money. Edie took Sally to the town watering trough, tied him to the hitching post, and let him drink. She went to the general store and found the proprietor.

"Sir?" she said tentatively. The proprietor looked her up and down, curious.

"It's a long story," she said. "I need help, and I don't have time. Rachel Daffern helped me escape a bad man. She's at the surgery with her injured grandmother now."

Wrinkling his brow, he asked, "Did you hurt Vern?"

"No, no!" Edie said. "Rachel and I rescued her and brought her to the doctor."

"Please. Vern will be fine after a while. She was helping me. If you can give me a container of water and food for the horse Rachel lent me, I promise to return and pay you in a few days. I have a long way to ride, and I don't have much time."

"You're riding Sally?" he asked.

"He's pulling the buckboard. I promised Rachel I'd have him back in a few days."

His look softened. He put some oats in an empty canvas bag, picked up a loaf of bread and a bundle of carrots, and filled a goatskin with water. He walked with Edie to the water trough. He scratched Sally and handed the bread and water to Edie. He gave Sally a carrot and dropped the rest of the supplies in the passenger seat of the buckboard.

"Eat one or two yourself. They'll keep you going. I'll walk up to the surgery and see how Vern is doing."

Edie thanked the man. Grateful for his trust and generosity, she climbed into the buckboard seat and directed Sally out of town. Edie needed to find out how to get to the farm, but she knew if she drove the buckboard in the direction of London, she could eventually find her way. When Edie saw carriages on the road, she was aware that any of them could be Henderson's cronies and pulled off to give Sally a break and make herself less visible. She eventually found signposts with town names she recognized and dirt roads she had traveled before. Edie drove for more than three hours, covering a reasonable distance, but she still had many more miles to go. She hoped Sally was up to it. She hoped *she* was up to it. She ate half the last carrot, saving the rest for Sally.

Edie finally pulled into the farmyard at dusk and was immediately met by all the boys and men who weren't still in the fields or elsewhere. Her sense of freedom and safety returned. It had only been a couple of weeks since she visited the farm, but it felt like she was returning from an epic journey.

"Are you all right, Edie?" Brian asked.

"I'm sore and tired but unharmed. I'll tell you everything, but please, someone take care of this dear horse—he deserves special treatment. His name is Sally."

Two boys stepped up, unhitched Sally, and led him off for a rub-down, water, and a decent meal.

"I see you've been clothes shopping," Brian said.

"Funny," Edie replied. "Do I have any clothes left here?"

Ralph, one of the other old-timers around Edie's age, said, "We'll find you something."

They helped her down and took an arm, leading her into the farmhouse. Her legs were suddenly rubber, and her feet hurt; she could hardly hold herself up. Brian put her arm around his neck and helped her.

"Is Benji here?"

"No. He hasn't been since you were last here," Brian said.

Suddenly overcome with emotion, Edie broke down in tears and held on to Brian.

Brian and the two boys put Edie in a vacant room in the farmhouse. The room was tidy, and the bed was made. She continued to sob intermittently. It had been years since she'd cried like this, and she didn't know why it was happening now. She accepted a pitcher of water but declined any food, and the boys left her alone to rest. Edie felt safe—as if this were her home, which in a way it was. She needed Benji safe and with her. Her dreams of wealth and being a proper lady felt empty and juvenile. She let her thoughts continue wherever they were headed. *What do I want besides Benji? A peaceful life. Perhaps Benji and I could have children.* At that thought, she started crying again. She paused; there was only one thing to do now. She needed to find Benji and help him.

In the morning, she saw a neatly folded pile of boy's farm clothes, a washbasin of water, and a towel on the bureau near the door. She changed and sat on a wicker chair, her feet on the discarded coveralls spread on the floor. She removed the bandages and found that the bleeding had stopped, but her feet and the bandages smelled horrible. The skin was wrinkled where the boar fat hadn't been spread, but it appeared that healing was already progressing. She put the washbasin on the floor and cleaned her feet. She found a small hole in the flannel shirt she had been wearing and worked it to tear off several strips of cloth, then tied a smaller bandage around each foot. She dressed in the boys' clothes: a light flannel shirt, indigo-dyed cotton pants, and wool socks. She recognized the pair of leather boots. They were the ones she'd left at the farm. *It was like encountering old friends,* she thought, and smiled to herself.

She was about to join the boys for breakfast when there was a light knock at the door.

"Come in, please," she said, expecting Brian. Mrs. Hill entered, standing very erect. She was casually but finely dressed. "Hello, Edie." The corners of her mouth turned up slightly. "I have some tea and biscuits coming up from the kitchen. May I sit?"

Edie—staring, mouth open, eyes wide—failed to regain her composure and voice. The best she could manage was to stammer, "Of course!"

They sat silently. Mrs. Hill turned one of the wicker chairs to face Edie. She fixed her eyes on Edie's face. After a minute, one of the boys knocked, and Mrs. Hill told him to come in. He set a tray of tea and food on the bed. Mrs. Hill stood and poured the tea, handing a cup to Edie and sitting back down.

Edie's hands were shaking. She didn't know where to begin or how she felt—angry, relieved, afraid? And Mrs. Hill didn't reveal anything.

"What are you doing here, Mrs. Hill?" Edie asked.

Now, her jaw set, Mrs. Hill leaned into Edie's face and spoke sternly. "I'm here for answers, Edie. I've been moving between my tenant properties since leaving the mansion, waiting for an opportunity to catch up with you. I lost track of you after you were kidnapped. I trust that was Henderson's doing?"

"Yes, Henderson was behind it. Some goons in flat caps were working with him, and they kept me in a box."

Mrs. Hill leaned back in her chair and sipped her tea. "The Velvet Vipers. They're a dangerous gang. But Henderson is now being held in lockup and will probably be transported back to Australia. I'm afraid he may try to use information on me to bargain. But for now, let's talk about you and me. You've survived your capture, and now I need some answers."

Edie resented the tone that Mrs. Hill had set for the conversation. "I'll tell you what I know," Edie said.

"Tell me where the diamonds are."

Edie was surprised, and couldn't keep the anger out of her voice. "You never even told me they were diamonds, let alone stolen diamonds, until they disappeared, along with the captain."

Mrs. Hill's face softened a little. "Edie, you grew to be like a daughter to me, but I don't know how much I trust you. You were the only person, other than the captain, on the ship who knew he had a special assignment from me to transport a package to a contact in Cape Town."

"And that went as planned. I had nothing further to do with this mess other than sending Benji to follow him as you ordered."

"And Benji could have discovered the contents of the package, and the two of you could have planned for its disappearance—or made a deal with the captain."

"Mrs. Hill, that didn't happen. I'm loyal to you. I always have been. I resent your implication otherwise."

Mrs. Hill ignored Edie's comment. "I think we can safely rule out the captain," Mrs. Hill said. "That leaves Benji and you as my suspects."

"Why rule out Watkins?" Edie asked.

"About two weeks after the *Scott* returned from Bermuda, the naked body of a dark-skinned man washed up on shore in the Great Sound. He had gray hair, but the body was too decomposed and nibbled on to make a proper identification." Mrs. Hill paused.

Eddie shuddered.

"There was a bullet wound in his chest," Mrs. Hill continued.

"Oh dear," Edie managed, thinking of the kind and gentle captain.

"Did Henderson pressure you to reveal the package's existence once the captain and Benji left the ship?"

"No!" Edie answered sharply, now more annoyed. "I hated him. I barely spoke to him. I continued to tolerate him because of you. I was trying to do my best for you." She was on the verge of tears again. Her fatigue washed over her. She felt her pulse speeding, her heart pounding. She leaned forward, her hands forming fists.

"I said I had nothing to do with your missing diamonds!" Edie took a deep breath to calm herself. "You can believe me or not. I don't care. I *have* been loyal to you."

Mrs. Hill paused and said nothing. She leaned back in her chair, evaluating the sincerity in Edie's voice. She sipped her tea. Edie had put hers aside.

After a long pause, Mrs. Hill said, "If I believe you, that leaves Benji. You're angry, Edie, but so am I. I'm told you were with the investigator for Lloyd's when you were kidnapped. Are you assisting in their investigation?"

"Would I do that if I stole your damn diamonds?"

"You might. It's a good cover-up."

Edie abruptly stood. Mrs. Hill leaned back in her chair just slightly, surprised.

"I contacted Lloyd's investigator, Jack Cramer, to help me find you and Benji. I'd lost track of Benji, and he wasn't here. You had disappeared. I needed help. I was desperate."

"You're telling me you haven't heard from Benji since you returned? You two were very close."

Edie looked at her, wondering how much she knew about Edie's relationship with Benji.

"That's correct," Edie said.

"Then Benji could have the diamonds—or the answers I need."

"He didn't take them, Mrs. Hill."

Mrs. Hill rose. "You don't know that, Edie."

"Mrs. Hill, I can assume the answer, but did *you* arrange for the theft of the diamonds?"

"You might assume, but you might assume wrong, Edie. I agreed to be the courier for a substantial fee. Still, I don't have the resources for such an elaborate robbery. I also wasn't originally informed that the cargo was diamonds. I learned that later. I expect that I was exposed to the authorities in retaliation for the diamonds' disappearance."

"If you didn't arrange the theft, then who did? And might they be involved in the diamonds' disappearance? What could possibly be the reason, though?"

Mrs. Hill hesitated. She stood and paced for a minute, a hand on her chin.

"I'm not sure, Edie. I'll trust you for now, but you're not leaving my sight until we solve this."

"Can you give me some background?" Edie asked.

Mrs. Hill hesitated but then said, "Harley Blake approached me. Harley and I have done a lot of ventures together. He was asked to arrange the theft of a ship for contacts in South Africa. My assignment was to organize and fund the *Ferret* theft. Harley promised a great deal of money, including the proceeds from the gun trade. I was asked to arrange for a package to be picked up in Brazil and delivered in Cape Town, which I entrusted to you and the captain. That was it."

"You gave me the address, but the package came from António Velez."

"After you wired me from Brazil, I got further instructions that the Cape Town contact would engage the captain to deliver a second package back to London, to be stored at Sterling Union International Bank of London. Watkins had delivered for them for years for added income, substantial income. Harley wired me that our client wanted me to arrange to have the captain followed and protected until the package was delivered. That's when I learned what the package really was."

"Do you think Harley arranged the theft?"

"That would have been difficult. Harley represents the bank and the bank's interests, but the group of bankers in Cape Town has the contacts and resources. Harley had the information from the Taylor syndicate, so he could have been involved. But then, why turn me in? Who benefits? The theft will likely ruin the Taylor syndicate and set in motion huge losses for Harley and his bank. Large losses for you and me as well. There must be more to the story."

Edie relaxed and tried to think like the detectives from her favorite novels. "How does Velez fit in?" she asked.

"He's a major gunrunner. He does a lot of jobs for the bank in Cape Town and anyone else willing to pay him substantial sums."

"What was in the package he gave me?"

"I don't know, Edie. My charge was to send the package to Robertson. He's involved in gun trading as well, but for the African banks. He brokers deals."

They both paced the room, the tension lessening between them as they explored ideas together.

"Mrs. Hill, if the diamonds hadn't disappeared, if they'd arrived as planned, what was to happen with them?"

Mrs. Hill looked taken aback. "You ask a good question. The banks were involved somehow; the diamonds would end up in storage at the Sterling Union International Bank. We were to be paid a substantial amount for stealing the ship and delivering the package and another substantial fee for protecting the cargo, the diamonds, to their destination. Perhaps they were to be held hostage for a ransom."

"The Lloyd's syndicate organized by Taylor is the party in the greatest financial trouble because of the theft," Edie said. "They have to pay the claim, regardless of the diamond's second disappearance. How would the successful delivery of the stolen diamonds, if they hadn't disappeared, benefit Fredrick's syndicate?"

"I've been a little nearsighted, Edie. Harley indicated that he and the Sterling Union were brokering this 'transaction' for a client and stood to earn substantial profits. Not everything these banks do is legal—the gun trading, for instance."

"How does that benefit Fredrick's syndicate?" Edie asked again.

"That's the part I'm not sure of . . . unless Fredrick arranged the theft. I suppose he could recover the diamonds, be a hero, and save the syndicate, but that doesn't make sense. Or he could sell the diamonds for his benefit, knowing the syndicate would pay the insurance and go broke—and to hell with the rest of us. The diamonds are worth more than their coverage." Mrs. Hill looked shaken.

"And Harley, as the middleman, could have arranged the disappearance of the diamonds for his benefit. To hell with Fredrick." Edie added.

Mrs. Hill just looked at her, dazed.

"Let's find Blake and Fredrick and get some answers," Edie said.

They decided to leave as soon as possible to return to London together and get to the bottom of the mystery.

Mrs. Hill was better known by all the boys and farm workers than Edie expected. *It makes sense*, Edie thought. *She provides their property and invests in their operation, and they all make money.*

Brian arranged for two boys to bring Sally and the wagon back to Rachel. Meanwhile, Edie decided to look through the chest of valuables she'd left at the farm. She hadn't opened the trunk in years. She found the sock her mother had made for her long ago. Memories flooded her brain. The chest was filled with all her savings from the stall and the Forty Elephants days, but the sock was the most precious thing she found. She looked skyward. *There's still time, Mum. I will make you proud of me.* She took six gold coins from her money and arranged to send two to Rachel, two to Vern, and two to the general store proprietor who had helped her. To them, it would be substantial wealth. She locked her chest and gave it back to the protection of Brian. Edie recognized that she now saw wealth as a necessary evil, a means to an end—but not the reward in life she had been seeking. *But I'm glad I can do something for good people*, she thought.

Mrs. Hill had an enclosed carriage prepared and asked Edie to drive in her farm clothes so it looked like a carriage for hire. Mrs. Hill didn't want to be recognized in London for fear of arrest. Edie was getting used to dressing in farm clothes again, and she liked it.

It took several hours to drive from the farm to London. The women spent most of the time in silence, each considering what could happen next and what they might do. When they drove by the Farnsworth farm, Edie was sad to see that it had fallen into disrepair. *Widow Farnsworth has probably died,* she thought. She recalled Benji's kindness to the woman; it was the time when she'd first realized she was in love with Benji.

When they arrived in London, they went first to Harley Blake's office, where his assistant told them that Harley was on holiday with his family. They next drove to Lloyd's. Edie's appearance in the trading room drew a few glances from the uniformed and suited traders. She asked for Fredrick Taylor and was soon greeted by Herbert Archer.

"If he's not here, Mr. Archer, you'd best step outside with me. I have Mrs. Hill waiting in a carriage."

Herbert was speechless. After hesitating, he said, "Just a minute. I'll go to my office and come right back."

Edie grabbed his arm and squeezed. She stared him down. "*Now*, Herbert," she said. Herbert blanched, but he nodded, following Edie to the carriage and stepping in.

"Herbert, what has happened since our last board meeting?"

Herbert stammered as he spoke, and his hands shook.

"Blake has fronted the entire deficit, including your portion. It's in escrow at the bank, pending signed demand notes from all investors. I signed the assignment of your ownership on your behalf, on Fredrick's orders."

"I don't think you have the authority to do that, Herbert," Mrs. Hill snarled at him.

Edie was sitting between them, the only thing saving Herbert from physical contact with the irate Mrs. Hill.

"The bylaws say that if an investor's money is found to be illegally gained, then ownership must be forfeited."

Hill paused. "We'll have to deal with that later. I want to know where Fredrick is. I'm going to visit, and if he finds out I'm coming before I get there, I'll make sure that I come back and wring your neck. I'll wring it now if you don't give me the address."

Herbert was shaking uncontrollably. Edie found herself impressed with Mrs. Hill.

At Mrs. Hill's request, Edie went with him into the offices, and when he returned with the address written on a note card, he gave it to Mrs. Hill and hurried away from the carriage. Turning back, he said, "You should know I gave Jack Cramer the address too."

◆ ◆ ◆

Edie approached the ticket window at London Bridge Station. The attendant wrinkled his forehead and lips at her farm clothes like he expected her to stink. When she requested a private sleeper car for the short trip to Chelsea, the ticket clerk raised his eyebrows quizzically at her. She explained that her grandmother was ill and wanted private accommodations where she could lie down. Sleepers had outside doors, and passengers boarded from the platform directly into the compartment. Mrs. Hill boarded with a scarf over her head, bending forward as if in pain, with Edie holding her arm. Mrs. Hill fell asleep before the train departed. Edie looked at her as the train sped along: she no longer trusted her as she once had, nor did she need her like she once did. But her instincts told her she needed to stick with Mrs. Hill for now while they wrapped up their business and found Benji.

CHAPTER 40

TRAIN TO TILEHURST

Johnny arrived back at the inn before Jack did. He'd found his mother at the bar, pulling beers for early dinner guests and sneaking a few sips from a glass of ale she had stowed under the bar.

"Are you supposed to be up and working?" he asked.

"Yes," she said. "I feel fine."

She still wore a bandage around her neck. Jenny came over.

"I couldn't stop her," she said to Johnny.

"I know," Johnny said, shaking his head, surrendering to his mother as always.

Jack arrived. Mrs. Riley handed both of them a beer and smiled.

"Oh," Mrs. Riley said, "the Trunk boy brought you a message. You should probably read it now. Jenny brought it to the attic."

"You know about the attic, and you read the note?" Johnny said.

"Nothing escapes me, son—you should know that by now."

They rushed to the attic.

The earliest train to Tilehurst was the following morning. Benji was already on his way; he would arrive earlier than they could. The next day, Jack and Johnny boarded the first-class train car twenty minutes before departure, a privilege of traveling first class. They chose seats facing each other, with a fold-down table between them.

"I got up during the night," Jack said, "and copied our wallpaper charts onto paper. I couldn't sleep. We're close, but I don't have the answers yet. If we figure out the motive, we'll have it."

"Where do you want to start?" Johnny asked.

Jack spread his copies of the wall scrolls on the table. They each took a few pages and studied the notes and diagrams.

"Mrs. Hill is connected to almost everyone on the charts, yet she's been targeted by someone wanting to expose her, and I can't see why anyone here would want to turn her in," Johnny said. "It seems like there are negative consequences to each for doing so."

"We're missing something," Jack said. "Saving Edie and turning Henderson over to the police is important. I hope we get there before Benji gets in over his head. We're not much closer to solving the diamond heist or the disappearance of the stolen diamonds than when we started—except I'm pretty sure Benji didn't do it."

Jack paused, brushed the hair out of his face, and stared at the paperwork.

"Evidence makes it look like Mrs. Hill arranged the theft of the ship, and my instinct says the ship was involved with the diamond theft," Jack continued.

"But what is Hill's motive for stealing the diamonds? As you said, it jeopardizes her investments if the Taylor syndicate fails. As to the diamonds disappearing, she would need to be working with someone, and again, what's the motive? She'd be trading investment value for diamonds—a risky proposition."

"What else do you see, Johnny?"

"Could it be Fredrick?" Johnny asked.

"If Fredrick arranged the diamond theft, how could he benefit? His syndicate was in default if the diamonds were stolen. And how could he benefit by turning Hill in? I don't think Fredrick would scuttle his operation, and turning Hill in wouldn't serve any purpose I can see. She was a source of money to him."

Jack shuffled some of the papers around on the table.

"Blake is in a similar position," he continued. "He and his bank have a large investment in the syndicate, and now he's in for much more, covering the loss of the diamonds."

"Could it be Lady Black?" Johnny asked cautiously. "It appears Henderson thinks so."

Jack sat back; he hadn't wanted to contemplate that possibility. Jack took a pencil and jotted some notes on the papers as Johnny watched. She was a lieutenant of Mrs. Hill. She was involved with stealing the *Ferret* and all its illegal activities. She was in Cape Town when the diamonds were stolen. She and Benji were very close, she'd said that. She knew the diamonds were transported to London, and she sent Benji to follow Watkins on Mrs. Hill's orders—so she claimed. The syndicate's failure would destroy her investment, but she might not have known the syndicate couldn't cover the loss, and her investment was much smaller than the value of the diamonds. How would she benefit from exposing Hill? A falling out, a release from obligations, or removing an obstacle.

"Johnny, it's a possibility."

"We still have more questions than answers, Jack."

"Of course, the Hill exposure might not be connected," Jack said. "It could be outside this case altogether."

The train whistle blew to signal their departure.

Detective Wells and Sergeant Lindy made it to their second-class car as the conductor shut the doors.

"All aboard," he said. He had already shouted the length of the train several minutes before. Wells brushed sweat from his forehead, and they looked for seats near the front of the car.

Wells glanced through the glass into the first-class car in front of them. He spotted Johnny Riley and assumed the back of the head he could see belonged to Jack Cramer. They were deep in conversation over a table full of papers. Wells looked for a conductor.

When the conductor entered the car, Wells said, "We'd like to upgrade to first. Can we do that?"

"You can. Why don't you take a seat while I finish checking tickets in second class, and I'll come right back and complete the transaction with you?"

They reluctantly took their seats. It was a frustrating twenty-minute wait.

Did Jack find out about Henderson? Wells thought. *If he did, how?*

The conductor returned and said, "The balance is one quid each for the upgrade."

Wells paid, and the conductor wrote new tickets and a receipt. "You can move up at the next stop," the conductor told them.

After Wells cited official police business, the conductor allowed him and the sergeant to exit the moving carriage onto the open platform and hop onto the platform of the first-class car at their own risk. Wells carried his case of papers.

"May we join you?" Wells asked when Jack turned his head. Jack smiled.

"Delighted!" Jack said. "Are you following us?"

"No! Are you following us? Let me introduce Sergeant Lindy." They exchanged greetings.

"You go first," Jack said.

Wells told them about the note from a teenage girl claiming Henderson was hog-tied in a farmhouse kitchen. They had checked out the ownership of the farm. "It had been the girl's grandfather's farm, but he died a year ago, and it's for sale. Henderson is in custody, being held in the Reading lockup. He's not happy about it."

"Any sign of Mrs. Hill?" Jack asked.

"No, but that's a question for Henderson."

"Was it a pig farm?" Jack asked.

"No, it used to be cows and corn," Wells answered. "Your turn."

Jack was curious as to the circumstances of Henderson's capture. How was Lady Black involved? Was she free, injured, or dead? What would Benji encounter at the pig farm?

"Did you get anything out of the Viper, Cap Sam?" Jack asked.

"Not a word. He knows we don't have any evidence and have to let him go soon."

"I thought we were sharing. Why didn't you let me know about Henderson sooner."

"Ran out of time," Wells said. "And you haven't told me why you're on this train."

"Detective, you're turning the tables on me. We are looking for Mrs. Hill. It's a long shot, but we found out that she owns a pig farm in Tilehurst with partners, and she may be in hiding there," Jack lied.

"The farm where Henderson was apprehended is near Tilehurst," Wells said.

"There could be a connection," Jack said. "As you know, Hill and Henderson have been acquainted for years, and I suspect her involvement in the *Ferret* heist. But they aren't on the best terms."

"Jack, I should send someone with you to investigate. I need Sergeant Lindy with me, but I can arrange for someone from Reading."

Jack ignored the comment and asked, "Will you share what you learn from Henderson?"

"I will. He's a little foggy from a heavy blow to the head, but he'll talk. The sergeant will make sure of that." Lindy smiled at Jack.

"Any word from your lavender ink lady?" Wells asked.

Jack froze and said nothing for a while.

"Sorry," he finally said. "Will you repeat that?"

"Sure. I asked if you'd found or heard from your lavender ink lady."

"No," Jack said. "Will you excuse me for a while? I need some time to think."

"I guess so," the Detective said, slightly put off. "We can find another seat."

"No need, just give me twenty minutes or so."

Jack gathered some of his paperwork on the table, took it and his document folder, and moved to an empty seat.

Wells glanced down at the notes that Jack had left, taking in the details he could while chatting with Johnny.

Jack pulled the note threatening Fredrick from the document folder and held it close to his face as Mr. Lackson had done; he sniffed. He turned it over to the blank side and sniffed. He did the same with the note from Herbert with Fredrick's address. He slipped both notes into his jacket pocket. He stood up and returned to the table with the other three men.

"Detective Wells, this is especially important to this case. Do you have the note you received exposing Mrs. Hill among the papers you have with you?"

"I do. I intend to quiz Henderson about it to see if he was the one who sent it."

"May I have it for a few minutes? It's important," he repeated.

The detective assented, passing the note to Jack.

Jack took it to his seat. He held it close and sniffed, turned it over, and sniffed again. He did the same with the two cards he had. He picked up his papers and returned to the table. The detective slid over to allow Jack to sit. Jack handed the note card back to Wells. He placed his own cards on the table.

"Well?" Wells said.

"I haven't thought of this in a long time. I spent a year at Harvard Law School in Boston. During that time, I attended a series of talks by a British lecturer who spoke at length on an area of crime-solving called forensics. He said the process can be traced back to sixth-century China but was just now becoming part of the methods used by Scotland Yard. One of his lectures was on the composition of materials as clues."

Jack took his two cards and again reached for the card about Mrs. Hill.

"Your question about the ink, Detective, reminded me of that lecture. There have been thousands of different ink formulas: each manufacturer has its recipe. Some use soot, turpentine, and walnut oil to bind them, some use graphite, multiple arrays of pigments, dyes, resins, fabricants, and other materials. Some add perfume, like lavender, to cover the scent. In other words, each ink has a distinct odor and a slight variation in blackness due to its ingredients. Furthermore, the pulpy composition of these cards makes them more absorbent. Every building has its unique smell. When I walk into Lloyd's, I anticipate its signature smell. In smoking rooms, the books on the shelves often acquire the smell of smoke."

The detective handled the cards, turning them over and smelling them.

Jack continued. "When Lackson examined the cards close to his eyes on both sides, I thought his sight was failing, but that wasn't the case—he was smelling. The back of these three cards has the distinct odor of Lloyd's. These three inks have the same shine: a little purple when you look closely. More importantly, they have identical smells. They all come from Fredrick Taylor's office."

Making a decision, he showed the third card to Detective Wells. "Taylor asked me not to include it officially in evidence." He turned to his friend. "Johnny, you and I are getting off at the next station and booking trains to Chelsea."

"What's in Chelsea?" Wells asked.

Jack pointed to the third card. "Fredrick Taylor—and perhaps Mrs. Hill."

"I can't stop you," Wells said, "but I would feel better if you waited and we went together. Or we could wire the constable in Chelsea from Tilehurst."

"I won't have enough evidence unless I confront them."

"Them?"

"Taylor and Blake. Will you wire the constable, and one of us will go to his office and bring him to the mansion?"

"I'll do that, and we'll follow once we've questioned Henderson and locked him in the Black Maria for the ride back to London."

"Will you have someone from the Reading police check out the pig farm?"

Wells wrote down the address in Chelsea and the address of the farm.

Jack and Johnny left the train at the next stop.

Wells got off and wired the chief in Reading, asking him to check out the pig farm, and sent a message to the chief in Chelsea that an investigator from Lloyd's would be arriving.

CHAPTER 41

THE GATHERING

Jack found a quiet spot at the train station to let Johnny know what he had surmised. "Fredrick sent *himself* the threatening note as an excuse to stay away from Lloyd's and tend to his shady enterprises—and to discourage me from investigating the *Ferret* theft. If that's so, he's also the one who sent the information on Mrs. Hill and the Forty Elephants to the Metropolitan Police."

"Why would he do that?"

"To get her out of the way."

"But why?" Johnny asked.

"Not completely sure yet, but I have a hunch we'll find out soon enough."

Jack kept scribbling in his notebook as they waited for the train to Chelsea, drawing circles and connecting them. He nodded a few times. Johnny left him to his thoughts.

As the train pulled into the Chelsea station, Jack said, "Johnny, you've got the address, right?"

"Yes."

"Take a cab and get the chief constable. Bring him to the house with backup in about a half hour. Tell them to be armed."

"Oh dear!" Johnny said, going pale.

"Tell him he'll have arrests to make."

Johnny took off to catch the next cab.

Jack hailed a hackney. Giving the driver the address, he said, "Stop a couple hundred feet short of the property."

The driver doffed his cap. "Sure, mate. Second trip to the location today. Brought two ladies earlier."

"Two ladies?"

"Yup, and not what I usually see. One was a real nice looker but dressed like a farmer. The older one was a fancy dresser, and boy she was angry. I get to make up a lot of stories looking at fares, but I haven't quite got this one yet."

Jack flashed an uneasy smile. "I hope I do."

The driver snapped the horses into motion, and as the houses of Chelsea flew by, Jack patted the bulldog revolver in his belt to ensure it was still there. The cab stopped twenty minutes later. Jack paid the driver and began walking toward the property, which was fully fenced and gated.

Waiting until the road was clear, he climbed a side fence, where shrubs protected his position. He headed down a sloping lawn to what he hoped was the rear entrance. The kitchen door was unlocked and the kitchen unoccupied, so he entered and began looking for a stair-case to the upper floor.

Making his way up to the main floor, he could hear voices. Keeping low, with his back to a staircase wall, he followed the sound. It was coming from a set of double doors on the wall to the left of the stairs. Looking around, he skirted the grand center staircase to the upper floors, turned, and put his back to the wall. He heard a voice he thought he recognized, then another. He inched toward the door and leaned against the panel to listen. A pistol pressed into his back. "Welcome, Jack. You've been expected. You *are* a little cleverer than I'd given you credit for." It was Fredrick. "My trustworthy Herbert sent a message that I had a lot of company coming."

Jack said nothing, rapidly assessing his predicament.

Fredrick reached around Jack's waist and removed the revolver.

"I bet you never checked. I had the firing pin filed on this beauty before it went to you, just in case." He poked Jack in the ribs to urge him through the double doors.

Mrs. Hill and Lady Black sat on high-backed wooden dining chairs in the middle of the sparse dining room, their hands tied behind them. Harley Blake was seated facing them with a gun on his lap.

"Jack!" Edie exclaimed.

He nodded. "Hello, er . . . Lady Black."

"I'll get another chair for our new guest," Fredrick said. "Please keep an eye on him, Harley. He's tricky."

Harley gave Jack a squinting and unfriendly smile. "Indeed, I will."

Once Jack's hands were securely tied, Fredrick said, "We were just chatting about all that's gone on in the recent past, Jack. Perhaps you can assist on some of the details."

"I think you can offer more," Jack said. He was shocked to see that Fredrick looked normal; his frail appearance had all been an act.

"There's a loose end or two that we need your help on. After all, you work for me," Fredrick chided.

Jack looked at the gun in Harley's lap, and cold sweat ran down his spine. He had to stall to give Johnny time.

"I figured out that no one threatened you, Fredrick. You sent that note to yourself, and you sent the note to the police exposing Mrs. Hill."

"Correct, Jack! And why would I have done that?"

He needed to draw Fredrick out.

"To divert my attention from the *Ferret* investigation so that I wouldn't find out that you and Blake orchestrated it with Mrs. Hill. You needed to avoid having it tied to the diamond theft."

"Very good, Jack. And why would I expose our friend Lillian?"

Jack looked at Mrs. Hill and hesitated. She looked vacant; her head was bowed to one side, and she seemed smaller than he remembered. She was devastated—her empire had been collapsed by that one note Fredrick had sent to the police. Jack caught Edie's eyes; they moved to the left. She tilted slightly in the same direction, directing Jack to look behind the chairs. He turned his head slightly and glanced behind them; about three feet from Edie's chair was a set of eight dynamite sticks lying on the floor and a blasting cap with a fuse that hadn't yet been inserted into the center of the dynamite. The fuse wire was still coiled around a wooden spool.

He turned his gaze to Blake. "You plan on killing all of us and getting away with it?" Jack asked, not expecting an answer.

He waited and continued.

"You instructed Fredrick to expose Hill, am I right?"

Blake's face hardened as he glowered at Jack. "To your first question, investigator, I would kill each of you this instant, if we had the diamonds, and yes, we will get away with it. Our plan is flawless. If you want a chance to save your friends, I need the missing diamonds delivered to me now! Can you do that?"

"You had Mrs. Hill exposed because she was an obstacle to you owning the Taylor Syndicate outright, and the diamonds would facilitate your purchase, correct?"

Fredrick shot a glance at Blake.

"Too clever, Jack. It was all working fine until the diamonds disappeared. I went ahead with my plan at the board meeting."

"You didn't want Mrs. Hill's investment in the bailout of the syndicate because you needed to own her interests in the syndicate as well, right, Harley?"

Blake snarled at Jack. "I have a gun, and we have dynamite to blast you all into little pieces and burn this beautiful place down. When we do, evidence will be found in the remains that pins it all on Mrs. Hill, the known criminal. We'll collect the insurance. You have no chance of leaving here alive; none of you do. Unless you can provide me with the location of the diamonds."

"Then you'd let us go?" Jack was still stalling.

"I'd consider it." Blake almost laughed as he said it.

Jack gave him a mocking smile in reply.

Blake flashed Jack a fierce glare, his eyebrows in a deep scowl, his lips curling, his jaw set. "I made provisions for the package to be delivered directly to my representatives at the bank, but someone upset our applecart. Can you tell us about that, Mr. Cramer?" Blake said. "We suspect Mrs. Hill can shed light on it, but she's not talking. She's a little groggy, but a bump on the head should loosen her tongue. I received a forwarded letter from Benji Diamond to our damsel in distress over here." He nodded toward Edie. "It contained a diamond. This one's not talking yet either. We want to know where to find Benji Diamond. Any ideas?"

"I know nothing about the missing diamonds, Harley, and neither does Benji," Edie said.

Leaning toward Edie and pointing his pistol, he said, "I just don't believe you."

Mrs. Hill suddenly came alive and spat, "I do, and I don't have your diamonds either, Harley. I don't know what happened to them. I arranged for a stolen boat, for your package to be picked up in Brazil and delivered to Cape Town, and for Benji to follow and protect the captain and the diamonds."

"Lillian, it's that last part, the protection part, that I have a problem with. If you know where the diamonds are, I'll set you free. I promise. I know you're not going to the authorities."

"Tell me this, Harley. Why expose me to the police? My source of income was helping fund the deficit that you and Fredrick needed to save the syndicate and our investments."

"You missed the point, Lillian. Didn't you hear Jack? I don't want your money in the syndicate. I don't want anyone's money in the syndicate! Fredrick asked for my help because he'd been skimming money for years, and it was about to catch up to him. The actuary was about to expose him; he's dead now. In return for my assistance, I want to own the syndicate, just me—and a little for our founding skimmer Fredrick. The syndicate is a gold mine. I orchestrated most of the losses in the last year and got a portion of the proceeds. I got Fredrick to stop skimming and arranged with my Cape Town bankers to use their criminal partners in Brazil to arrange the diamond heist. That's why we needed the ship. Velez is our mastermind. Once the syndicate defaulted, its value would be greatly diminished, almost nil. I'd then call in the demand notes from all the investors. No one would pay since the notes are for much more money than their shares' value. I would then put my bank's money in and own and control the syndicate and its earnings. Plus, I'd be a hero to Lloyd's. I'd get the syndicate back to making money."

Fredrick stood by silently, listening to the exchange. Jack needed the conversation to go on just a bit longer.

"Your bank would have a great deal of money invested and would need to be repaid, I presume," Jack said.

"Jack, I thought you had this all figured out. The key is the diamonds. I would have them safely stored in the bank. They are worth a great deal more than the coverage being paid."

"Why transport the diamonds back to London instead of working through your partners in Cape Town?" Jack asked.

"Watkins has been a trusted courier for years. Once the diamonds were received here in London, I could store them securely and confidentially in safe deposit boxes. We would have brokered them through normal marketing channels in small batches, allowing us to return three times the insurance value—instead of selling hot goods at a discount."

"Truly brilliant," Jack said. "Only you don't have them."

Fredrick broke in. "Enough of all this worthless banter. Let's get on with it. We can use Benji Diamond and Watkins to find the diamonds."

"Watkins is dead," Lillian said.

"What?" Harley asked.

"Washed up in the bay in Bermuda."

"That only leaves Benji Diamond, whom I've suspected all along."

"Why kill us?" Jack asked. "You'll get caught." *What the hell happened to Johnny?* he thought. *He should have been here by now.*

"You underestimate us, Jack," Harley said. "Records show one Lillian Hill purchased this dynamite; her name is on this property with mine. We've planted evidence that will survive the blast and the fire, documenting how she lured all of us here. Your bodies will be unrecognizable. I'll tell the story of how I escaped at the last minute. She's already a criminal; I'm a respected banker. It will be believed."

Fredrick took a small vial out of his pocket, poured the contents on his pocket square, and placed it over Mrs. Hill's nose; she instantly passed out. He put the pocket square and vial on top of the dynamite. He untied Mrs. Hill and pushed her to the floor.

"Can't have our villain tied to a chair," he told his audience.

Fredrick inserted an end of the fuse-wire coil into the center of the dynamite, cut a length, and placed the end into the blasting cap, carefully setting it on the floor. He inserted the coil end into the opposite end of the blasting cap and then unrolled the spool toward the dining room doors and into the hall, where he cut the end. Harley followed, and with one last look back at his captives, he lit the fuse and closed the door.

The previous afternoon

Benji turned his road-weary steed over to the local stable in Tilehurst. He gave her a good pat and a scratch. He took out his coin purse and paid the stable boy. He tipped a little extra and said, "Give her some water and some oats and wipe her down. I need to be back on the road quickly." His horse was exhausted, and he needed her as strong as possible for whatever would happen at the pig farm. He got directions and reclaimed his horse an hour later; she seemed rejuvenated. He thanked the stable boy. "She took a nap," he said. Benji gave him an additional coin.

Benji stopped his horse and wagon short of the farm and tied her to a tree. He skirted the tree line as close as he could. He saw no one in the yard. Benji crouched low and ran to the side of the farmhouse. He ducked under the front window and went to the door. It was locked. He thought there might be a second entrance off the pigpen area. He saw no one, so he opened the gate—the pigs all noticed and ambled toward him. Benji saw that the feeding trough was empty. Entering the pig's enclosure, he saw the open box, the footprints, and blood on the floor. He shuddered; his heartbeat quickened. Was he too late? He carefully opened the door leading into an open breezeway to the farmhouse's back door. He walked to the back door, listening for any sound. He reached for the knob. Two hands grabbed him from behind and pushed him to the ground. His hands were bound behind him, and a gag was tied over his mouth.

Three weeks earlier

Rohwedder had concluded that he couldn't work his way into getting a piece of the diamond fortune while he was sitting in Australia. He hadn't received a reply to the message he'd asked Dutch Hamill to send to Lady Black. Henderson had ignored several messages sent to him. Rohwedder felt everyone was using him for their gain. He decided his future lay in his own hands.

Over the next ten days, he executed his plan. Still employed by the Melbourne Gaol, he went to the medical library and removed two volumes: *The Nomenclature of Diseases* from the Royal College of Physicians of London and *Anatomy: Descriptive and Surgical* by Sir Henry Gray. *Anyone can cut up a body,* he thought. He hid the books in his canvas clothes bag and left the prison. He packed his belongings at his apartment and loaded them in his wagon. He stopped at a printer in Melbourne to pick up the order he'd placed a few days prior. He untied the string in his wagon seat and unwrapped the brown paper covering. He read his new card: *Thaddeus Snow.* He had picked the name from the Edinburgh medical register the week before. The card read *Anatomist and Medical Doctor, Private Practice, Sydney, Australia.* He had one final stop to make before heading up the coast to his new life. He carefully loaded the three trunks in the rear of the wagon. (They were heavy, he knew.) *Let them have their diamonds. I'll live a life of luxury and won't have to do anyone's errands any longer.*

Chelsea

The fuse began its slow burn toward the stack of dynamite.

The door knocker clanked on the front door. Blake stepped back into the dining room; they had little time. Fredrick would have to deal with this quickly. Fredrick opened the door; it was Johnny.

"Welcome, Johnny," Fredrick said. "Jack and the others are in the dining room. Why don't you join them?" Johnny entered; Fredrick stepped behind him and stuck his pistol in his back. "Go in quickly." Suddenly, the chief constable stepped in the door behind Fredrick and held his revolver to Fredrick's head.

"Drop it immediately, or you're dead." Fredrick made a quick move, but the constable was faster. He brought a heavy rubber cosh down on Fredrick's gun hand, and the gun fell to the floor. Johnny grabbed Fredrick and wrapped him in his arms. As one of the constable's men entered, Harley Blake came through the door with his pistol ready. The constable, now free of Fredrick, stepped toward Blake with his gun pointed at his face.

"You or me, sir?" the constable said. Blake quickly fell to the floor and rolled into the legs of Fredrick and Johnny, collapsing them. They fell backward over Blake's body into the constable. The constable fell forward into Fredrick. Blake jumped up and ran out the door.

Fredrick yelled, "The dynamite is lit."

Jack had an excellent knowledge of explosives from his work as a fire insurance consultant and investigator in Boston. The fuse wouldn't take long to burn its way to the blasting cap, the explosion of which would cause the nitroglycerin in the dynamite to blow, killing them all. His hands were tied securely; he had to act. Using his head and torso, he flung his head back violently while pushing his feet to the floor. It worked! The chair was top heavy enough that he began falling backward. *I can't fall on the blasting cap; the impact will cause the dynamite to explode.*

He twisted to his left, landing next to the fuse wire and missing the cap; the chair back cracked, but he was still bound.

His hands behind him stretched to find the fuse; he reached it and pulled it slowly. As he moved his fingers, the fuse wire inched away. He pulled again. He could see the gunpowder flame of the fuse getting closer; it would go right by his face. He pulled again gently. If he were too forceful, it would ignite the cap. The wire leading from the dynamite to the cap came out of the center of the dynamite and fell to the floor. It would still ignite if the cap blew. Jack strained to push himself away from the dynamite, gripping the ignition fuse. He needed to pull the cap farther away. The crossbars on the back of the chair broke with the strain. He turned—the cap moved. Part of the chair broke free, and with one hand loose, Jack grabbed the fuse and tried to roll. He would be hurt if it went off, but perhaps it was far enough away to avoid setting the dynamite off and killing everyone. Johnny entered just then and immediately assessed the danger. He grabbed the hot fuse wire, pulled it quickly away from Jack's body, and flung it to the back of the room. The cap exploded when it hit, but it was a safe distance from the dynamite.

The chief constable had Fredrick handcuffed on the front lawn. They both turned to the house when they heard the explosion.

Johnny untied Jack and helped him to his feet. Jack went to Edie and untied her, then untied Mrs. Hill; she was moaning, slowly coming to. Johnny wrapped his burned hand with a dining napkin from a pile on the floor. He picked Mrs. Hill up in his arms. A small fire was burning in the corner as they left the room. One of the constable's men went to deal with the fire, another to safely remove the dynamite. Jack, Johnny, and Edie exited the front door and joined the chief constable in time to see Benji walking up the street carrying Harley Blake, his arms around Blake's arms and chest. He walked up the lawn and dropped him at the feet of one of the chief constable's men.

"He's all yours," Benji said. "His gun is in the street down that way. It fell when he tried to run away from me, and I grabbed him. He just looked like he should be grabbed," Benji added with a smile.

"Quite a gathering," the chief constable said.

Edie burst into tears as she ran into Benji's arms.

"I'm turning into a real girly girl lately," she said, sobbing.

"That suits me fine," Benji said, his voice cracking and his eyes watery. "You're safe; that's what matters to me. I love you."

The chief constable said, "We'll sort this out at the station. We can all walk."

"Benji, how did you get here?" Jack asked.

"After I sent you the note, I headed to Tilehurst to rescue Edie; I was sure Henderson had her at the pig farm," Benji said. "As I entered the farmhouse, two police officers from Reading jumped me; they handcuffed me and took me into the station. Luckily, Detective Wells was there, and I told him who I was. He had a warrant for my arrest for the diamond heist. He had them release me into his custody. The three of us took the train from Reading to Chelsea. I told Wells my entire story on the trip. Wells let me run ahead here while they went to the station. He said he was convinced it wasn't me who stole the diamonds. Wells gave me the address. I guess my timing was good."

"Impeccable," Jack said.

Detective Wells and Sergeant Lindy were waiting at the police station, which suddenly became overcrowded. They borrowed the lawn of a friendly neighbor, where they handcuffed Taylor and Blake to the iron fence. The station attendant bandaged Johnny's hand.

Wells formally arrested Mrs. Hill. He'd spared her the handcuffs; she was sleeping on the lawn, still affected by the drugs. Wells was introduced to Lady Black of Melbourne, Australia, by Jack Cramer. Wells greeted her and nodded to Jack. No one mentioned any connection. The chief constable and Wells took statements.

London officers would return the next day to move Blake and Taylor to London. Wells and Sergeant Lindy escorted Mrs. Hill to the train station to travel to the London lockup with them for further prosecution. She slept most of the trip.

Mrs. Hill was booked for the standing warrant issued on her for crimes associated with the Forty Elephants gang. Taylor and Archer were held on suspicion of conspiracy, theft, and fraud associated with financial activities related to Lloyd's and the Taylor syndicate. Though there was no concrete evidence, the police were investigating the entire affair. No trace of the diamonds had been found.

Edie maintained her Lady Black identity with the authorities. As Lady Black, she had not committed any crime, according to the London police. The question of why she was there was simple enough to answer: she and Mrs. Hill were social acquaintances. She knew nothing about any Forty Elephants, she said with a disapproving ring to her voice. She was in Chelsea to volunteer at the public gardens.

♦ ♦ ♦

Detective Wells joined Jack and Johnny at the inn for a couple of beers after work a few days later. Mrs. Riley was thrilled to meet a "real detective." Jack and Johnny traded glances.

"The Taylor syndicate has been put on immediate suspension," Wells said. "I advised the administration of Taylor's arrest and charges as soon as we were back in London, and a quick review on their part led to evidence of suspicious activity. The actuary is missing, which is under investigation. The bank confirmed the syndicate was in an overdraft situation but had sizeable funds that had yet to clear and post to the account from Harley Blake. The bank board has put a stop order on the transfer of funds."

"There are still a lot of loose ends, but I suspect they'll be exposed in time," Johnny said. "I don't understand why the scheme had to be so elaborate, a stolen ship to assist with a diamond robbery."

Jack rubbed the stubble on his chin. "Who would suspect a ship arriving in the harbor to be part of a significant theft? The ship made money on its own. Mrs. Hill was being paid additional funds to provide the ship to assist in the setup of the heist, even though she wasn't fully aware of the purpose."

Wells added, "A little more has come to light about the ship and Mrs. Hill's activities from Henderson. He's trying to cooperate for a lesser sentence and is afraid the Vipers are after him. He wants us to protect him. Blake has also opened up a bit."

"What about Velez?" Jack asked.

"He's a significant operator in stolen guns. He's supported by the Chilean government and paid well by them and many others. He sold guns to the *Ferret* and was paid handsomely. The *Ferret* transferred the firearms to Peruvian guerillas for almost double what they paid Velez. The catch was that when the Peruvian guerillas reached the jungle path in Brazil, Velez's men were waiting for them. The fighters ran into the jungle, most of them leaving their cargo. Velez's men took possession of the weapons to sell again; they now had the boats and their contents, including chests of money and cases of wine with the *Ferret* name on the crates.

"How did you learn that?" Johnny asked.

"Communications with authorities in Brazil. Three of the Peruvian guerillas turned themselves in, begging for protection. The others were left to return to Bolivia on foot with whatever they had on them when they fled into the jungle."

"Whose idea was the ship?" Jack asked.

"The ship served multiple purposes," Wells said. "Hill made a bundle on the gun transfer, and I understand there were other trades. Still, the package that Mrs. Hill was charged with delivering, we suspect, contained details for the diamond heist and payoff money to gunrunning partners; it needed an elaborate and private method of delivery. I don't know who came up with the idea."

"What's going to happen to Mrs. Hill?" Johnny asked.

"Good question," Wells replied. "The Forty Elephants thefts, which she didn't commit personally, are old and will be hard to prove. We don't have the perpetrators or victims to provide testimony pointing directly to Hill. Old stolen goods and the elaborate setup at the mansion are suspicious but circumstantial. Blake has confirmed her involvement in the *Ferret* theft, which has already been prosecuted. The courts will have to decide what to do about her. Three men have already been convicted, and the previous owner isn't pressing any additional charges: they want nothing to do with it. On Taylor, we have had a flood of civil and regulatory lawsuits naming him for financial claims since the collapse of the Taylor syndicate at Lloyd's. There's suspicion he's involved in other criminal activity. Hill owns substantial assets in the syndicate, which I suspect are lost. She owns many other assets in various names and covers that could take a while to sort out—if they ever can be. Taylor is ruined; there's significant evidence that he used the syndicate as his personal bank and bought his properties, including the one in Chelsea, with funds that belonged to the syndicate. Learning this opened the door for Blake to make his move. We're talking about international crimes. His partners in Cape Town are involved in everything from gunrunning to diamond theft for hire. Taylor and Blake will serve long and hard sentences, I believe."

"What happens to the investors in Taylor's syndicate?" Jack asked.

"They lose everything invested unless the diamonds and other assets can be recovered, and, legally, they're still on the hook for any coverages. However, policies are being reviewed and picked up by other syndicates."

When they'd had one more pint and decided to call it a night, Wells asked Jack, "Will we see you again in London?"

"I suspect so," Jack replied. "I've done work for smaller syndicates, and there are several growing competitors to Lloyd's now. They'll need investigators. I hope we can renew our relationship if I return, Detective."

"By all means! You paid for the beer. Be aware you also may be needed at the trials."

"Of course. You'll let me know."

Jack went to the general clerk's office at Lloyd's and filed a bill for his services, an expense report accounting for what he had been advanced, and a bill for the balance. Since the activity of Fredrick's syndicate was suspended, it would take a little longer to get the invoices paid. Still, Jack was assured they'd be covered. There were contingency funds for general oversight.

Jack talked to one of the syndicate managers he knew and discovered that the entire diamond claim had been paid to Kimberley Mines, although coverage was far less than consignees in London would have paid. The *Ferret* payments had been made long ago. Still, a partial repayment would eventually be made—the ship had been sold for passenger and cargo service around Australia.

Jack headed back to the inn to start preparing for his return to America. Mrs. Riley was now back to her work at the helm of the inn. She was a little weaker physically, but she made up for it in colorful banter. A messenger delivered an envelope smelling of lavender. Jack smiled at the scent. The envelope was addressed to Mr. Jack Cramer and Mr. Johnny Riley. Jack opened the envelope, finding an invitation to join Edie Black, Benji Diamond, and a group of friends for dinner at the farm on Friday, two days hence. A carriage would pick them up and return them to the inn the following evening. They both accepted and gave the messenger a return acceptance.

The trial of Mrs. Hill was still weeks away, but she would wait behind bars since enough evidence had surfaced. Fredrick was being held and would not be released on bail. The authorities were still piecing together evidence to define the crimes he would be charged with. Harley Blake would not be out on bail either. Herbert Archer was suspended from activity at Lloyd's, pending investigation.

Dinner at the farm was delightful. Benji and fourteen young and middle-aged men, all sharing a common history of thievery and farming, dined on roast chickens, potatoes, squash, freshly baked rolls, and farm-made butter. The beer flowed freely during the meal, which ended with hot apple pies and tea. The men and boys who'd once made up Benji's gang excused themselves to the bunkhouse, where they would play checkers and retire soon because of early morning chores.

After the three-hour feast, Edie, Benji, Johnny, and Jack moved to the main house's living room, where a fire burned, fending off the evening chill. Benji added a couple more logs. Edie served brandy, and the talk turned to past and future events.

"First, the important news," Edie said. "Benji and I are moving to Melbourne and getting married!"

Johnny and Jack stood, wobbling slightly, and toasted the newly engaged couple.

"What will happen to the farm?" Johnny asked.

"I don't know," Benji said, "but I have a lawyer who will attempt to buy it when the trial of Mrs. Hill is over. Edie and I have some savings; we should be able to cover it."

Edie added, "I have the money in the bank in Melbourne. It might not be fully legal, but I can't turn it in and implicate myself. I have my trunk here and substantial assets I transported to Australia. Also, I have a trunk that belongs to Mrs. Hill and one of Henderson's."

"The big question is, where are the diamonds?" Benji said.

CHAPTER 42

MELBOURNE

Spring 1882

"I'm bored," Edie said.

Benji moaned to let her know he was listening. Then he said, "I'm tired."

"We haven't even had dinner. Let's talk first. I can't just spend my days working in the gardens and attending boring meetings."

"You could return to a life of crime. That's exciting."

"Not funny, Benji. We both know that life is behind us. We're lucky to be well off and not in prison. Crime took us out of poverty, but it's not recommended. I need to do something to help others make a better life. When I was ten, I promised myself I would do that. It was after I saw *you* doing good things for people. I need to do something meaningful to help the truly down-and-out. I'm going to see Chief Inspector McElroy in the morning; perhaps he has suggestions."

"He's got a crush on you."

"I know. That could help," she said, smiling at Benji and batting her eyelashes.

"You're hopeless, Edie. I'm opening wine. Shiraz fine?"

She stopped pacing and sat on the couch.

Benji opened the wine and returned with two glasses.

◆ ◆ ◆

The doorbell rang, and Benji went to answer it.

A smartly dressed delivery boy wearing a bow tie smiled and announced, "Package for Minnie Rose c/o Lady Edith Black."

"They're me," Edie answered from the couch. She stood and walked to the door, where she signed the receipt. She took a few coins from the bowl she kept by the door and tipped the boy.

"No indication of the sender," she said. "Postmark in Saint Vincent, Grenadine Islands."

Benji sat next to her. "Open it."

Edie untied the string and removed the brown paper wrapper. Inside was a blue metallic box with gold trim. It had a sliding top. She slid it back to reveal a note. She removed the message, revealing a box full of sparkling diamonds.

They both stared.

Benji said, "Do you want me to read the note?"

Coming out of her trance, Edie said, "No, I'll do it." She unfolded it and read aloud.

My dear Edie,

Thank you for the kindness you showed me during our adventures on the Ferret. I enjoyed our time in the wheelhouse, me telling stories and you asking stimulating questions. I especially enjoyed our final dinner together before I left. I now have the comfort of my own sailing vessel. I'm traveling the world. I live on the sea with no one to order me around or disrupt my thoughts.

I tracked you down through an acquaintance I have in Melbourne, a former lady friend. Congratulations to you and Benji on your marriage. Live happily.

By way of explanation, I was confronted on the Scott at gunpoint as we approached the port of Bermuda. I won the fight, but I'm afraid Mr. Robertson was mortally wounded with his own gun. Conveniently, the noise was muffled by a pillow he intended to shoot me through.

I couldn't stay around and become involved in a killing while holding an abundance of stolen diamonds, so I hoisted Mr. Robertson over the railing into the ocean before we docked. I added my personal belongings to the ocean. I decided then and there it was fate. I left the ship and disappeared. I have a new name. I will enjoy life on the water.

I'm pleased to have known you. Do good things for others as you always said you wanted to do.

Your former captain, Wilford Watkins.

The statement usually reads: Names, characters, places, and incidents are either the product of the author's imagination or are used fictitiously. Any resemblance to actual persons, living or dead, events, or locales is entirely coincidental. In this case, I felt you, the reader, should know that the *Ferret* was a real ship and the theft of the ship as well as the changes of name and appearance of the ship, are mostly factual. The characters in this novel are mostly fictional, but Henderson, Walker, Carlyon, and Captain Watkins are based on real people involved in the *Ferret* heist. Other names in the narrative are from real people, including some of the crew, the constable who recognized the *Ferret* in Australia, and Rohwedder, who was mentioned in newspaper accounts of the arrest of Henderson at the remote inn. I could find no additional information on Rohwedder. Most of the actions of the characters based on real people are fictional.

Based on my research, there was never any explanation of the motives behind the steamship theft or how the extravagant heist was financed, so I made that up. News reports and investigations revealed that when Henderson boarded the *Ferret* in Cardiff, he was accompanied by his wife, beautiful and elaborately dressed for boarding. None of my research revealed a wife, and there was no further mention of her beyond her arrival on the ship. That brief mention and image became the focus of this novel—the mysterious woman became my protagonist. Edie Black is a product of my imagination, as is Benji Diamond. Some of the other minor details in this novel are facts, like the bill for the wine to be stored on the ship, of which I was duly impressed. The coffee theft was real. All my research could not account for Henderson or Walker after they were sentenced to jail. I made those parts up.

The Forty Elephants gang really did exist. This gang of lady thieves was extremely successful, and it survived well into the twentieth century. It operated without being implicated in major criminal investigations, and it was very profitable. Mrs. Hill is not real. There were really gangs similar to the Velvet Vipers, but their involvement in the events of this novel was purely fiction.

And though much of the story of the criminal events in this book is from my imagination, the diamond heist was real. It occurred at a time close to when the *Ferret*, also known as the *India*, was in port in Cape Town. The heist was a late discovery in my research and a compelling extension of my narrative. Though I've embellished and fabricated many of the details, the post office crime scene is based on historical records. I provide a solution to the heist, but as of my last inquiry, the theft has never been solved, the diamonds never recovered . . . and a reward is still offered.

As an interesting note, the *Ferret*'s history continued after the events adapted for this book. The owners had no need of the *Ferret*'s return, so an Australian shipping company purchased it. Later she entered the passenger service and became Australia's best-known coaster. During this time, a steward served aboard the ship who would become immortalized, one Bill Bailey (not the one of "Won't you come home?" fame). Bill Bailey was really a woman disguised as a man to serve on shipboard. She served for many years. The *Ferret* was in service until 1920, when on November 14 the ship and its crew encountered a dense fog, and the ship became stranded beneath the towering cliffs at Reef Head with Bill Bailey aboard. All the crew escaped, but ongoing storms destroyed the ship. Remnants remain today on the rocky shore where her service ended. Bill Bailey served aboard another steamer until she became ill and her secret was discovered.

Writing this novel has been a long effort, but every minute has been enjoyable. I hope you have also enjoyed the story and will continue to follow Lady Black as she enters her new career in amateur investigating and righting wrongs, beginning with saving her best friend, Britina, from a cruel death. A teaser text follows for book two in the series, *Asylum Murders*.

I am deeply grateful to my early readers, who were kind but honest in their criticism. The input led to rewrites, character changes, and the deletion of unnecessary background information (but I probably still have a little too much).

Thank you to Mary Esther Treat, Ellen Wolfson, Charlotte Dalton, Barbara York, and Deborah Sliz.

Without my marvelous editor, Celia Blue Johnson, cofounder of the Pub Pros and Slice Literary, this book would never have been completed. Her experience at Random House and Grand Central Publishing gave her the perfect background to critique and guide me through three rewrites, always with a compliment and positive attitude to encourage me to get it done better. Thank you, Celia.

As in my nonfiction books, Maria Gagliano, a cofounder of the Pub Pros, leads and supervises me. Her team of professionals is second to none. Special thanks to Beth Blachman for copy editing and excellent advice and to Karl Spurzem for a captivating cover design and to Dan Avant for proofread corrections. Thank you, Maria, Beth, Karl and Dan.

A PREVIEW OF BOOK TWO...

ASYLUM MURDERS

A Lady Black Mystery

PROLOGUE

She felt and smelled blood. Her head hit something hard when he pushed her to the ground. She kicked with the strength she had left, but she didn't make contact. He let go of her right wrist. She felt a hard object on the ground, grasped it, and tried to hit him, but he put his hand on her throat and squeezed; she gasped. The night had been so promising just hours ago—prominent men, big money. He loosened his grip as he undid his belt with his free hand and wiggled his trousers down. Pinning her to the ground with his body, he hovered over her, sweat dripping from his face onto her skin; his eyes were violent, with a halo of fire red illuminated by the gas streetlamp that overlooked the rat-infested alley. Her damaged mind asked, *Why him? Why here?* He squeezed her throat harder as he tried to enter her. He failed and tried again. She struggled, then laughed.

He can't perform! It was the last thought before he hit her head again with his fist. She was broken; she knew it.

She was taken by horse cart to the Royal Melbourne Hospital and left at the delivery door. No one knew who brought the injured woman, where she came from, or who she was.

She was breathing, but she'd slipped into a coma. The nurses dressed her wounds, gave her pain medication, put her in a hospital gown, and got her into a bed. The doctor in charge the next morning was Dr. Bran Brookfield, a short, thin man with curly black hair and small, round hazel eyes that looked like they were pushing their way out of his eye sockets. He was an import from Edinburgh University Medical School, which he and others considered superior to the medical schools in Australia, which were in their infancy. He examined the new arrival and tried to get a verbal response from her. He pulled her eyelids open and tried to get a reaction, but none came. He was pressed for time. He wrote on her chart: *Unlikely to regain full cognitive function. Commit to Kew Asylum, the medical ward, for continued observation. Name unknown, assigned Jane Doe.*